My Little Pony™

Friendship is Magic

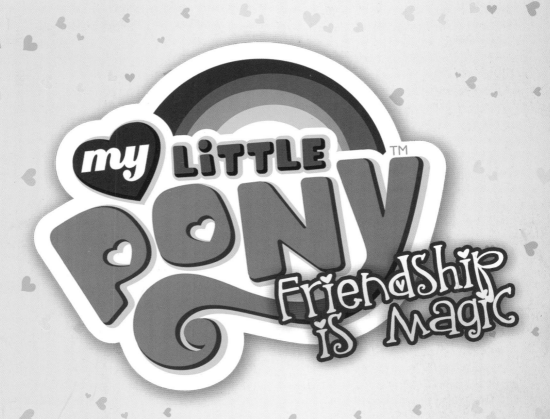

My Little Pony™ Friendship is Magic

Written By
Katie Cook

Art By
Andy Price

Colors By
Heather Breckel

Letters By
Robbie Robbins & Neil Uyetake

Edited By
Bobby Curnow

Cover By
Amanda Conner

Cover Colors By
Paul Mounts

Collection Edits By
Justin Eisinger & Alonzo Simon

Collection Design By
Neil Uyetake

For Grayson, my own lil' Cutie Mark Crusader. -Katie

With great love to friends and family, for my wife Alice and our cats Spooky, Tabitha, Boris, Bela, and Mina. And above all, especially for Sam. -Andy

Special thanks to Erin Comella, Robert Fewkes, Heather Hopkins, Valerie Jurries, Ed Lane, Brian Lenard, Marissa Mansolillo, Donna Tobin, Michael Vogel, Mark Wiesenhahn, and Michael Kelly for their invaluable assistance.

For international rights, please contact licensing@idwpublishing.com

ISBN: 978-1-61377-605-6

21 20 19 18 10 11 12 13

IDW® www.IDWPUBLISHING.com

Licensed By: Hasbro

Ted Adams, CEO & Publisher • Greg Goldstein, President & COO • Robbie Robbins, EVP/Sr. Graphic Artist • Chris Ryall, Chief Creative Officer • David Hedgecock, Editor-in-Chief • Laurie Windrow, Senior Vice President of Sales & Marketing • Matthew Ruzicka, CPA, Chief Financial Officer • Lorelei Bunjes, VP of Digital Services • Jerry Bennington, VP of New Product Development

Facebook: facebook.com/idwpublishing • Twitter: @idwpublishing • YouTube: youtube.com/idwpublishing
Tumblr: tumblr.idwpublishing.com • Instagram: instagram.com/idwpublishing

Originally published as MY LITTLE PONY: FRIENDSHIP IS MAGIC Issues #1–4.

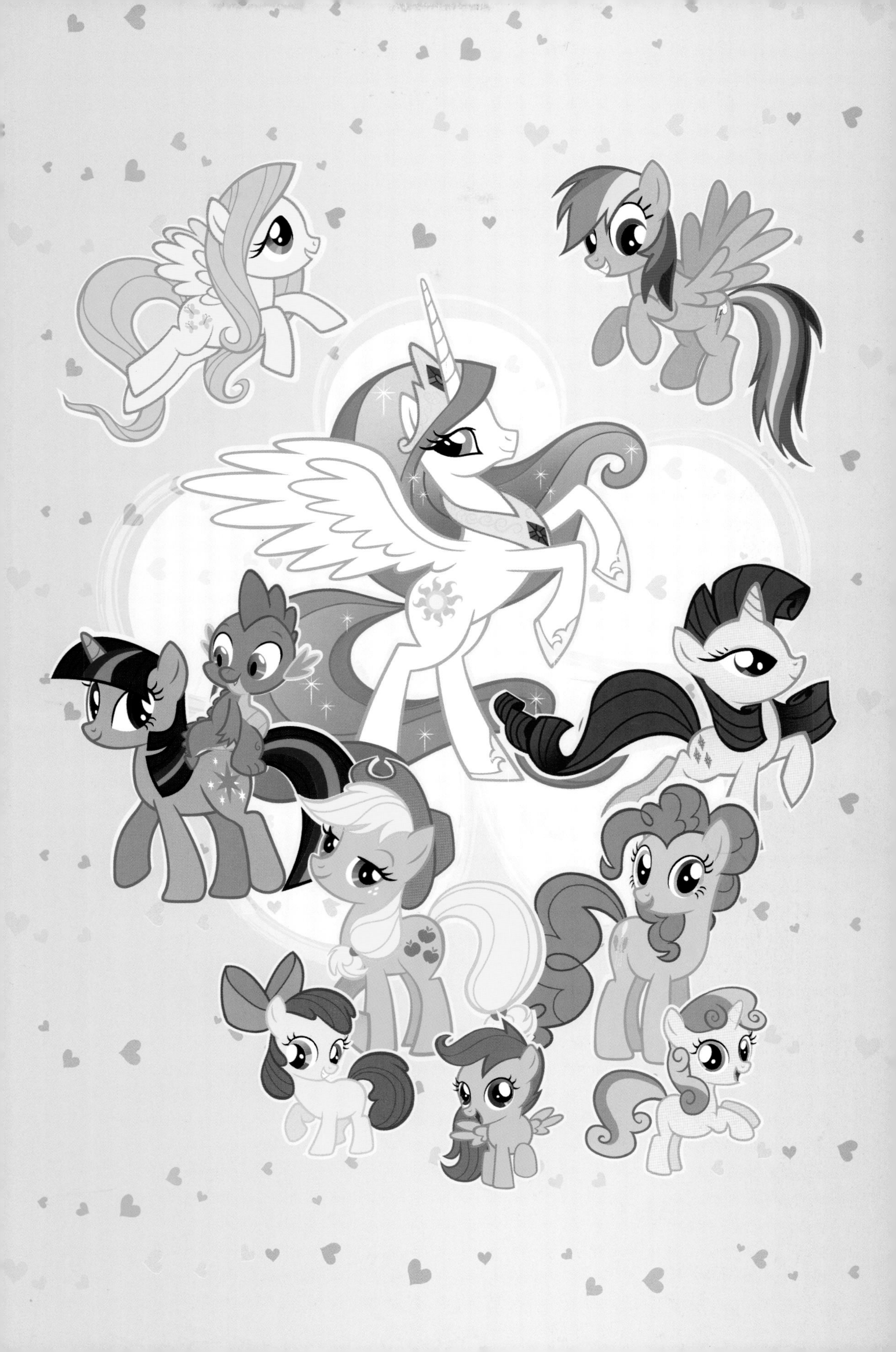

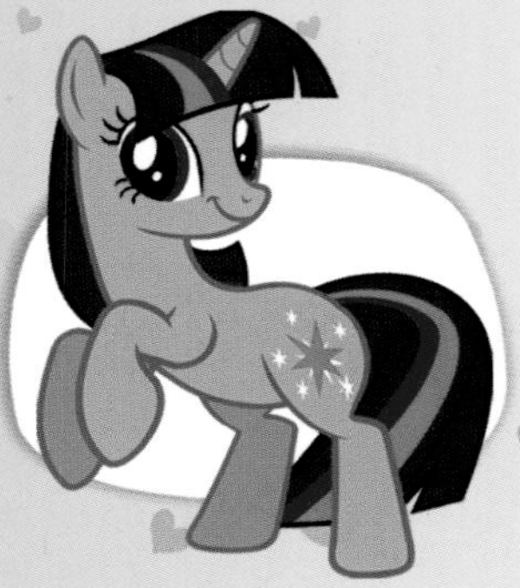

TWILIGHT SPARKLE

Twilight Sparkle is a unicorn with a big heart. Even though she prefers to have her muzzle stuck in a book, she's always willing to put her work aside to help her friends! She's also one of the most magically gifted unicorns there is, thanks to her studies and the personal guidance of Princess Celestia.

RARITY

Rarity is a unicorn who has dedicated her life to making beautiful things... She's a fashion designer in Ponyville and has aspirations to be "the biggest thing in Equestria." She has big dreams, but she's very dedicated to her Ponyville friends who have always been there for her.

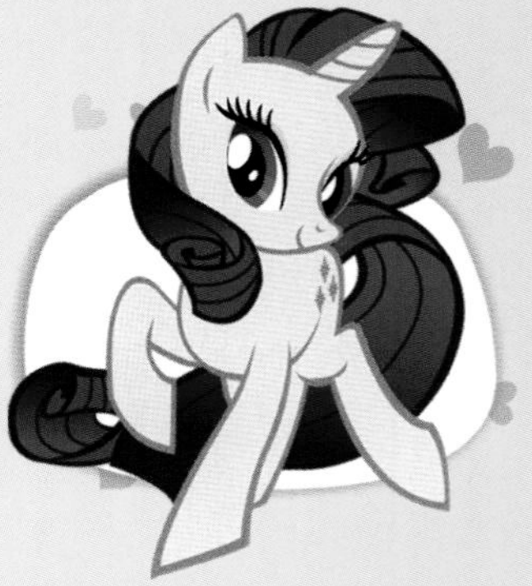

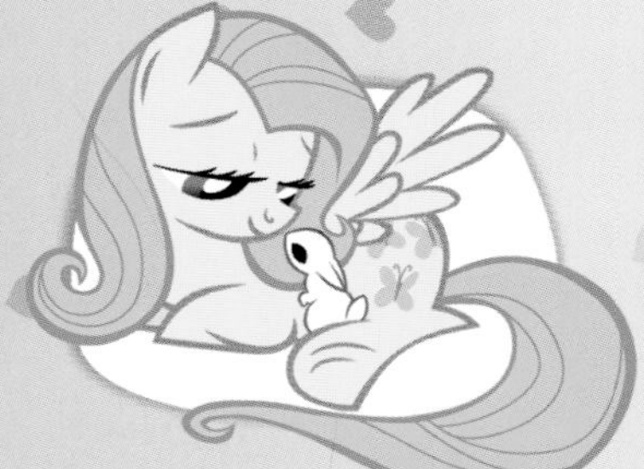

FLUTTERSHY

Fluttershy is a shy pegasus with a gentle hoof. Her love and understanding of animals is almost legendary to the ponies around her. She's calm and collected, even when faced with some of the scariest beings in the Everfree Forest!

APPLEJACK

Applejack is a pony you can trust. She's the hardest worker in all of Ponyville and will always be there to lend a helping hoof! She and her family run Sweet Apple Acres, the foremost place to acquire apples and apple-related goodies in Ponyville.

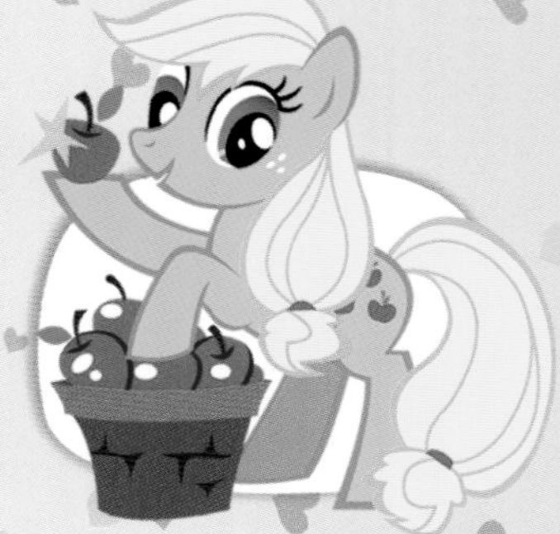

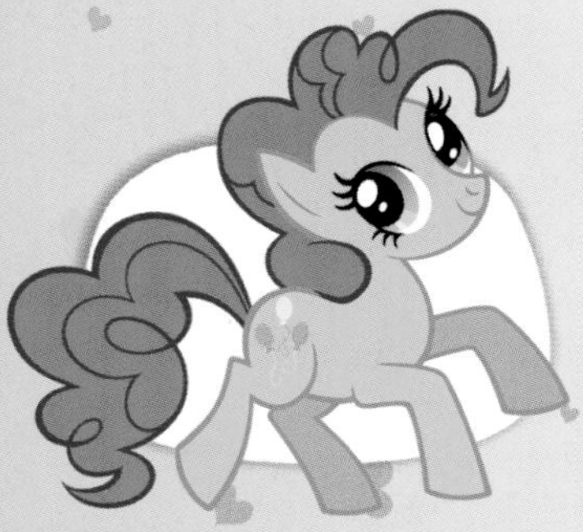

PINKIE PIE

Pinkie Pie is a pony that likes to PAR-TAY. Friendly, funny... and maybe a little weird, Pinkie Pie is always on hoof for a celebration for any occasion! She's always there with a smile and an elaborate cake, even if she's just saying "thanks for pet-sitting my alligator."

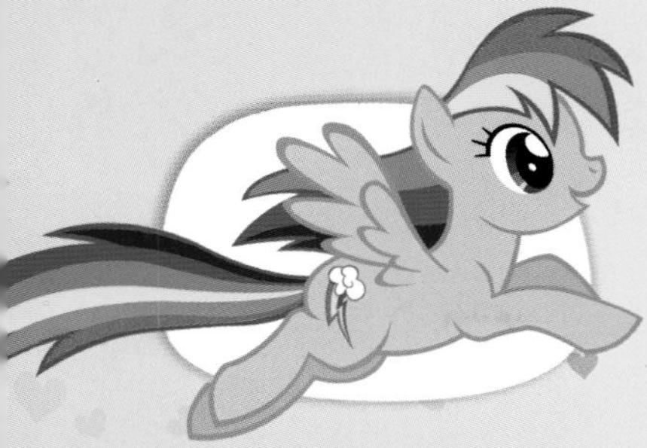

RAINBOW DASH

Rainbow Dash is the fastest pegasus around... and she KNOWS it! Never one to turn down a challenge, she's always ready to seize the day (in the spirit of friendly competition of course!).

SPIKE

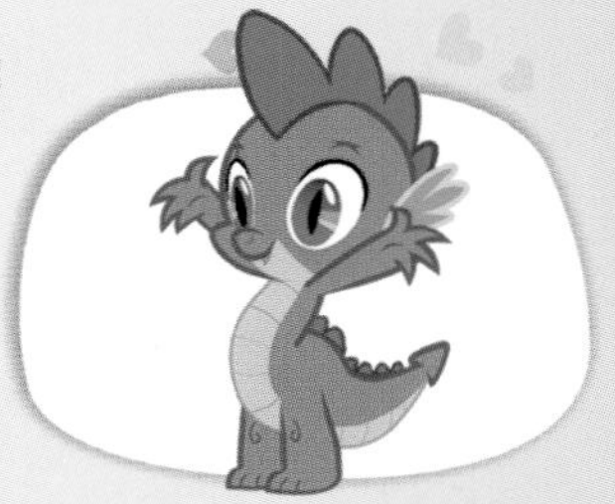

Spike the Dragon is the pint-sized assistant to Twilight Sparkle. Besides helping her out in the Ponyville library, he helps her practice spells and the duties of her daily life... he may be in the designated role of "helper," but he's also her dear friend.

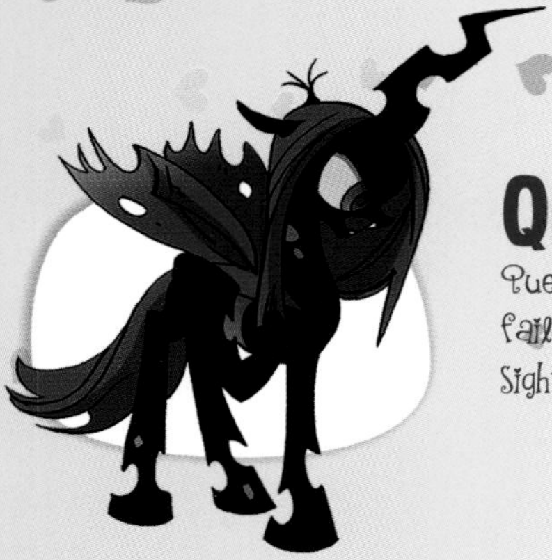

QUEEN CHRYSALIS

Queen Chrysalis is the Queen of the Changelings. After a failed attempt to take over Equestria, she now has her sights set on Twilight and her friends.

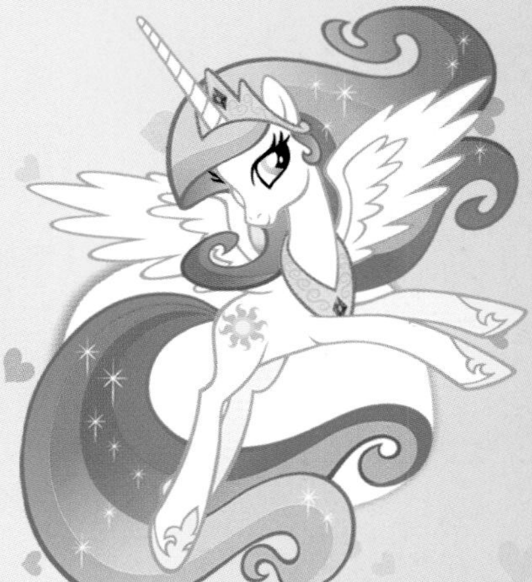

PRINCESS CELESTIA

Princess Celestia is the ruler of Equestria and Twilight Sparkle's mentor. Princess Celestia is kind, gentle, and powerful... everything she needs to be to rule and protect her kingdom.

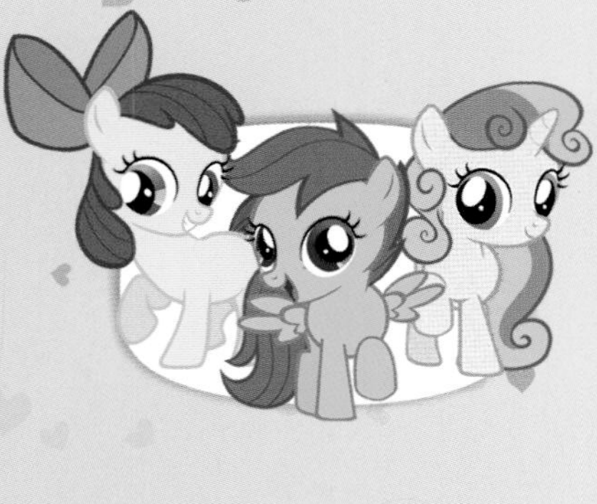

THE CUTIE MARK CRUSADERS

The Cutie Mark Crusaders are comprised of Sweetie Belle, Apple Bloom, and Scootaloo. These young fillies have yet to earn their cutie marks (the image on a pony's flank depicting their special talent!) and they are dashing through task after task together with the sole purpose of finding what makes them unique.

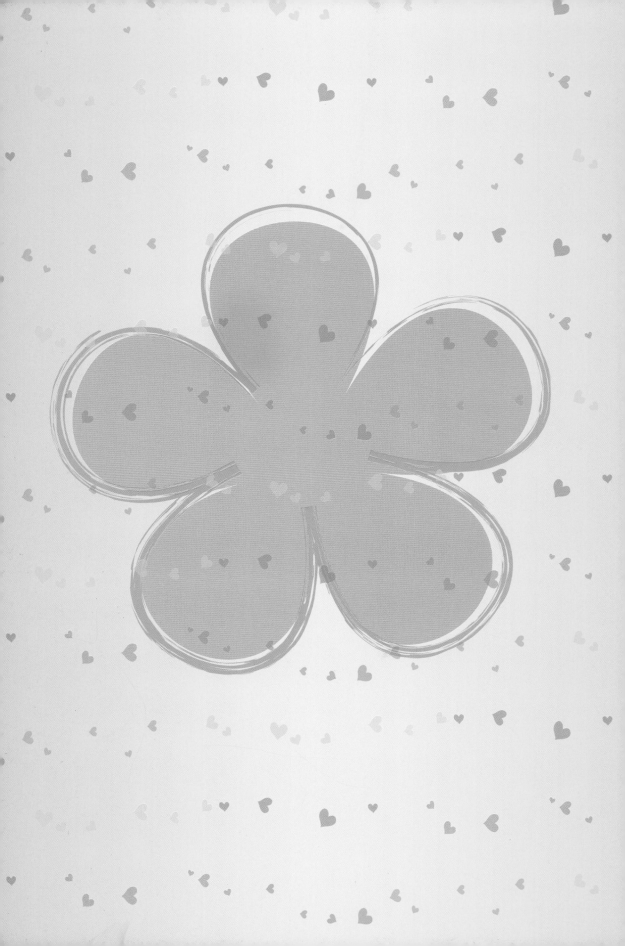

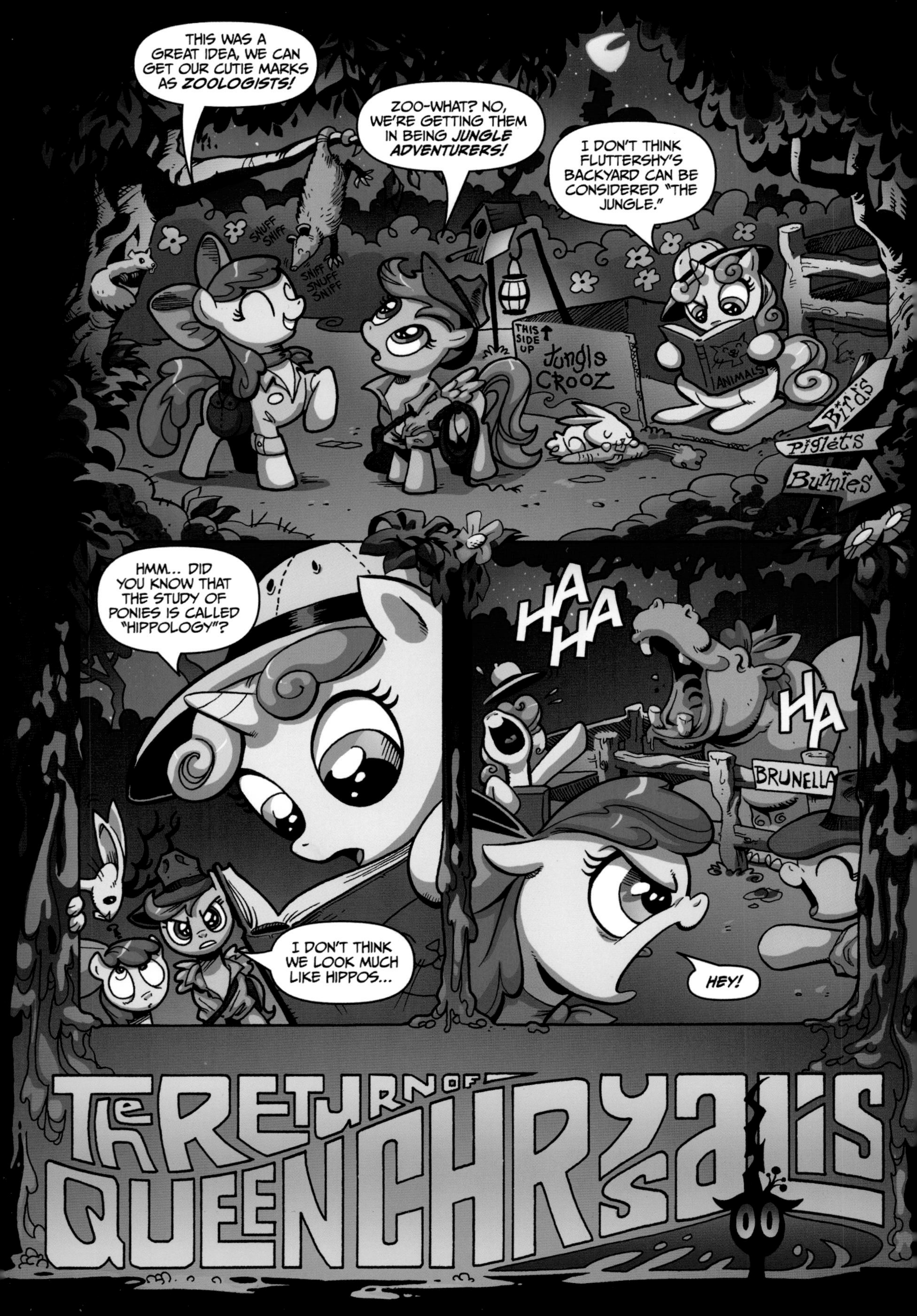
THIS WAS A GREAT IDEA, WE CAN GET OUR CUTIE MARKS AS ZOOLOGISTS!
ZOO-WHAT? NO, WE'RE GETTING THEM IN BEING JUNGLE ADVENTURERS!
I DON'T THINK FLUTTERSHY'S BACKYARD CAN BE CONSIDERED "THE JUNGLE."
SNUFF SNIFF
SNIFF SNUFF SNIFF
THIS SIDE UP
Jungle CROOZ
ANIMALS
Birds
Piglets
Bunnies
HMM... DID YOU KNOW THAT THE STUDY OF PONIES IS CALLED "HIPPOLOGY"?
I DON'T THINK WE LOOK MUCH LIKE HIPPOS...
HA HA HA
HA
BRUNELLA
HEY!
The RETURN OF QUEEN CHRYSALIS

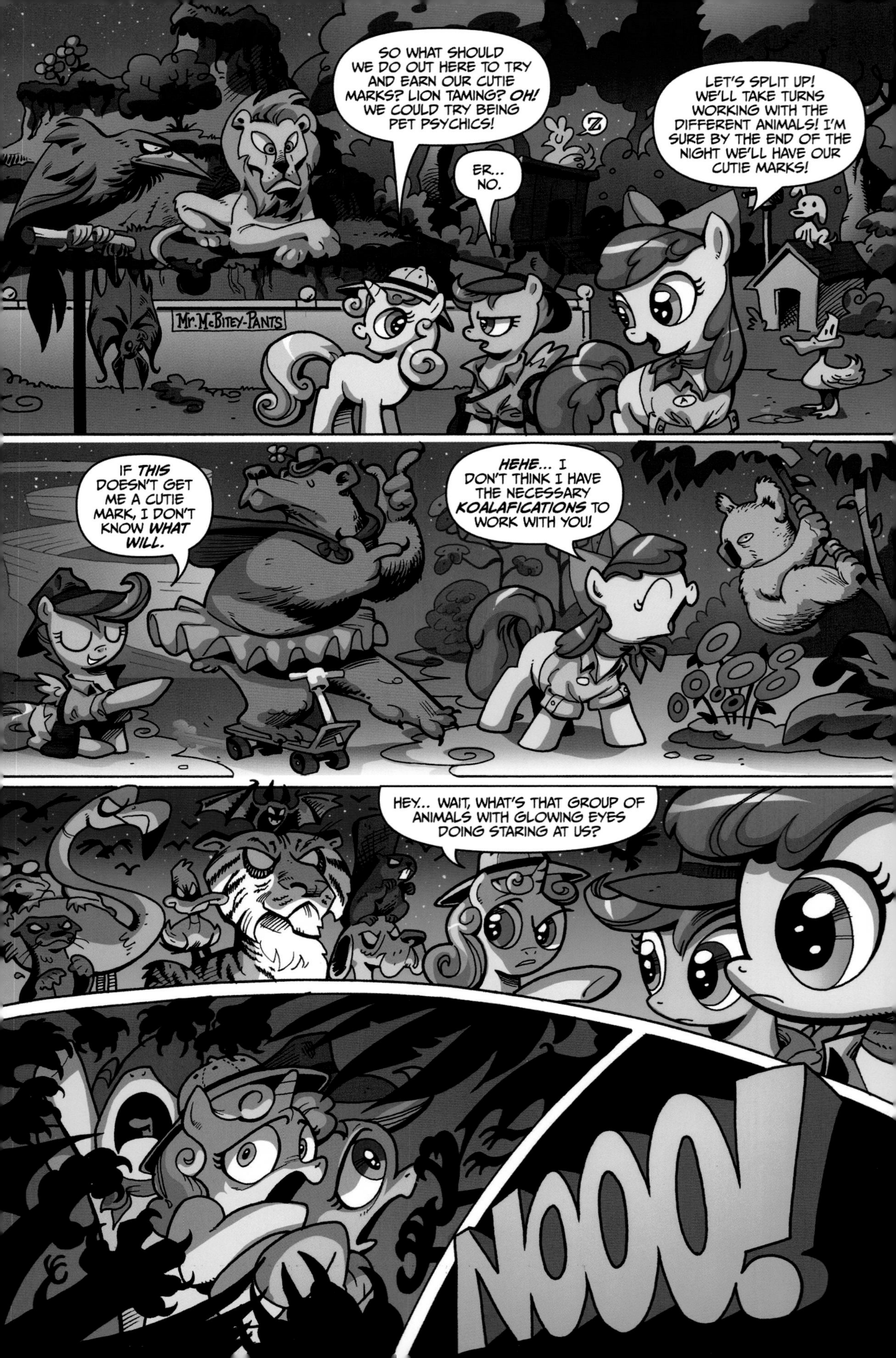
SO WHAT SHOULD WE DO OUT HERE TO TRY AND EARN OUR CUTIE MARKS? LION TAMING? *OH!* WE COULD TRY BEING PET PSYCHICS!
ER... NO.
LET'S SPLIT UP! WE'LL TAKE TURNS WORKING WITH THE DIFFERENT ANIMALS! I'M SURE BY THE END OF THE NIGHT WE'LL HAVE OUR CUTIE MARKS!
Z
Mr. McBitey-Pants
IF *THIS* DOESN'T GET ME A CUTIE MARK, I DON'T KNOW *WHAT WILL.*
HEHE... I DON'T THINK I HAVE THE NECESSARY *KOALAFICATIONS* TO WORK WITH YOU!
HEY... WAIT, WHAT'S THAT GROUP OF ANIMALS WITH GLOWING EYES DOING STARING AT US?
NOOO!

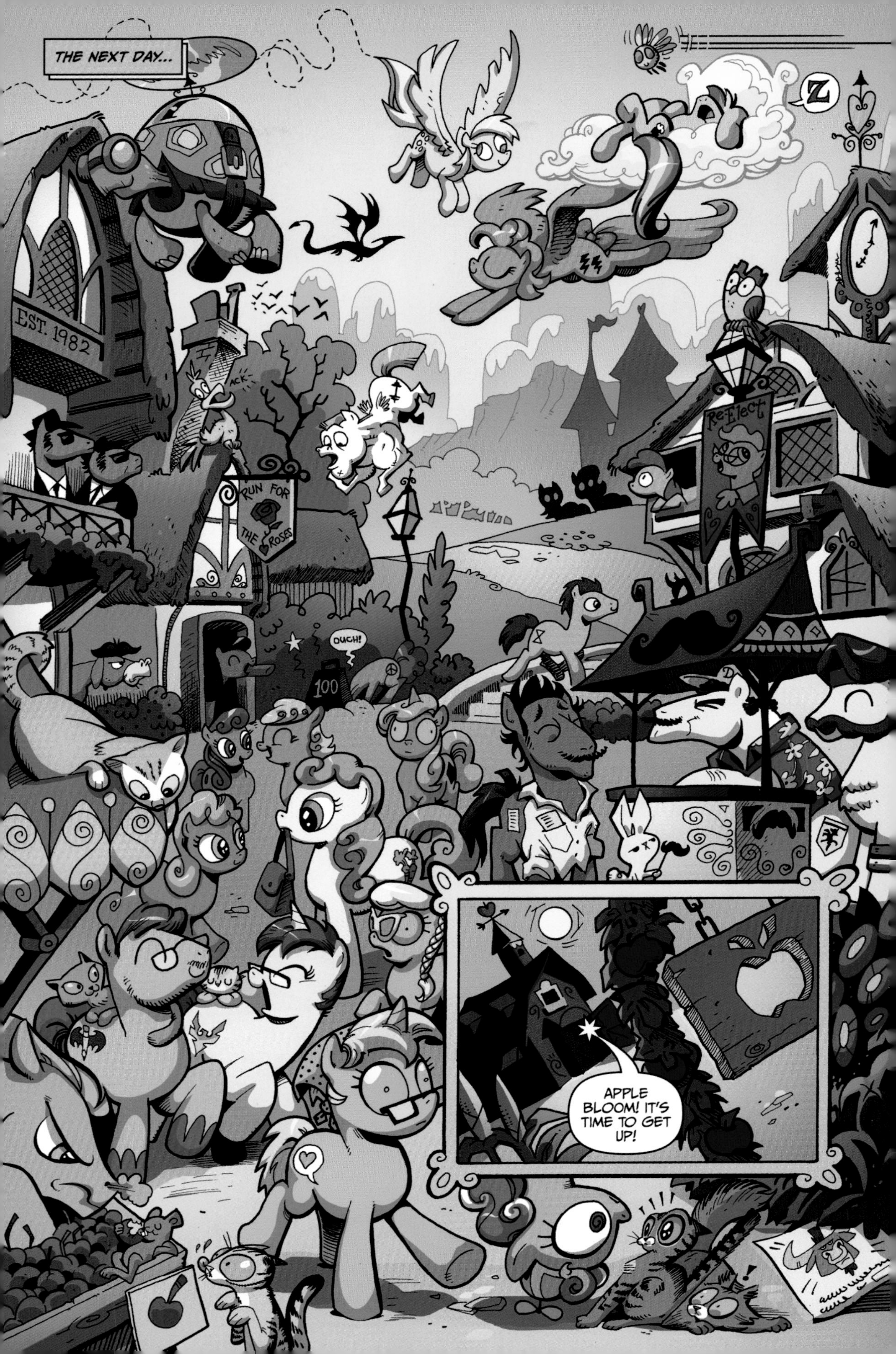
THE NEXT DAY...
Z
EST. 1982
ACK
RUN FOR THE ROSES
Re-Elect
OUCH!
100
APPLE BLOOM! IT'S TIME TO GET UP!

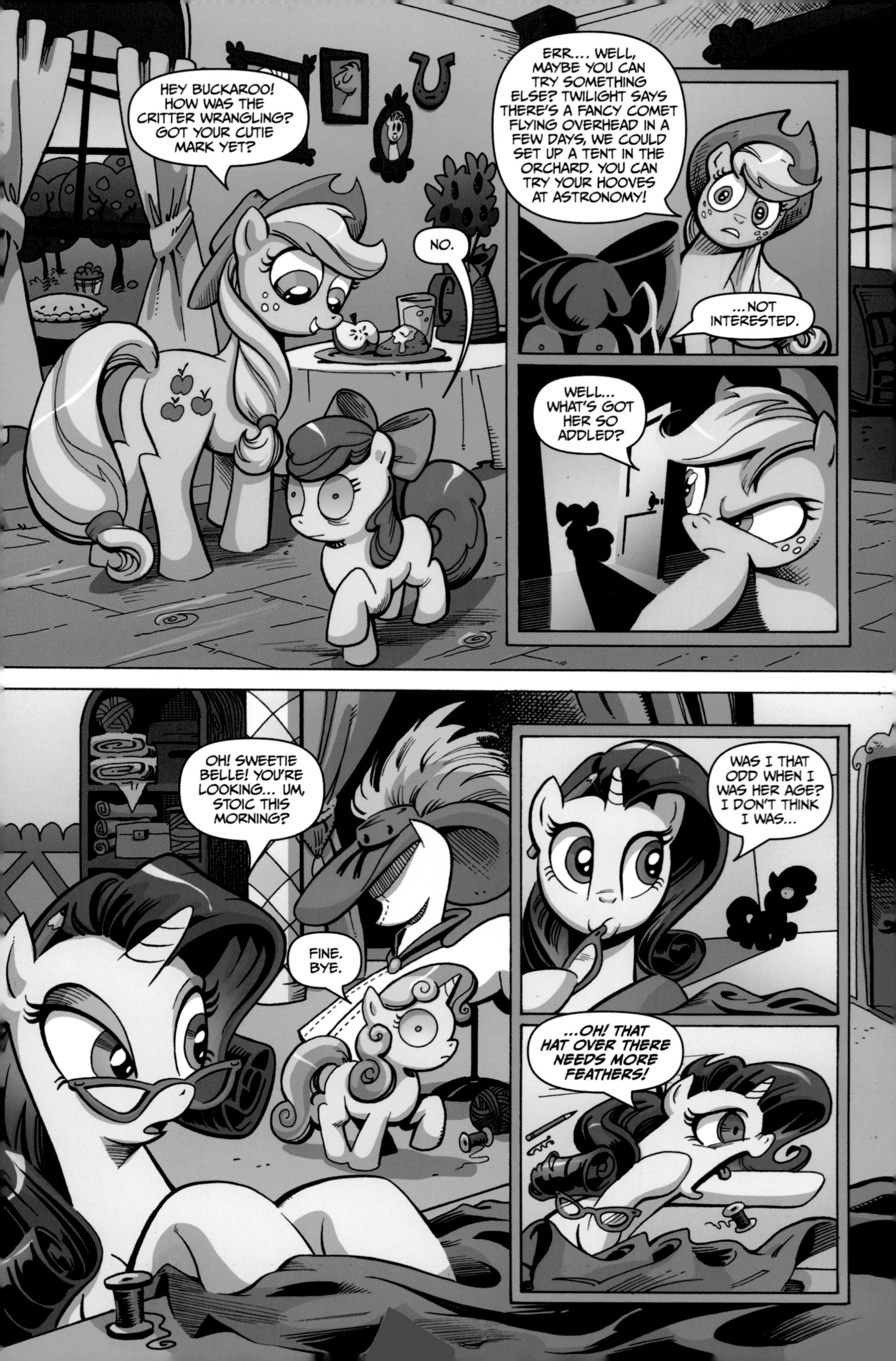
HEY BUCKAROO! HOW WAS THE CRITTER WRANGLING? GOT YOUR CUTIE MARK YET?
NO.
ERR... WELL, MAYBE YOU CAN TRY SOMETHING ELSE? TWILIGHT SAYS THERE'S A FANCY COMET FLYING OVERHEAD IN A FEW DAYS, WE COULD SET UP A TENT IN THE ORCHARD. YOU CAN TRY YOUR HOOVES AT ASTRONOMY!
...NOT INTERESTED.
WELL... WHAT'S GOT HER SO ADDLED?
OH! SWEETIE BELLE! YOU'RE LOOKING... UM, STOIC THIS MORNING?
FINE. BYE.
WAS I THAT ODD WHEN I WAS HER AGE? I DON'T THINK I WAS...
...OH! THAT HAT OVER THERE NEEDS MORE FEATHERS!

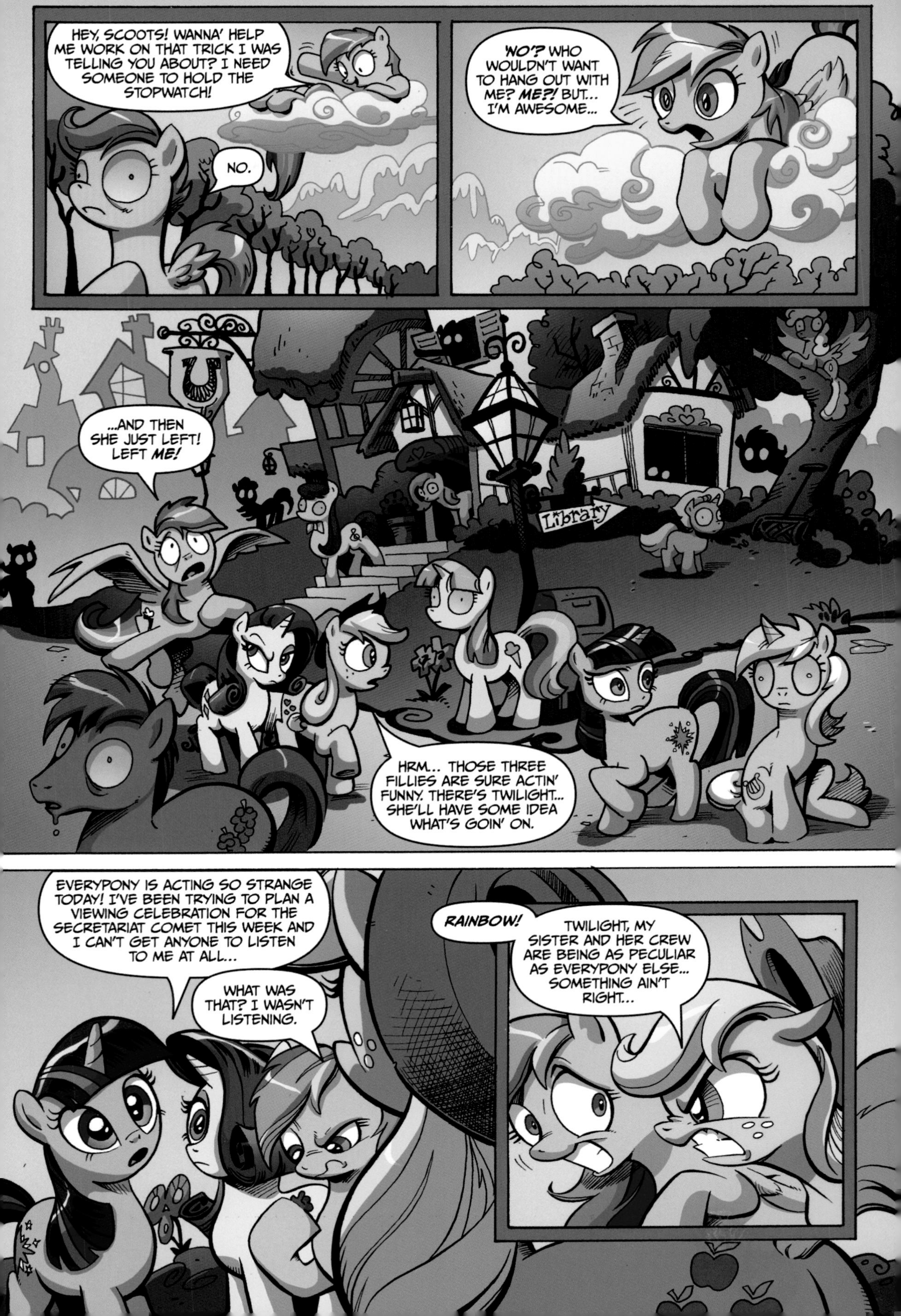
HEY, SCOOTS! WANNA' HELP ME WORK ON THAT TRICK I WAS TELLING YOU ABOUT? I NEED SOMEONE TO HOLD THE STOPWATCH!
NO.
'NO'? WHO WOULDN'T WANT TO HANG OUT WITH ME? ME?! BUT... I'M AWESOME...
...AND THEN SHE JUST LEFT! LEFT ME!
Library
HRM... THOSE THREE FILLIES ARE SURE ACTIN' FUNNY. THERE'S TWILIGHT... SHE'LL HAVE SOME IDEA WHAT'S GOIN' ON.
EVERYPONY IS ACTING SO STRANGE TODAY! I'VE BEEN TRYING TO PLAN A VIEWING CELEBRATION FOR THE SECRETARIAT COMET THIS WEEK AND I CAN'T GET ANYONE TO LISTEN TO ME AT ALL...
WHAT WAS THAT? I WASN'T LISTENING.
RAINBOW!
TWILIGHT, MY SISTER AND HER CREW ARE BEING AS PECULIAR AS EVERYPONY ELSE... SOMETHING AIN'T RIGHT...

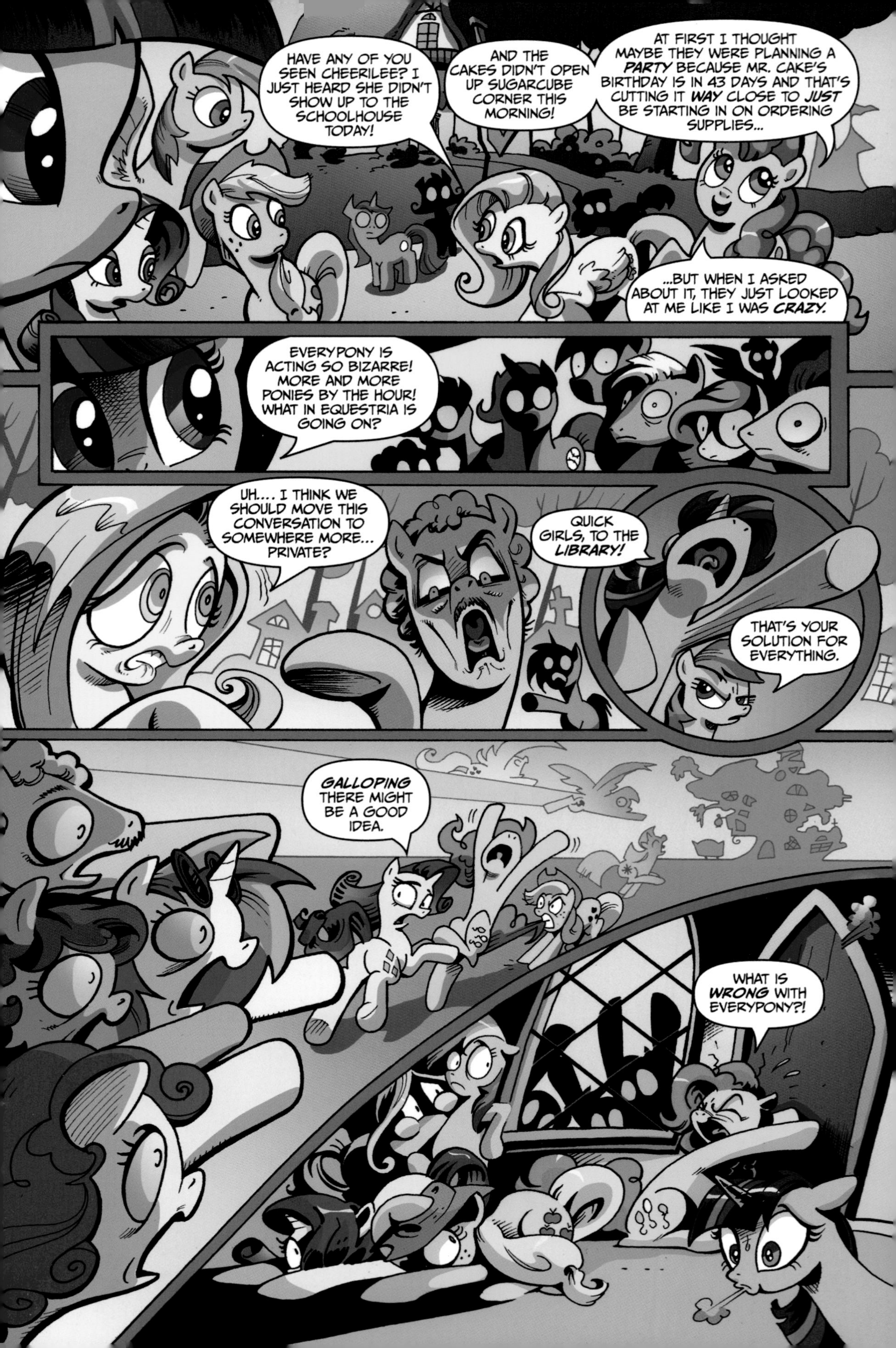
HAVE ANY OF YOU SEEN CHEERILEE? I JUST HEARD SHE DIDN'T SHOW UP TO THE SCHOOLHOUSE TODAY!
AND THE CAKES DIDN'T OPEN UP SUGARCUBE CORNER THIS MORNING!
AT FIRST I THOUGHT MAYBE THEY WERE PLANNING A PARTY BECAUSE MR. CAKE'S BIRTHDAY IS IN 43 DAYS AND THAT'S CUTTING IT WAY CLOSE TO JUST BE STARTING IN ON ORDERING SUPPLIES...
...BUT WHEN I ASKED ABOUT IT, THEY JUST LOOKED AT ME LIKE I WAS CRAZY.
EVERYPONY IS ACTING SO BIZARRE! MORE AND MORE PONIES BY THE HOUR! WHAT IN EQUESTRIA IS GOING ON?
UH.... I THINK WE SHOULD MOVE THIS CONVERSATION TO SOMEWHERE MORE... PRIVATE?
QUICK GIRLS, TO THE LIBRARY!
THAT'S YOUR SOLUTION FOR EVERYTHING.
GALLOPING THERE MIGHT BE A GOOD IDEA.
WHAT IS WRONG WITH EVERYPONY?!

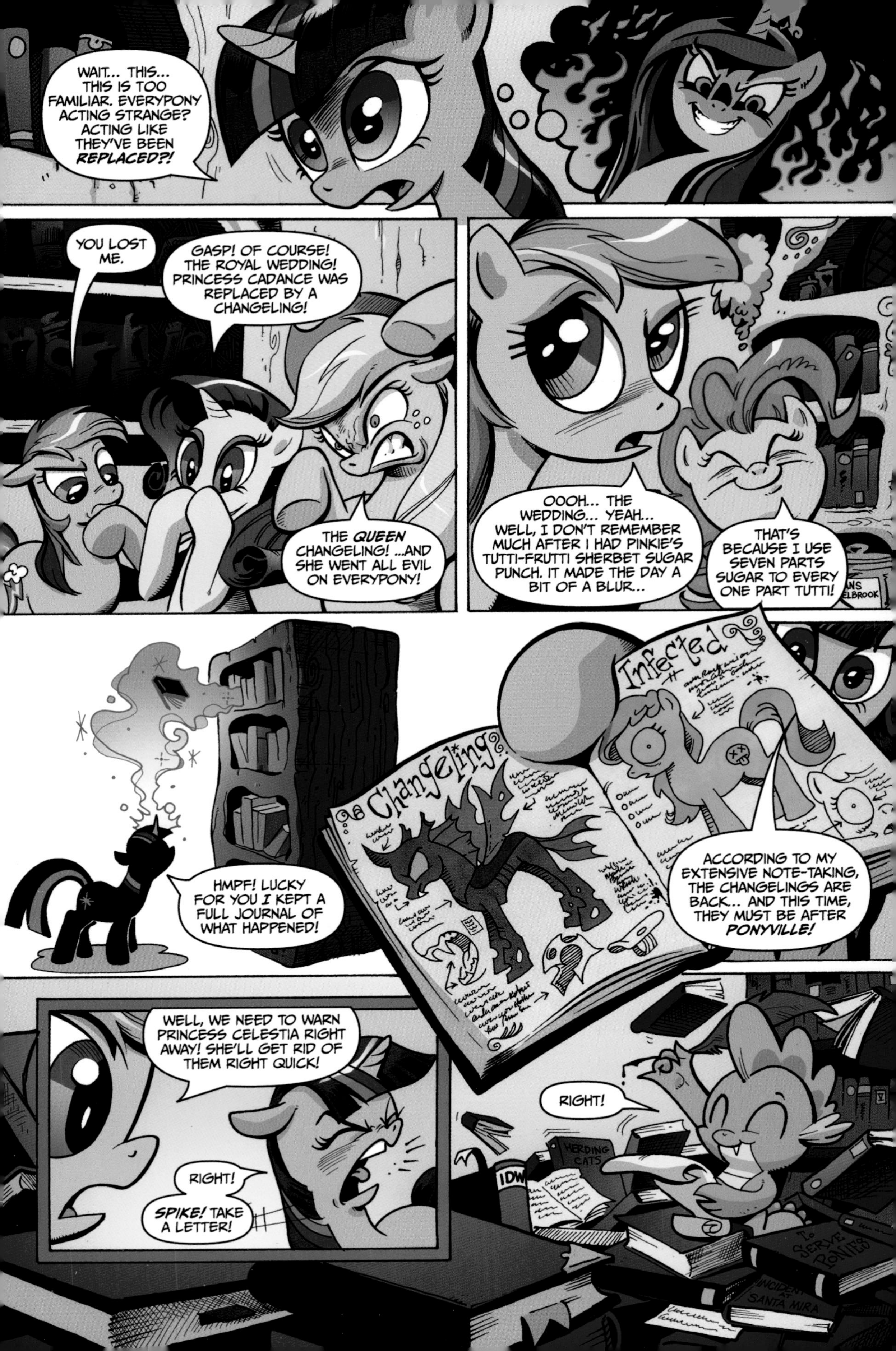
WAIT... THIS... THIS IS TOO FAMILIAR. EVERYPONY ACTING STRANGE? ACTING LIKE THEY'VE BEEN REPLACED?!
YOU LOST ME.
GASP! OF COURSE! THE ROYAL WEDDING! PRINCESS CADANCE WAS REPLACED BY A CHANGELING!
THE QUEEN CHANGELING! ...AND SHE WENT ALL EVIL ON EVERYPONY!
OOOH... THE WEDDING... YEAH... WELL, I DON'T REMEMBER MUCH AFTER I HAD PINKIE'S TUTTI-FRUTTI SHERBET SUGAR PUNCH. IT MADE THE DAY A BIT OF A BLUR...
THAT'S BECAUSE I USE SEVEN PARTS SUGAR TO EVERY ONE PART TUTTI!
HMPF! LUCKY FOR YOU I KEPT A FULL JOURNAL OF WHAT HAPPENED!
Changeling
Infected
ACCORDING TO MY EXTENSIVE NOTE-TAKING, THE CHANGELINGS ARE BACK... AND THIS TIME, THEY MUST BE AFTER PONYVILLE!
WELL, WE NEED TO WARN PRINCESS CELESTIA RIGHT AWAY! SHE'LL GET RID OF THEM RIGHT QUICK!
RIGHT!
SPIKE! TAKE A LETTER!
RIGHT!
HERDING CATS
IDW
TO SERVE PONIES
INCIDENT AT SANTA MIRA

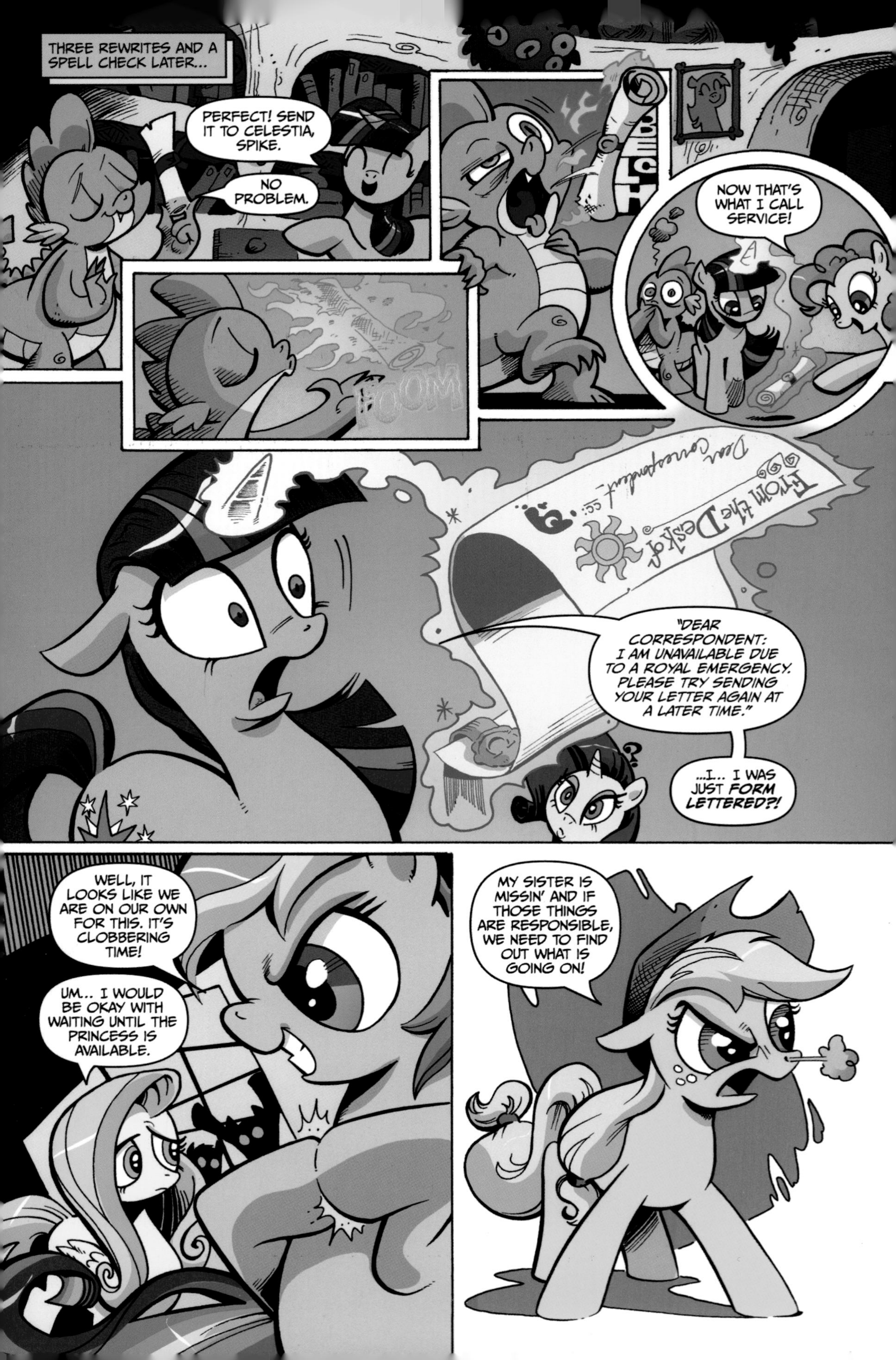
THREE REWRITES AND A SPELL CHECK LATER...
PERFECT! SEND IT TO CELESTIA, SPIKE.
NO PROBLEM.
BELCH
FOOM
NOW THAT'S WHAT I CALL SERVICE!
From the Desk of
Dear Correspondent
"DEAR CORRESPONDENT: I AM UNAVAILABLE DUE TO A ROYAL EMERGENCY. PLEASE TRY SENDING YOUR LETTER AGAIN AT A LATER TIME."
...I... I WAS JUST FORM LETTERED?!
WELL, IT LOOKS LIKE WE ARE ON OUR OWN FOR THIS. IT'S CLOBBERING TIME!
UM... I WOULD BE OKAY WITH WAITING UNTIL THE PRINCESS IS AVAILABLE.
MY SISTER IS MISSIN' AND IF THOSE THINGS ARE RESPONSIBLE, WE NEED TO FIND OUT WHAT IS GOING ON!

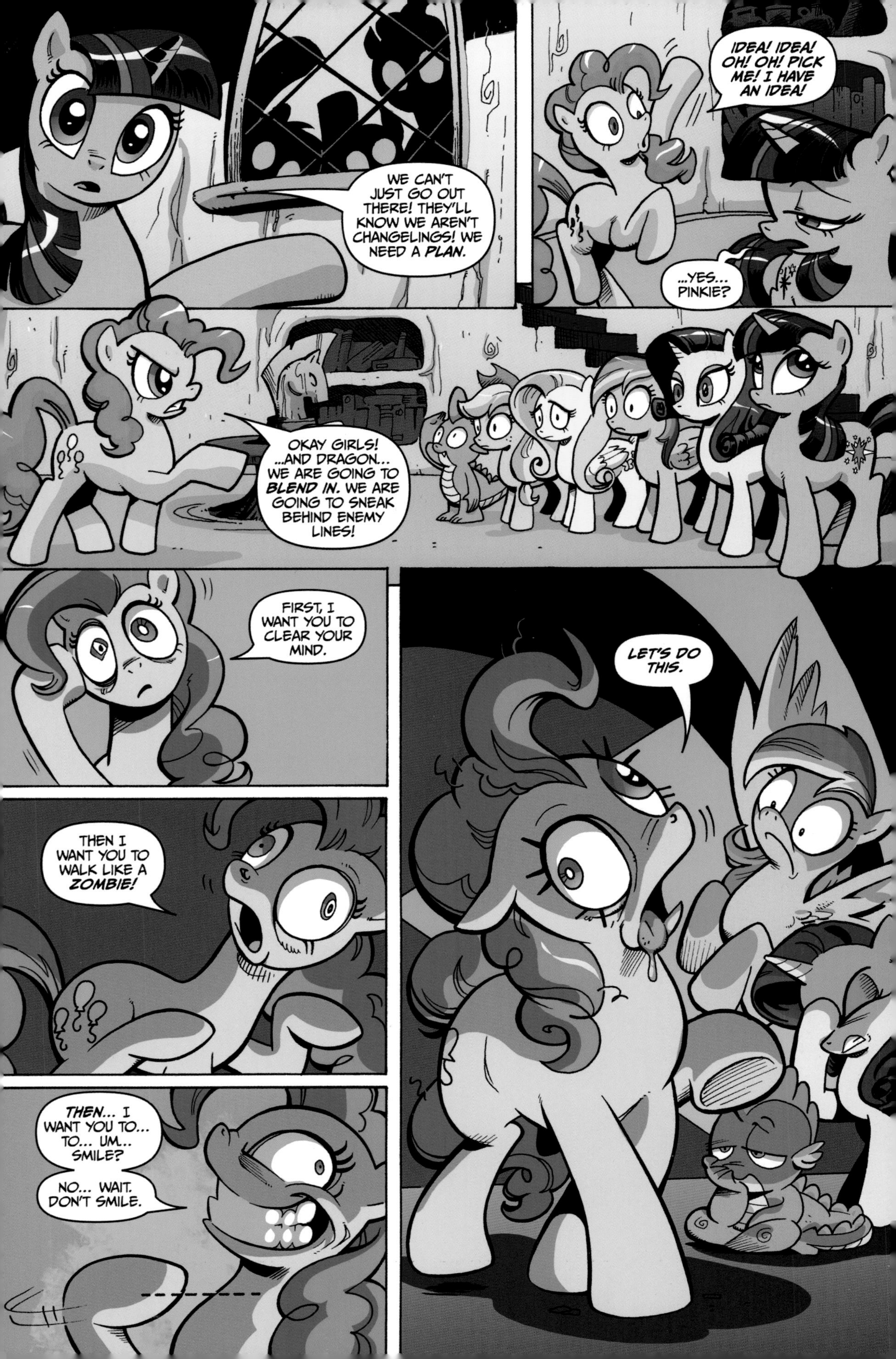
WE CAN'T JUST GO OUT THERE! THEY'LL KNOW WE AREN'T CHANGELINGS! WE NEED A *PLAN*.
IDEA! IDEA! OH! OH! PICK ME! I HAVE AN IDEA!
...YES... PINKIE?
OKAY GIRLS! ...AND DRAGON... WE ARE GOING TO *BLEND IN*. WE ARE GOING TO SNEAK BEHIND ENEMY LINES!
FIRST, I WANT YOU TO CLEAR YOUR MIND.
THEN I WANT YOU TO WALK LIKE A *ZOMBIE!*
THEN... I WANT YOU TO... TO... UM... SMILE?
NO... WAIT. DON'T SMILE.
LET'S DO THIS.

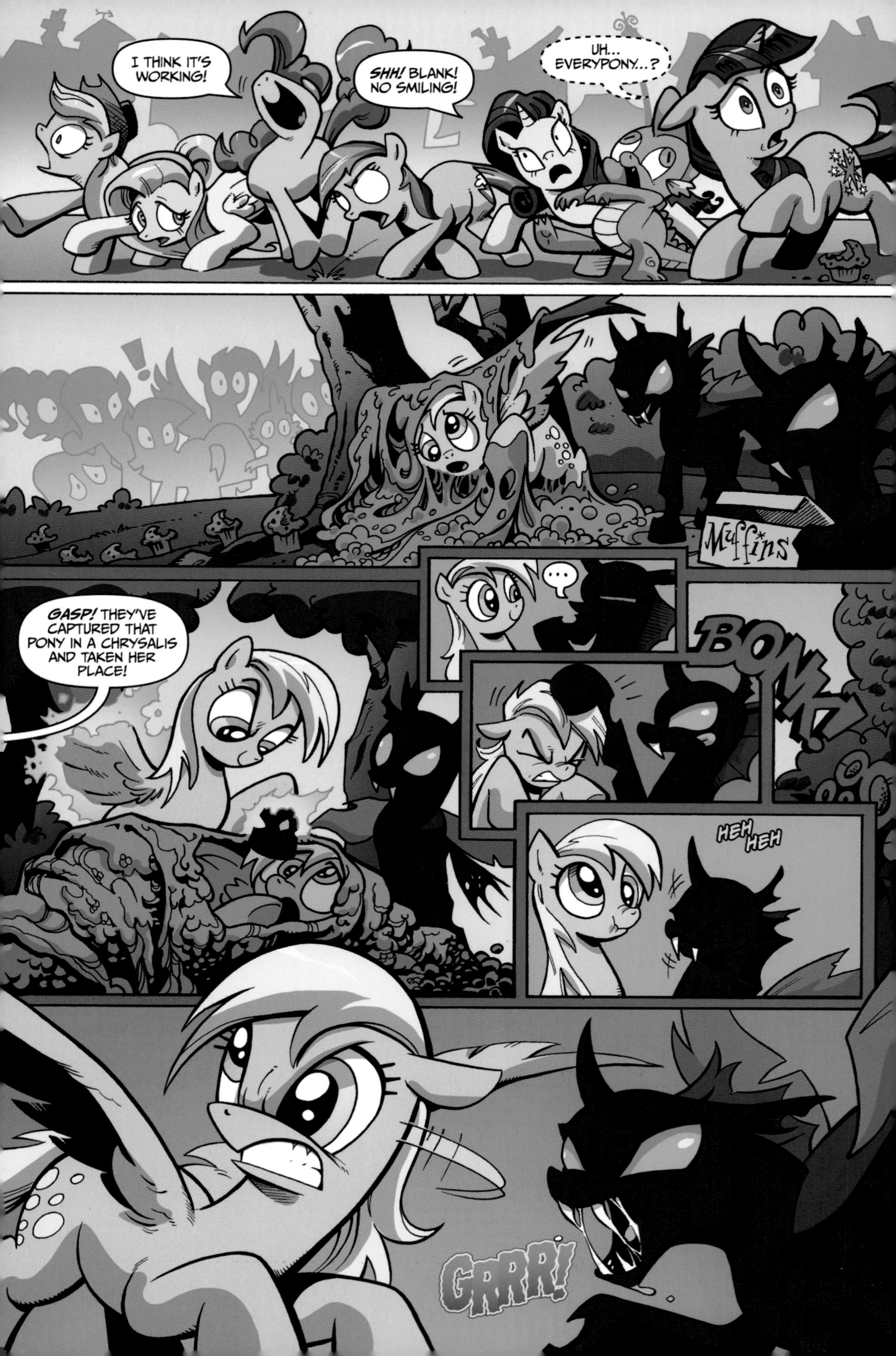
I THINK IT'S WORKING!
SHH! BLANK! NO SMILING!
UH... EVERYPONY...?
Muffins
GASP! THEY'VE CAPTURED THAT PONY IN A CHRYSALIS AND TAKEN HER PLACE!
...
BONK!
HEH HEH
GRRR!

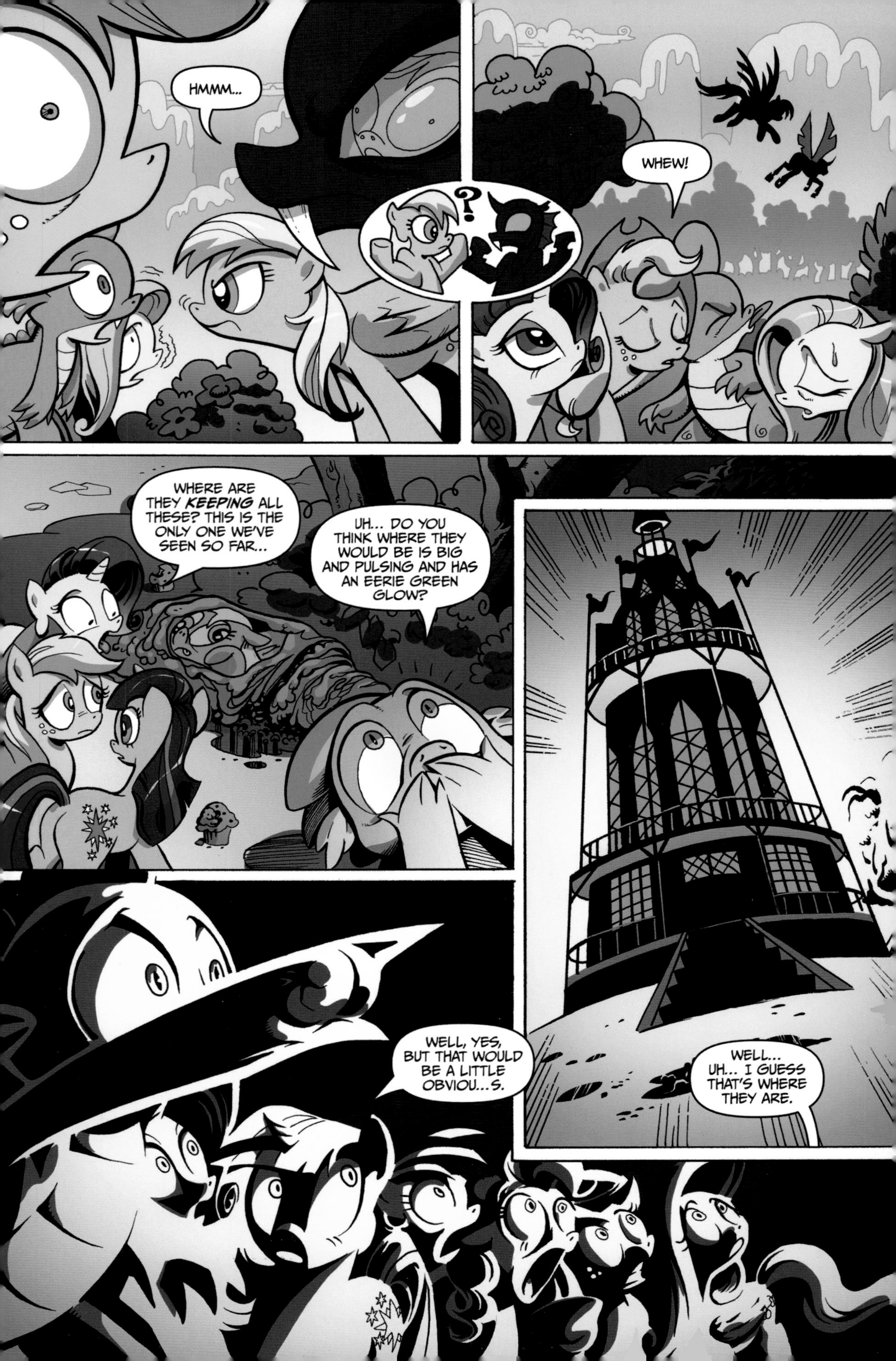
HMMM...
WHEW!
WHERE ARE THEY KEEPING ALL THESE? THIS IS THE ONLY ONE WE'VE SEEN SO FAR...
UH... DO YOU THINK WHERE THEY WOULD BE IS BIG AND PULSING AND HAS AN EERIE GREEN GLOW?
WELL, YES, BUT THAT WOULD BE A LITTLE OBVIOU...S.
WELL... UH... I GUESS THAT'S WHERE THEY ARE.

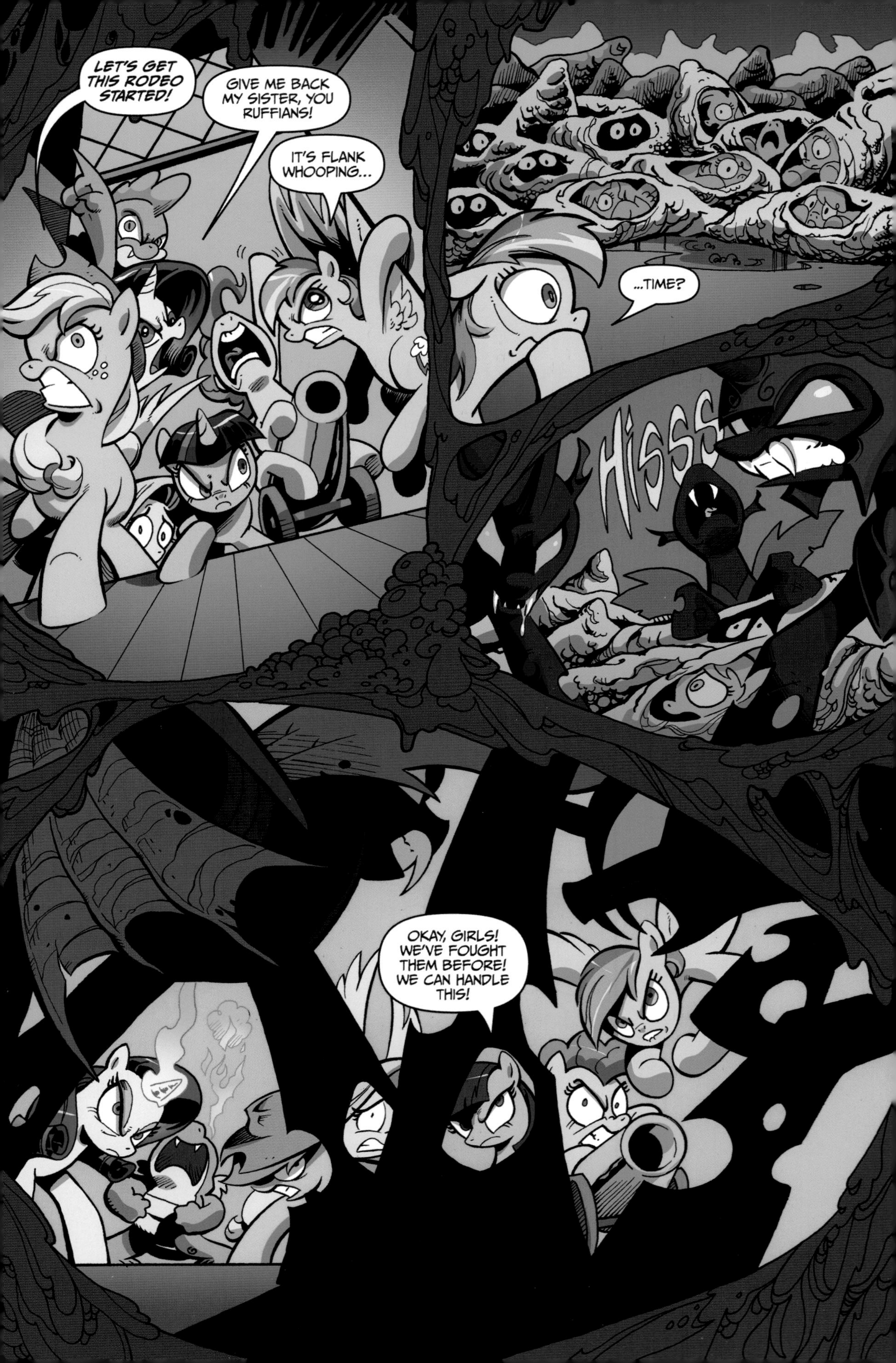
LET'S GET THIS RODEO STARTED!
GIVE ME BACK MY SISTER, YOU RUFFIANS!
IT'S FLANK WHOOPING...
...TIME?
HISSS
OKAY, GIRLS! WE'VE FOUGHT THEM BEFORE! WE CAN HANDLE THIS!

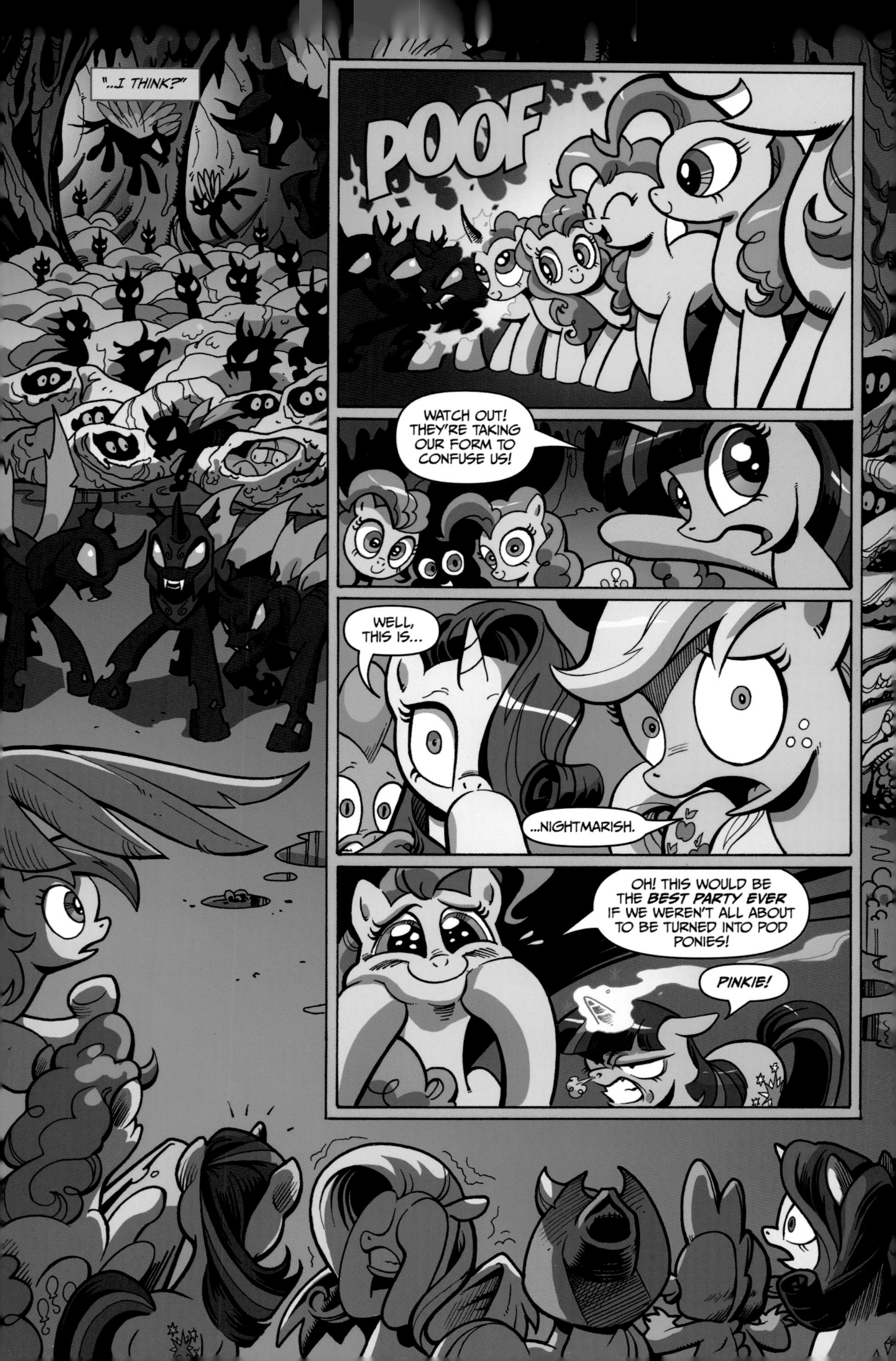
"...I THINK?"
POOF
WATCH OUT! THEY'RE TAKING OUR FORM TO CONFUSE US!
WELL, THIS IS...
...NIGHTMARISH.
OH! THIS WOULD BE THE BEST PARTY EVER IF WE WEREN'T ALL ABOUT TO BE TURNED INTO POD PONIES!
PINKIE!

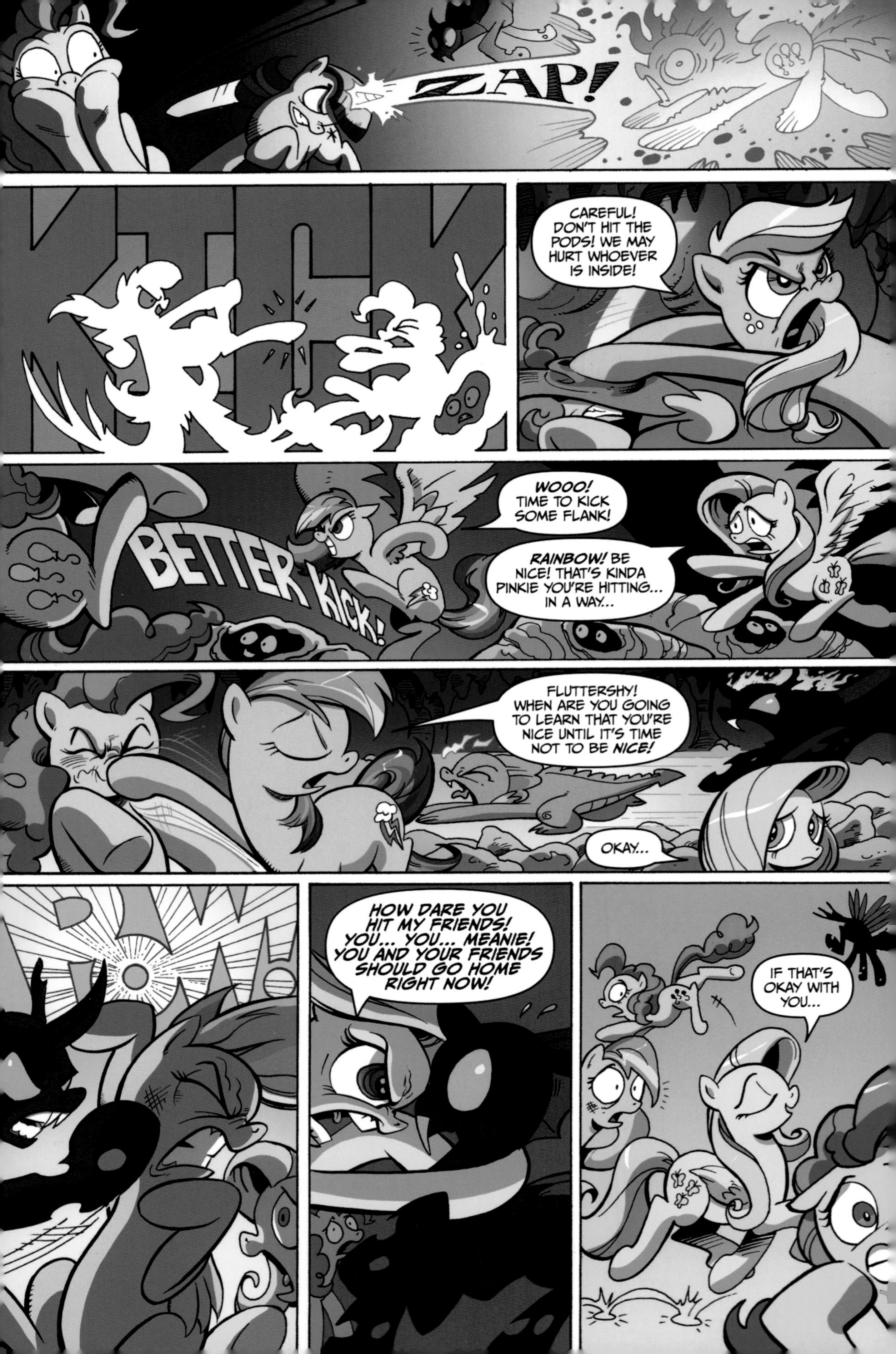
ZAP!
CAREFUL! DON'T HIT THE PODS! WE MAY HURT WHOEVER IS INSIDE!
WOOO! TIME TO KICK SOME FLANK!
BETTER KICK!
RAINBOW! BE NICE! THAT'S KINDA PINKIE YOU'RE HITTING... IN A WAY...
FLUTTERSHY! WHEN ARE YOU GOING TO LEARN THAT YOU'RE NICE UNTIL IT'S TIME NOT TO BE NICE!
OKAY...
HOW DARE YOU HIT MY FRIENDS! YOU... YOU... MEANIE! YOU AND YOUR FRIENDS SHOULD GO HOME RIGHT NOW!
IF THAT'S OKAY WITH YOU...

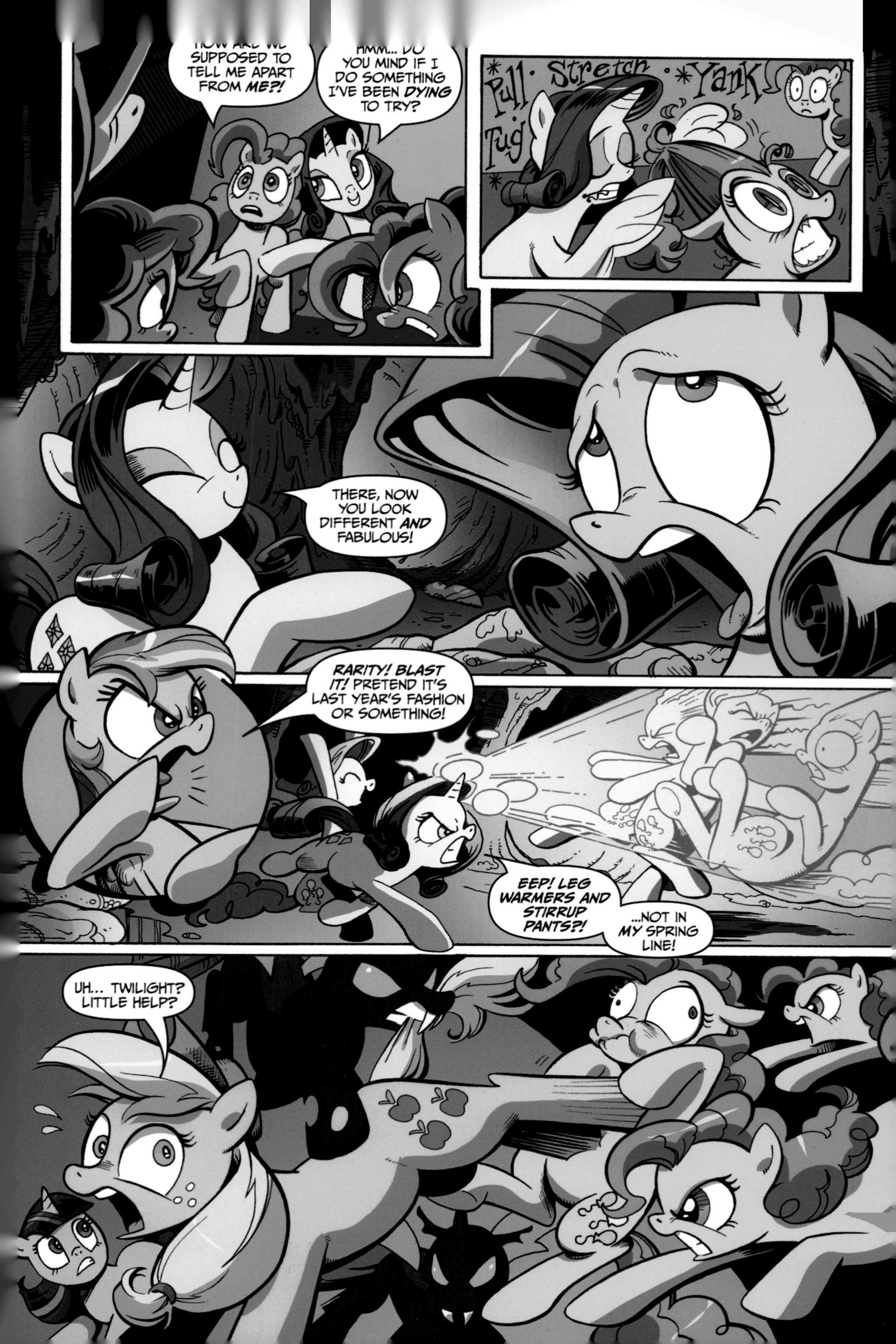
HOW ARE WE SUPPOSED TO TELL ME APART FROM *ME*?!
HMM... DO YOU MIND IF I DO SOMETHING I'VE BEEN *DYING* TO TRY?
Pull · Stretch · Yank! Tug
THERE, NOW YOU LOOK DIFFERENT *AND* FABULOUS!
RARITY! BLAST IT! PRETEND IT'S LAST YEAR'S FASHION OR SOMETHING!
EEP! LEG WARMERS AND STIRRUP PANTS?!
...NOT IN *MY* SPRING LINE!
UH... TWILIGHT? LITTLE HELP?

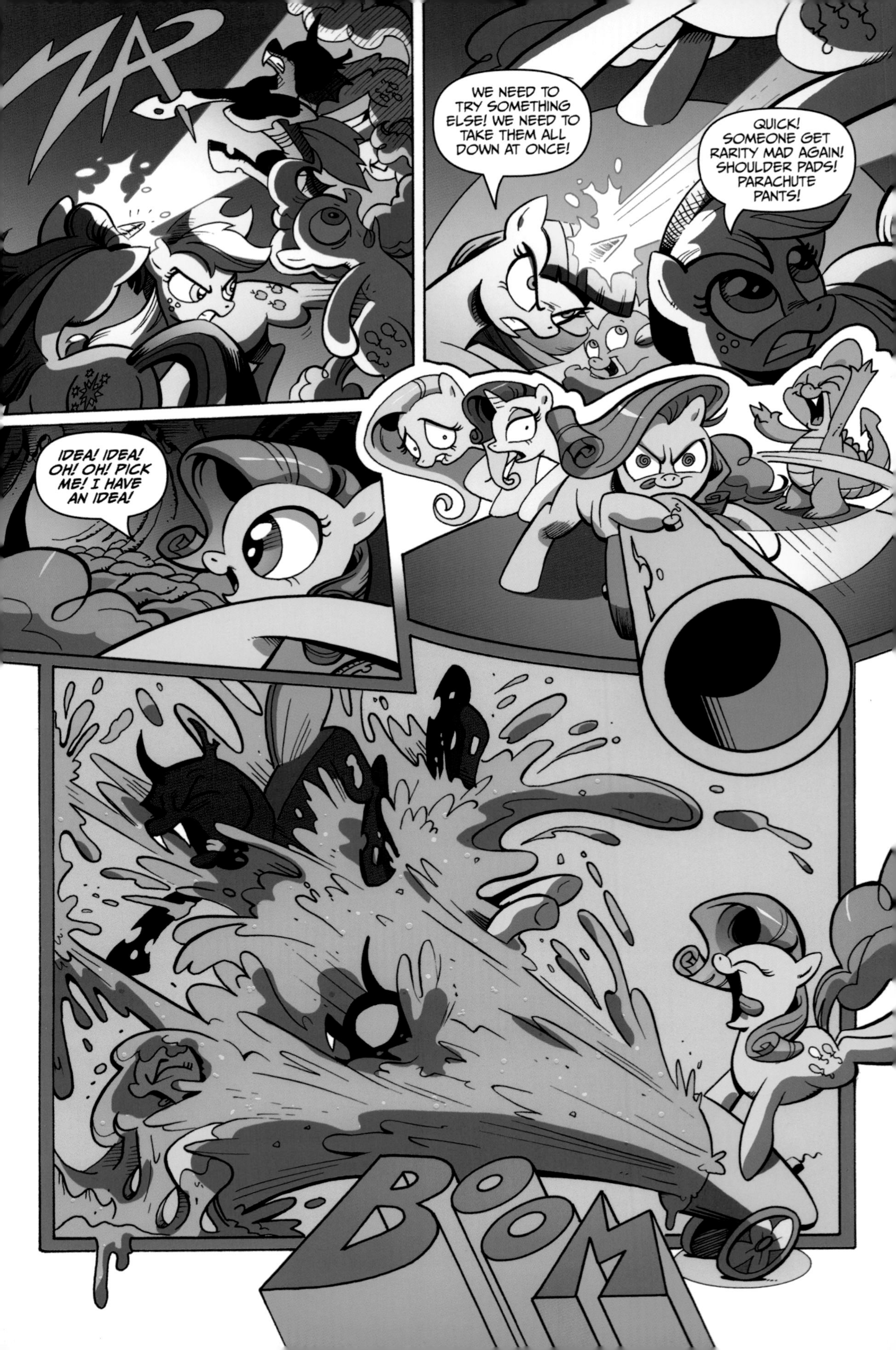
ZAP
WE NEED TO TRY SOMETHING ELSE! WE NEED TO TAKE THEM ALL DOWN AT ONCE!
QUICK! SOMEONE GET RARITY MAD AGAIN! SHOULDER PADS! PARACHUTE PANTS!
IDEA! IDEA! OH! OH! PICK ME! I HAVE AN IDEA!
BOOM

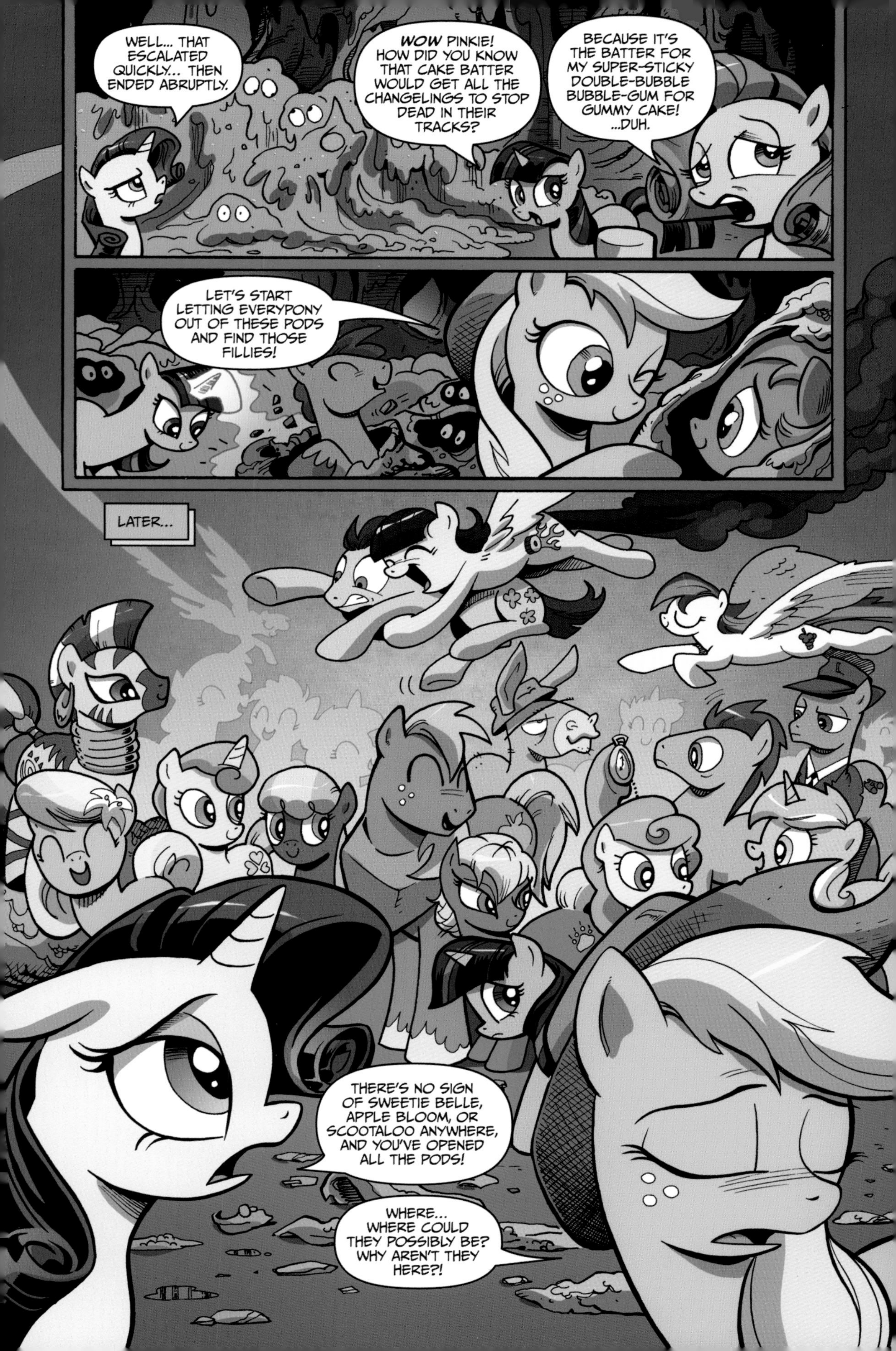
WELL... THAT ESCALATED QUICKLY... THEN ENDED ABRUPTLY.
WOW PINKIE! HOW DID YOU KNOW THAT CAKE BATTER WOULD GET ALL THE CHANGELINGS TO STOP DEAD IN THEIR TRACKS?
BECAUSE IT'S THE BATTER FOR MY SUPER-STICKY DOUBLE-BUBBLE BUBBLE-GUM FOR GUMMY CAKE! ...DUH.
LET'S START LETTING EVERYPONY OUT OF THESE PODS AND FIND THOSE FILLIES!
LATER...
THERE'S NO SIGN OF SWEETIE BELLE, APPLE BLOOM, OR SCOOTALOO ANYWHERE, AND YOU'VE OPENED ALL THE PODS!
WHERE... WHERE COULD THEY POSSIBLY BE? WHY AREN'T THEY HERE?!

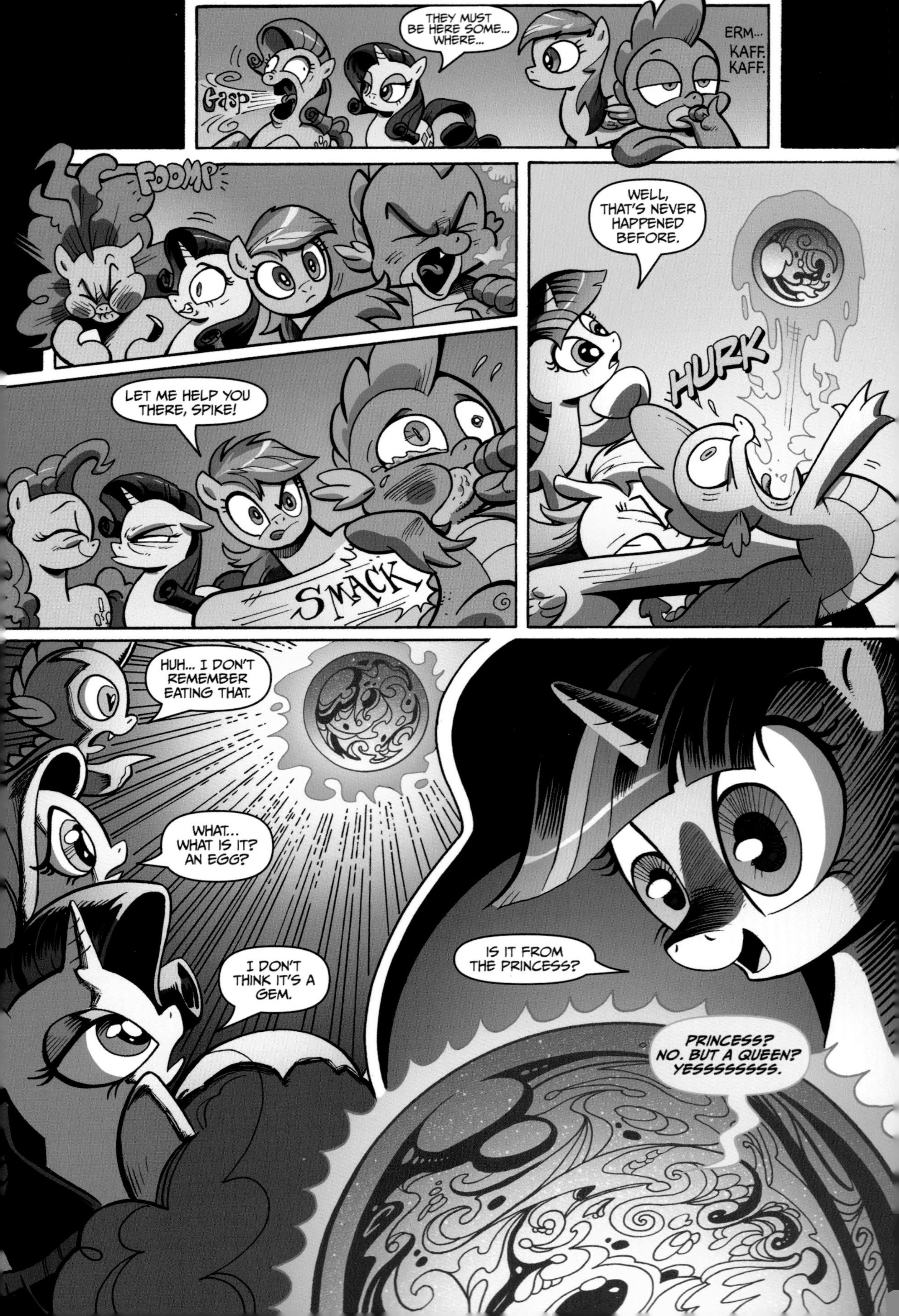
GASP
THEY MUST BE HERE SOME... WHERE...
ERM... KAFF. KAFF.
FOOMP
LET ME HELP YOU THERE, SPIKE!
SMACK
WELL, THAT'S NEVER HAPPENED BEFORE.
HURK
HUH... I DON'T REMEMBER EATING THAT.
WHAT... WHAT IS IT? AN EGG?
I DON'T THINK IT'S A GEM.
IS IT FROM THE PRINCESS?
PRINCESS? NO. BUT A QUEEN? YESSSSSSSS.

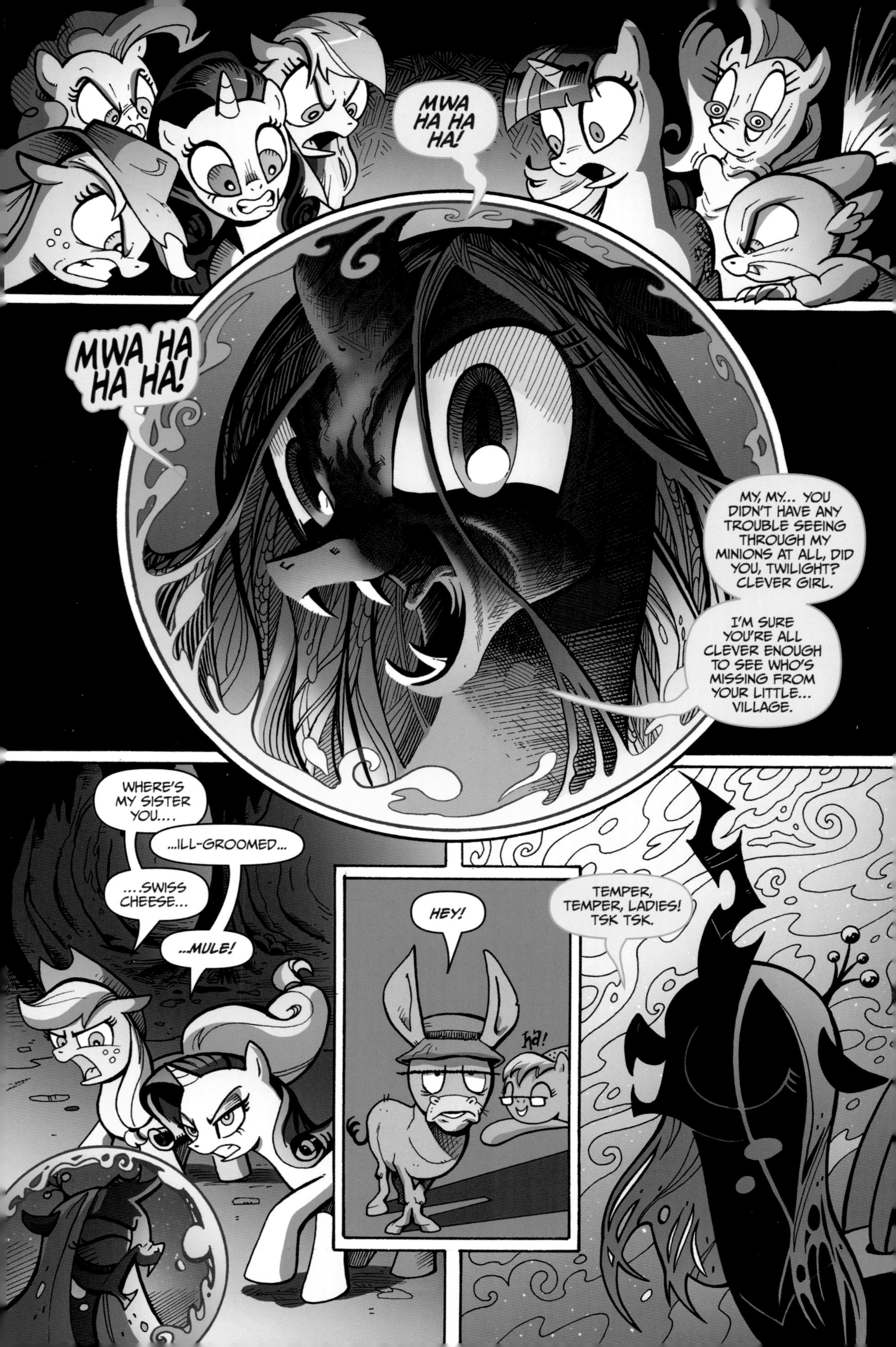
MWA HA HA HA!
MWA HA HA HA!
MY, MY... YOU DIDN'T HAVE ANY TROUBLE SEEING THROUGH MY MINIONS AT ALL, DID YOU, TWILIGHT? CLEVER GIRL.
I'M SURE YOU'RE ALL CLEVER ENOUGH TO SEE WHO'S MISSING FROM YOUR LITTLE... VILLAGE.
WHERE'S MY SISTER YOU....
...ILL-GROOMED...
....SWISS CHEESE...
...MULE!
HEY!
HA!
TEMPER, TEMPER, LADIES! TSK TSK.

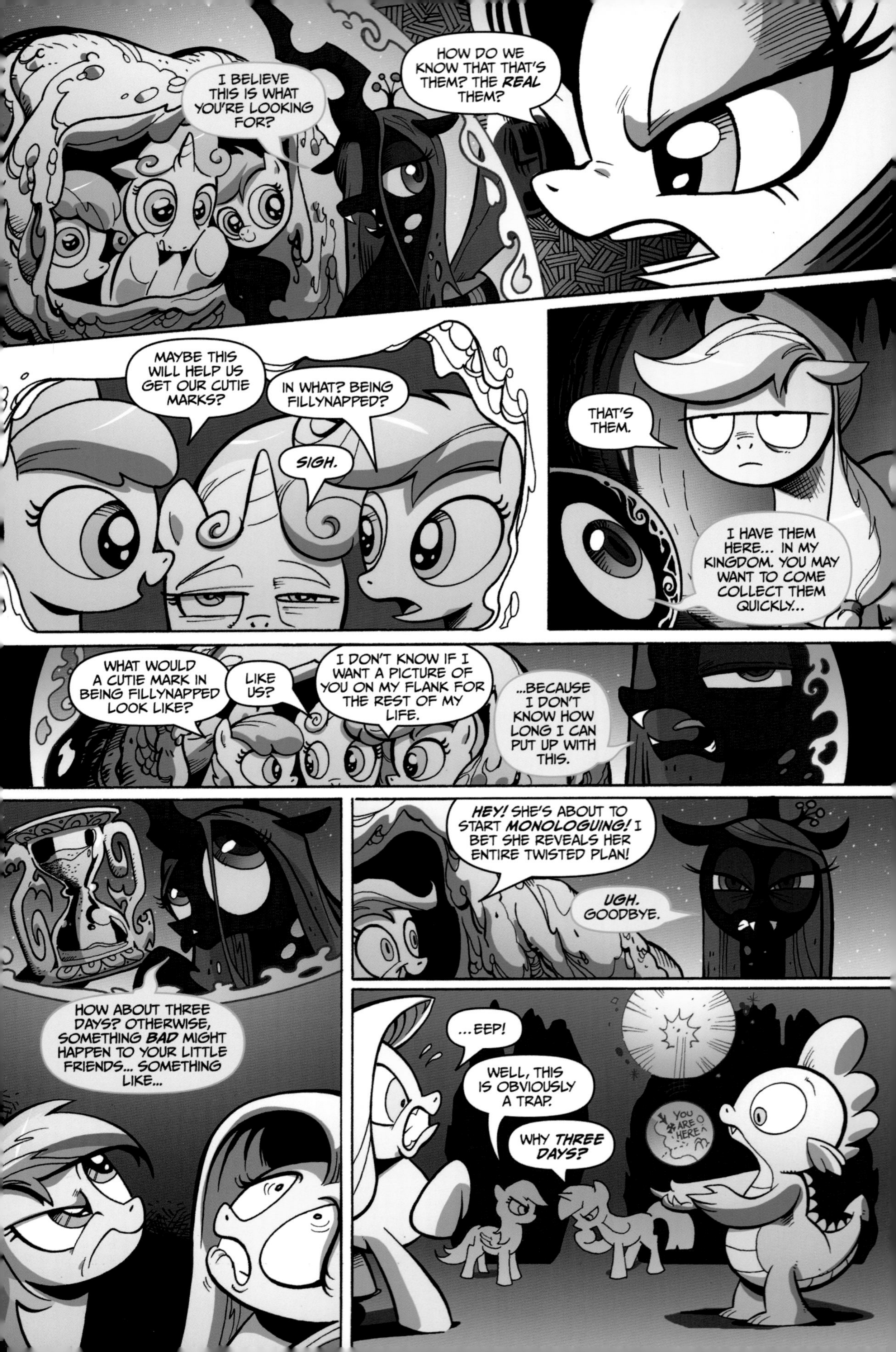
I BELIEVE THIS IS WHAT YOU'RE LOOKING FOR?
HOW DO WE KNOW THAT THAT'S THEM? THE *REAL* THEM?
MAYBE THIS WILL HELP US GET OUR CUTIE MARKS?
IN WHAT? BEING FILLYNAPPED?
SIGH.
THAT'S THEM.
I HAVE THEM HERE... IN MY KINGDOM. YOU MAY WANT TO COME COLLECT THEM QUICKLY...
WHAT WOULD A CUTIE MARK IN BEING FILLYNAPPED LOOK LIKE?
LIKE US?
I DON'T KNOW IF I WANT A PICTURE OF YOU ON MY FLANK FOR THE REST OF MY LIFE.
...BECAUSE I DON'T KNOW HOW LONG I CAN PUT UP WITH THIS.
HOW ABOUT THREE DAYS? OTHERWISE, SOMETHING *BAD* MIGHT HAPPEN TO YOUR LITTLE FRIENDS... SOMETHING LIKE...
HEY! SHE'S ABOUT TO START *MONOLOGUING!* I BET SHE REVEALS HER ENTIRE TWISTED PLAN!
UGH. GOODBYE.
...EEP!
WELL, THIS IS OBVIOUSLY A TRAP.
WHY *THREE DAYS?*
YOU ARE HERE

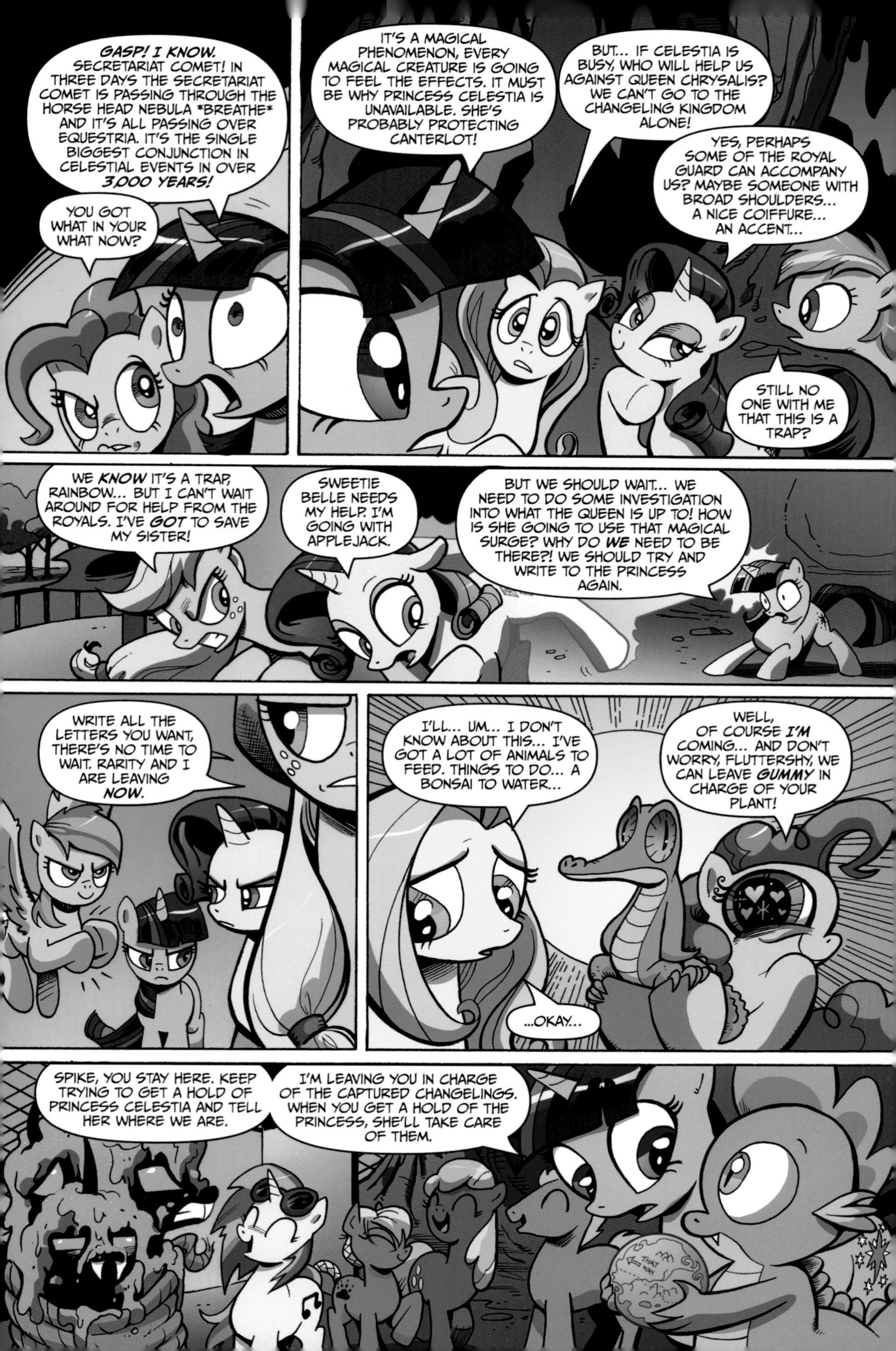
GASP! I KNOW. SECRETARIAT COMET! IN THREE DAYS THE SECRETARIAT COMET IS PASSING THROUGH THE HORSE HEAD NEBULA *BREATHE* AND IT'S ALL PASSING OVER EQUESTRIA. IT'S THE SINGLE BIGGEST CONJUNCTION IN CELESTIAL EVENTS IN OVER 3,000 YEARS!
YOU GOT WHAT IN YOUR WHAT NOW?
IT'S A MAGICAL PHENOMENON, EVERY MAGICAL CREATURE IS GOING TO FEEL THE EFFECTS. IT MUST BE WHY PRINCESS CELESTIA IS UNAVAILABLE. SHE'S PROBABLY PROTECTING CANTERLOT!
BUT... IF CELESTIA IS BUSY, WHO WILL HELP US AGAINST QUEEN CHRYSALIS? WE CAN'T GO TO THE CHANGELING KINGDOM ALONE!
YES, PERHAPS SOME OF THE ROYAL GUARD CAN ACCOMPANY US? MAYBE SOMEONE WITH BROAD SHOULDERS... A NICE COIFFURE... AN ACCENT...
STILL NO ONE WITH ME THAT THIS IS A TRAP?
WE KNOW IT'S A TRAP, RAINBOW... BUT I CAN'T WAIT AROUND FOR HELP FROM THE ROYALS. I'VE GOT TO SAVE MY SISTER!
SWEETIE BELLE NEEDS MY HELP. I'M GOING WITH APPLEJACK.
BUT WE SHOULD WAIT... WE NEED TO DO SOME INVESTIGATION INTO WHAT THE QUEEN IS UP TO! HOW IS SHE GOING TO USE THAT MAGICAL SURGE? WHY DO WE NEED TO BE THERE?! WE SHOULD TRY AND WRITE TO THE PRINCESS AGAIN.
WRITE ALL THE LETTERS YOU WANT, THERE'S NO TIME TO WAIT. RARITY AND I ARE LEAVING NOW.
I'LL... UM... I DON'T KNOW ABOUT THIS... I'VE GOT A LOT OF ANIMALS TO FEED. THINGS TO DO... A BONSAI TO WATER...
WELL, OF COURSE I'M COMING... AND DON'T WORRY, FLUTTERSHY, WE CAN LEAVE GUMMY IN CHARGE OF YOUR PLANT!
...OKAY...
SPIKE, YOU STAY HERE. KEEP TRYING TO GET A HOLD OF PRINCESS CELESTIA AND TELL HER WHERE WE ARE.
I'M LEAVING YOU IN CHARGE OF THE CAPTURED CHANGELINGS. WHEN YOU GET A HOLD OF THE PRINCESS, SHE'LL TAKE CARE OF THEM.
THAT WAY

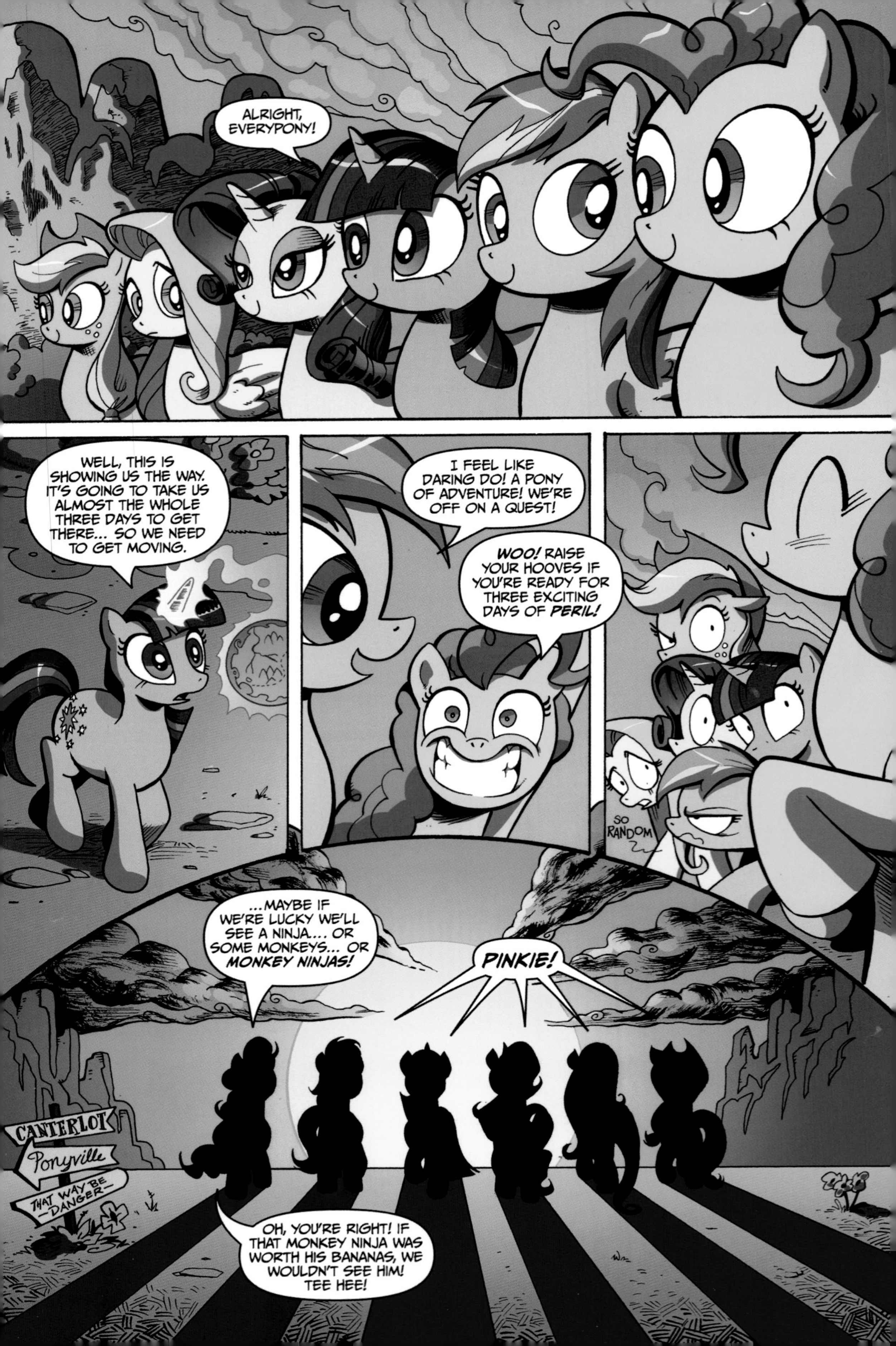
ALRIGHT, EVERYPONY!
WELL, THIS IS SHOWING US THE WAY. IT'S GOING TO TAKE US ALMOST THE WHOLE THREE DAYS TO GET THERE... SO WE NEED TO GET MOVING.
I FEEL LIKE DARING DO! A PONY OF ADVENTURE! WE'RE OFF ON A QUEST!
WOO! RAISE YOUR HOOVES IF YOU'RE READY FOR THREE EXCITING DAYS OF PERIL!
SO RANDOM
...MAYBE IF WE'RE LUCKY WE'LL SEE A NINJA... OR SOME MONKEYS... OR MONKEY NINJAS!
PINKIE!
CANTERLOT
Ponyville
THAT WAY BE DANGER
OH, YOU'RE RIGHT! IF THAT MONKEY NINJA WAS WORTH HIS BANANAS, WE WOULDN'T SEE HIM! TEE HEE!

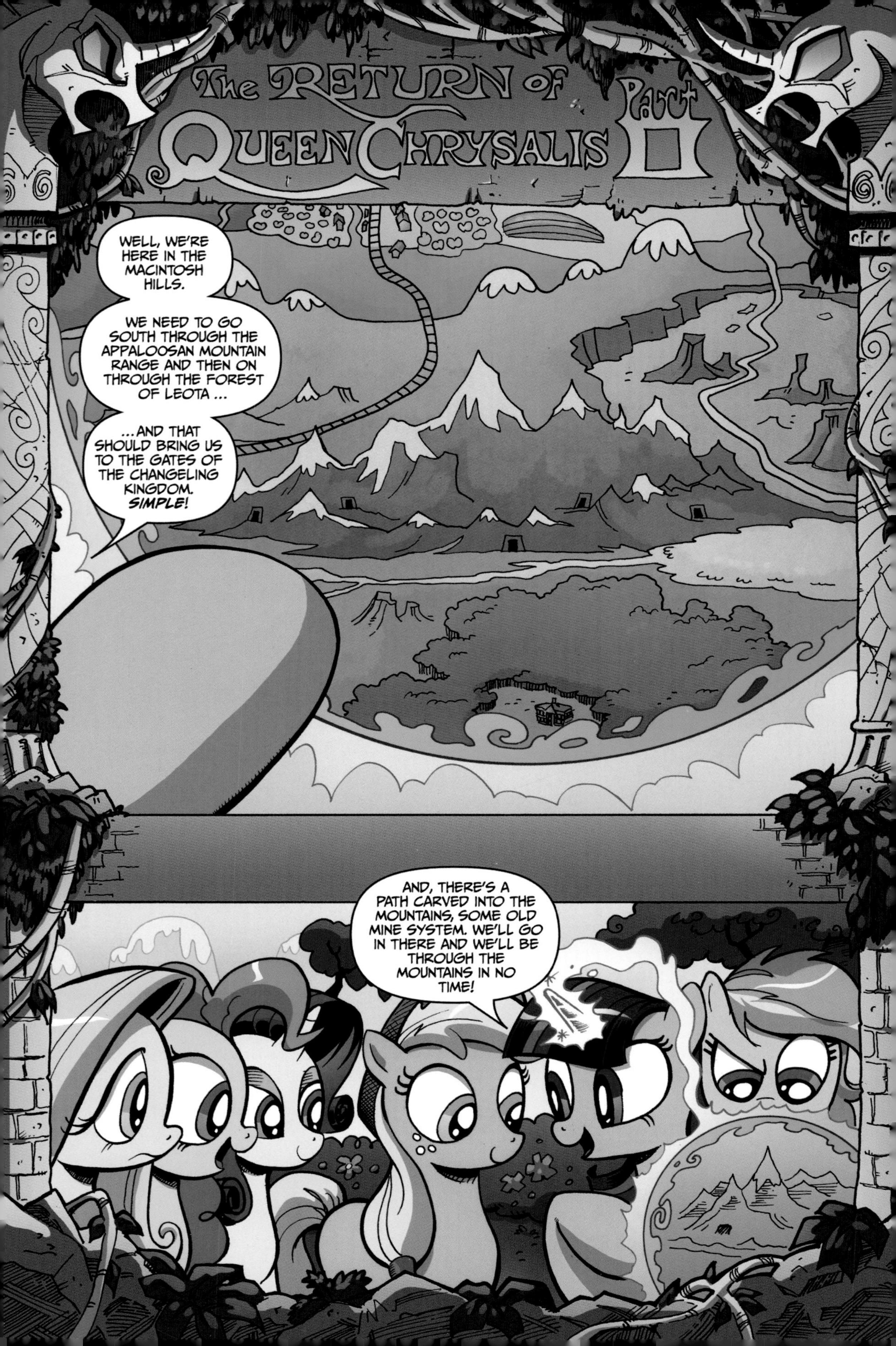

The RETURN of QUEEN CHRYSALIS Part II
WELL, WE'RE HERE IN THE MACINTOSH HILLS.
WE NEED TO GO SOUTH THROUGH THE APPALOOSAN MOUNTAIN RANGE AND THEN ON THROUGH THE FOREST OF LEOTA ...
...AND THAT SHOULD BRING US TO THE GATES OF THE CHANGELING KINGDOM. SIMPLE!
AND, THERE'S A PATH CARVED INTO THE MOUNTAINS, SOME OLD MINE SYSTEM. WE'LL GO IN THERE AND WE'LL BE THROUGH THE MOUNTAINS IN NO TIME!

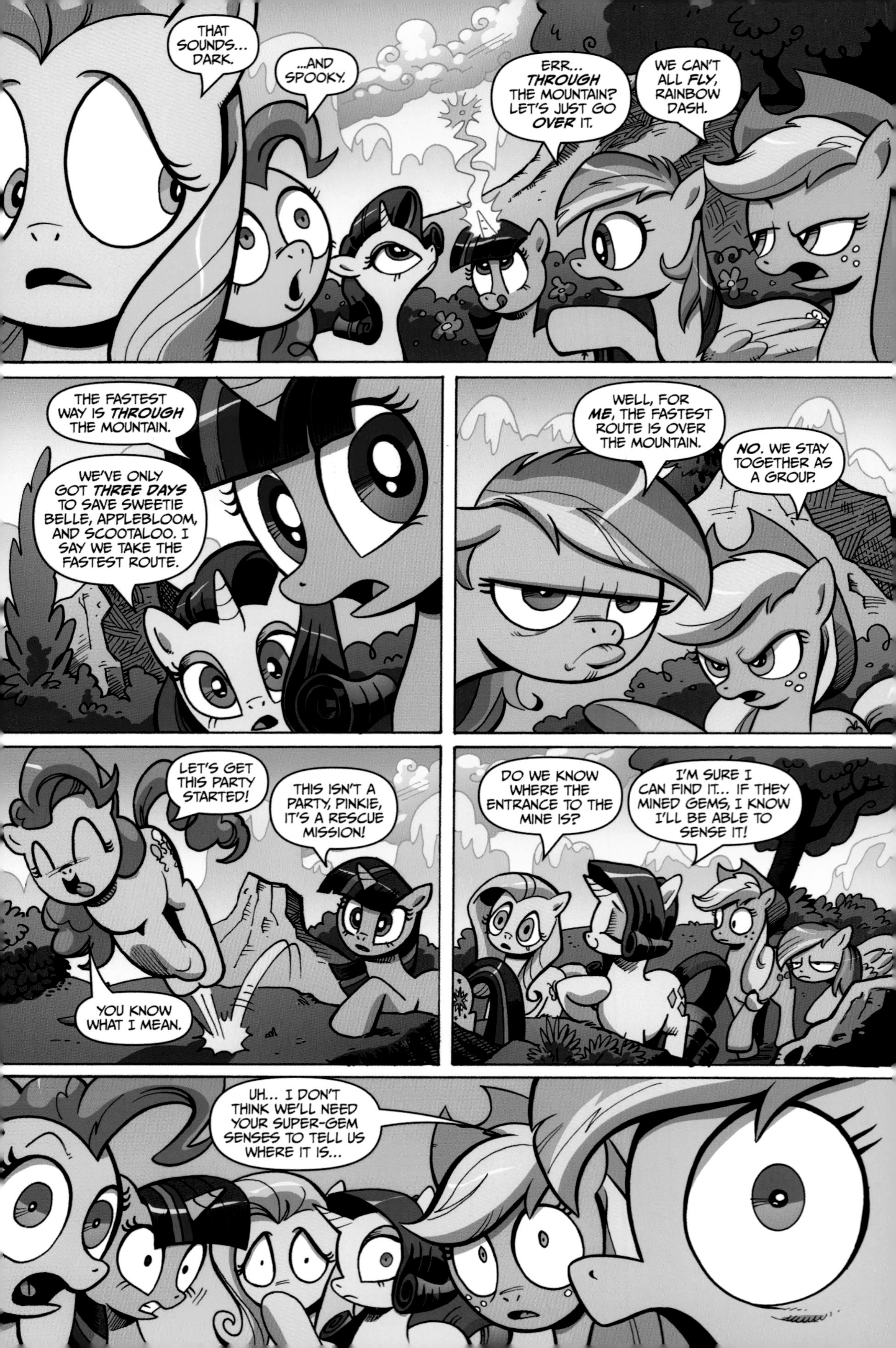
THAT SOUNDS... DARK.
...AND SPOOKY.
ERR... THROUGH THE MOUNTAIN? LET'S JUST GO OVER IT.
WE CAN'T ALL FLY, RAINBOW DASH.
THE FASTEST WAY IS THROUGH THE MOUNTAIN.
WE'VE ONLY GOT THREE DAYS TO SAVE SWEETIE BELLE, APPLEBLOOM, AND SCOOTALOO. I SAY WE TAKE THE FASTEST ROUTE.
WELL, FOR ME, THE FASTEST ROUTE IS OVER THE MOUNTAIN.
NO. WE STAY TOGETHER AS A GROUP.
LET'S GET THIS PARTY STARTED!
THIS ISN'T A PARTY, PINKIE, IT'S A RESCUE MISSION!
YOU KNOW WHAT I MEAN.
DO WE KNOW WHERE THE ENTRANCE TO THE MINE IS?
I'M SURE I CAN FIND IT... IF THEY MINED GEMS, I KNOW I'LL BE ABLE TO SENSE IT!
UH... I DON'T THINK WE'LL NEED YOUR SUPER-GEM SENSES TO TELL US WHERE IT IS...

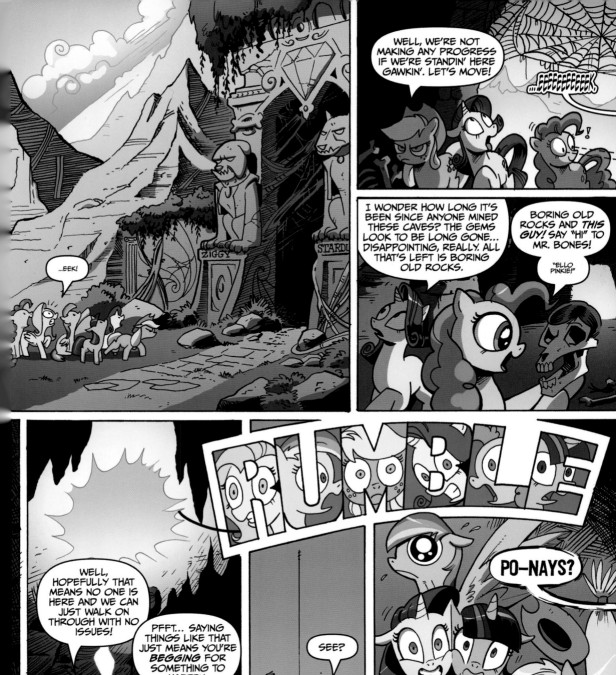

...EEK!

WELL, WE'RE NOT MAKING ANY PROGRESS IF WE'RE STANDIN' HERE GAWKIN'. LET'S MOVE!

...EEEEEEEEEEEK.

I WONDER HOW LONG IT'S BEEN SINCE ANYONE MINED THESE CAVES? THE GEMS LOOK TO BE LONG GONE... DISAPPOINTING, REALLY. ALL THAT'S LEFT IS BORING OLD ROCKS.

BORING OLD ROCKS AND *THIS GUY!* SAY "HI" TO MR. BONES!

"'ELLO PINKIE!"

RUMBLE

WELL, HOPEFULLY THAT MEANS NO ONE IS HERE AND WE CAN JUST WALK ON THROUGH WITH NO ISSUES!

PFFT... SAYING THINGS LIKE THAT JUST MEANS YOU'RE *BEGGING* FOR SOMETHING TO HAPPEN.

SEE?

PO-NAYS?

PWETAH
PONAY!

EEK!

PO-NAYS!

A *CAVE TROLL!* HOW EXCITING! THEY'RE MUCH BIGGER THAN THE "CAVE DWELLER'S REFERENCE GUIDE" SAYS THEY ARE!

EXCITING? WHAT IS *WRONG* WITH YOU?

Brush ♡

Brush ♡

PWETAH HAR ON DAH PWETAH PONAY

WELL THAT'S... ER... STRANGE.

HEY! PUT HER DOWN YA' BIG LUG!

YES! PUT HER DOWN THIS INSTANT! JUST LOOK WHAT YOU'RE DOING TO HER POOR MANE!

NEXT PONAY!

HEY!

PONAY!

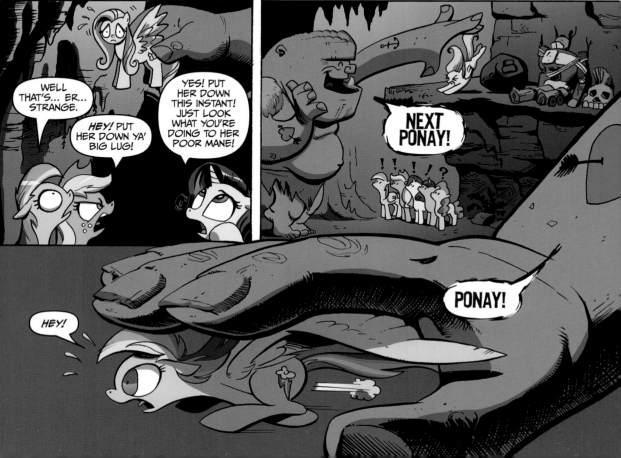

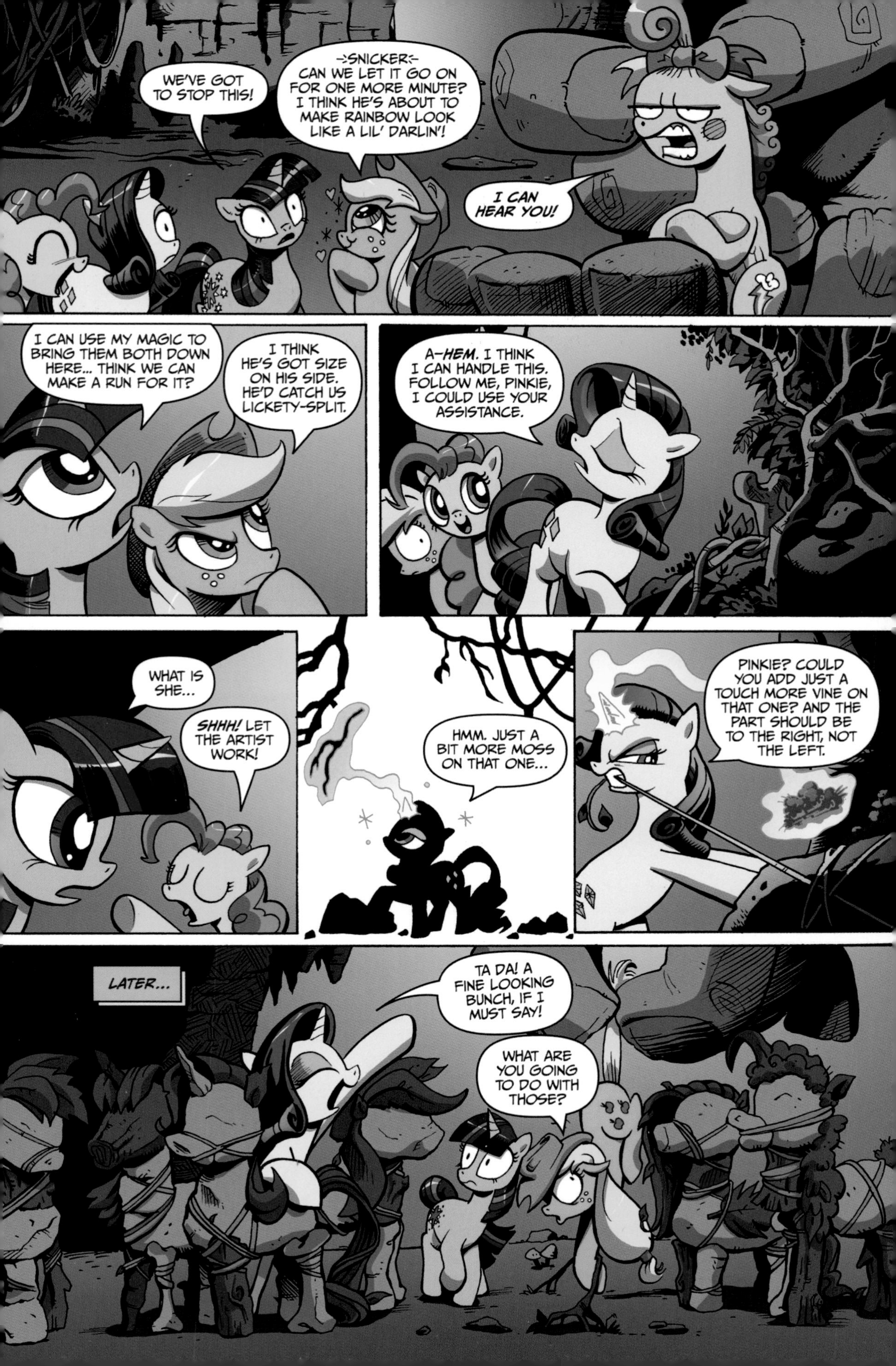
WE'VE GOT TO STOP THIS!
-SNICKER- CAN WE LET IT GO ON FOR ONE MORE MINUTE? I THINK HE'S ABOUT TO MAKE RAINBOW LOOK LIKE A LIL' DARLIN'!
I CAN HEAR YOU!
I CAN USE MY MAGIC TO BRING THEM BOTH DOWN HERE... THINK WE CAN MAKE A RUN FOR IT?
I THINK HE'S GOT SIZE ON HIS SIDE. HE'D CATCH US LICKETY-SPLIT.
A-HEM. I THINK I CAN HANDLE THIS. FOLLOW ME, PINKIE, I COULD USE YOUR ASSISTANCE.
WHAT IS SHE...
SHHH! LET THE ARTIST WORK!
HMM. JUST A BIT MORE MOSS ON THAT ONE...
PINKIE? COULD YOU ADD JUST A TOUCH MORE VINE ON THAT ONE? AND THE PART SHOULD BE TO THE RIGHT, NOT THE LEFT.
LATER...
TA DA! A FINE LOOKING BUNCH, IF I MUST SAY!
WHAT ARE YOU GOING TO DO WITH THOSE?

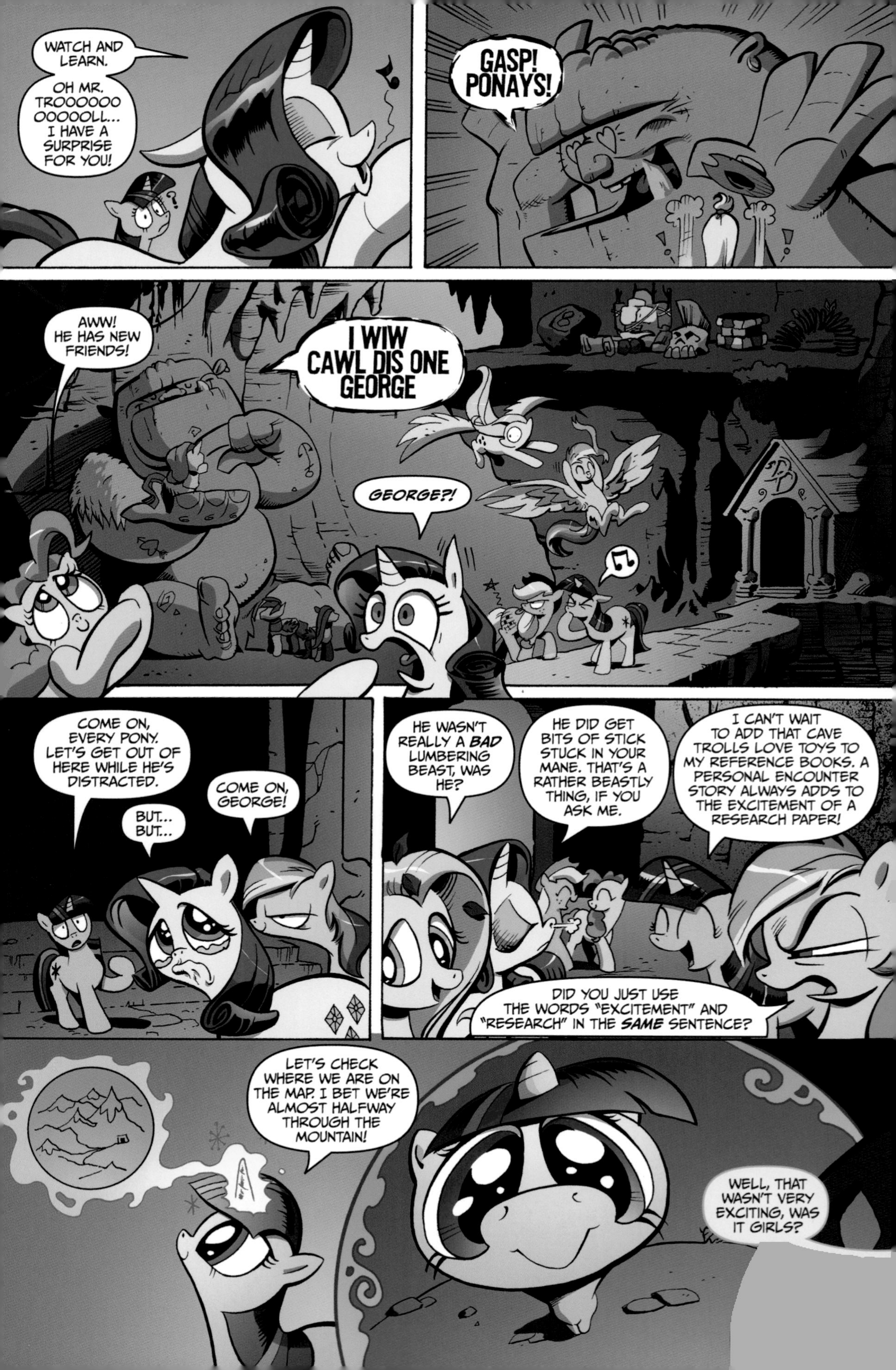
WATCH AND LEARN.
OH MR. TROOOOOO OOOOOLL... I HAVE A SURPRISE FOR YOU!
GASP! PONAYS!
AWW! HE HAS NEW FRIENDS!
I WIW CAWL DIS ONE GEORGE
GEORGE?!
COME ON, EVERY PONY. LET'S GET OUT OF HERE WHILE HE'S DISTRACTED.
BUT... BUT...
COME ON, GEORGE!
HE WASN'T REALLY A BAD LUMBERING BEAST, WAS HE?
HE DID GET BITS OF STICK STUCK IN YOUR MANE. THAT'S A RATHER BEASTLY THING, IF YOU ASK ME.
I CAN'T WAIT TO ADD THAT CAVE TROLLS LOVE TOYS TO MY REFERENCE BOOKS. A PERSONAL ENCOUNTER STORY ALWAYS ADDS TO THE EXCITEMENT OF A RESEARCH PAPER!
DID YOU JUST USE THE WORDS "EXCITEMENT" AND "RESEARCH" IN THE SAME SENTENCE?
LET'S CHECK WHERE WE ARE ON THE MAP. I BET WE'RE ALMOST HALFWAY THROUGH THE MOUNTAIN!
WELL, THAT WASN'T VERY EXCITING, WAS IT GIRLS?

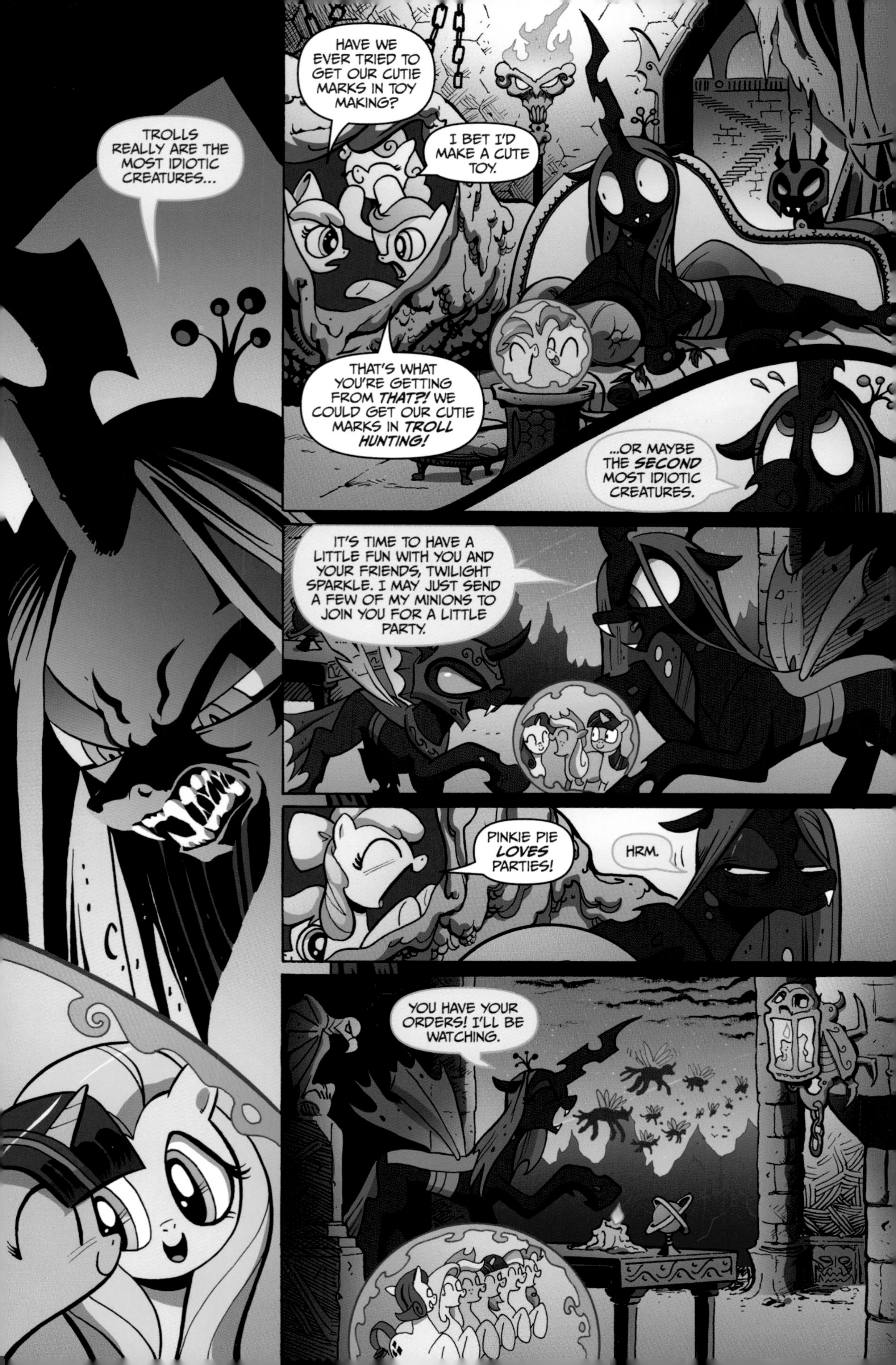
TROLLS REALLY ARE THE MOST IDIOTIC CREATURES...
HAVE WE EVER TRIED TO GET OUR CUTIE MARKS IN TOY MAKING?
I BET I'D MAKE A CUTE TOY.
THAT'S WHAT YOU'RE GETTING FROM THAT?! WE COULD GET OUR CUTIE MARKS IN TROLL HUNTING!
...OR MAYBE THE SECOND MOST IDIOTIC CREATURES.
IT'S TIME TO HAVE A LITTLE FUN WITH YOU AND YOUR FRIENDS, TWILIGHT SPARKLE. I MAY JUST SEND A FEW OF MY MINIONS TO JOIN YOU FOR A LITTLE PARTY.
PINKIE PIE LOVES PARTIES!
HRM.
YOU HAVE YOUR ORDERS! I'LL BE WATCHING.

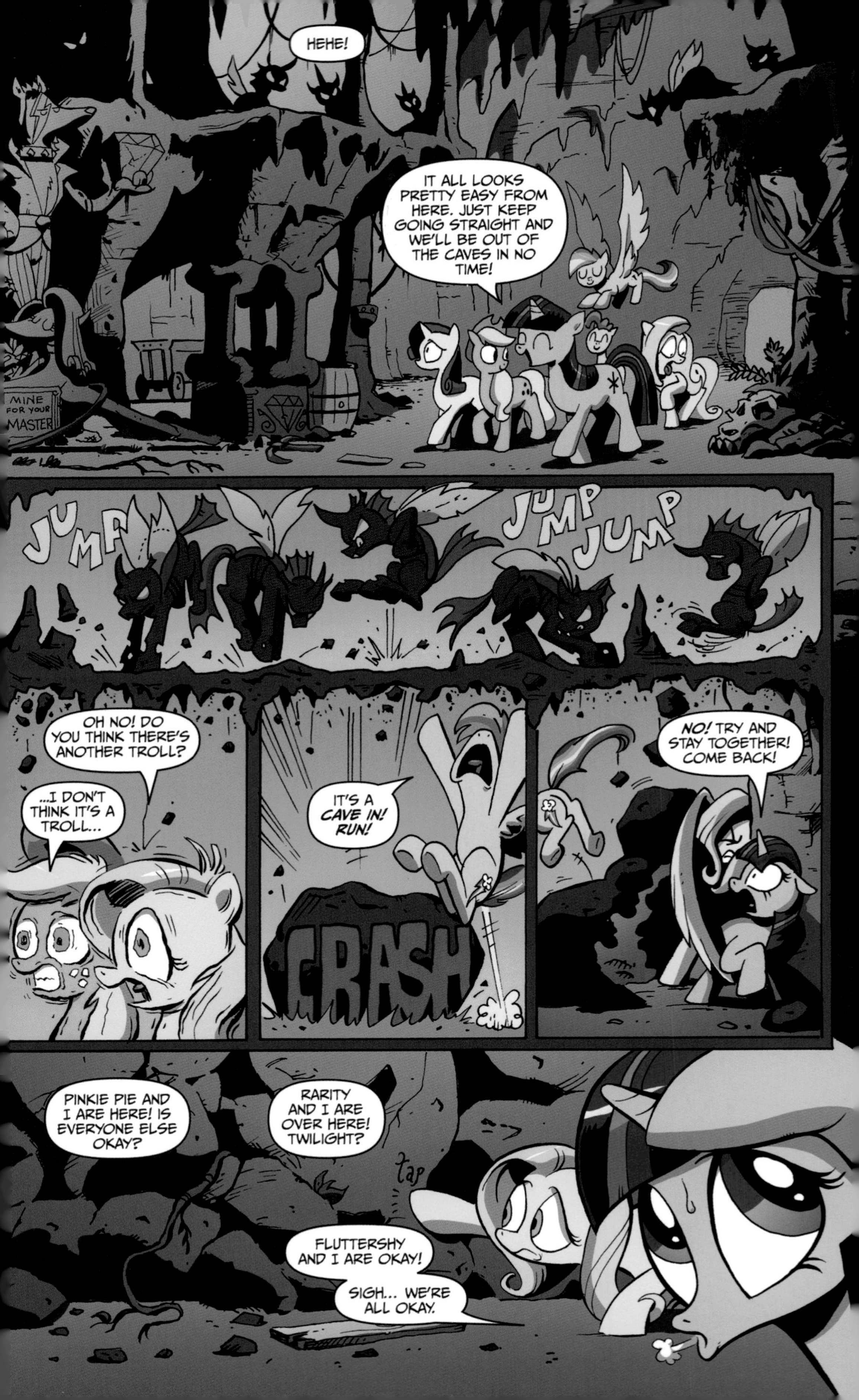
HEHE!
MINE FOR YOUR MASTER
IT ALL LOOKS PRETTY EASY FROM HERE. JUST KEEP GOING STRAIGHT AND WE'LL BE OUT OF THE CAVES IN NO TIME!
JUMP
JUMP
JUMP
OH NO! DO YOU THINK THERE'S ANOTHER TROLL?
...I DON'T THINK IT'S A TROLL...
IT'S A CAVE IN! RUN!
CRASH
NO! TRY AND STAY TOGETHER! COME BACK!
PINKIE PIE AND I ARE HERE! IS EVERYONE ELSE OKAY?
RARITY AND I ARE OVER HERE! TWILIGHT?
tap
FLUTTERSHY AND I ARE OKAY!
SIGH... WE'RE ALL OKAY.

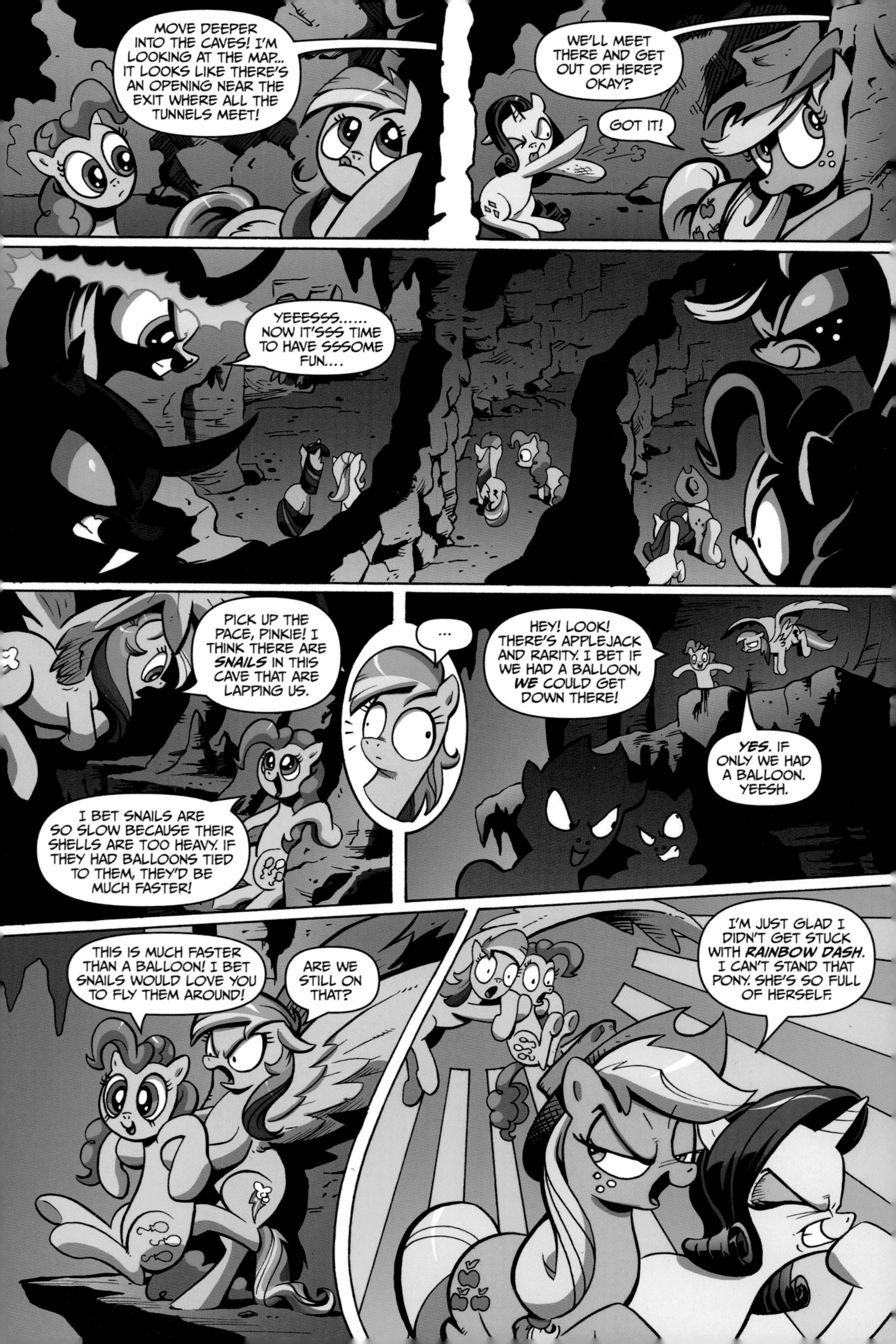
MOVE DEEPER INTO THE CAVES! I'M LOOKING AT THE MAP... IT LOOKS LIKE THERE'S AN OPENING NEAR THE EXIT WHERE ALL THE TUNNELS MEET!
WE'LL MEET THERE AND GET OUT OF HERE? OKAY?
GOT IT!
YEEESSS...... NOW IT'SSS TIME TO HAVE SSSOME FUN....
PICK UP THE PACE, PINKIE! I THINK THERE ARE SNAILS IN THIS CAVE THAT ARE LAPPING US.
I BET SNAILS ARE SO SLOW BECAUSE THEIR SHELLS ARE TOO HEAVY. IF THEY HAD BALLOONS TIED TO THEM, THEY'D BE MUCH FASTER!
...
HEY! LOOK! THERE'S APPLEJACK AND RARITY. I BET IF WE HAD A BALLOON, WE COULD GET DOWN THERE!
YES. IF ONLY WE HAD A BALLOON. YEESH.
THIS IS MUCH FASTER THAN A BALLOON! I BET SNAILS WOULD LOVE YOU TO FLY THEM AROUND!
ARE WE STILL ON THAT?
I'M JUST GLAD I DIDN'T GET STUCK WITH RAINBOW DASH. I CAN'T STAND THAT PONY. SHE'S SO FULL OF HERSELF.

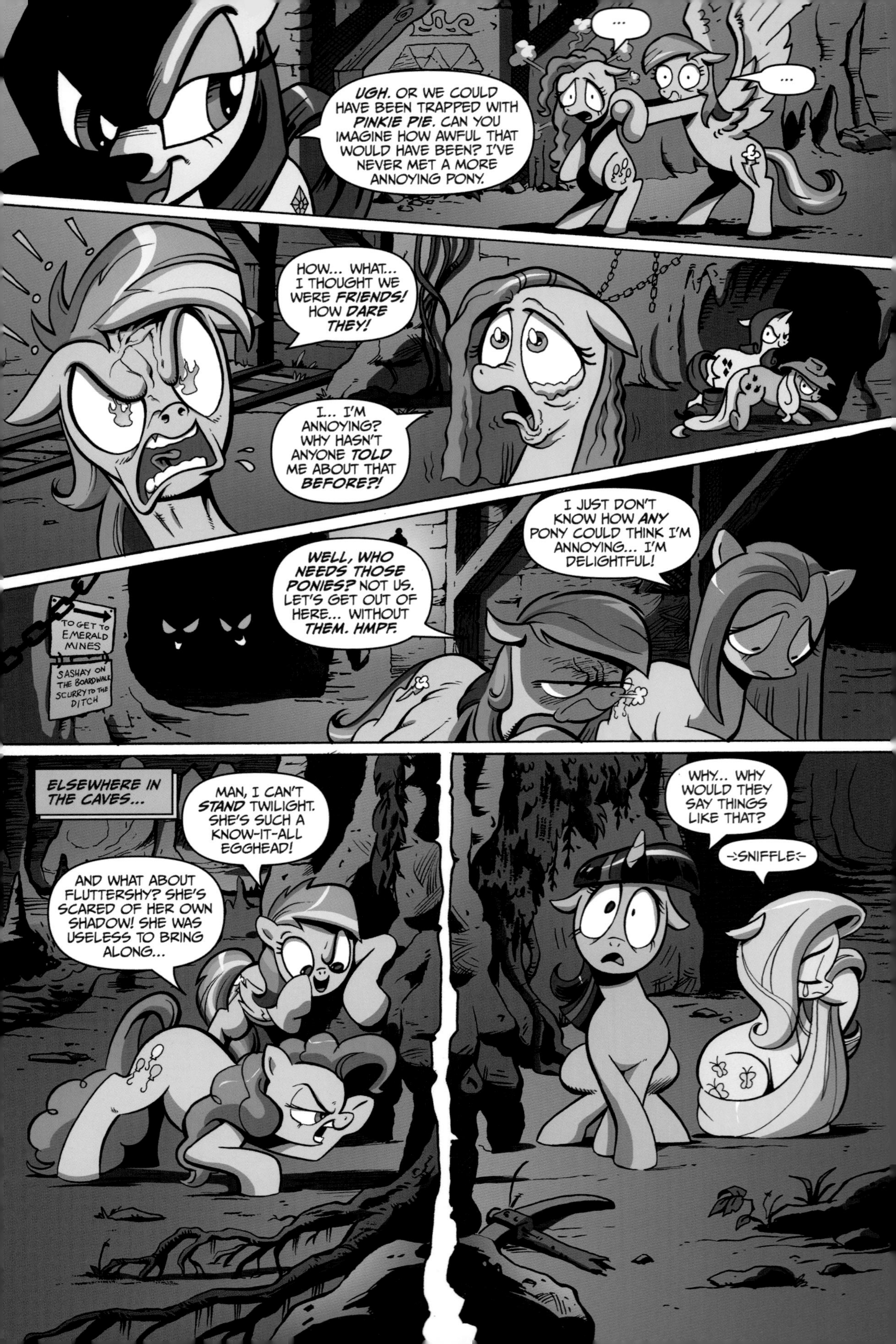
UGH. OR WE COULD HAVE BEEN TRAPPED WITH PINKIE PIE. CAN YOU IMAGINE HOW AWFUL THAT WOULD HAVE BEEN? I'VE NEVER MET A MORE ANNOYING PONY.
...
...
HOW... WHAT... I THOUGHT WE WERE FRIENDS! HOW DARE THEY!
I... I'M ANNOYING? WHY HASN'T ANYONE TOLD ME ABOUT THAT BEFORE?!
TO GET TO EMERALD MINES
SASHAY ON THE BOARDWALK SCURRY TO THE DITCH
WELL, WHO NEEDS THOSE PONIES? NOT US. LET'S GET OUT OF HERE... WITHOUT THEM. HMPF.
I JUST DON'T KNOW HOW ANY PONY COULD THINK I'M ANNOYING... I'M DELIGHTFUL!
ELSEWHERE IN THE CAVES...
MAN, I CAN'T STAND TWILIGHT. SHE'S SUCH A KNOW-IT-ALL EGGHEAD!
AND WHAT ABOUT FLUTTERSHY? SHE'S SCARED OF HER OWN SHADOW! SHE WAS USELESS TO BRING ALONG...
WHY... WHY WOULD THEY SAY THINGS LIKE THAT?
SNIFFLE

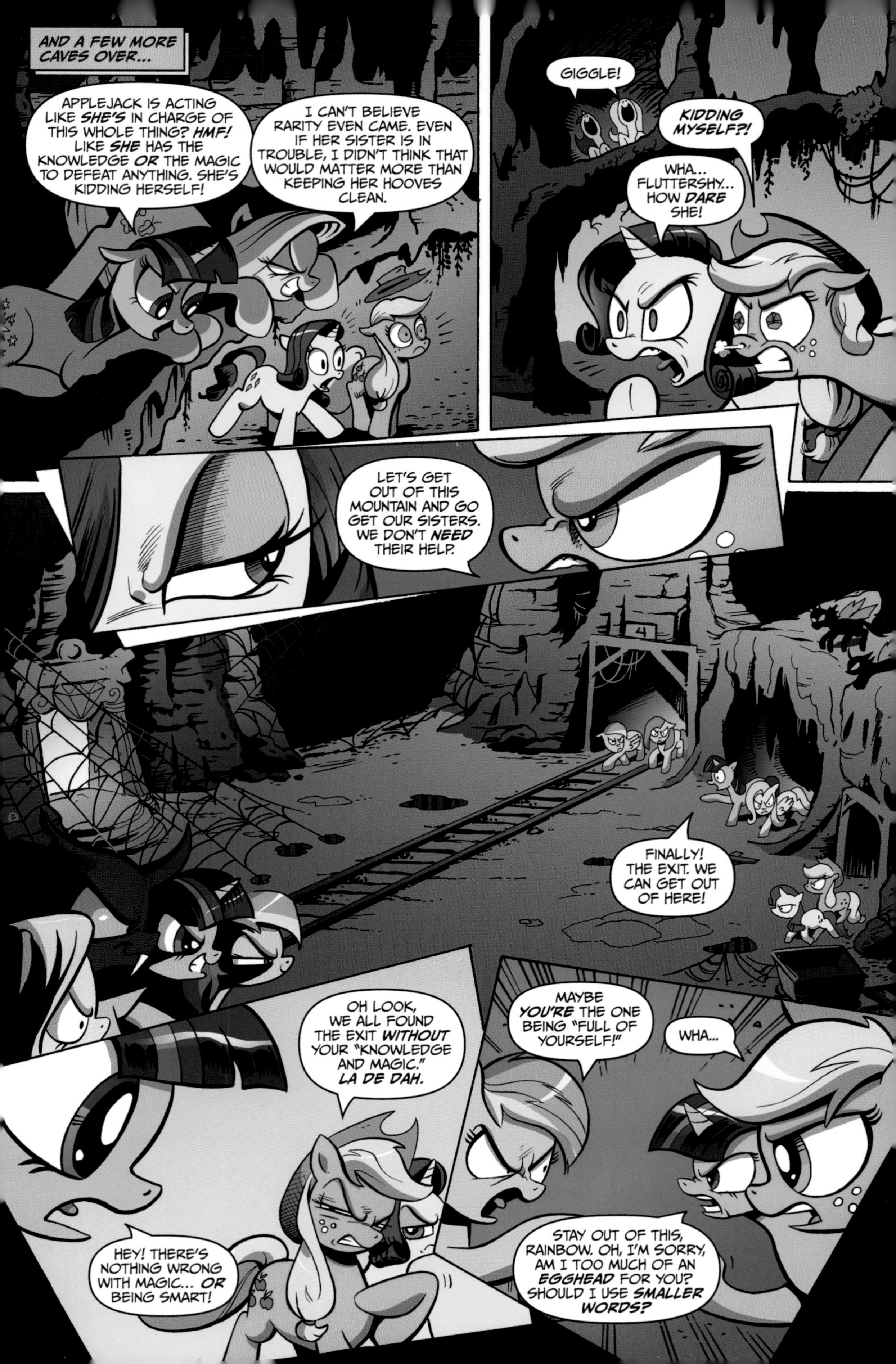
AND A FEW MORE CAVES OVER...
APPLEJACK IS ACTING LIKE SHE'S IN CHARGE OF THIS WHOLE THING? HMF! LIKE SHE HAS THE KNOWLEDGE OR THE MAGIC TO DEFEAT ANYTHING. SHE'S KIDDING HERSELF!
I CAN'T BELIEVE RARITY EVEN CAME. EVEN IF HER SISTER IS IN TROUBLE, I DIDN'T THINK THAT WOULD MATTER MORE THAN KEEPING HER HOOVES CLEAN.
GIGGLE!
KIDDING MYSELF?!
WHA... FLUTTERSHY... HOW DARE SHE!
LET'S GET OUT OF THIS MOUNTAIN AND GO GET OUR SISTERS. WE DON'T NEED THEIR HELP.
4
FINALLY! THE EXIT. WE CAN GET OUT OF HERE!
OH LOOK, WE ALL FOUND THE EXIT WITHOUT YOUR "KNOWLEDGE AND MAGIC." LA DE DAH.
MAYBE YOU'RE THE ONE BEING "FULL OF YOURSELF!"
WHA...
HEY! THERE'S NOTHING WRONG WITH MAGIC... OR BEING SMART!
STAY OUT OF THIS, RAINBOW. OH, I'M SORRY, AM I TOO MUCH OF AN EGGHEAD FOR YOU? SHOULD I USE SMALLER WORDS?

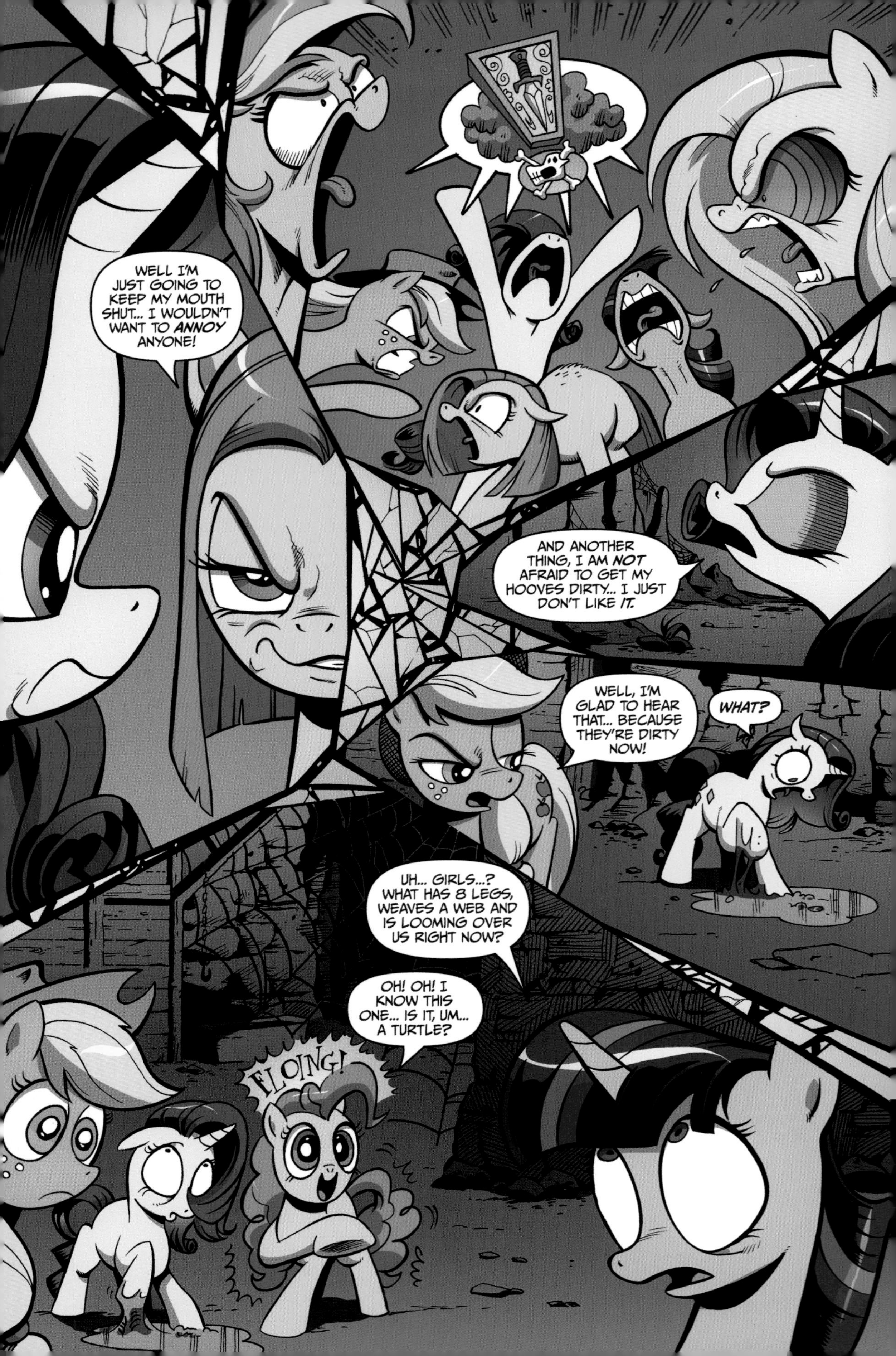

WELL I'M JUST GOING TO KEEP MY MOUTH SHUT... I WOULDN'T WANT TO ANNOY ANYONE!
AND ANOTHER THING, I AM NOT AFRAID TO GET MY HOOVES DIRTY... I JUST DON'T LIKE IT.
WELL, I'M GLAD TO HEAR THAT... BECAUSE THEY'RE DIRTY NOW!
WHAT?
UH... GIRLS...? WHAT HAS 8 LEGS, WEAVES A WEB AND IS LOOMING OVER US RIGHT NOW?
OH! OH! I KNOW THIS ONE... IS IT, UM... A TURTLE?
FLOING!

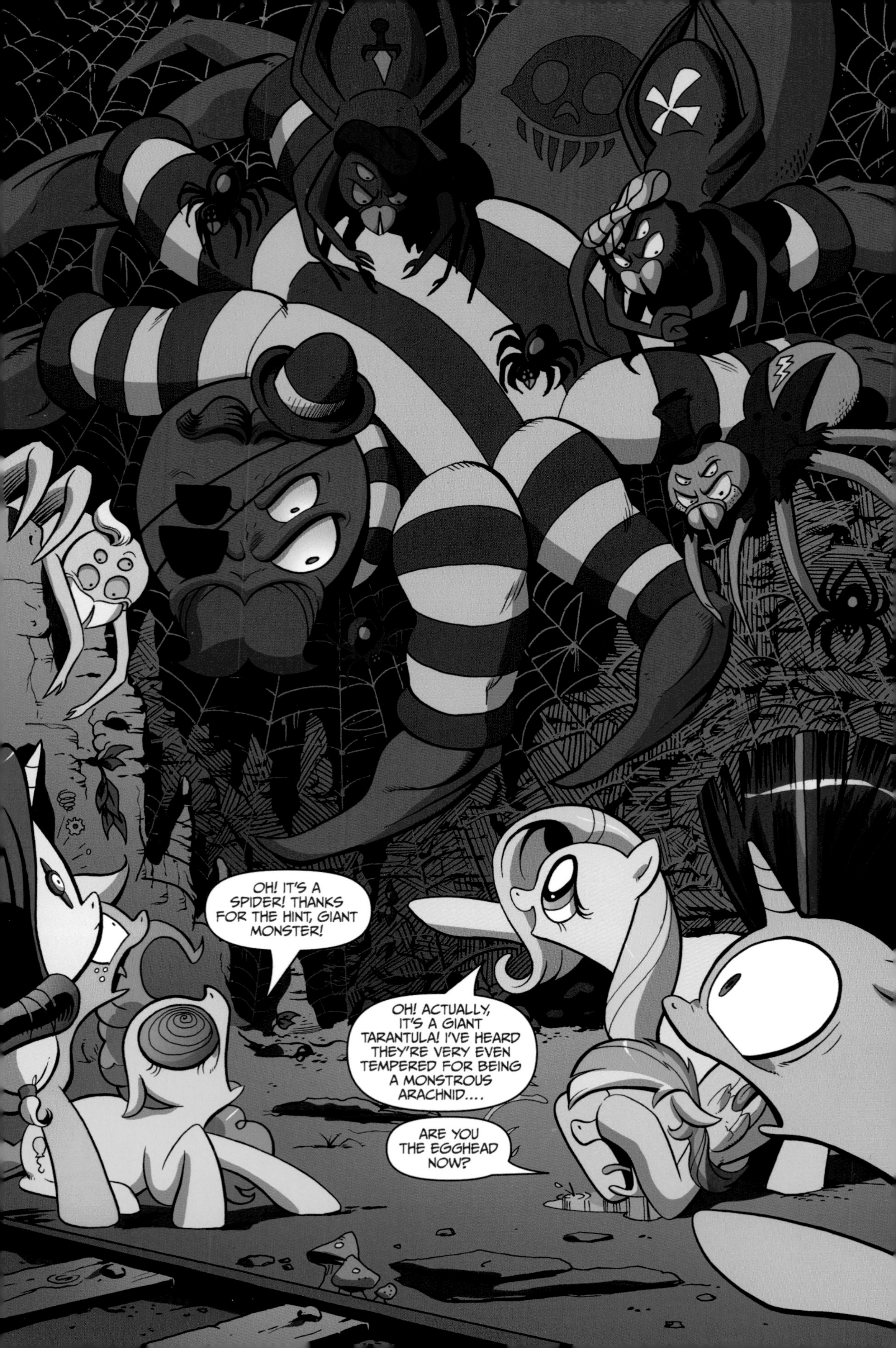
OH! IT'S A SPIDER! THANKS FOR THE HINT, GIANT MONSTER!
OH! ACTUALLY, IT'S A GIANT TARANTULA! I'VE HEARD THEY'RE VERY EVEN TEMPERED FOR BEING A MONSTROUS ARACHNID....
ARE YOU THE EGGHEAD NOW?

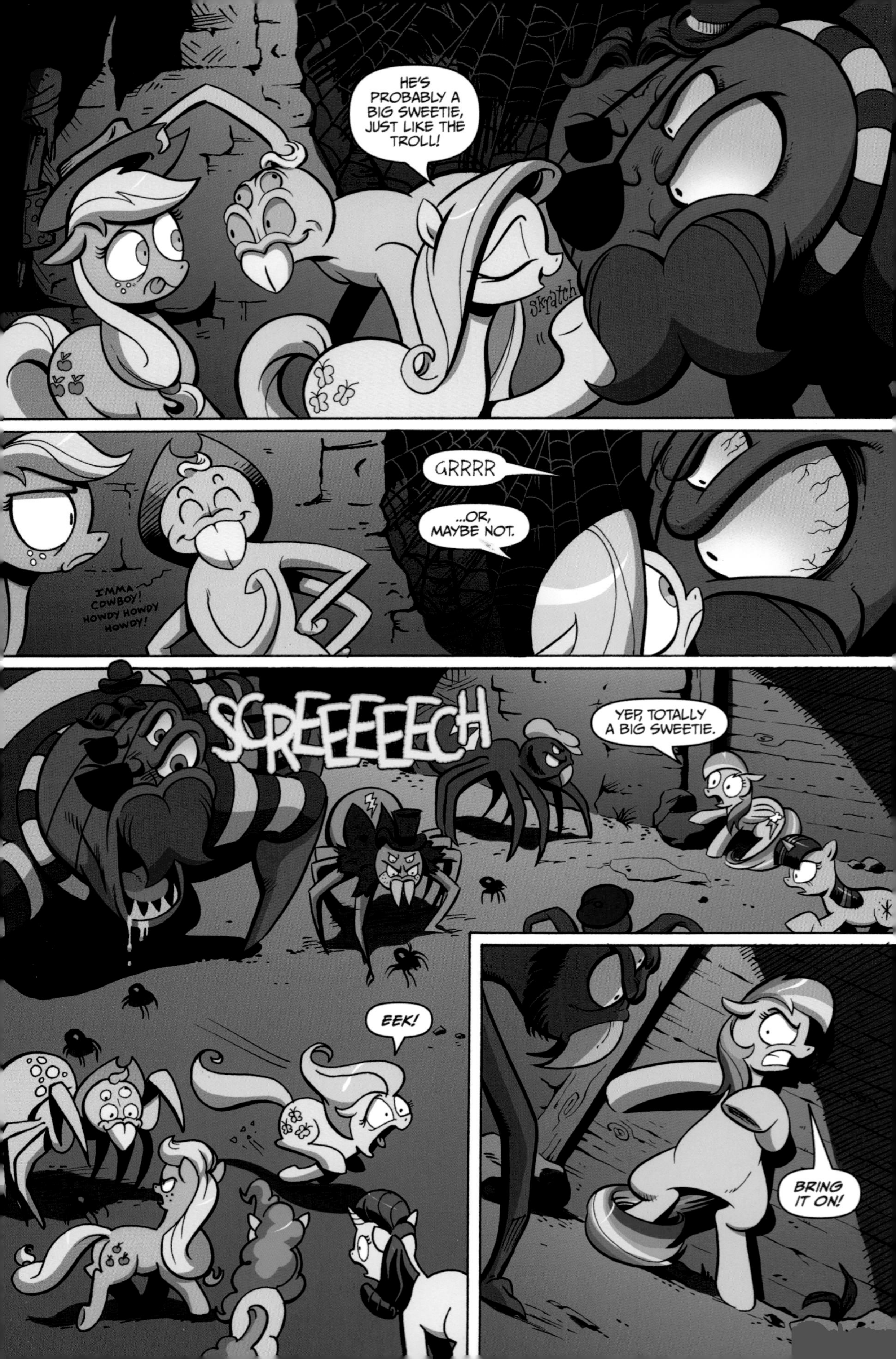

HE'S PROBABLY A BIG SWEETIE, JUST LIKE THE TROLL!
SKRATCH
GRRRR
...OR, MAYBE NOT.
IMMA COWBOY! HOWDY HOWDY HOWDY!
SCREEEEECH
YEP, TOTALLY A BIG SWEETIE.
EEK!
BRING IT ON!

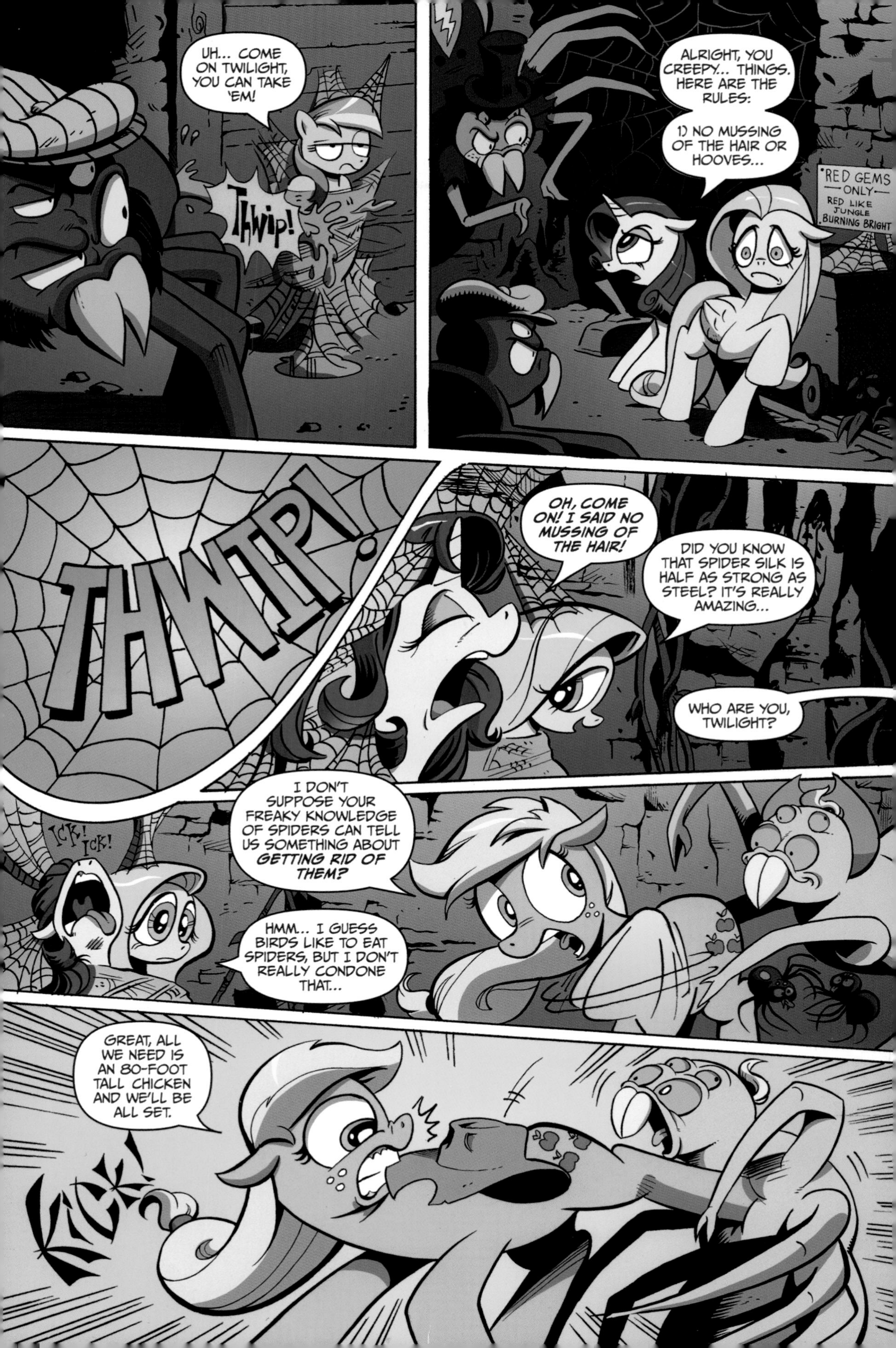
UH... COME ON TWILIGHT, YOU CAN TAKE 'EM!
THWIP!
ALRIGHT, YOU CREEPY... THINGS. HERE ARE THE RULES:
1) NO MUSSING OF THE HAIR OR HOOVES...
RED GEMS ONLY
RED LIKE JUNGLE BURNING BRIGHT
THWIP!
OH, COME ON! I SAID NO MUSSING OF THE HAIR!
DID YOU KNOW THAT SPIDER SILK IS HALF AS STRONG AS STEEL? IT'S REALLY AMAZING...
WHO ARE YOU, TWILIGHT?
ICK! ICK!
I DON'T SUPPOSE YOUR FREAKY KNOWLEDGE OF SPIDERS CAN TELL US SOMETHING ABOUT GETTING RID OF THEM?
HMM... I GUESS BIRDS LIKE TO EAT SPIDERS, BUT I DON'T REALLY CONDONE THAT...
GREAT, ALL WE NEED IS AN 80-FOOT TALL CHICKEN AND WE'LL BE ALL SET.
KICK!

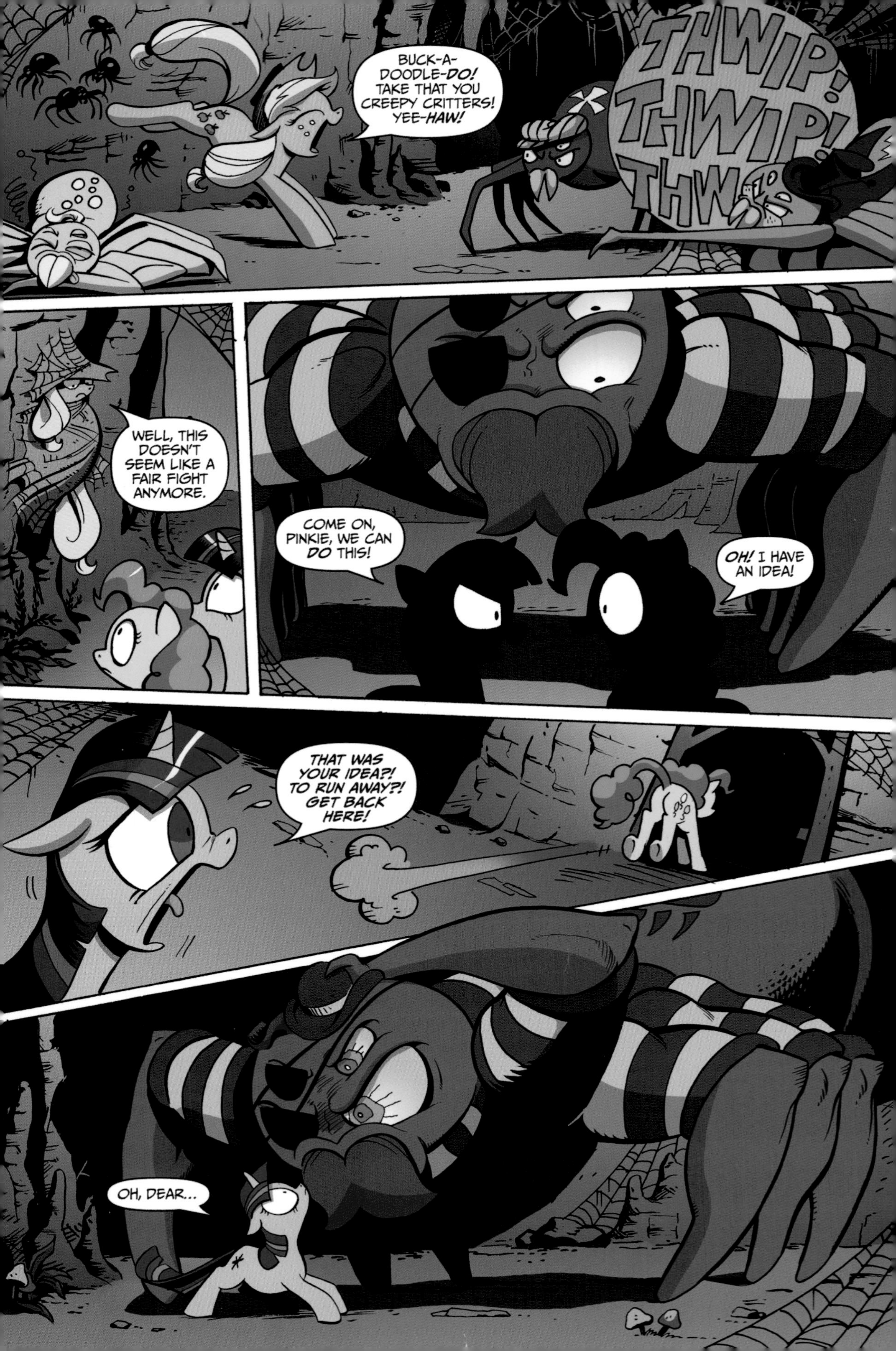
BUCK-A-DOODLE-*DO!* TAKE THAT YOU CREEPY CRITTERS! YEE-*HAW!*
THWIP! THWIP! THW
WELL, THIS DOESN'T SEEM LIKE A FAIR FIGHT ANYMORE.
COME ON, PINKIE, WE CAN *DO* THIS!
OH! I HAVE AN IDEA!
THAT WAS YOUR IDEA?! TO RUN AWAY?! GET BACK HERE!
OH, DEAR...

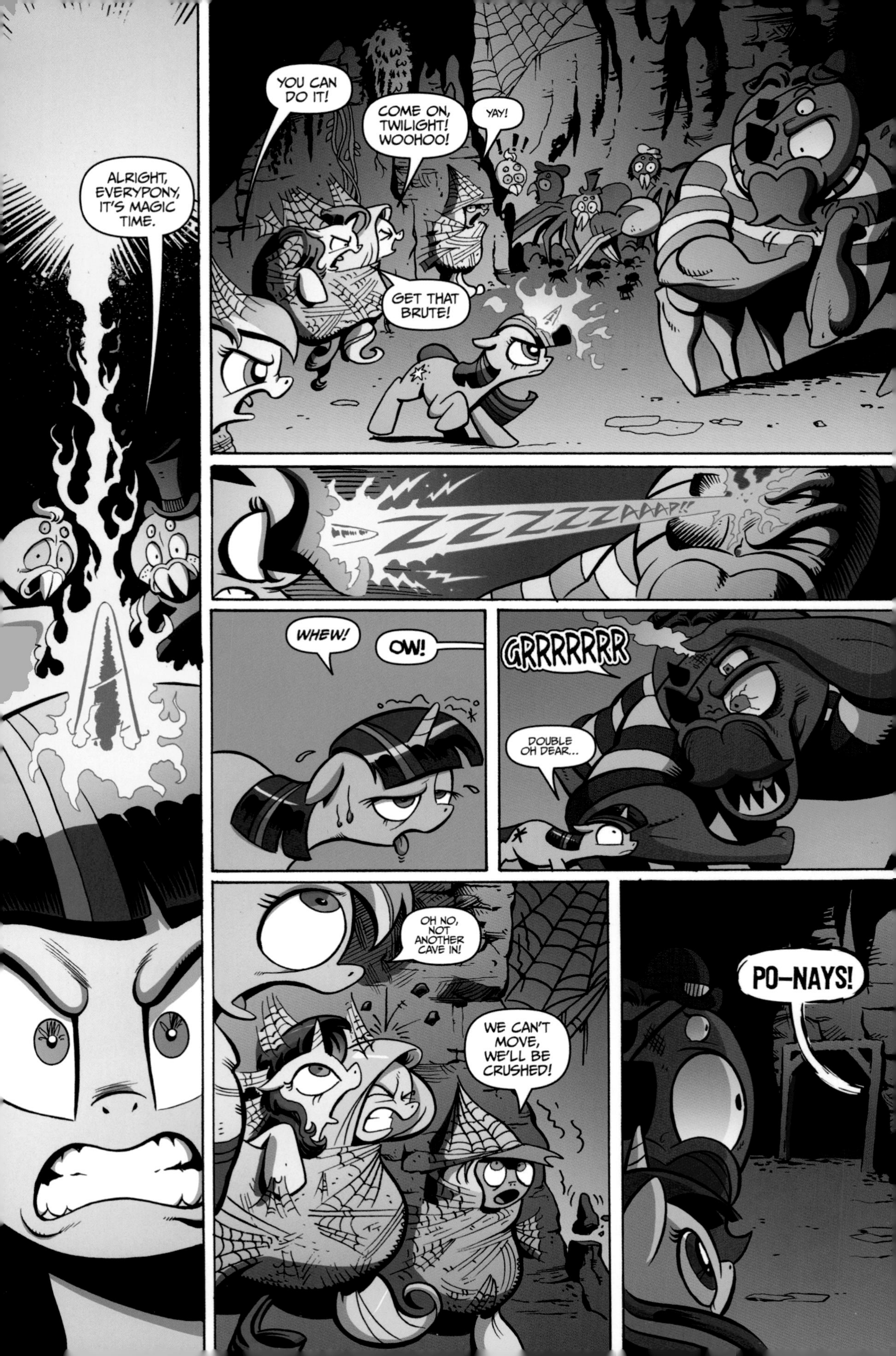
ALRIGHT, EVERYPONY, IT'S MAGIC TIME.
YOU CAN DO IT!
COME ON, TWILIGHT! WOOHOO!
YAY!
GET THAT BRUTE!
ZZZZZZZAAAP!!
WHEW!
OW!
GRRRRRRR
DOUBLE OH DEAR...
OH NO, NOT ANOTHER CAVE IN!
WE CAN'T MOVE, WE'LL BE CRUSHED!
PO-NAYS!

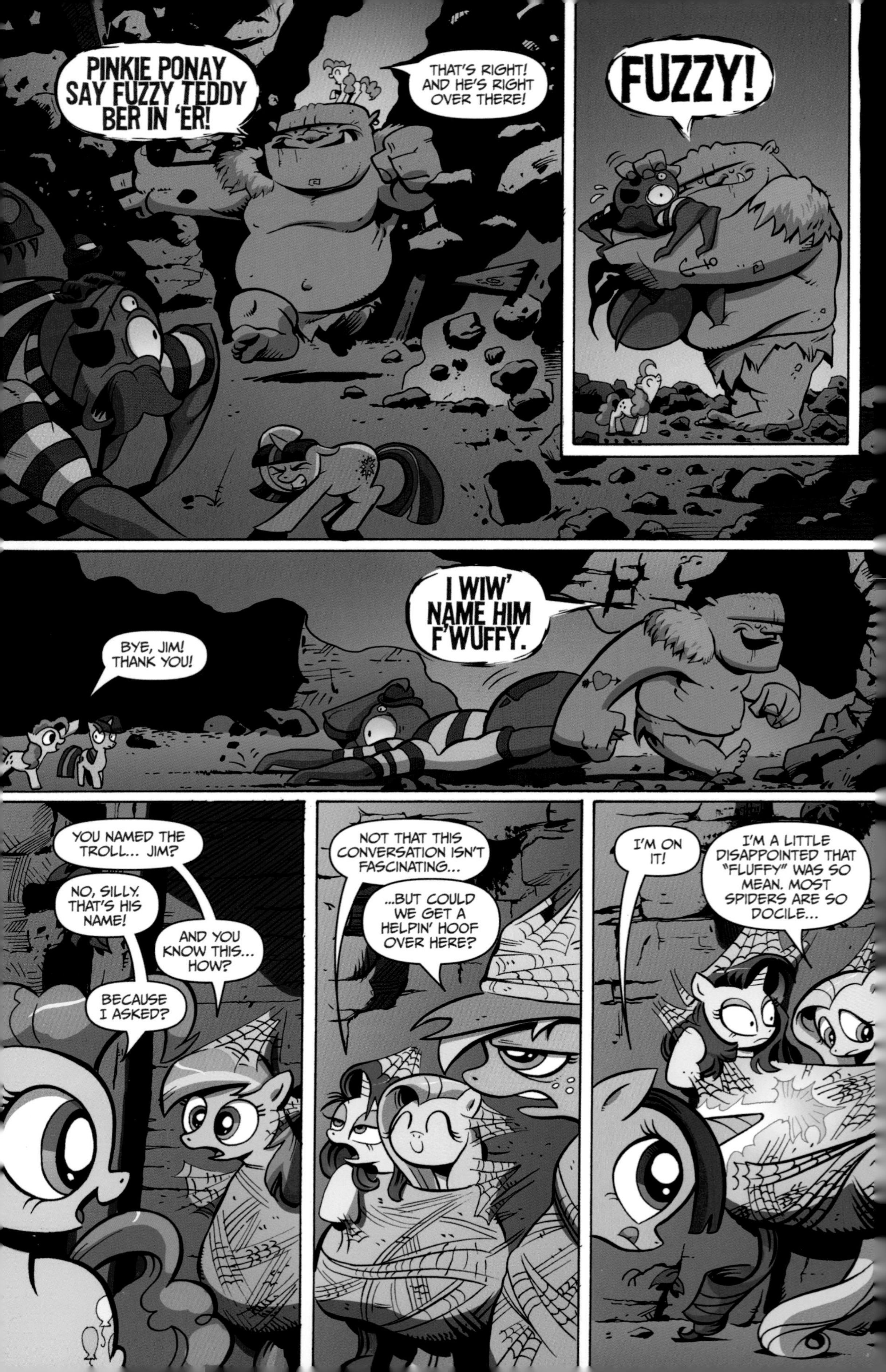
PINKIE PONAY SAY FUZZY TEDDY BER IN 'ER!
THAT'S RIGHT! AND HE'S RIGHT OVER THERE!
FUZZY!
BYE, JIM! THANK YOU!
I WIW' NAME HIM F'WUFFY.
YOU NAMED THE TROLL... JIM?
NO, SILLY. THAT'S HIS NAME!
AND YOU KNOW THIS... HOW?
BECAUSE I ASKED?
NOT THAT THIS CONVERSATION ISN'T FASCINATING...
...BUT COULD WE GET A HELPIN' HOOF OVER HERE?
I'M ON IT!
I'M A LITTLE DISAPPOINTED THAT "FLUFFY" WAS SO MEAN. MOST SPIDERS ARE SO DOCILE...

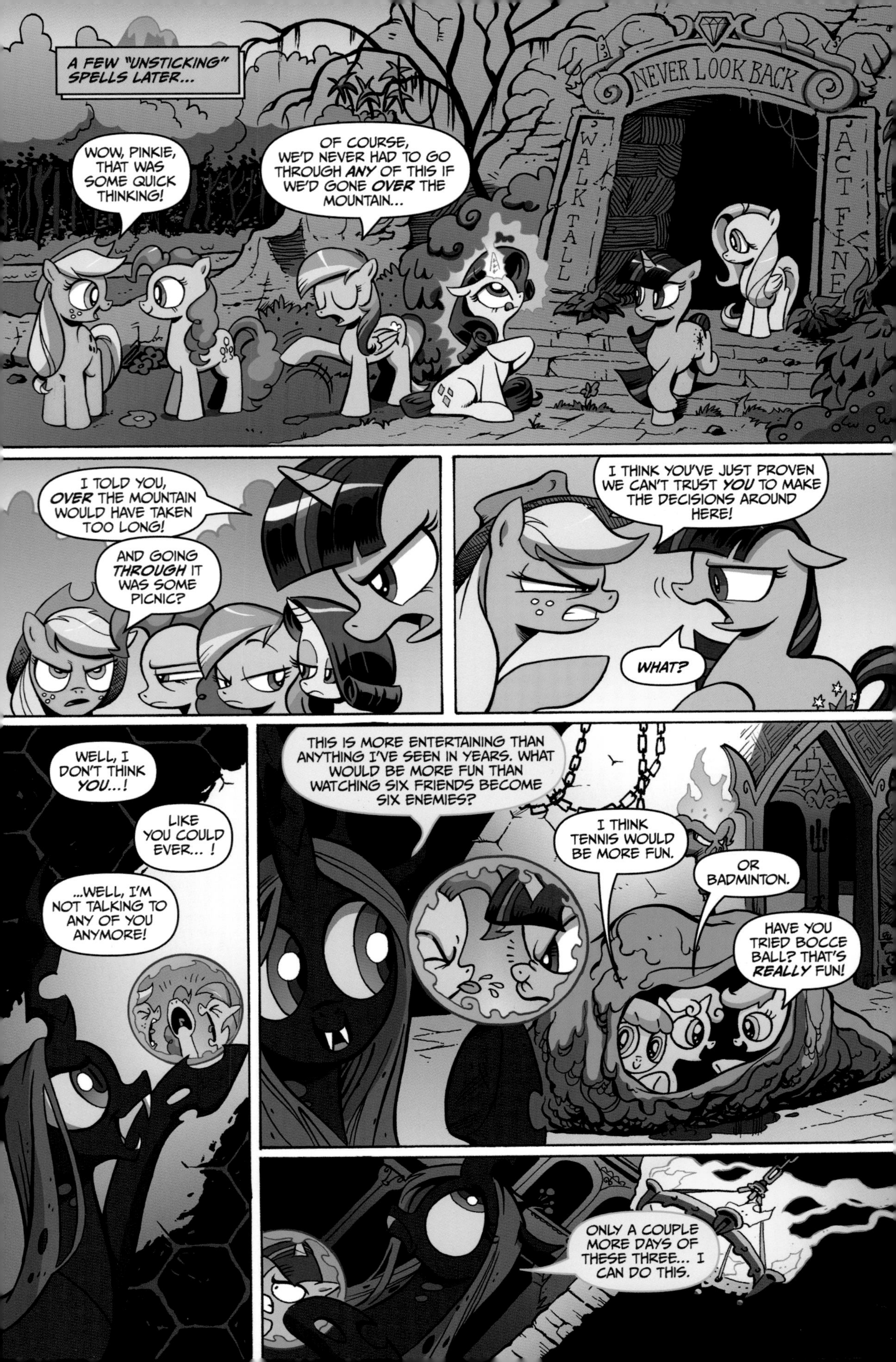
A FEW "UNSTICKING" SPELLS LATER...
NEVER LOOK BACK
WALK TALL
ACT FINE
WOW, PINKIE, THAT WAS SOME QUICK THINKING!
OF COURSE, WE'D NEVER HAD TO GO THROUGH ANY OF THIS IF WE'D GONE OVER THE MOUNTAIN...
I TOLD YOU, OVER THE MOUNTAIN WOULD HAVE TAKEN TOO LONG!
AND GOING THROUGH IT WAS SOME PICNIC?
I THINK YOU'VE JUST PROVEN WE CAN'T TRUST YOU TO MAKE THE DECISIONS AROUND HERE!
WHAT?
WELL, I DON'T THINK YOU...!
LIKE YOU COULD EVER... !
...WELL, I'M NOT TALKING TO ANY OF YOU ANYMORE!
THIS IS MORE ENTERTAINING THAN ANYTHING I'VE SEEN IN YEARS. WHAT WOULD BE MORE FUN THAN WATCHING SIX FRIENDS BECOME SIX ENEMIES?
I THINK TENNIS WOULD BE MORE FUN.
OR BADMINTON.
HAVE YOU TRIED BOCCE BALL? THAT'S REALLY FUN!
ONLY A COUPLE MORE DAYS OF THESE THREE... I CAN DO THIS.

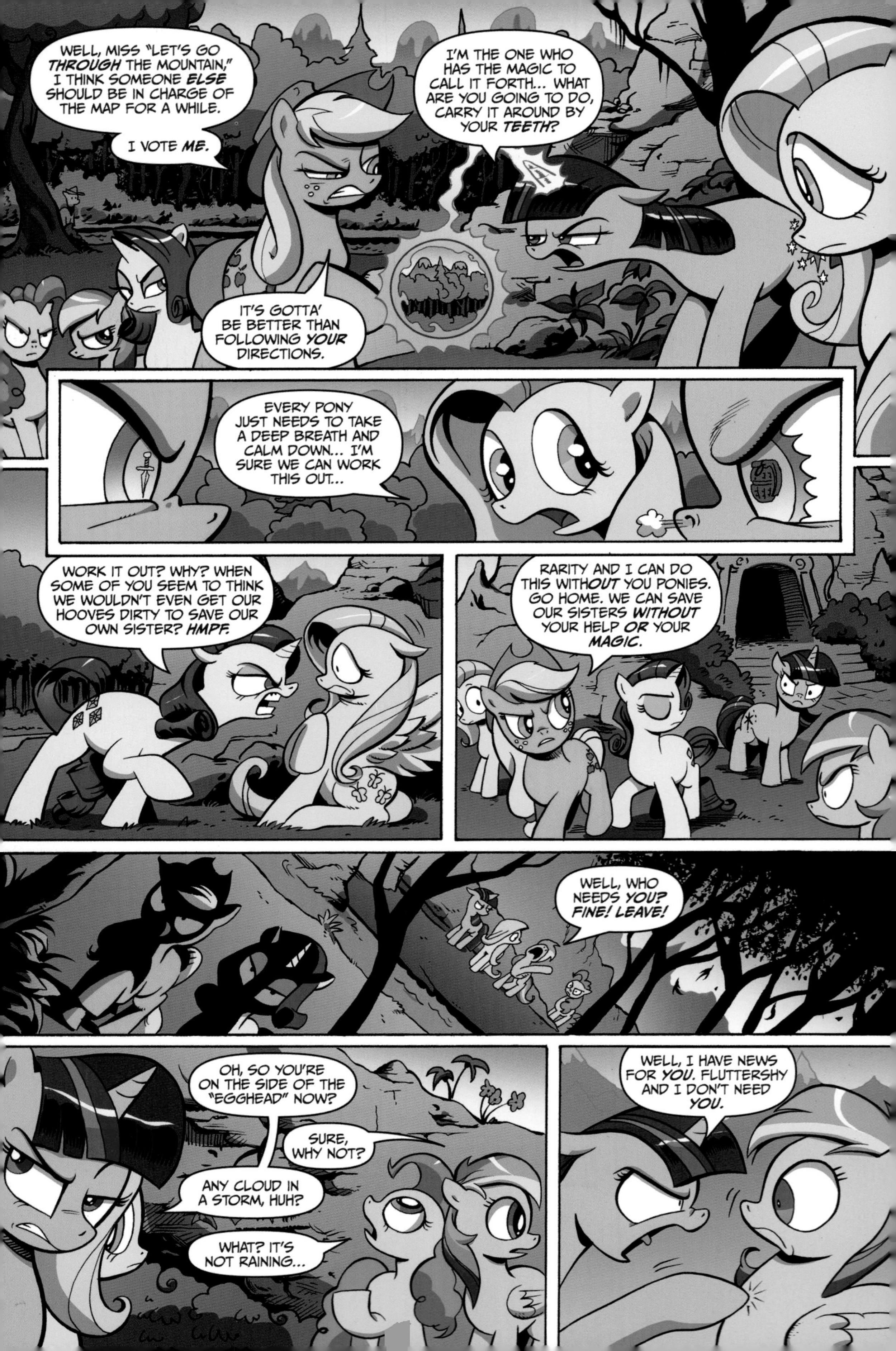
WELL, MISS "LET'S GO THROUGH THE MOUNTAIN," I THINK SOMEONE ELSE SHOULD BE IN CHARGE OF THE MAP FOR A WHILE.
I VOTE ME.
I'M THE ONE WHO HAS THE MAGIC TO CALL IT FORTH... WHAT ARE YOU GOING TO DO, CARRY IT AROUND BY YOUR TEETH?
IT'S GOTTA' BE BETTER THAN FOLLOWING YOUR DIRECTIONS.
EVERY PONY JUST NEEDS TO TAKE A DEEP BREATH AND CALM DOWN... I'M SURE WE CAN WORK THIS OUT...
WORK IT OUT? WHY? WHEN SOME OF YOU SEEM TO THINK WE WOULDN'T EVEN GET OUR HOOVES DIRTY TO SAVE OUR OWN SISTER? HMPF.
RARITY AND I CAN DO THIS WITHOUT YOU PONIES. GO HOME. WE CAN SAVE OUR SISTERS WITHOUT YOUR HELP OR YOUR MAGIC.
WELL, WHO NEEDS YOU? FINE! LEAVE!
OH, SO YOU'RE ON THE SIDE OF THE "EGGHEAD" NOW?
SURE, WHY NOT?
ANY CLOUD IN A STORM, HUH?
WHAT? IT'S NOT RAINING...
WELL, I HAVE NEWS FOR YOU. FLUTTERSHY AND I DON'T NEED YOU.

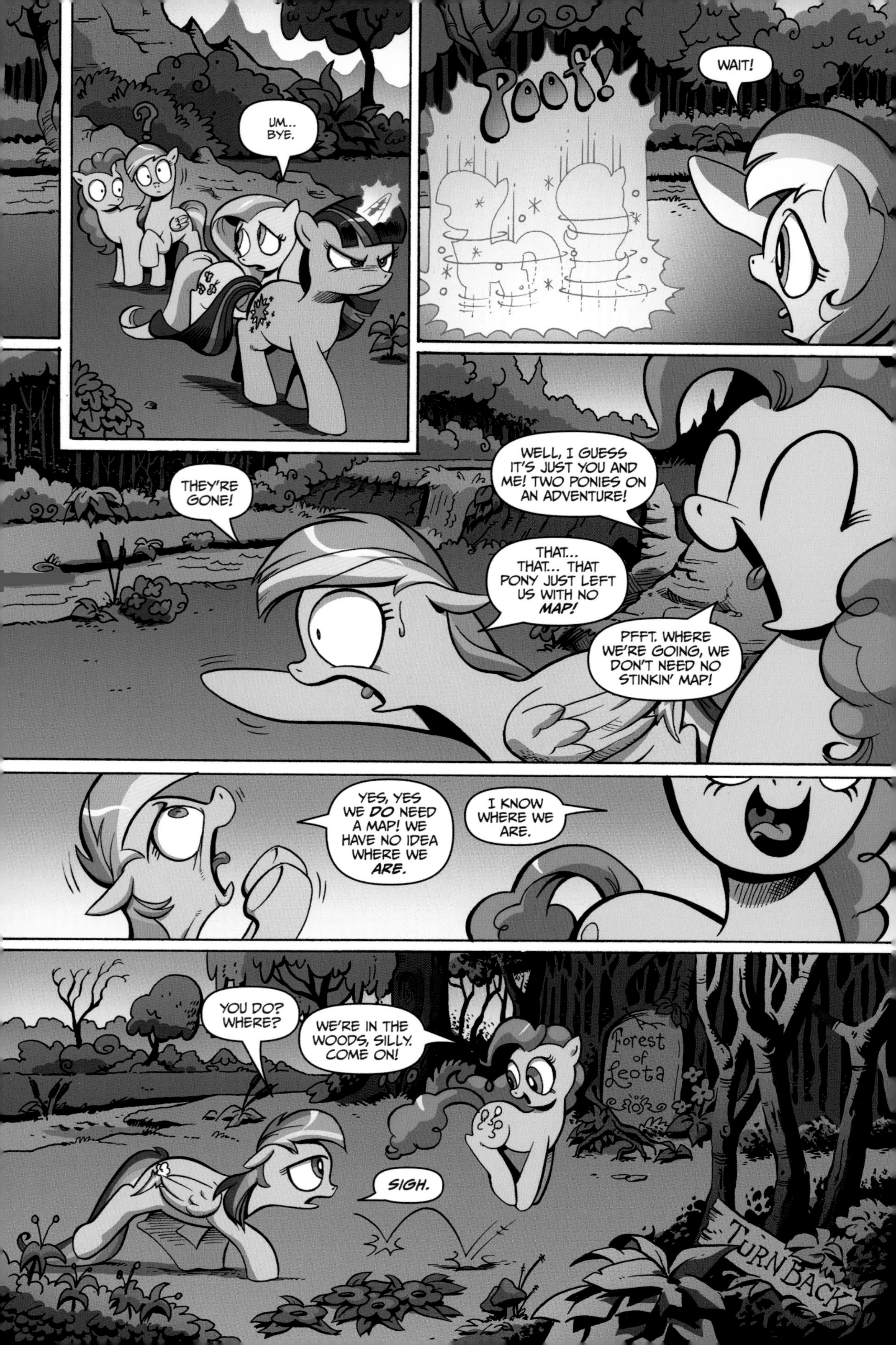
?
UM... BYE.
POOF!
WAIT!
THEY'RE GONE!
WELL, I GUESS IT'S JUST YOU AND ME! TWO PONIES ON AN ADVENTURE!
THAT... THAT... THAT PONY JUST LEFT US WITH NO *MAP!*
PFFT. WHERE WE'RE GOING, WE DON'T NEED NO STINKIN' MAP!
YES, YES WE *DO* NEED A MAP! WE HAVE NO IDEA WHERE WE *ARE.*
I KNOW WHERE WE ARE.
YOU DO? WHERE?
WE'RE IN THE WOODS, SILLY. COME ON!
Forest of Leota
SIGH.
TURN BACK

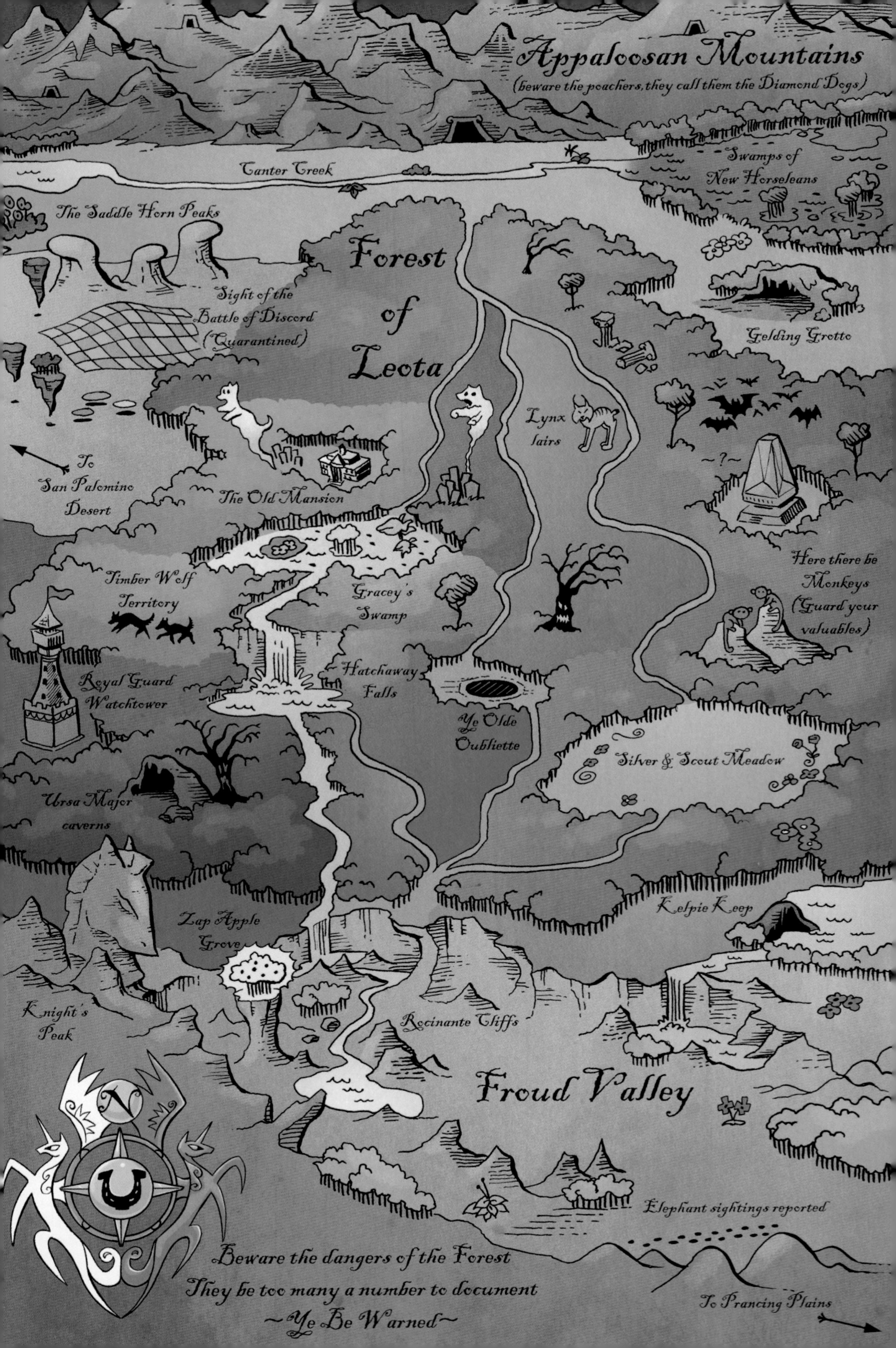

Appaloosan Mountains
(beware the poachers, they call them the Diamond Dogs)
Canter Creek
Swamps of New Horseleans
The Saddle Horn Peaks
Forest of Leota
Sight of the Battle of Discord (Quarantined)
Gelding Grotto
Lynx lairs
To San Palomino Desert
~?~
The Old Mansion
Here there be Monkeys (Guard your valuables)
Timber Wolf Territory
Gracey's Swamp
Royal Guard Watchtower
Hatchaway Falls
Ye Olde Oubliette
Silver & Scout Meadow
Ursa Major caverns
Kelpie Keep
Zap Apple Grove
Knight's Peak
Rocinante Cliffs
Froud Valley
Elephant sightings reported
Beware the dangers of the Forest
They be too many a number to document
~Ye Be Warned~
To Prancing Plains

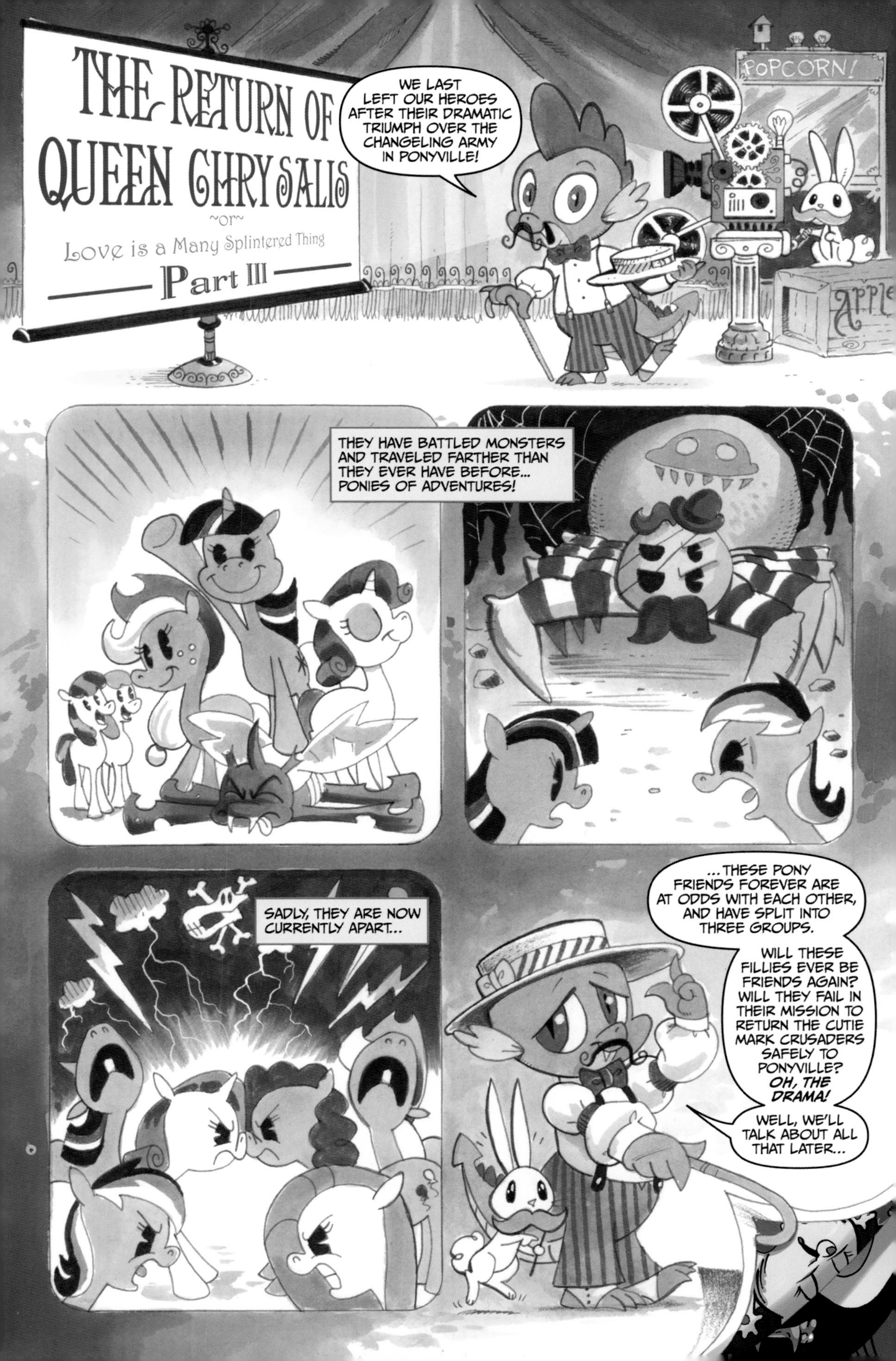
THE RETURN OF QUEEN CHRYSALIS
~or~
Love is a Many Splintered Thing
Part II
POPCORN!
WE LAST LEFT OUR HEROES AFTER THEIR DRAMATIC TRIUMPH OVER THE CHANGELING ARMY IN PONYVILLE!
APPLE
THEY HAVE BATTLED MONSTERS AND TRAVELED FARTHER THAN THEY EVER HAVE BEFORE... PONIES OF ADVENTURES!
SADLY, THEY ARE NOW CURRENTLY APART...
...THESE PONY FRIENDS FOREVER ARE AT ODDS WITH EACH OTHER, AND HAVE SPLIT INTO THREE GROUPS.
WILL THESE FILLIES EVER BE FRIENDS AGAIN? WILL THEY FAIL IN THEIR MISSION TO RETURN THE CUTIE MARK CRUSADERS SAFELY TO PONYVILLE? OH, THE DRAMA!
WELL, WE'LL TALK ABOUT ALL THAT LATER...

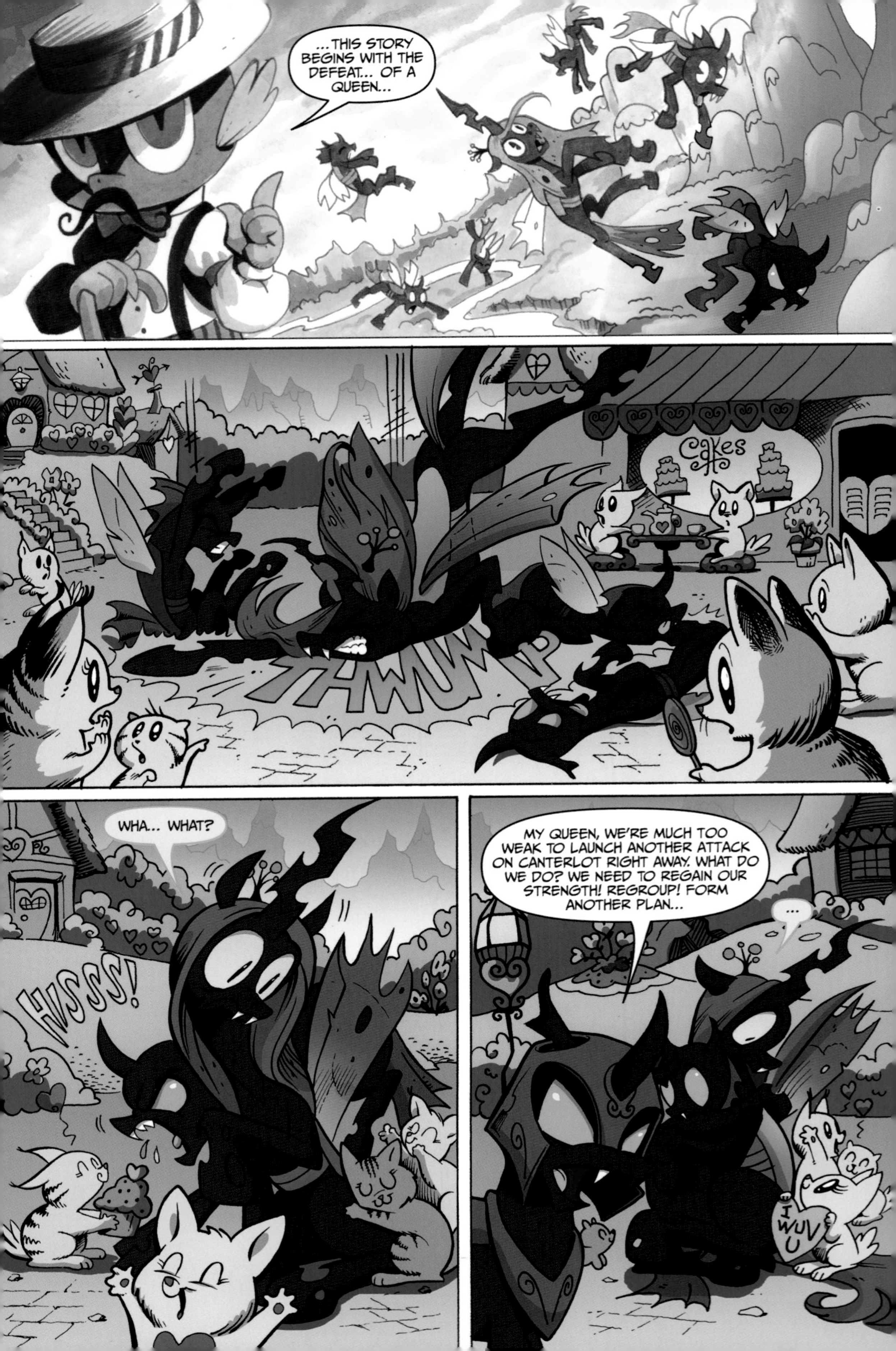
...THIS STORY BEGINS WITH THE DEFEAT... OF A QUEEN...
CAKES
THWUMP
WHA... WHAT?
HISSS!
MY QUEEN, WE'RE MUCH TOO WEAK TO LAUNCH ANOTHER ATTACK ON CANTERLOT RIGHT AWAY. WHAT DO WE DO? WE NEED TO REGAIN OUR STRENGTH! REGROUP! FORM ANOTHER PLAN...
...
I WUV U

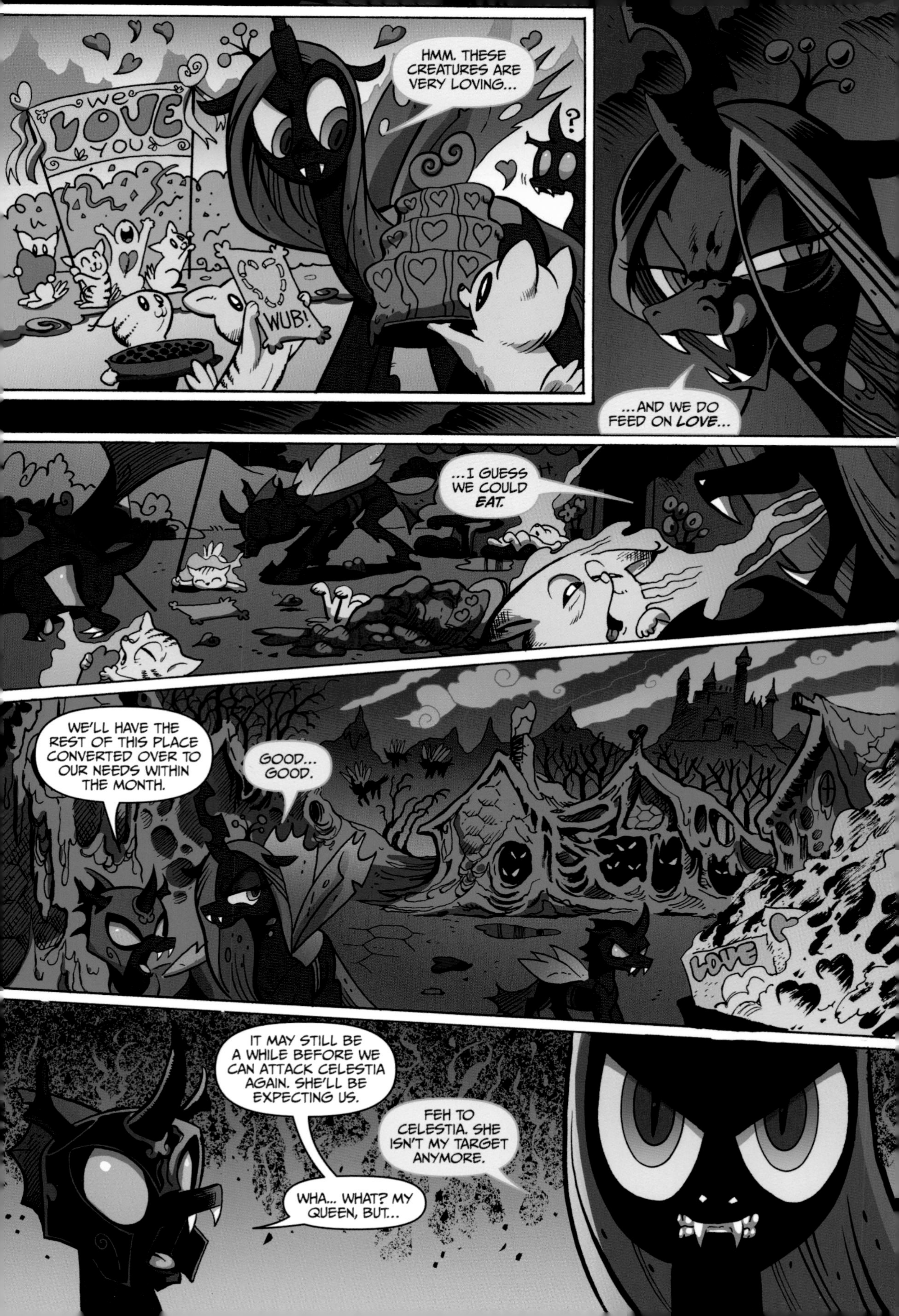

WE LOVE YOU
HMM. THESE CREATURES ARE VERY LOVING...
?
WUB!
...AND WE DO FEED ON LOVE...
...I GUESS WE COULD EAT.
WE'LL HAVE THE REST OF THIS PLACE CONVERTED OVER TO OUR NEEDS WITHIN THE MONTH.
GOOD... GOOD.
LOVE
IT MAY STILL BE A WHILE BEFORE WE CAN ATTACK CELESTIA AGAIN. SHE'LL BE EXPECTING US.
FEH TO CELESTIA. SHE ISN'T MY TARGET ANYMORE.
WHA... WHAT? MY QUEEN, BUT...

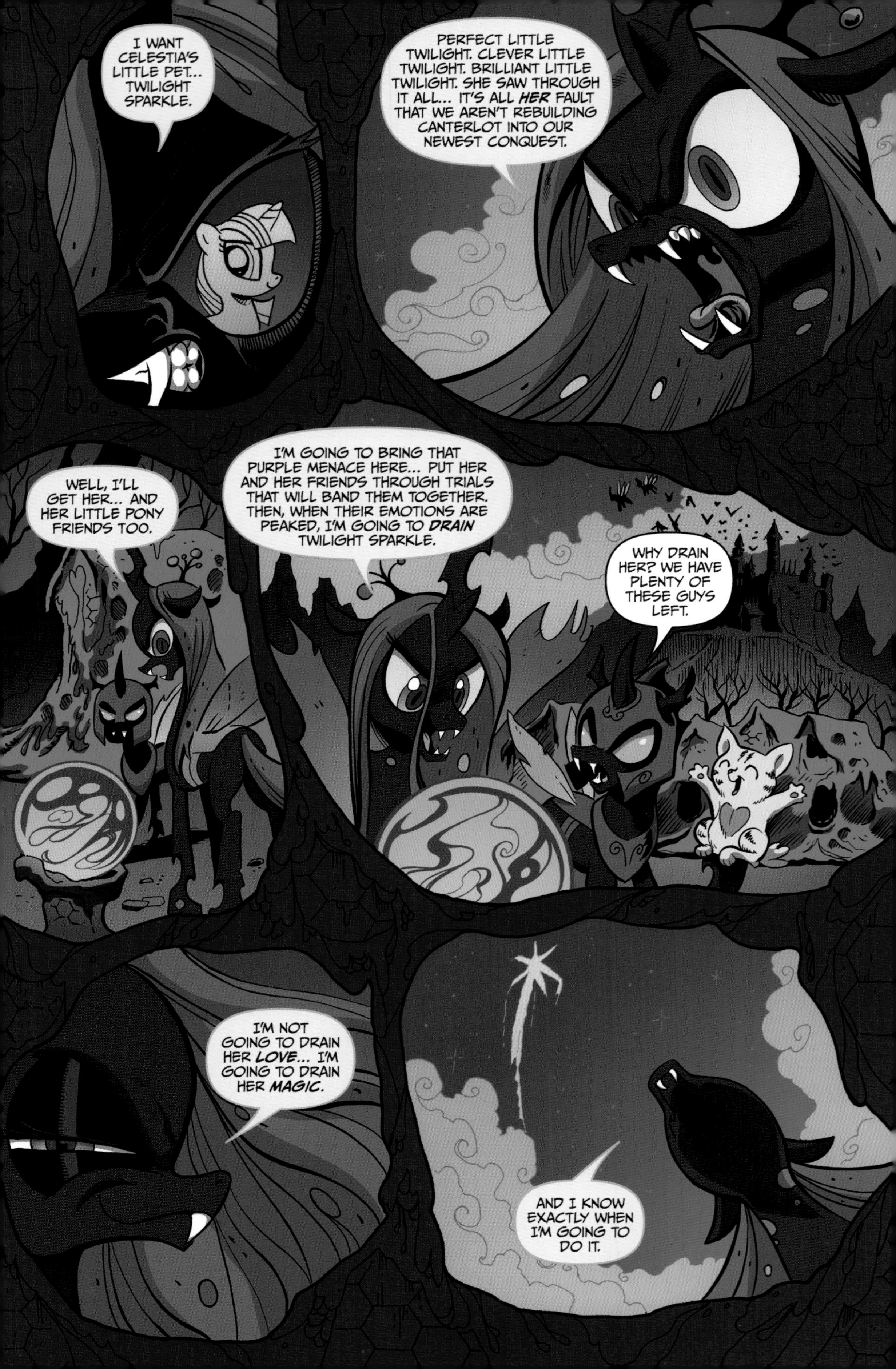

I WANT CELESTIA'S LITTLE PET... TWILIGHT SPARKLE.
PERFECT LITTLE TWILIGHT. CLEVER LITTLE TWILIGHT. BRILLIANT LITTLE TWILIGHT. SHE SAW THROUGH IT ALL... IT'S ALL *HER* FAULT THAT WE AREN'T REBUILDING CANTERLOT INTO OUR NEWEST CONQUEST.
WELL, I'LL GET HER... AND HER LITTLE PONY FRIENDS TOO.
I'M GOING TO BRING THAT PURPLE MENACE HERE... PUT HER AND HER FRIENDS THROUGH TRIALS THAT WILL BAND THEM TOGETHER. THEN, WHEN THEIR EMOTIONS ARE PEAKED, I'M GOING TO *DRAIN* TWILIGHT SPARKLE.
WHY DRAIN HER? WE HAVE PLENTY OF THESE GUYS LEFT.
I'M NOT GOING TO DRAIN HER *LOVE*... I'M GOING TO DRAIN HER *MAGIC*.
AND I KNOW EXACTLY WHEN I'M GOING TO DO IT.

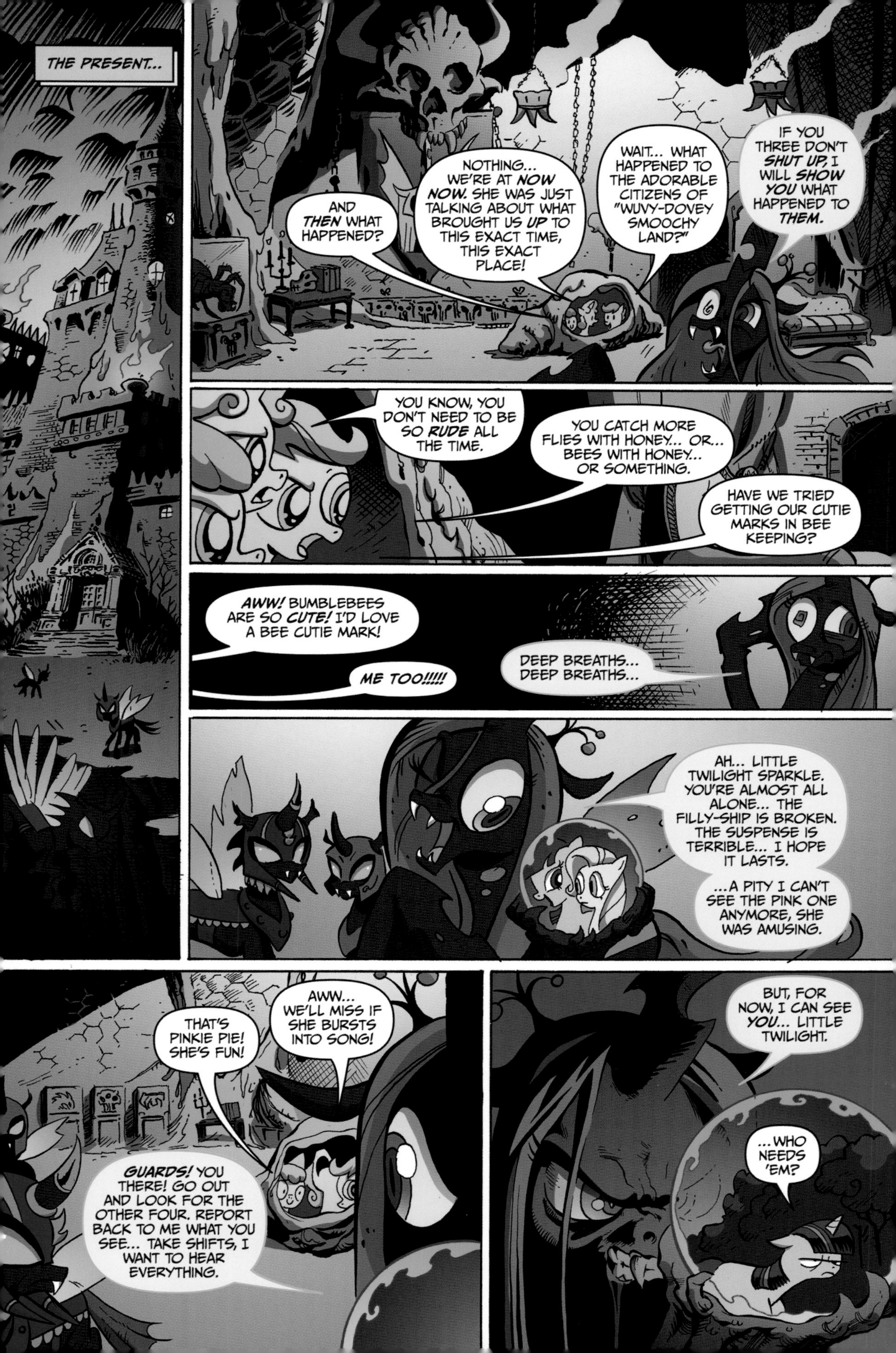
THE PRESENT...
AND THEN WHAT HAPPENED?
NOTHING... WE'RE AT NOW NOW. SHE WAS JUST TALKING ABOUT WHAT BROUGHT US UP TO THIS EXACT TIME, THIS EXACT PLACE!
WAIT... WHAT HAPPENED TO THE ADORABLE CITIZENS OF "WUVY-DOVEY SMOOCHY LAND?"
IF YOU THREE DON'T SHUT UP, I WILL SHOW YOU WHAT HAPPENED TO THEM.
YOU KNOW, YOU DON'T NEED TO BE SO RUDE ALL THE TIME.
YOU CATCH MORE FLIES WITH HONEY... OR... BEES WITH HONEY... OR SOMETHING.
HAVE WE TRIED GETTING OUR CUTIE MARKS IN BEE KEEPING?
AWW! BUMBLEBEES ARE SO CUTE! I'D LOVE A BEE CUTIE MARK!
ME TOO!!!!!
DEEP BREATHS... DEEP BREATHS...
AH... LITTLE TWILIGHT SPARKLE. YOU'RE ALMOST ALL ALONE... THE FILLY-SHIP IS BROKEN. THE SUSPENSE IS TERRIBLE... I HOPE IT LASTS.
...A PITY I CAN'T SEE THE PINK ONE ANYMORE, SHE WAS AMUSING.
THAT'S PINKIE PIE! SHE'S FUN!
AWW... WE'LL MISS IF SHE BURSTS INTO SONG!
GUARDS! YOU THERE! GO OUT AND LOOK FOR THE OTHER FOUR. REPORT BACK TO ME WHAT YOU SEE... TAKE SHIFTS, I WANT TO HEAR EVERYTHING.
BUT, FOR NOW, I CAN SEE YOU... LITTLE TWILIGHT.
...WHO NEEDS 'EM?

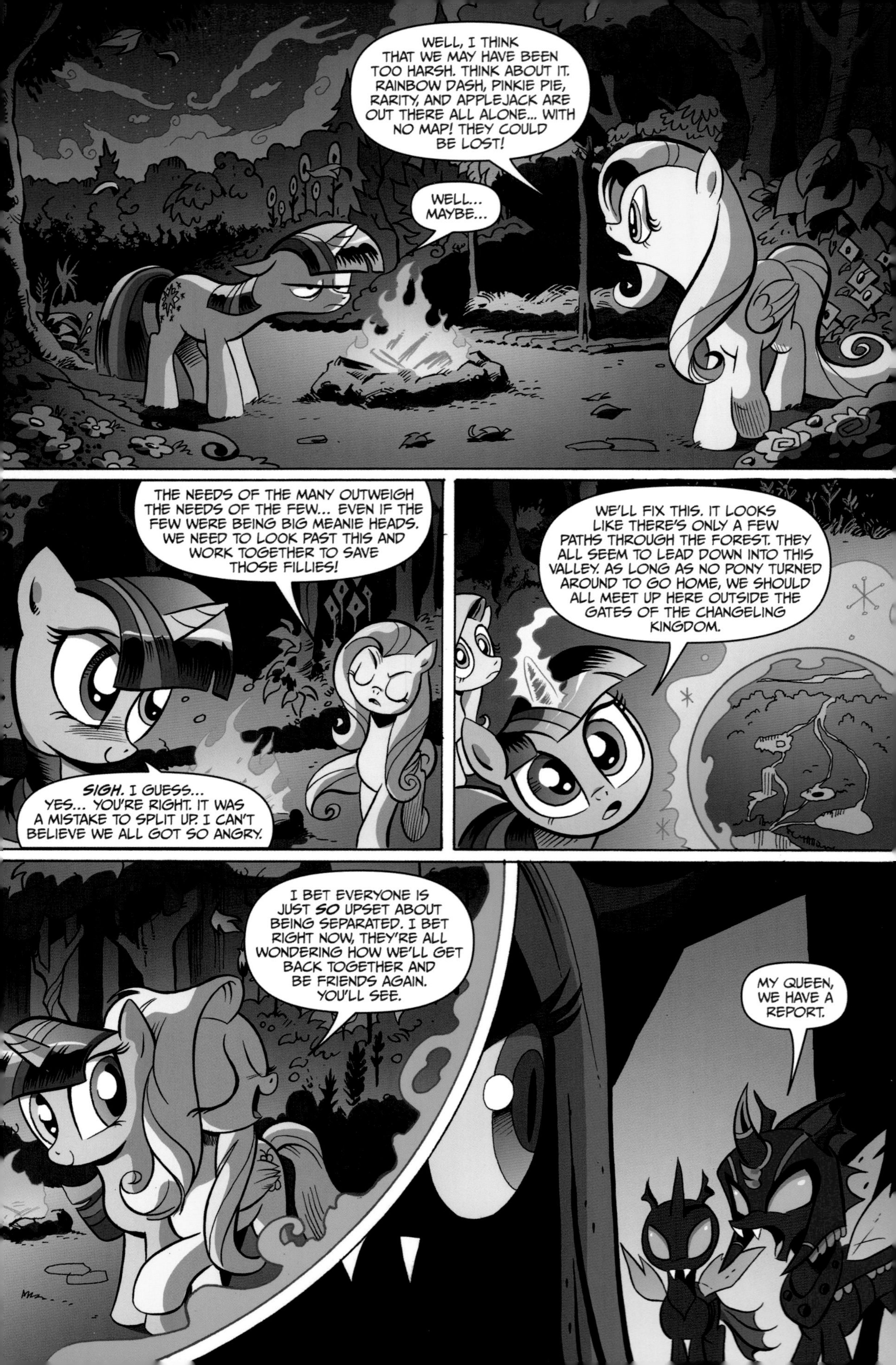
WELL, I THINK THAT WE MAY HAVE BEEN TOO HARSH. THINK ABOUT IT. RAINBOW DASH, PINKIE PIE, RARITY, AND APPLEJACK ARE OUT THERE ALL ALONE... WITH NO MAP! THEY COULD BE LOST!
WELL... MAYBE...
THE NEEDS OF THE MANY OUTWEIGH THE NEEDS OF THE FEW... EVEN IF THE FEW WERE BEING BIG MEANIE HEADS. WE NEED TO LOOK PAST THIS AND WORK TOGETHER TO SAVE THOSE FILLIES!
SIGH. I GUESS... YES... YOU'RE RIGHT. IT WAS A MISTAKE TO SPLIT UP. I CAN'T BELIEVE WE ALL GOT SO ANGRY.
WE'LL FIX THIS. IT LOOKS LIKE THERE'S ONLY A FEW PATHS THROUGH THE FOREST. THEY ALL SEEM TO LEAD DOWN INTO THIS VALLEY. AS LONG AS NO PONY TURNED AROUND TO GO HOME, WE SHOULD ALL MEET UP HERE OUTSIDE THE GATES OF THE CHANGELING KINGDOM.
I BET EVERYONE IS JUST *SO* UPSET ABOUT BEING SEPARATED. I BET RIGHT NOW, THEY'RE ALL WONDERING HOW WE'LL GET BACK TOGETHER AND BE FRIENDS AGAIN. YOU'LL SEE.
MY QUEEN, WE HAVE A REPORT.

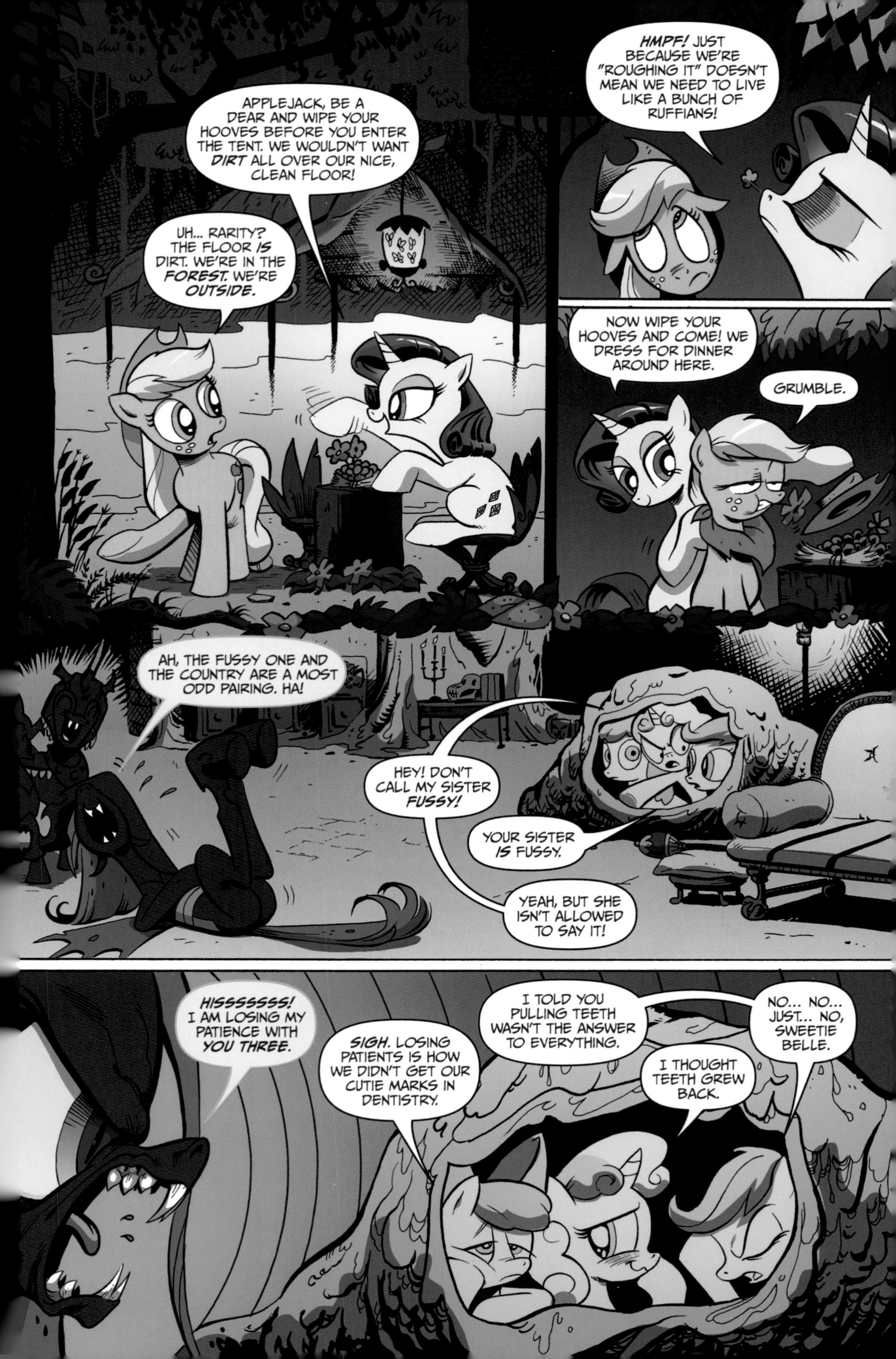
APPLEJACK, BE A DEAR AND WIPE YOUR HOOVES BEFORE YOU ENTER THE TENT. WE WOULDN'T WANT DIRT ALL OVER OUR NICE, CLEAN FLOOR!
UH... RARITY? THE FLOOR IS DIRT. WE'RE IN THE FOREST. WE'RE OUTSIDE.
HMPF! JUST BECAUSE WE'RE "ROUGHING IT" DOESN'T MEAN WE NEED TO LIVE LIKE A BUNCH OF RUFFIANS!
NOW WIPE YOUR HOOVES AND COME! WE DRESS FOR DINNER AROUND HERE.
GRUMBLE.
AH, THE FUSSY ONE AND THE COUNTRY ARE A MOST ODD PAIRING. HA!
HEY! DON'T CALL MY SISTER FUSSY!
YOUR SISTER IS FUSSY.
YEAH, BUT SHE ISN'T ALLOWED TO SAY IT!
HISSSSSSS! I AM LOSING MY PATIENCE WITH YOU THREE.
SIGH. LOSING PATIENTS IS HOW WE DIDN'T GET OUR CUTIE MARKS IN DENTISTRY.
I TOLD YOU PULLING TEETH WASN'T THE ANSWER TO EVERYTHING.
I THOUGHT TEETH GREW BACK.
NO... NO... JUST... NO, SWEETIE BELLE.

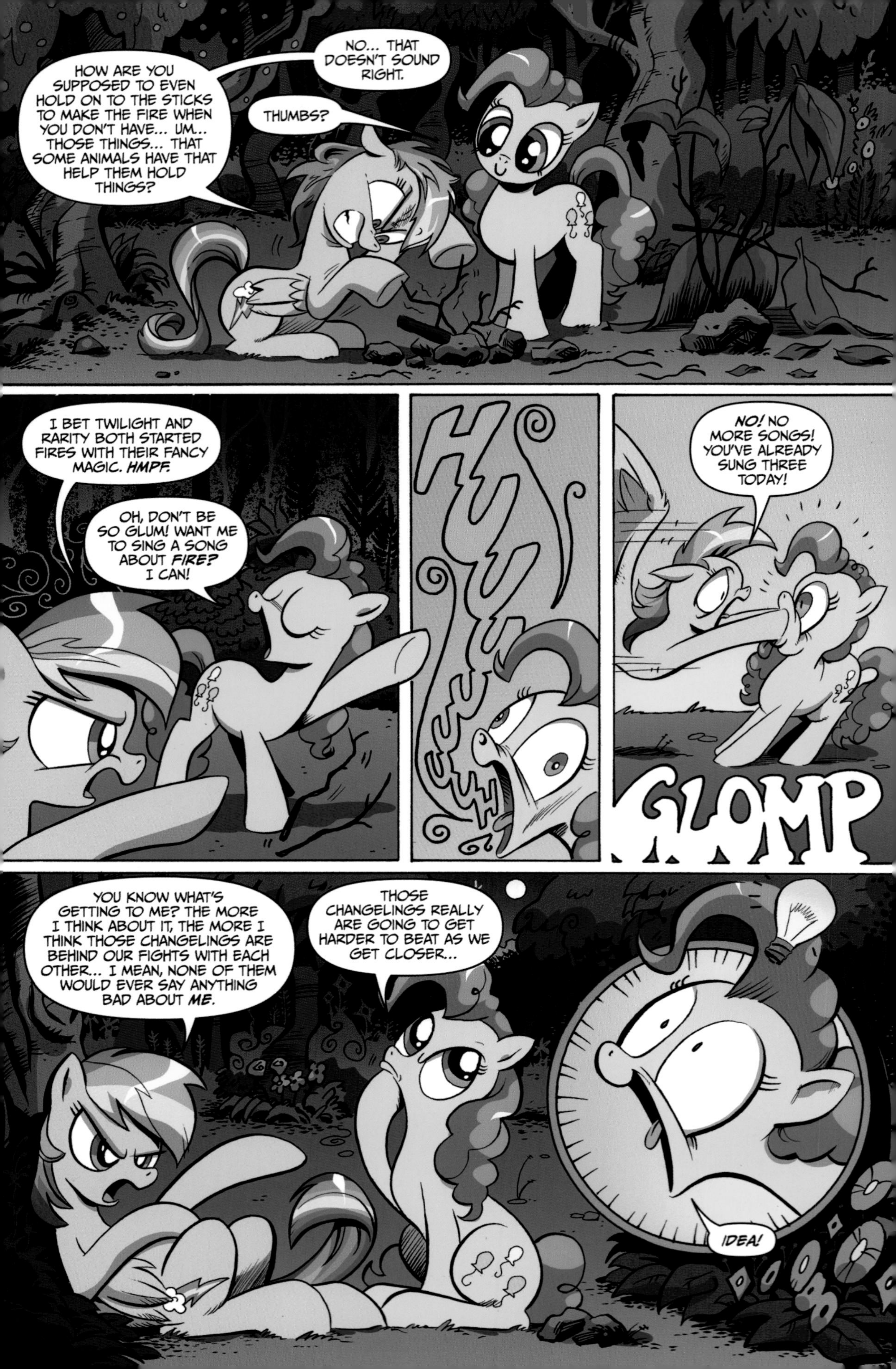
HOW ARE YOU SUPPOSED TO EVEN HOLD ON TO THE STICKS TO MAKE THE FIRE WHEN YOU DON'T HAVE... UM... THOSE THINGS... THAT SOME ANIMALS HAVE THAT HELP THEM HOLD THINGS?
THUMBS?
NO... THAT DOESN'T SOUND RIGHT.
I BET TWILIGHT AND RARITY BOTH STARTED FIRES WITH THEIR FANCY MAGIC. *HMPF.*
OH, DON'T BE SO GLUM! WANT ME TO SING A SONG ABOUT *FIRE?* I CAN!
HUUUUUH
NO! NO MORE SONGS! YOU'VE ALREADY SUNG THREE TODAY!
GLOMP
YOU KNOW WHAT'S GETTING TO ME? THE MORE I THINK ABOUT IT, THE MORE I THINK THOSE CHANGELINGS ARE BEHIND OUR FIGHTS WITH EACH OTHER... I MEAN, NONE OF THEM WOULD EVER SAY ANYTHING BAD ABOUT *ME*.
THOSE CHANGELINGS REALLY ARE GOING TO GET HARDER TO BEAT AS WE GET CLOSER...
IDEA!

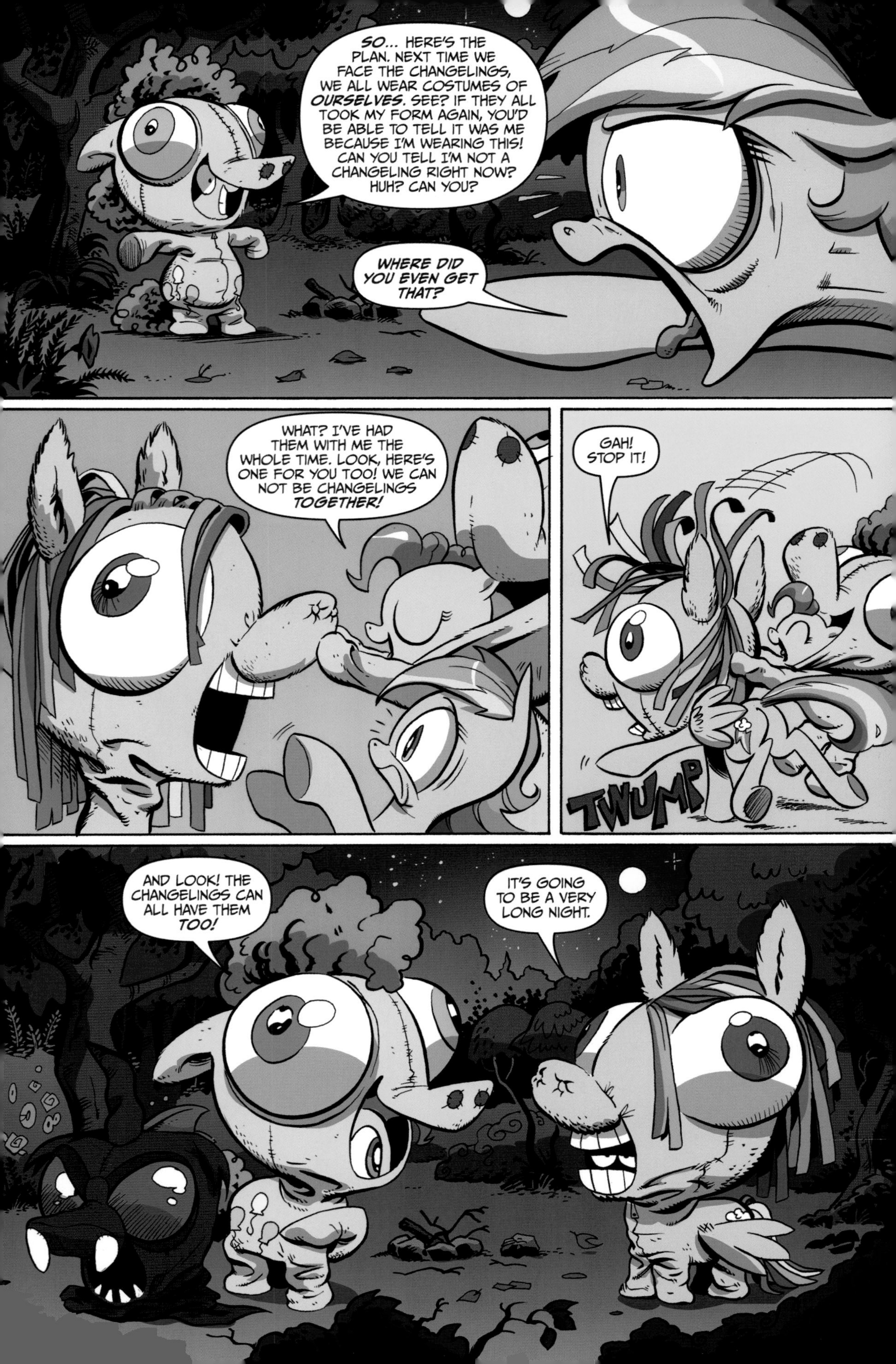
SO... HERE'S THE PLAN. NEXT TIME WE FACE THE CHANGELINGS, WE ALL WEAR COSTUMES OF OURSELVES. SEE? IF THEY ALL TOOK MY FORM AGAIN, YOU'D BE ABLE TO TELL IT WAS ME BECAUSE I'M WEARING THIS! CAN YOU TELL I'M NOT A CHANGELING RIGHT NOW? HUH? CAN YOU?
WHERE DID YOU EVEN GET THAT?
WHAT? I'VE HAD THEM WITH ME THE WHOLE TIME. LOOK, HERE'S ONE FOR YOU TOO! WE CAN NOT BE CHANGELINGS TOGETHER!
GAH! STOP IT!
TWUMP
AND LOOK! THE CHANGELINGS CAN ALL HAVE THEM TOO!
IT'S GOING TO BE A VERY LONG NIGHT.

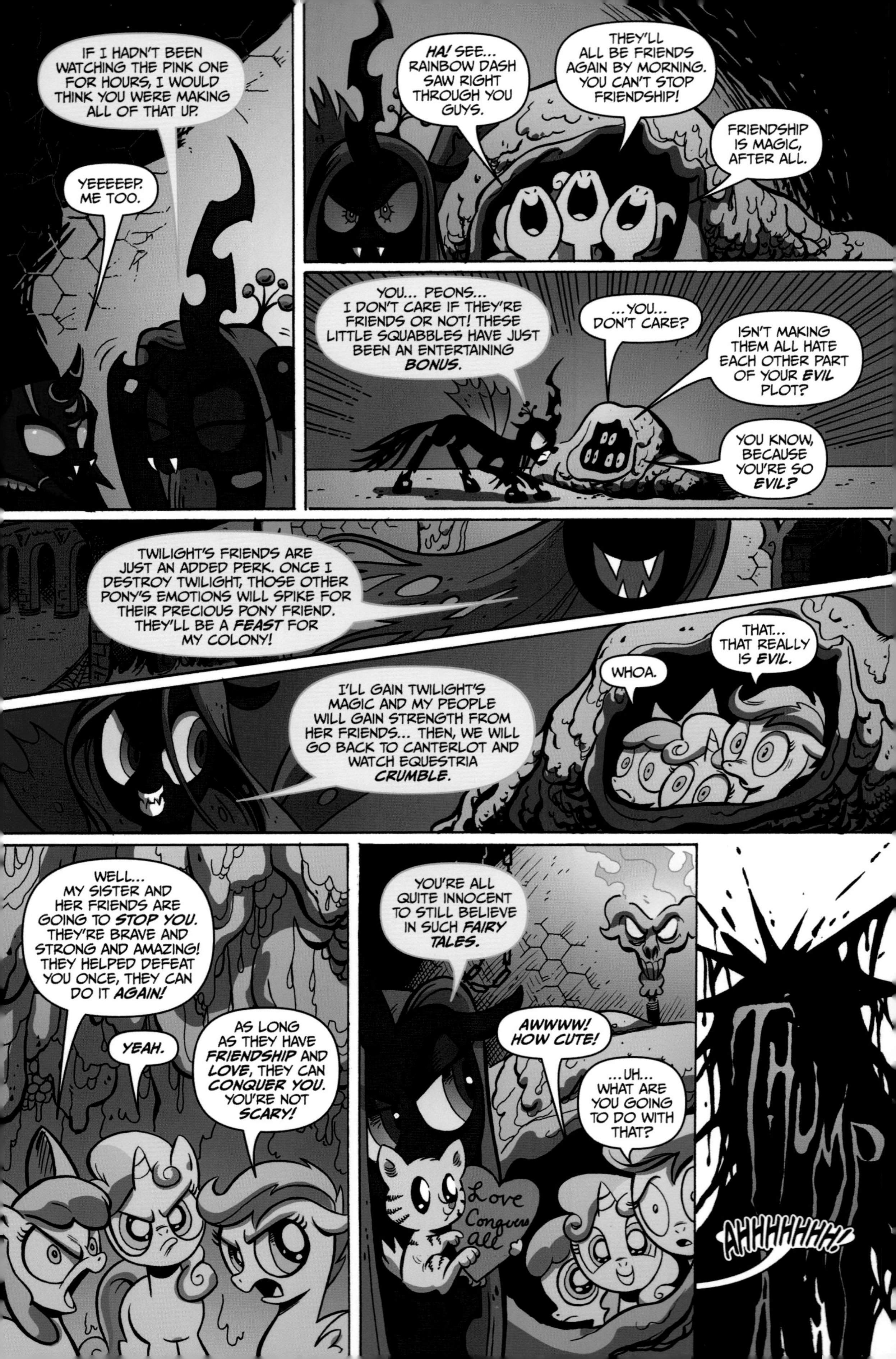
IF I HADN'T BEEN WATCHING THE PINK ONE FOR HOURS, I WOULD THINK YOU WERE MAKING ALL OF THAT UP.
YEEEEEP. ME TOO.
HA! SEE... RAINBOW DASH SAW RIGHT THROUGH YOU GUYS.
THEY'LL ALL BE FRIENDS AGAIN BY MORNING. YOU CAN'T STOP FRIENDSHIP!
FRIENDSHIP IS MAGIC, AFTER ALL.
YOU... PEONS... I DON'T CARE IF THEY'RE FRIENDS OR NOT! THESE LITTLE SQUABBLES HAVE JUST BEEN AN ENTERTAINING BONUS.
...YOU... DON'T CARE?
ISN'T MAKING THEM ALL HATE EACH OTHER PART OF YOUR EVIL PLOT?
YOU KNOW, BECAUSE YOU'RE SO EVIL?
TWILIGHT'S FRIENDS ARE JUST AN ADDED PERK. ONCE I DESTROY TWILIGHT, THOSE OTHER PONY'S EMOTIONS WILL SPIKE FOR THEIR PRECIOUS PONY FRIEND. THEY'LL BE A FEAST FOR MY COLONY!
I'LL GAIN TWILIGHT'S MAGIC AND MY PEOPLE WILL GAIN STRENGTH FROM HER FRIENDS... THEN, WE WILL GO BACK TO CANTERLOT AND WATCH EQUESTRIA CRUMBLE.
WHOA.
THAT... THAT REALLY IS EVIL.
WELL... MY SISTER AND HER FRIENDS ARE GOING TO STOP YOU. THEY'RE BRAVE AND STRONG AND AMAZING! THEY HELPED DEFEAT YOU ONCE, THEY CAN DO IT AGAIN!
YEAH.
AS LONG AS THEY HAVE FRIENDSHIP AND LOVE, THEY CAN CONQUER YOU. YOU'RE NOT SCARY!
YOU'RE ALL QUITE INNOCENT TO STILL BELIEVE IN SUCH FAIRY TALES.
AWWWW! HOW CUTE!
...UH... WHAT ARE YOU GOING TO DO WITH THAT?
Love Conquers all
THUMP
AHHHHHHH!

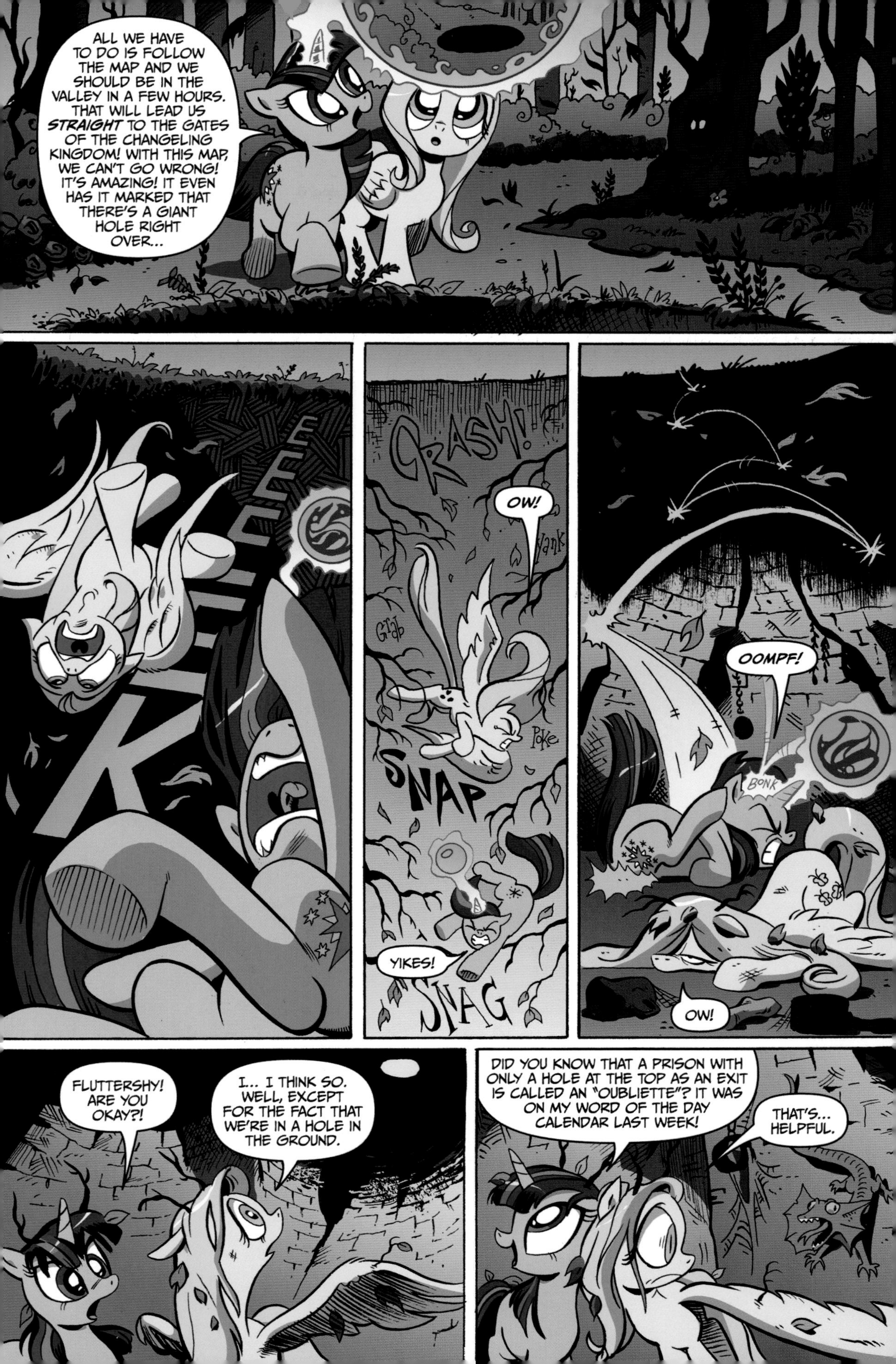
ALL WE HAVE TO DO IS FOLLOW THE MAP AND WE SHOULD BE IN THE VALLEY IN A FEW HOURS. THAT WILL LEAD US STRAIGHT TO THE GATES OF THE CHANGELING KINGDOM! WITH THIS MAP, WE CAN'T GO WRONG! IT'S AMAZING! IT EVEN HAS IT MARKED THAT THERE'S A GIANT HOLE RIGHT OVER...
EEEK
CRASH!
OW!
Yank
Grab
Poke
SNAP
YIKES!
SNAG
OOMPF!
BONK
OW!
FLUTTERSHY! ARE YOU OKAY?!
I... I THINK SO. WELL, EXCEPT FOR THE FACT THAT WE'RE IN A HOLE IN THE GROUND.
DID YOU KNOW THAT A PRISON WITH ONLY A HOLE AT THE TOP AS AN EXIT IS CALLED AN "OUBLIETTE"? IT WAS ON MY WORD OF THE DAY CALENDAR LAST WEEK!
THAT'S... HELPFUL.

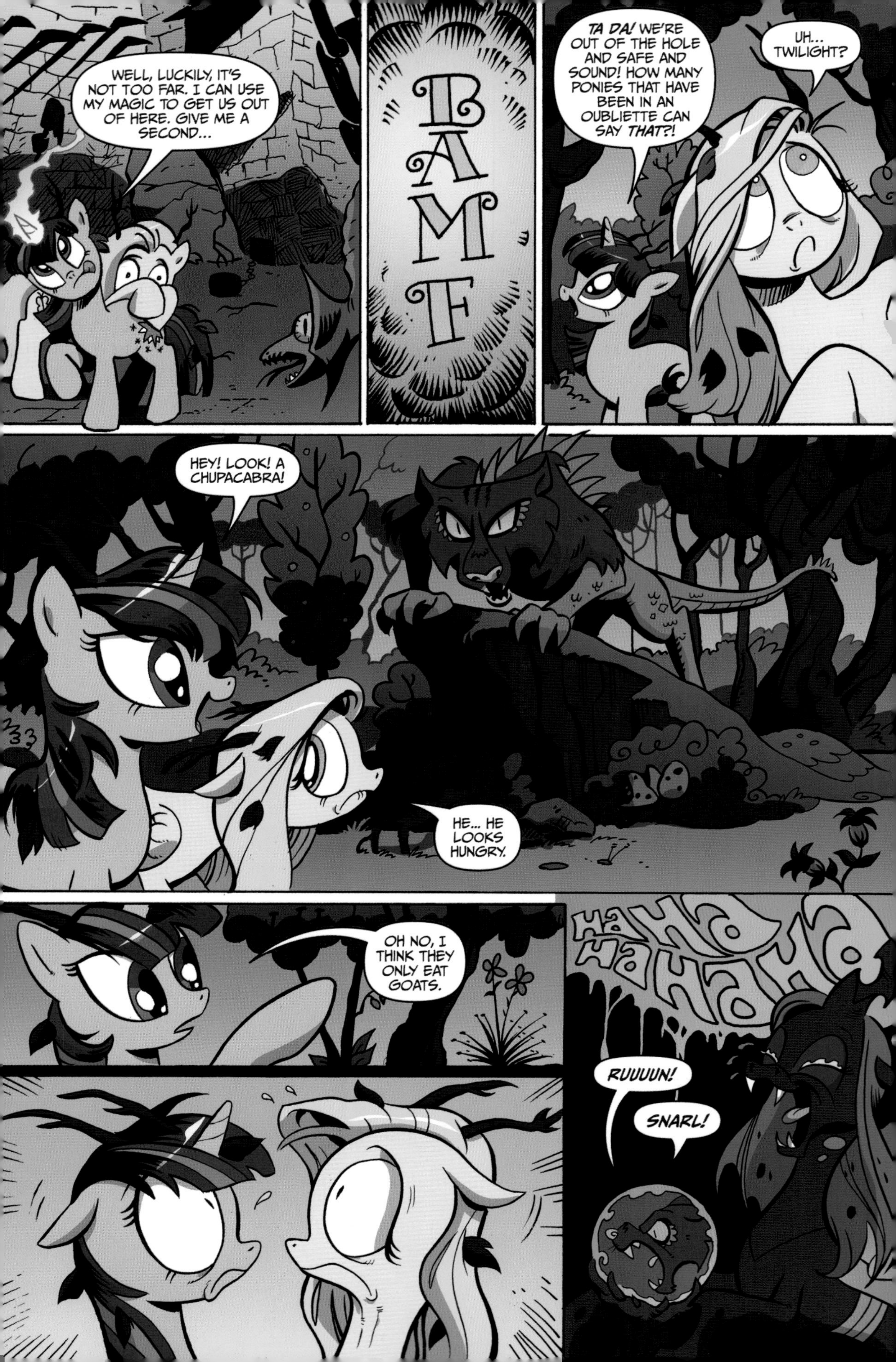

WELL, LUCKILY, IT'S NOT TOO FAR. I CAN USE MY MAGIC TO GET US OUT OF HERE. GIVE ME A SECOND...
BAMF
TA DA! WE'RE OUT OF THE HOLE AND SAFE AND SOUND! HOW MANY PONIES THAT HAVE BEEN IN AN OUBLIETTE CAN SAY THAT?!
UH... TWILIGHT?
HEY! LOOK! A CHUPACABRA!
HE... HE LOOKS HUNGRY.
OH NO, I THINK THEY ONLY EAT GOATS.
HaHaHa
HaHaHaHa
RUUUUN!
SNARL!

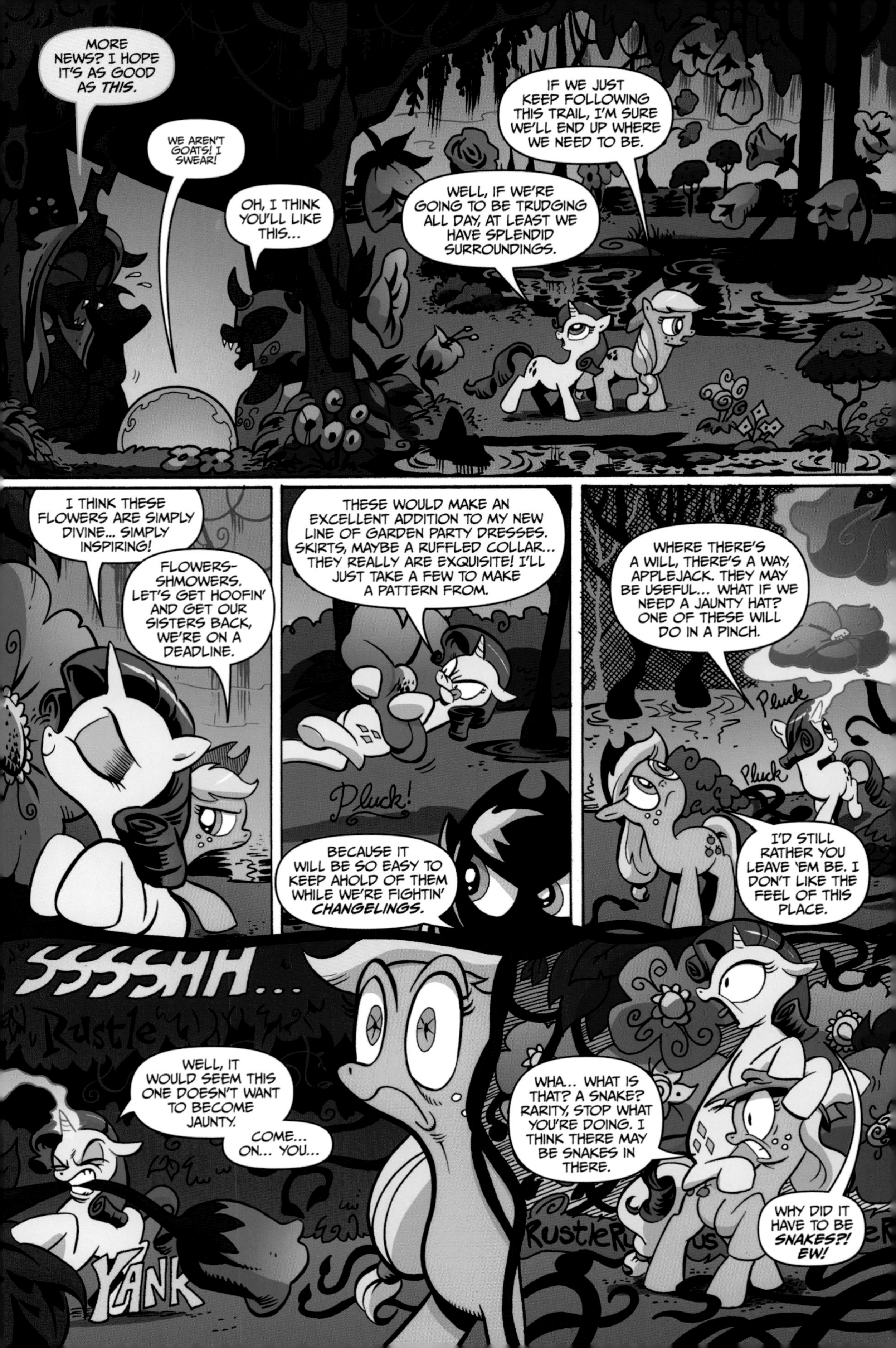

MORE NEWS? I HOPE IT'S AS GOOD AS *THIS*.
WE AREN'T GOATS! I SWEAR!
OH, I THINK YOU'LL LIKE THIS...
IF WE JUST KEEP FOLLOWING THIS TRAIL, I'M SURE WE'LL END UP WHERE WE NEED TO BE.
WELL, IF WE'RE GOING TO BE TRUDGING ALL DAY, AT LEAST WE HAVE SPLENDID SURROUNDINGS.
I THINK THESE FLOWERS ARE SIMPLY DIVINE... SIMPLY INSPIRING!
FLOWERS-SHMOWERS. LET'S GET HOOFIN' AND GET OUR SISTERS BACK, WE'RE ON A DEADLINE.
THESE WOULD MAKE AN EXCELLENT ADDITION TO MY NEW LINE OF GARDEN PARTY DRESSES. SKIRTS, MAYBE A RUFFLED COLLAR... THEY REALLY ARE EXQUISITE! I'LL JUST TAKE A FEW TO MAKE A PATTERN FROM.
Pluck!
BECAUSE IT WILL BE SO EASY TO KEEP AHOLD OF THEM WHILE WE'RE FIGHTIN' ***CHANGELINGS.***
WHERE THERE'S A WILL, THERE'S A WAY, APPLEJACK. THEY MAY BE USEFUL... WHAT IF WE NEED A JAUNTY HAT? ONE OF THESE WILL DO IN A PINCH.
Pluck
Pluck
I'D STILL RATHER YOU LEAVE 'EM BE. I DON'T LIKE THE FEEL OF THIS PLACE.
SSSSHH...
Rustle
WELL, IT WOULD SEEM THIS ONE DOESN'T WANT TO BECOME JAUNTY.
COME... ON... YOU...
YANK
WHA... WHAT IS THAT? A SNAKE? RARITY, STOP WHAT YOU'RE DOING. I THINK THERE MAY BE SNAKES IN THERE.
WHY DID IT HAVE TO BE ***SNAKES?! EW!***

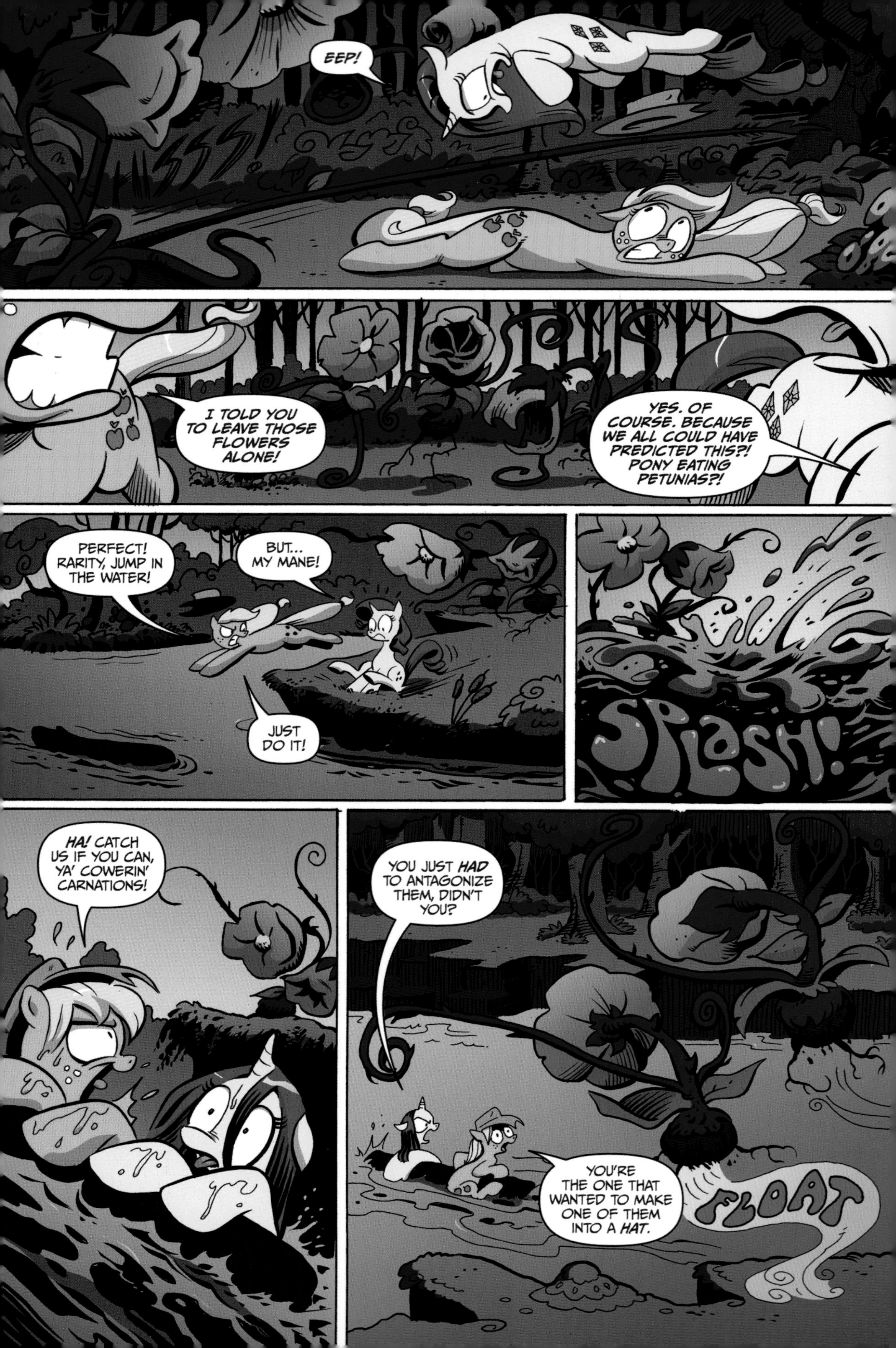

EEP!
HISSSS!
I TOLD YOU TO LEAVE THOSE FLOWERS ALONE!
YES. OF COURSE. BECAUSE WE ALL COULD HAVE PREDICTED THIS?! PONY EATING PETUNIAS?!
PERFECT! RARITY, JUMP IN THE WATER!
BUT... MY MANE!
JUST DO IT!
SPLASH!
HA! CATCH US IF YOU CAN, YA' COWERIN' CARNATIONS!
YOU JUST HAD TO ANTAGONIZE THEM, DIDN'T YOU?
YOU'RE THE ONE THAT WANTED TO MAKE ONE OF THEM INTO A HAT.
FLOAT

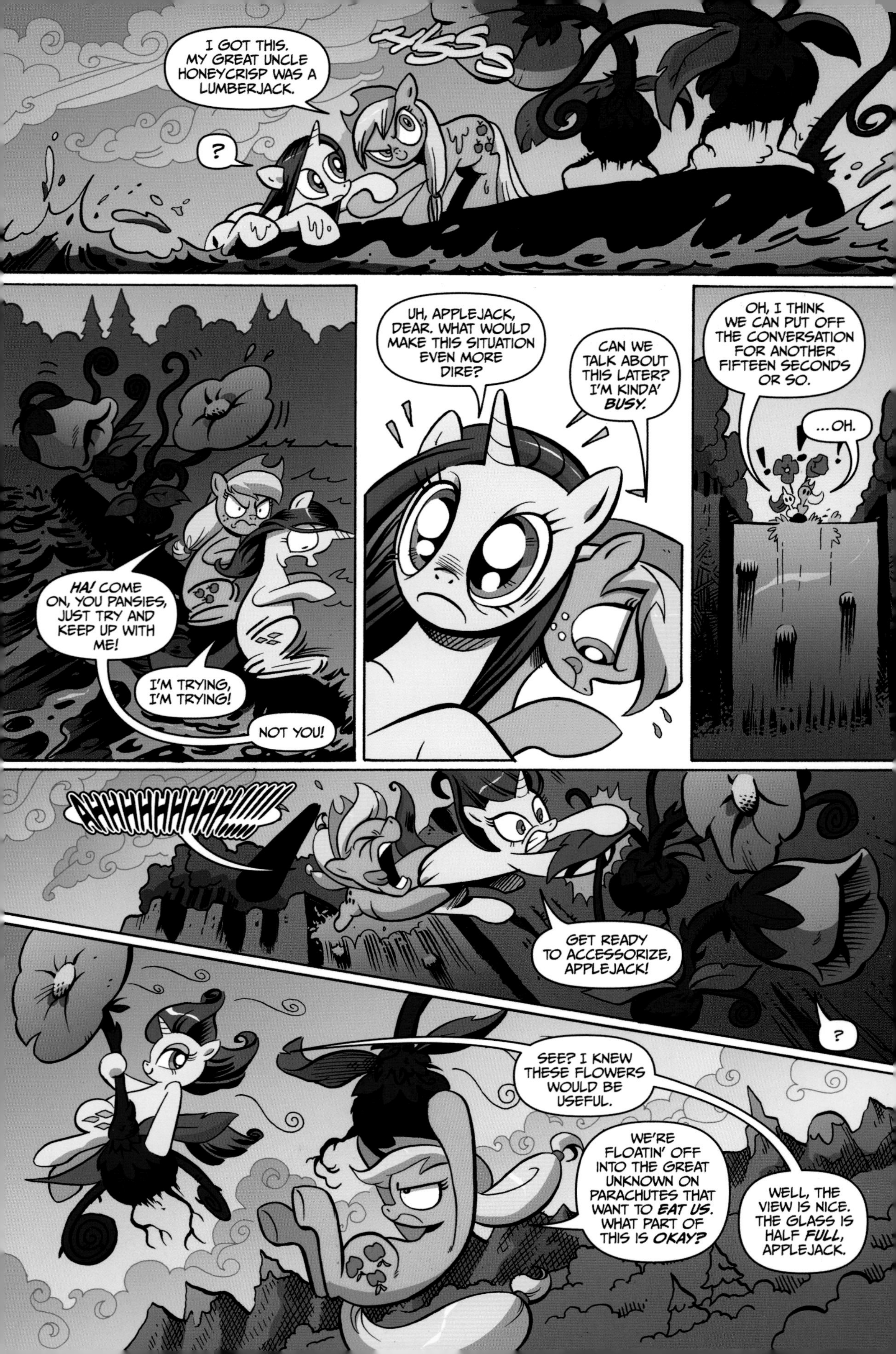

I GOT THIS. MY GREAT UNCLE HONEYCRISP WAS A LUMBERJACK.
HISSS
?
HA! COME ON, YOU PANSIES, JUST TRY AND KEEP UP WITH ME!
I'M TRYING, I'M TRYING!
NOT YOU!
UH, APPLEJACK, DEAR. WHAT WOULD MAKE THIS SITUATION EVEN MORE DIRE?
CAN WE TALK ABOUT THIS LATER? I'M KINDA' BUSY.
OH, I THINK WE CAN PUT OFF THE CONVERSATION FOR ANOTHER FIFTEEN SECONDS OR SO.
...OH.
AHHHHHHHHH!!!!!!!
GET READY TO ACCESSORIZE, APPLEJACK!
?
SEE? I KNEW THESE FLOWERS WOULD BE USEFUL.
WE'RE FLOATIN' OFF INTO THE GREAT UNKNOWN ON PARACHUTES THAT WANT TO EAT US. WHAT PART OF THIS IS OKAY?
WELL, THE VIEW IS NICE. THE GLASS IS HALF FULL, APPLEJACK.

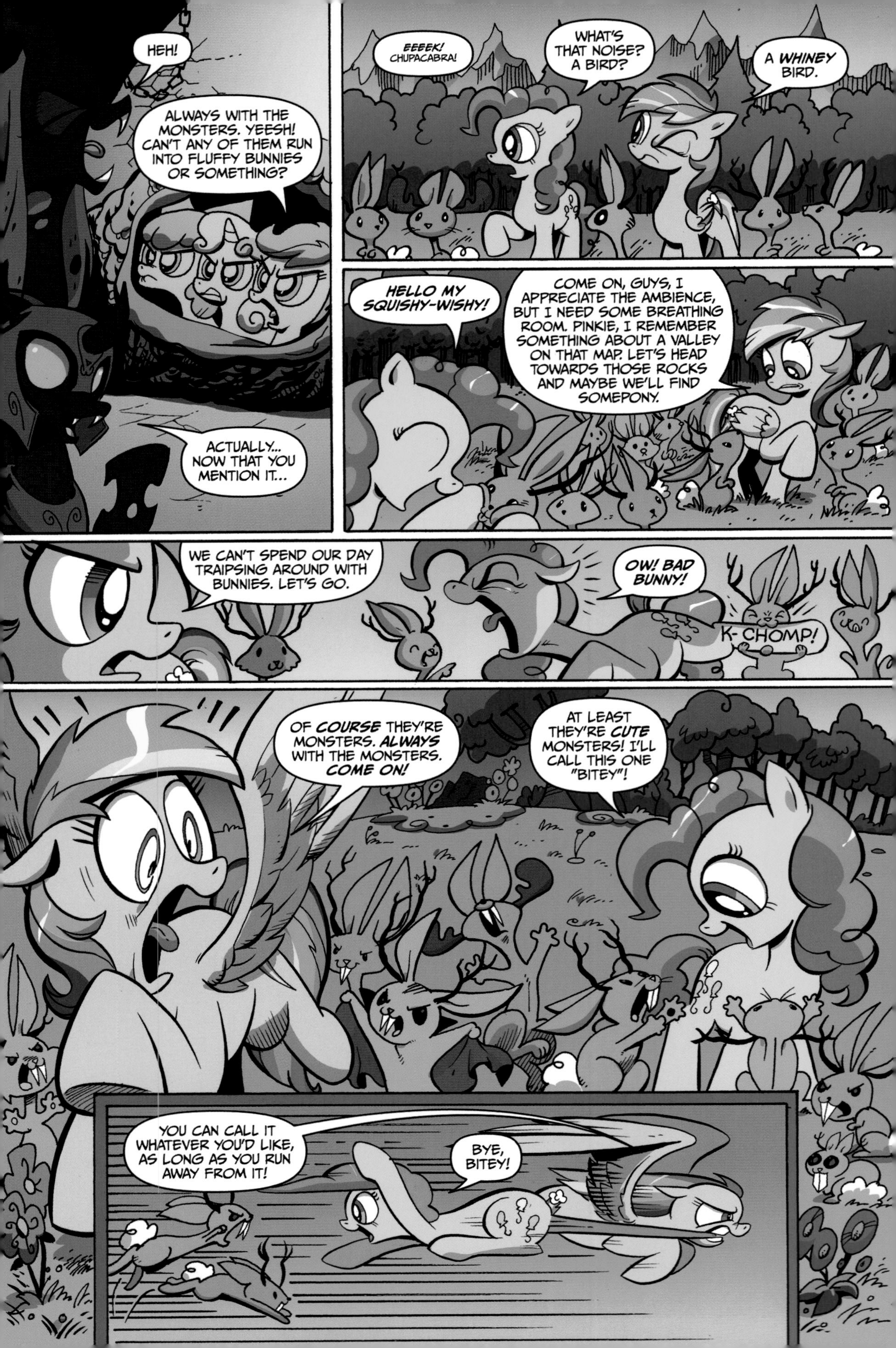
HEH!
ALWAYS WITH THE MONSTERS. YEESH! CAN'T ANY OF THEM RUN INTO FLUFFY BUNNIES OR SOMETHING?
ACTUALLY... NOW THAT YOU MENTION IT...
EEEEK! CHUPACABRA!
WHAT'S THAT NOISE? A BIRD?
A WHINEY BIRD.
HELLO MY SQUISHY-WISHY!
COME ON, GUYS, I APPRECIATE THE AMBIENCE, BUT I NEED SOME BREATHING ROOM. PINKIE, I REMEMBER SOMETHING ABOUT A VALLEY ON THAT MAP. LET'S HEAD TOWARDS THOSE ROCKS AND MAYBE WE'LL FIND SOMEPONY.
WE CAN'T SPEND OUR DAY TRAIPSING AROUND WITH BUNNIES. LET'S GO.
OW! BAD BUNNY!
K-CHOMP!
OF COURSE THEY'RE MONSTERS. ALWAYS WITH THE MONSTERS. COME ON!
AT LEAST THEY'RE CUTE MONSTERS! I'LL CALL THIS ONE "BITEY"!
YOU CAN CALL IT WHATEVER YOU'D LIKE, AS LONG AS YOU RUN AWAY FROM IT!
BYE, BITEY!

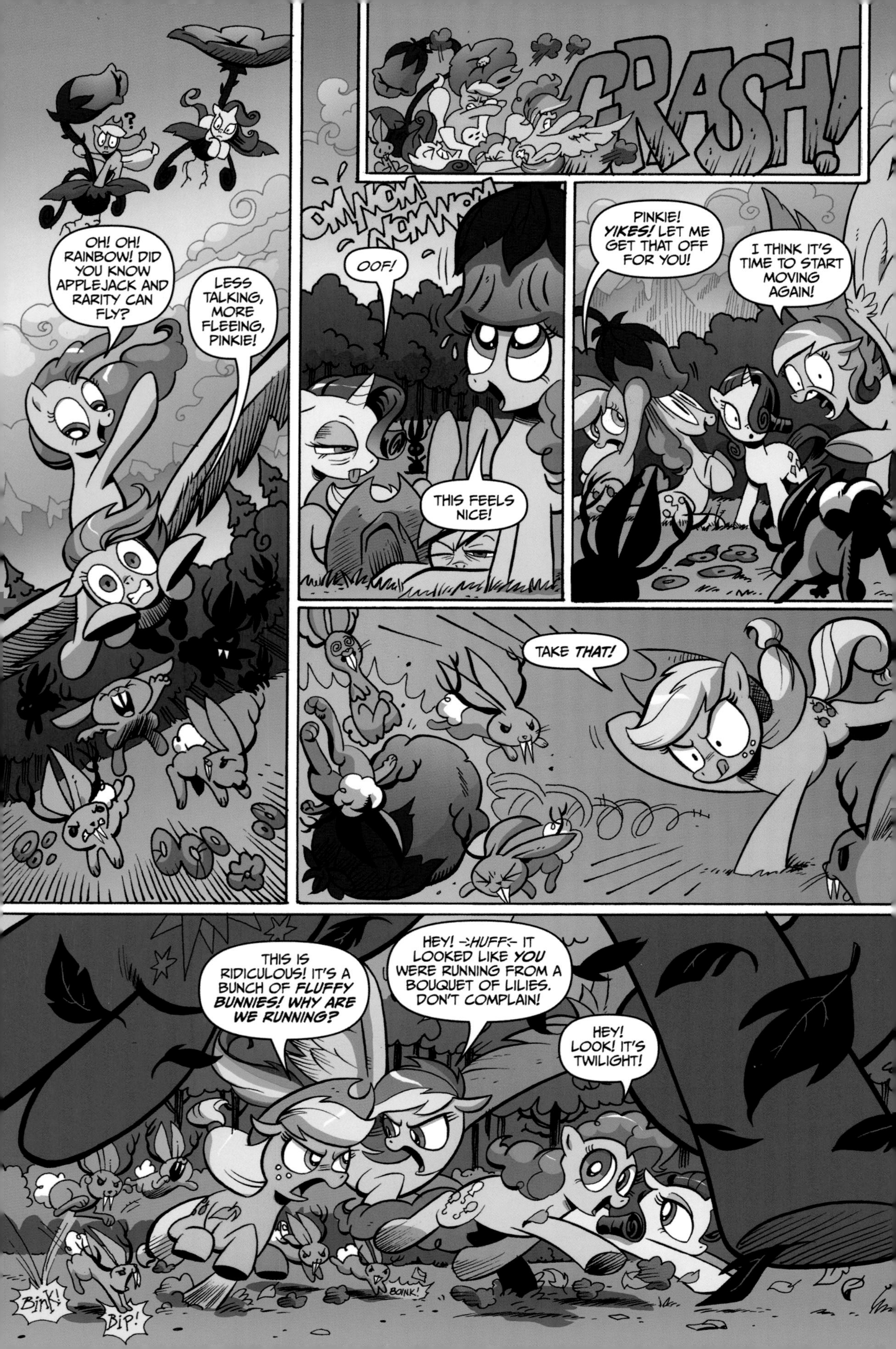

OH! OH! RAINBOW! DID YOU KNOW APPLEJACK AND RARITY CAN FLY?
LESS TALKING, MORE FLEEING, PINKIE!
CRASH!
OMNOM NOMNOMNOM
OOF!
THIS FEELS NICE!
PINKIE! *YIKES!* LET ME GET THAT OFF FOR YOU!
I THINK IT'S TIME TO START MOVING AGAIN!
TAKE *THAT!*
THIS IS RIDICULOUS! IT'S A BUNCH OF *FLUFFY BUNNIES! WHY ARE WE RUNNING?*
HEY! *HUFF* IT LOOKED LIKE *YOU* WERE RUNNING FROM A BOUQUET OF LILIES. DON'T COMPLAIN!
HEY! LOOK! IT'S TWILIGHT!
BOINK!
BINK!
BIP!

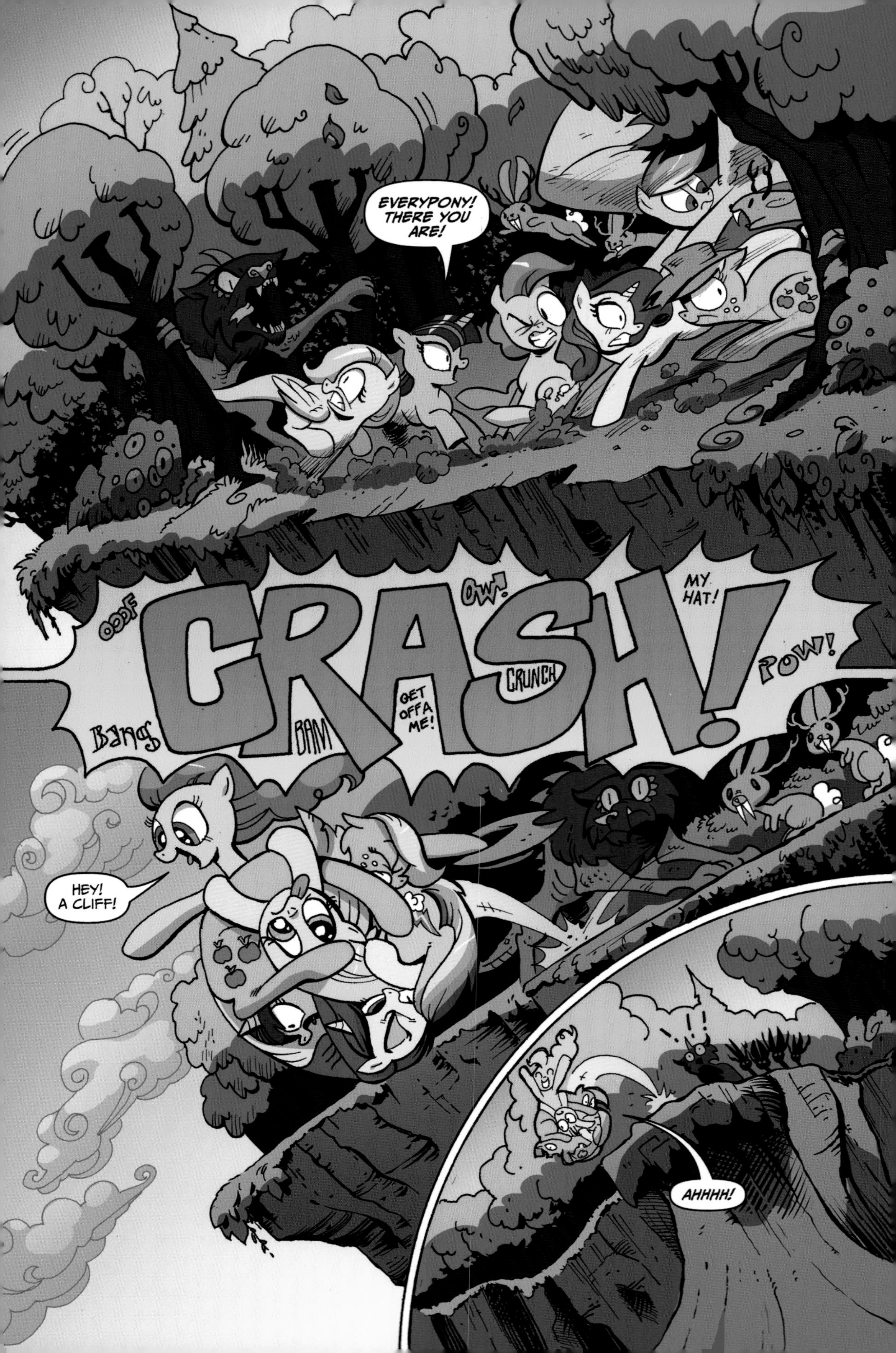
EVERYPONY! THERE YOU ARE!
OOF
OW!
MY HAT!
CRASH!
CRUNCH
POW!
Bang
BAM
GET OFFA ME!
HEY! A CLIFF!
AHHHH!

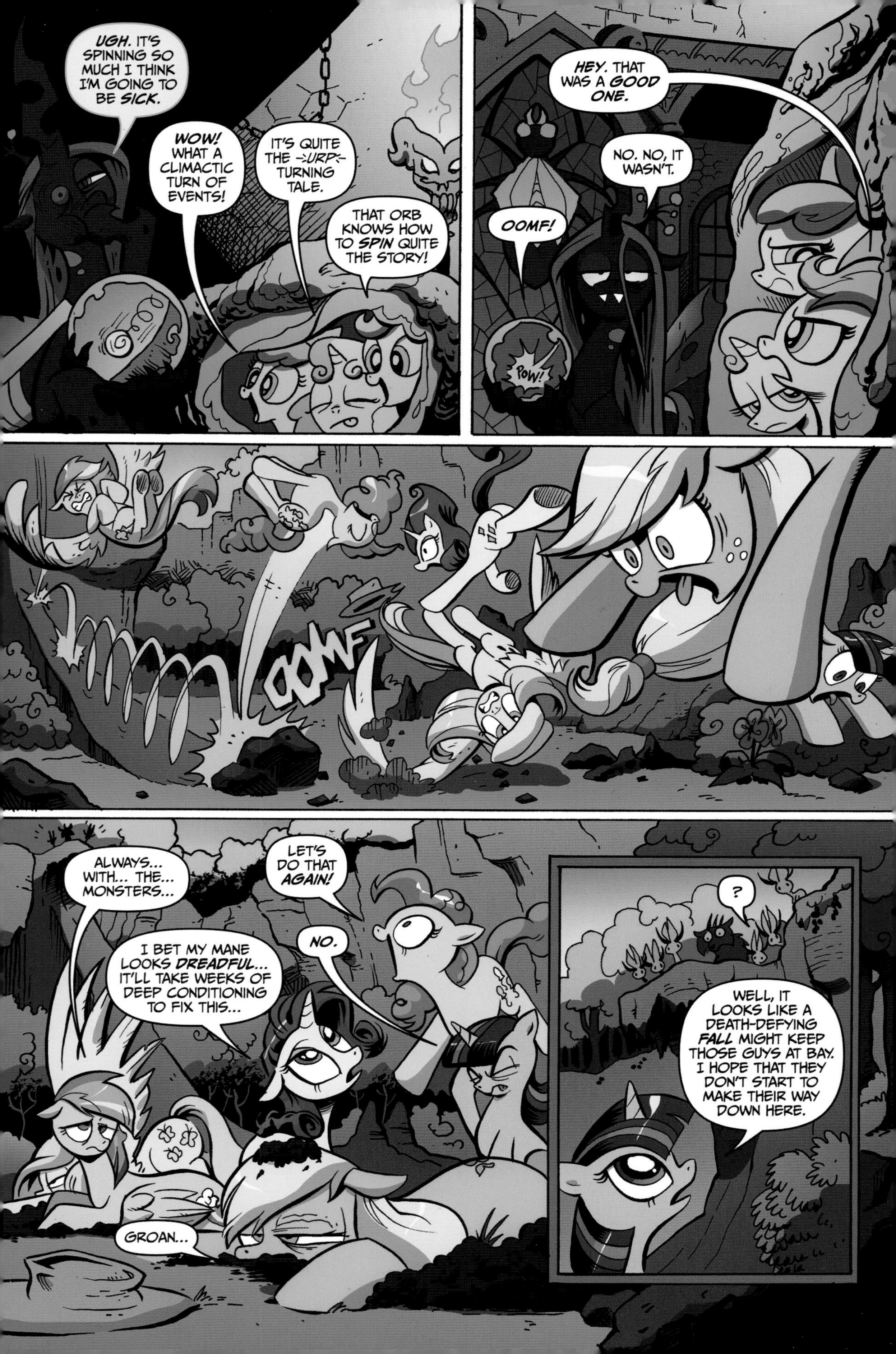
UGH. IT'S SPINNING SO MUCH I THINK I'M GOING TO BE SICK.
WOW! WHAT A CLIMACTIC TURN OF EVENTS!
IT'S QUITE THE -URP- TURNING TALE.
THAT ORB KNOWS HOW TO SPIN QUITE THE STORY!
HEY. THAT WAS A GOOD ONE.
NO. NO, IT WASN'T.
OOMF!
POW!
OOMF
ALWAYS... WITH... THE... MONSTERS...
LET'S DO THAT AGAIN!
NO.
I BET MY MANE LOOKS DREADFUL... IT'LL TAKE WEEKS OF DEEP CONDITIONING TO FIX THIS...
GROAN...
?
WELL, IT LOOKS LIKE A DEATH-DEFYING FALL MIGHT KEEP THOSE GUYS AT BAY. I HOPE THAT THEY DON'T START TO MAKE THEIR WAY DOWN HERE.

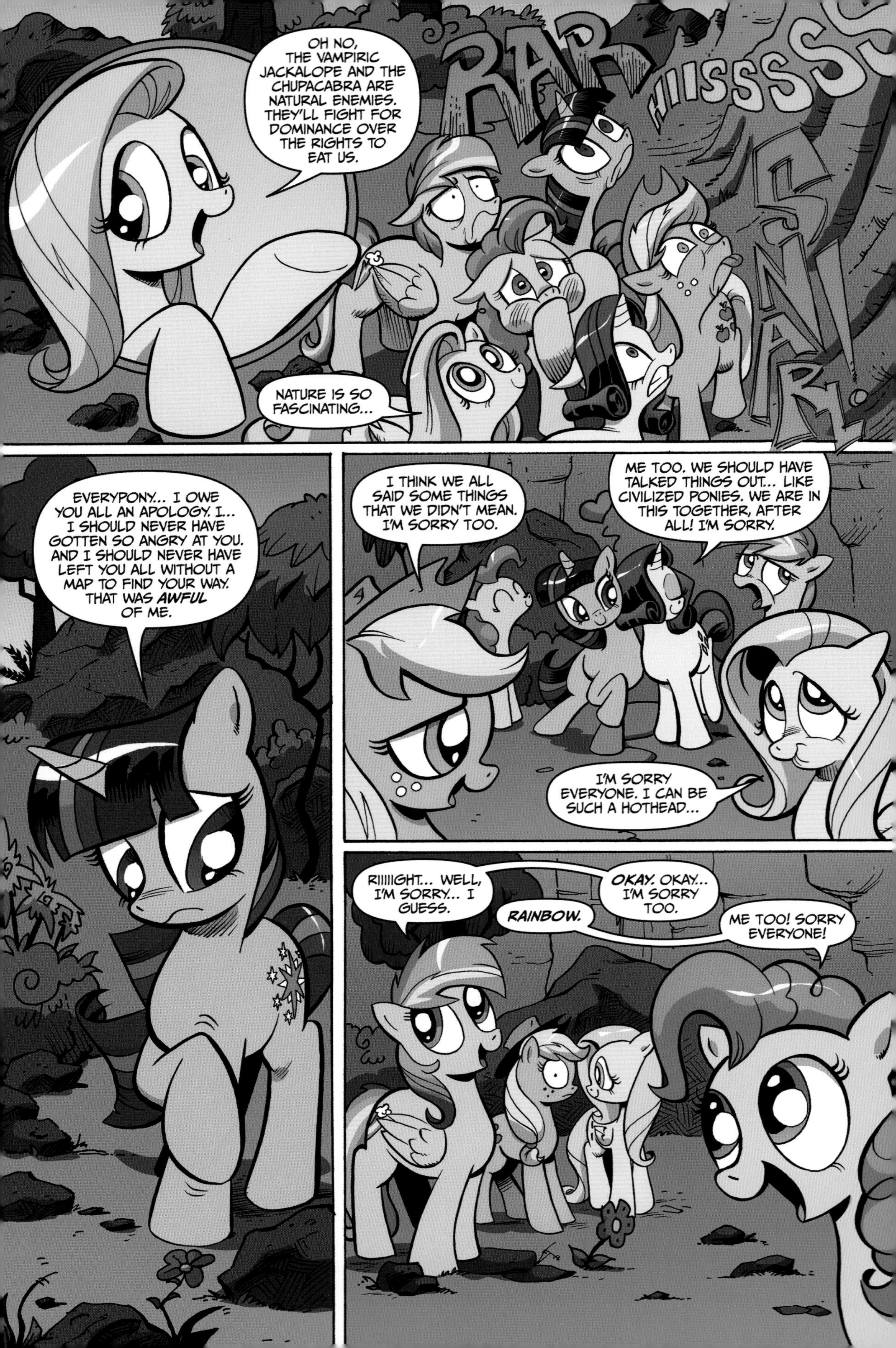
OH NO, THE VAMPIRIC JACKALOPE AND THE CHUPACABRA ARE NATURAL ENEMIES. THEY'LL FIGHT FOR DOMINANCE OVER THE RIGHTS TO EAT US.
RAR
HIISSSSS
SNARL!
NATURE IS SO FASCINATING...
EVERYPONY... I OWE YOU ALL AN APOLOGY. I... I SHOULD NEVER HAVE GOTTEN SO ANGRY AT YOU. AND I SHOULD NEVER HAVE LEFT YOU ALL WITHOUT A MAP TO FIND YOUR WAY. THAT WAS AWFUL OF ME.
I THINK WE ALL SAID SOME THINGS THAT WE DIDN'T MEAN. I'M SORRY TOO.
ME TOO. WE SHOULD HAVE TALKED THINGS OUT... LIKE CIVILIZED PONIES. WE ARE IN THIS TOGETHER, AFTER ALL! I'M SORRY.
I'M SORRY EVERYONE. I CAN BE SUCH A HOTHEAD...
RIIIIGHT... WELL, I'M SORRY... I GUESS.
RAINBOW.
OKAY. OKAY... I'M SORRY TOO.
ME TOO! SORRY EVERYONE!

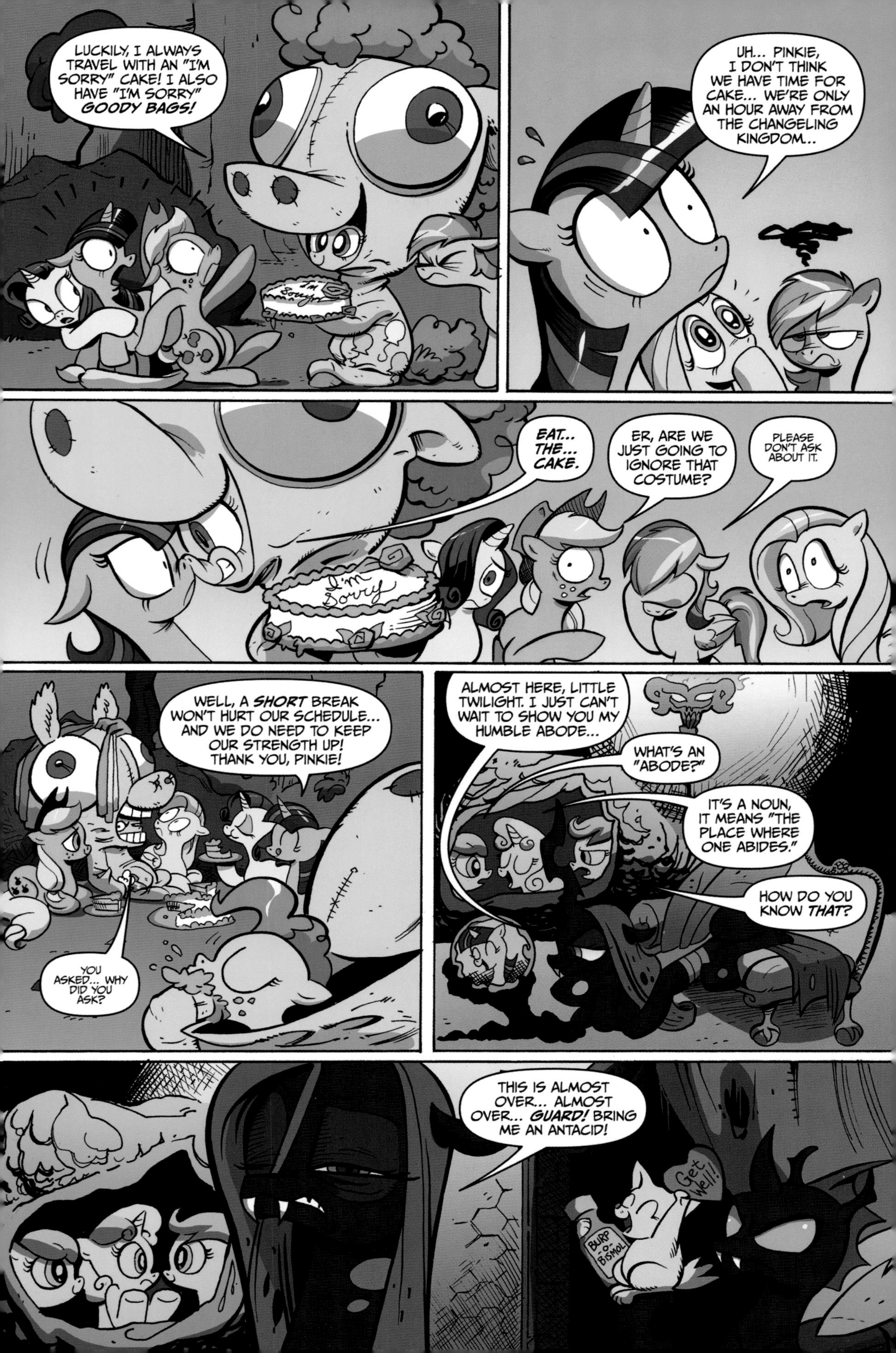
LUCKILY, I ALWAYS TRAVEL WITH AN "I'M SORRY" CAKE! I ALSO HAVE "I'M SORRY" GOODY BAGS!
I'm Sorry
UH... PINKIE, I DON'T THINK WE HAVE TIME FOR CAKE... WE'RE ONLY AN HOUR AWAY FROM THE CHANGELING KINGDOM...
EAT... THE... CAKE.
ER, ARE WE JUST GOING TO IGNORE THAT COSTUME?
PLEASE DON'T ASK ABOUT IT.
I'm Sorry
WELL, A SHORT BREAK WON'T HURT OUR SCHEDULE... AND WE DO NEED TO KEEP OUR STRENGTH UP! THANK YOU, PINKIE!
YOU ASKED... WHY DID YOU ASK?
ALMOST HERE, LITTLE TWILIGHT. I JUST CAN'T WAIT TO SHOW YOU MY HUMBLE ABODE...
WHAT'S AN "ABODE?"
IT'S A NOUN, IT MEANS "THE PLACE WHERE ONE ABIDES."
HOW DO YOU KNOW THAT?
THIS IS ALMOST OVER... ALMOST OVER... GUARD! BRING ME AN ANTACID!
Get Well!
BURP-O-BISMOL

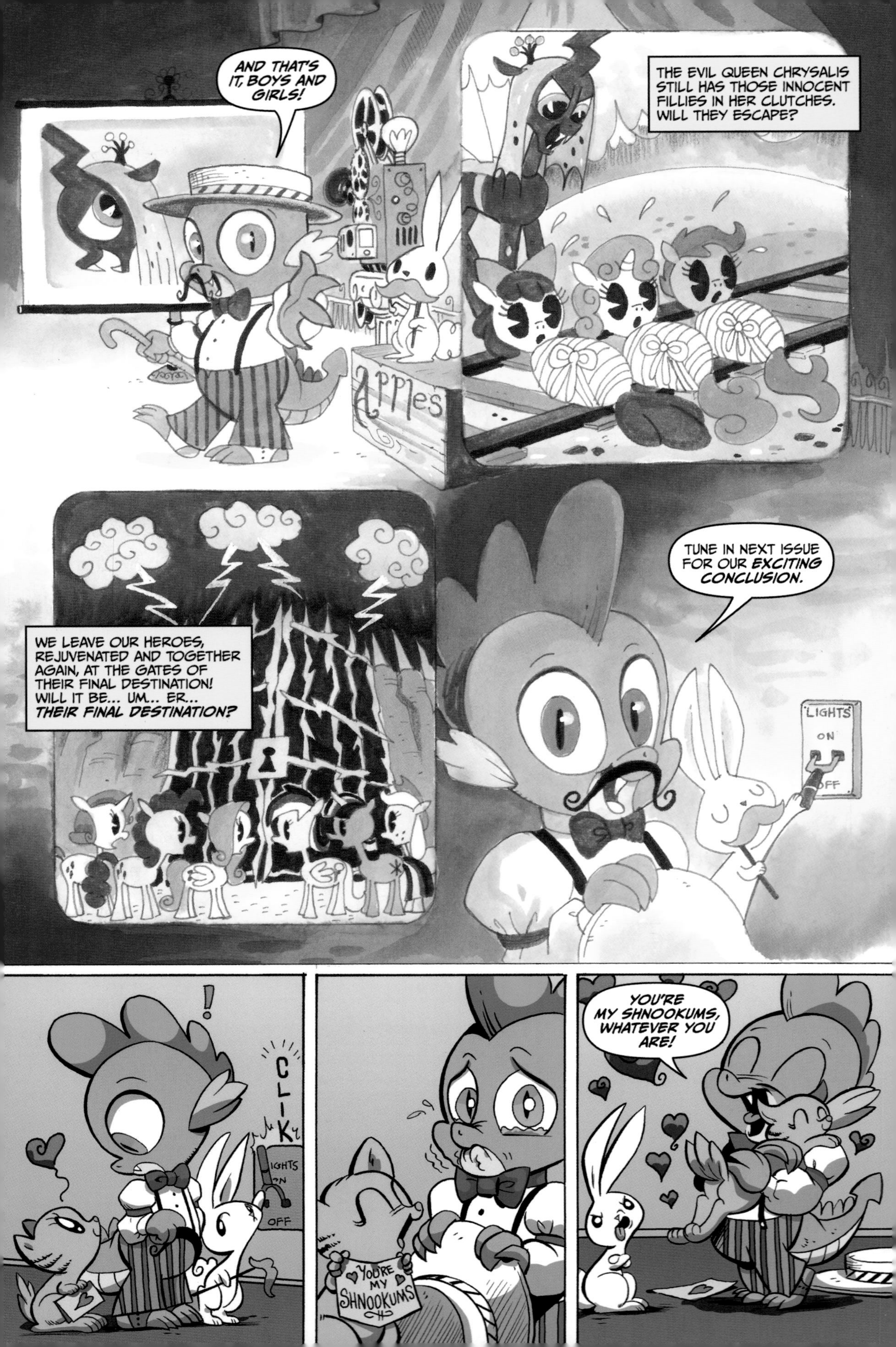
AND THAT'S IT, BOYS AND GIRLS!
THE EVIL QUEEN CHRYSALIS STILL HAS THOSE INNOCENT FILLIES IN HER CLUTCHES. WILL THEY ESCAPE?
APPLES
WE LEAVE OUR HEROES, REJUVENATED AND TOGETHER AGAIN, AT THE GATES OF THEIR FINAL DESTINATION! WILL IT BE... UM... ER... THEIR FINAL DESTINATION?
TUNE IN NEXT ISSUE FOR OUR EXCITING CONCLUSION.
LIGHTS
ON
OFF
!
CLIK
YOU'RE MY SHNOOKUMS
YOU'RE MY SHNOOKUMS, WHATEVER YOU ARE!

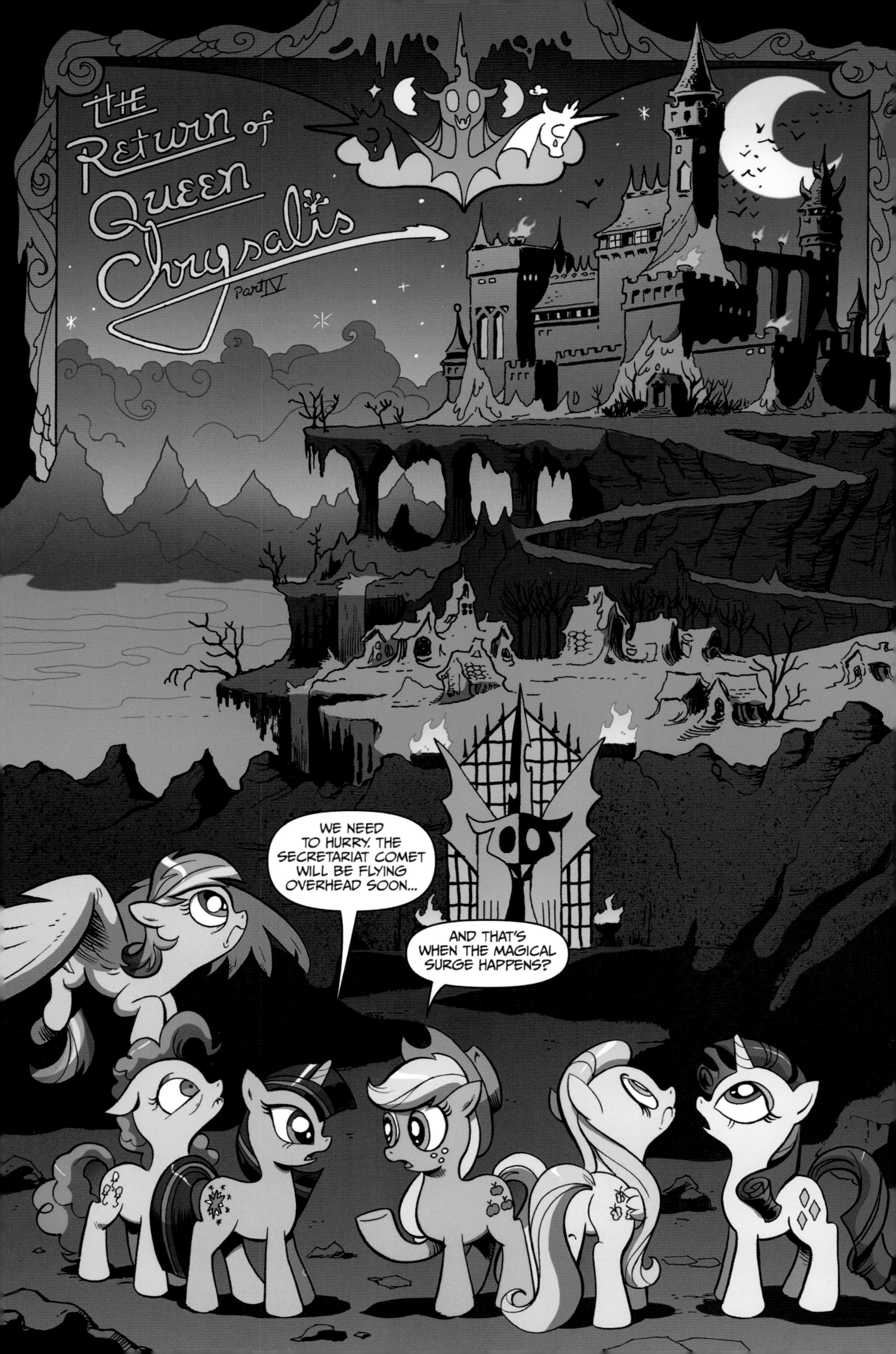
The Return of Queen Chrysalis
Part IV
WE NEED TO HURRY. THE SECRETARIAT COMET WILL BE FLYING OVERHEAD SOON...
AND THAT'S WHEN THE MAGICAL SURGE HAPPENS?

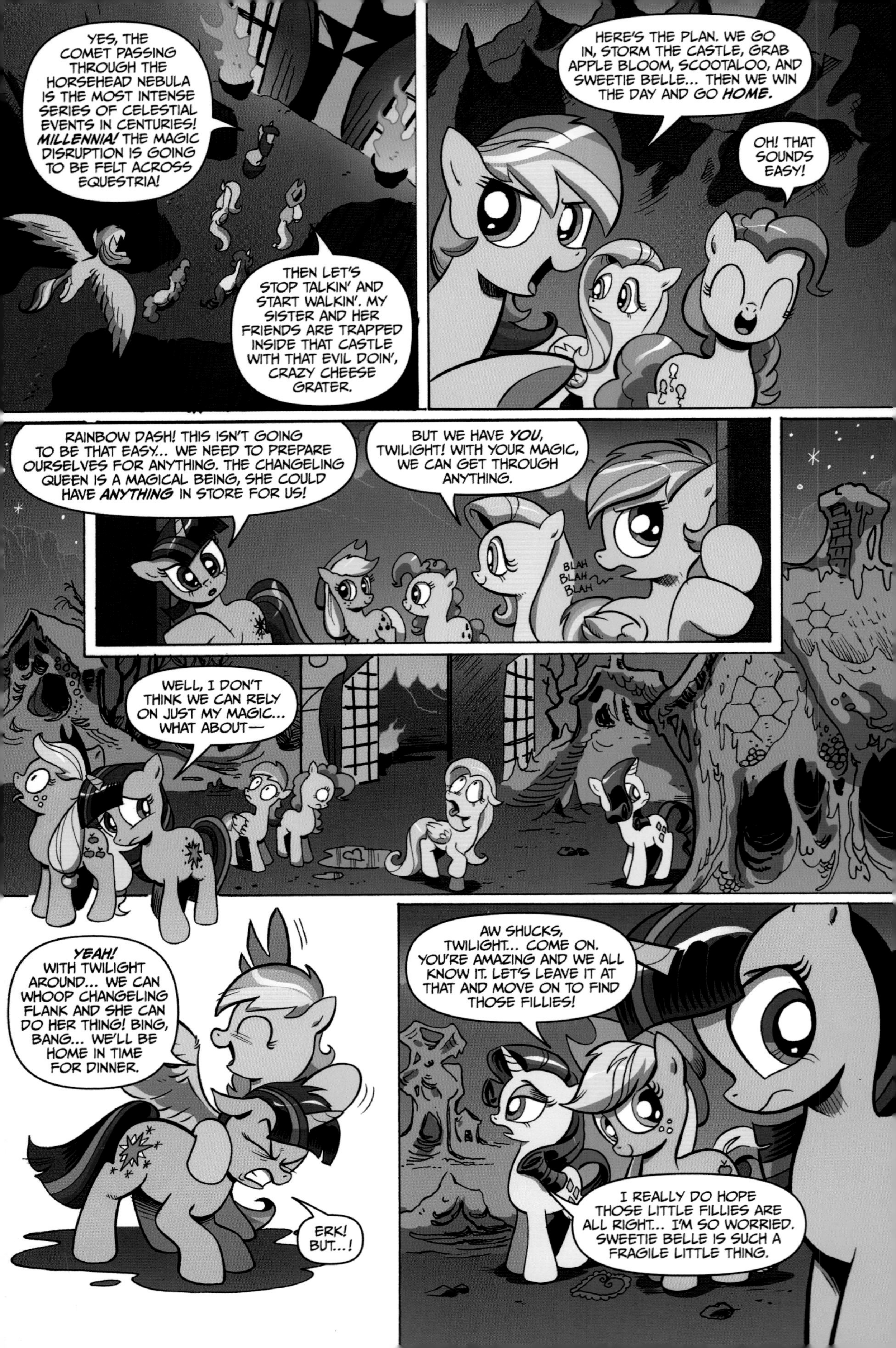
YES, THE COMET PASSING THROUGH THE HORSEHEAD NEBULA IS THE MOST INTENSE SERIES OF CELESTIAL EVENTS IN CENTURIES! MILLENNIA! THE MAGIC DISRUPTION IS GOING TO BE FELT ACROSS EQUESTRIA!
THEN LET'S STOP TALKIN' AND START WALKIN'. MY SISTER AND HER FRIENDS ARE TRAPPED INSIDE THAT CASTLE WITH THAT EVIL DOIN', CRAZY CHEESE GRATER.
HERE'S THE PLAN. WE GO IN, STORM THE CASTLE, GRAB APPLE BLOOM, SCOOTALOO, AND SWEETIE BELLE... THEN WE WIN THE DAY AND GO HOME.
OH! THAT SOUNDS EASY!
RAINBOW DASH! THIS ISN'T GOING TO BE THAT EASY... WE NEED TO PREPARE OURSELVES FOR ANYTHING. THE CHANGELING QUEEN IS A MAGICAL BEING, SHE COULD HAVE ANYTHING IN STORE FOR US!
BUT WE HAVE YOU, TWILIGHT! WITH YOUR MAGIC, WE CAN GET THROUGH ANYTHING.
BLAH BLAH BLAH
WELL, I DON'T THINK WE CAN RELY ON JUST MY MAGIC... WHAT ABOUT—
YEAH! WITH TWILIGHT AROUND... WE CAN WHOOP CHANGELING FLANK AND SHE CAN DO HER THING! BING, BANG... WE'LL BE HOME IN TIME FOR DINNER.
ERK! BUT...!
AW SHUCKS, TWILIGHT... COME ON. YOU'RE AMAZING AND WE ALL KNOW IT. LET'S LEAVE IT AT THAT AND MOVE ON TO FIND THOSE FILLIES!
I REALLY DO HOPE THOSE LITTLE FILLIES ARE ALL RIGHT... I'M SO WORRIED. SWEETIE BELLE IS SUCH A FRAGILE LITTLE THING.

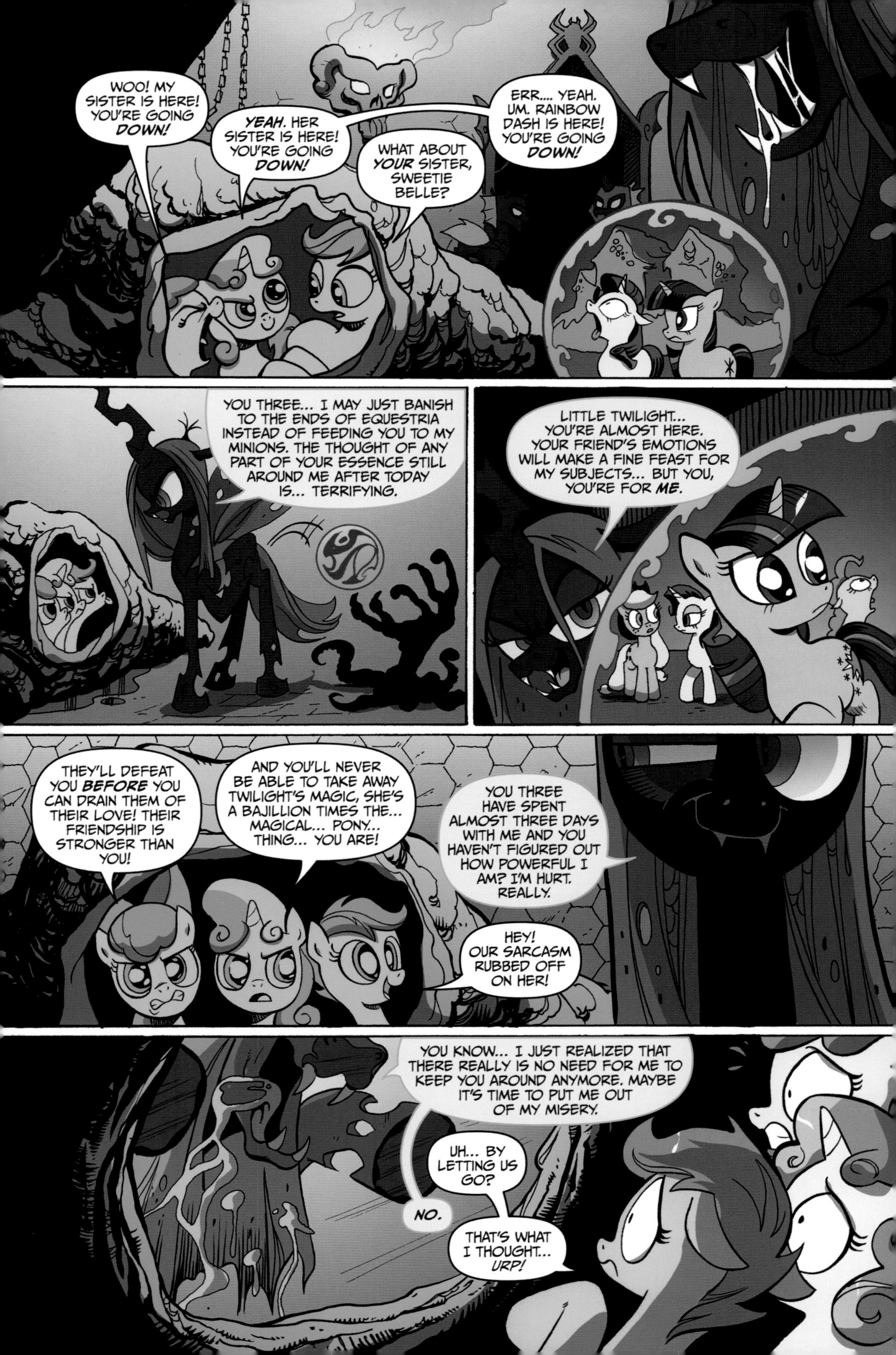
WOO! MY SISTER IS HERE! YOU'RE GOING *DOWN!*
YEAH. HER SISTER IS HERE! YOU'RE GOING *DOWN!*
WHAT ABOUT *YOUR* SISTER, SWEETIE BELLE?
ERR.... YEAH. UM. RAINBOW DASH IS HERE! YOU'RE GOING *DOWN!*
YOU THREE... I MAY JUST BANISH TO THE ENDS OF EQUESTRIA INSTEAD OF FEEDING YOU TO MY MINIONS. THE THOUGHT OF ANY PART OF YOUR ESSENCE STILL AROUND ME AFTER TODAY IS... TERRIFYING.
LITTLE TWILIGHT... YOU'RE ALMOST HERE. YOUR FRIEND'S EMOTIONS WILL MAKE A FINE FEAST FOR MY SUBJECTS... BUT YOU, YOU'RE FOR *ME*.
THEY'LL DEFEAT YOU *BEFORE* YOU CAN DRAIN THEM OF THEIR LOVE! THEIR FRIENDSHIP IS STRONGER THAN YOU!
AND YOU'LL NEVER BE ABLE TO TAKE AWAY TWILIGHT'S MAGIC, SHE'S A BAJILLION TIMES THE... MAGICAL... PONY... THING... YOU ARE!
YOU THREE HAVE SPENT ALMOST THREE DAYS WITH ME AND YOU HAVEN'T FIGURED OUT HOW POWERFUL I AM? I'M HURT. REALLY.
HEY! OUR SARCASM RUBBED OFF ON HER!
YOU KNOW... I JUST REALIZED THAT THERE REALLY IS NO NEED FOR ME TO KEEP YOU AROUND ANYMORE. MAYBE IT'S TIME TO PUT ME OUT OF MY MISERY.
UH... BY LETTING US GO?
NO.
THAT'S WHAT I THOUGHT... *URP!*

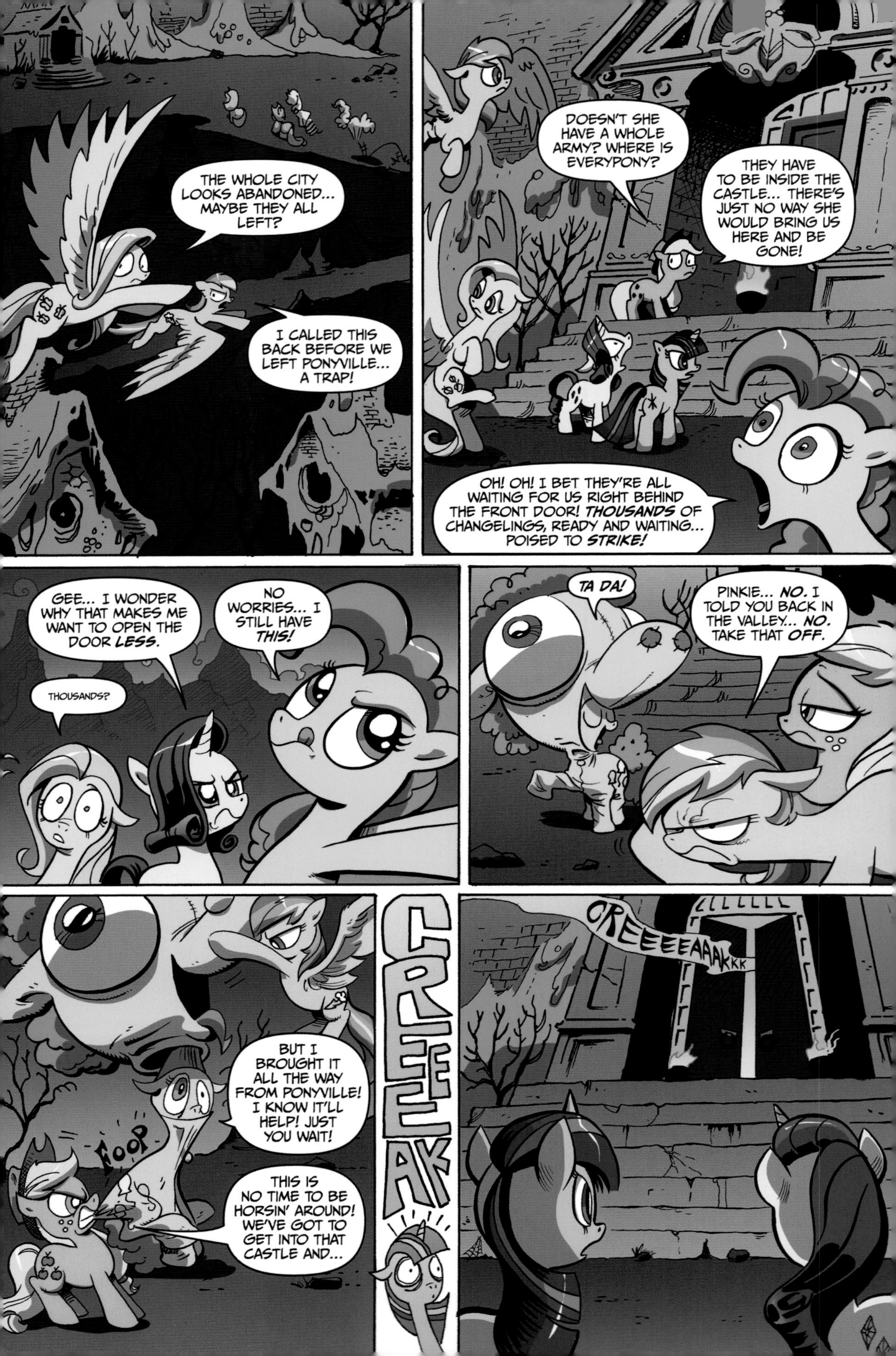
THE WHOLE CITY LOOKS ABANDONED... MAYBE THEY ALL LEFT?
I CALLED THIS BACK BEFORE WE LEFT PONYVILLE... A TRAP!
DOESN'T SHE HAVE A WHOLE ARMY? WHERE IS EVERYPONY?
THEY HAVE TO BE INSIDE THE CASTLE... THERE'S JUST NO WAY SHE WOULD BRING US HERE AND BE GONE!
OH! OH! I BET THEY'RE ALL WAITING FOR US RIGHT BEHIND THE FRONT DOOR! THOUSANDS OF CHANGELINGS, READY AND WAITING... POISED TO STRIKE!
GEE... I WONDER WHY THAT MAKES ME WANT TO OPEN THE DOOR LESS.
NO WORRIES... I STILL HAVE THIS!
THOUSANDS?
TA DA!
PINKIE... NO. I TOLD YOU BACK IN THE VALLEY... NO. TAKE THAT OFF.
BUT I BROUGHT IT ALL THE WAY FROM PONYVILLE! I KNOW IT'LL HELP! JUST YOU WAIT!
FOOP
THIS IS NO TIME TO BE HORSIN' AROUND! WE'VE GOT TO GET INTO THAT CASTLE AND...
CREEEAK
CREEEEEAAAKKK

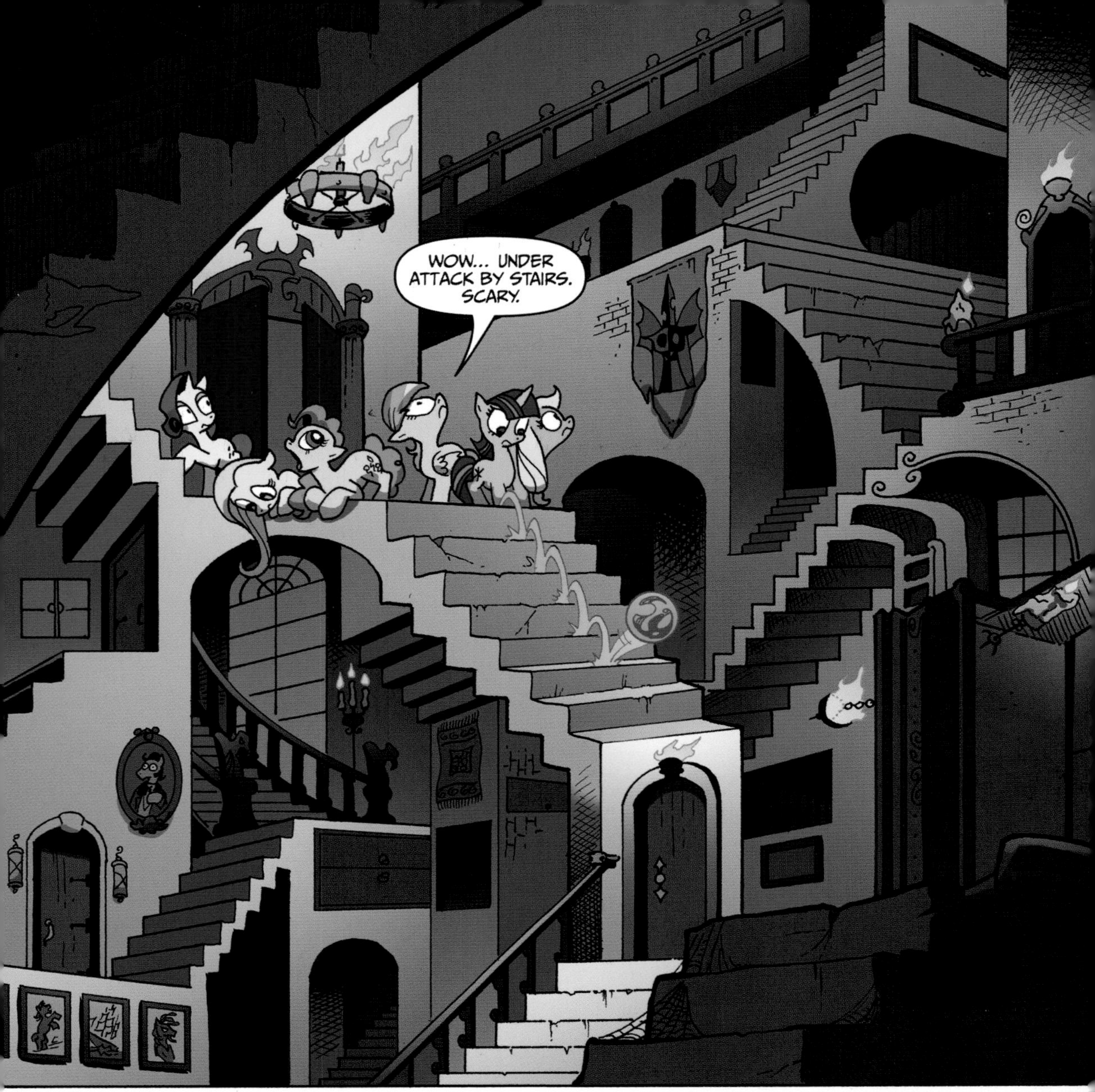
WOW... UNDER ATTACK BY STAIRS. SCARY.

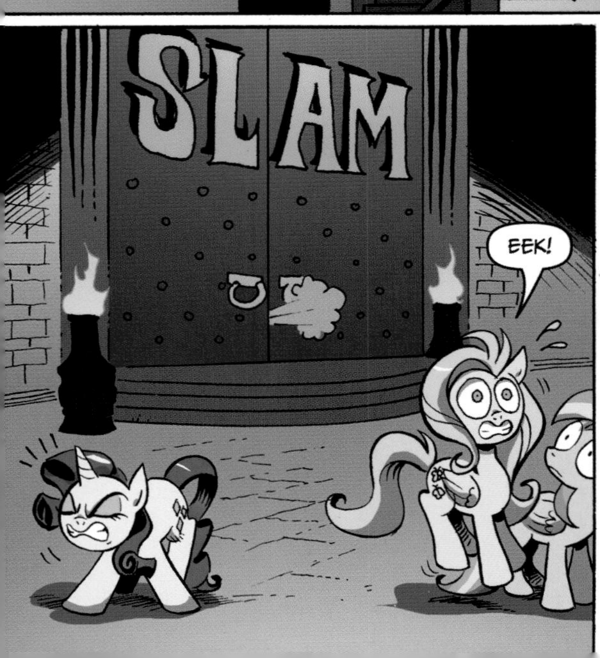
SLAM
EEK!

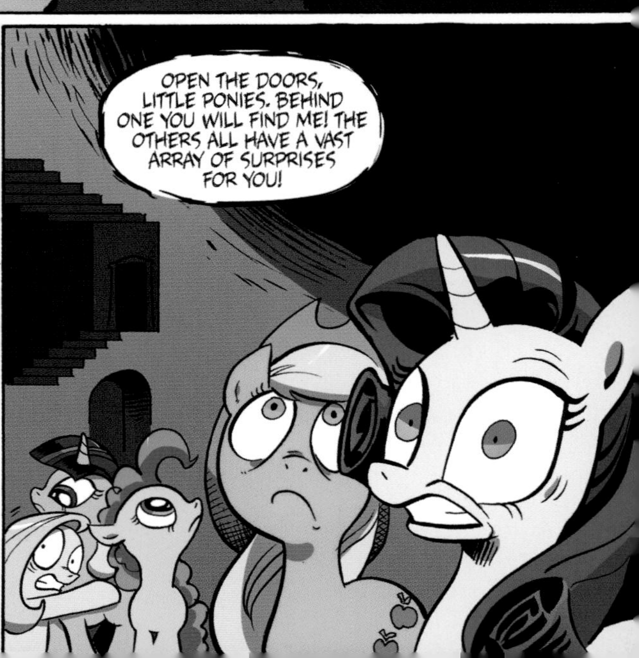
OPEN THE DOORS, LITTLE PONIES. BEHIND ONE YOU WILL FIND ME! THE OTHERS ALL HAVE A VAST ARRAY OF SURPRISES FOR YOU!

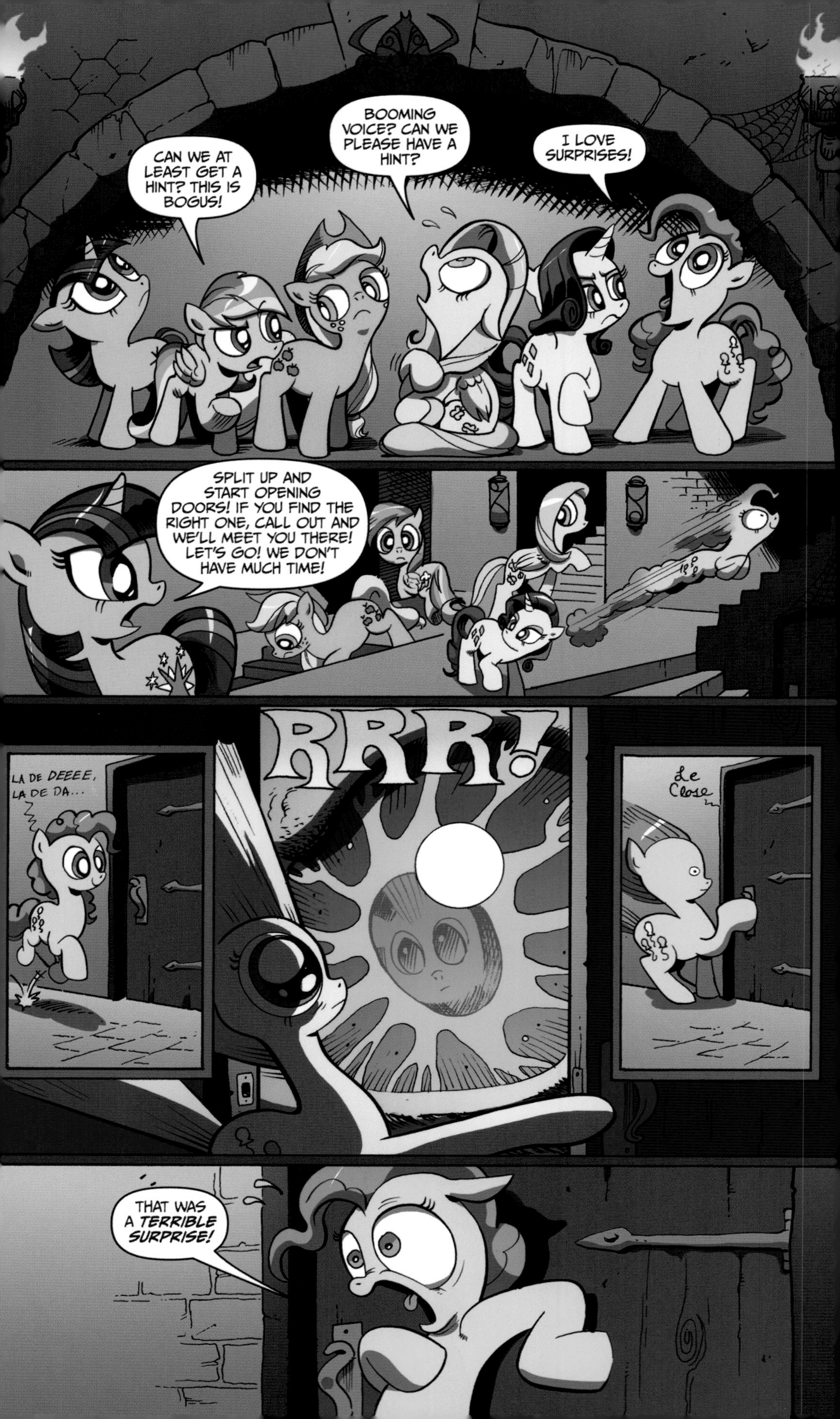
CAN WE AT LEAST GET A HINT? THIS IS BOGUS!
BOOMING VOICE? CAN WE PLEASE HAVE A HINT?
I LOVE SURPRISES!
SPLIT UP AND START OPENING DOORS! IF YOU FIND THE RIGHT ONE, CALL OUT AND WE'LL MEET YOU THERE! LET'S GO! WE DON'T HAVE MUCH TIME!
LA DE DEEEE, LA DE DA...
RRR!
Le Close
THAT WAS A *TERRIBLE SURPRISE!*

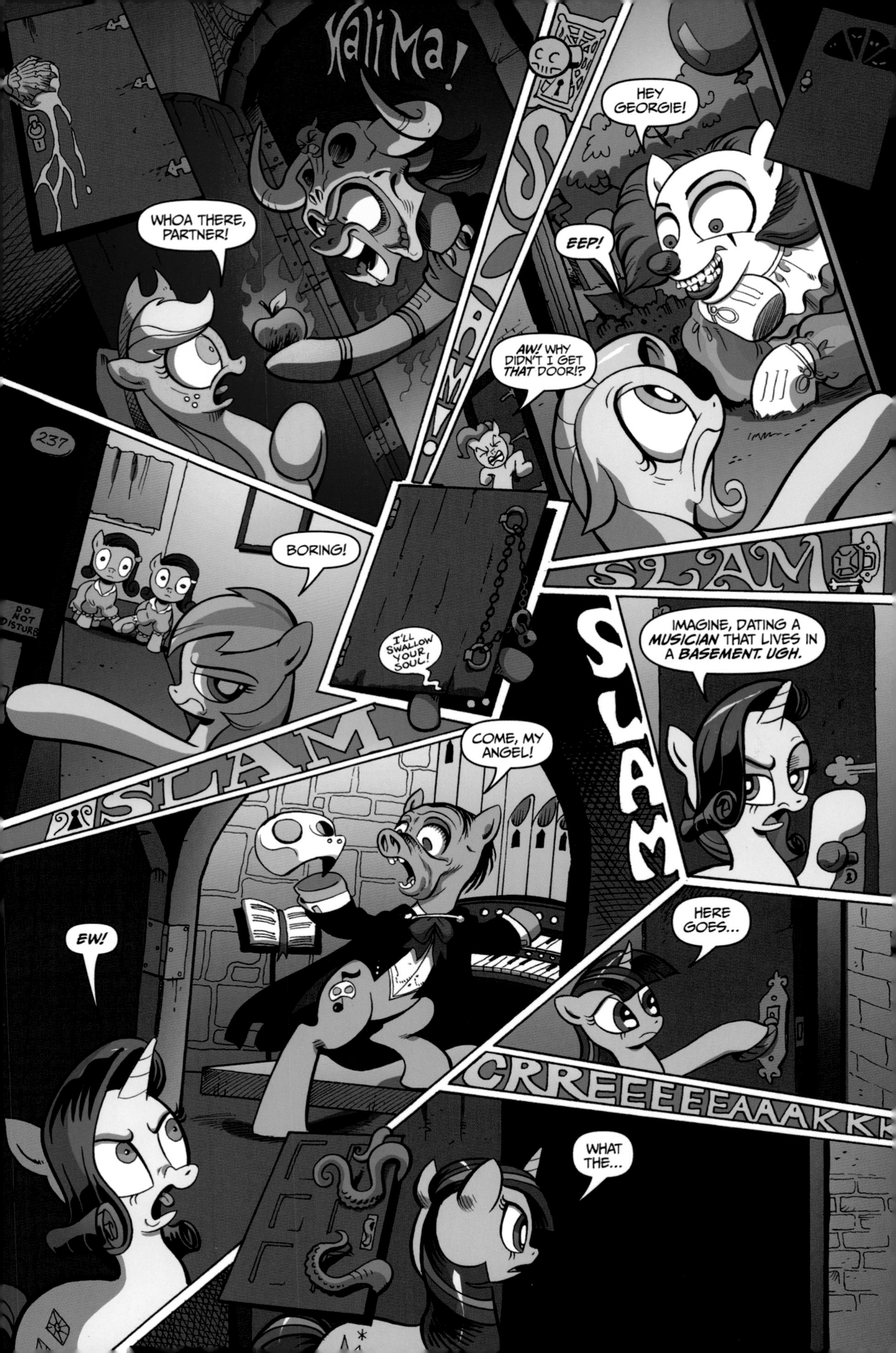
KALI MA!
WHOA THERE, PARTNER!
HEY GEORGIE!
EEP!
AW! WHY DIDN'T I GET THAT DOOR!?
SLAM
237
BORING!
DO NOT DISTURB
I'LL SWALLOW YOUR SOUL!
SLAM
SLAM
IMAGINE, DATING A MUSICIAN THAT LIVES IN A BASEMENT. UGH.
SLAM
COME, MY ANGEL!
EW!
HERE GOES...
CRREEEEEEAAAKKK
WHAT THE...

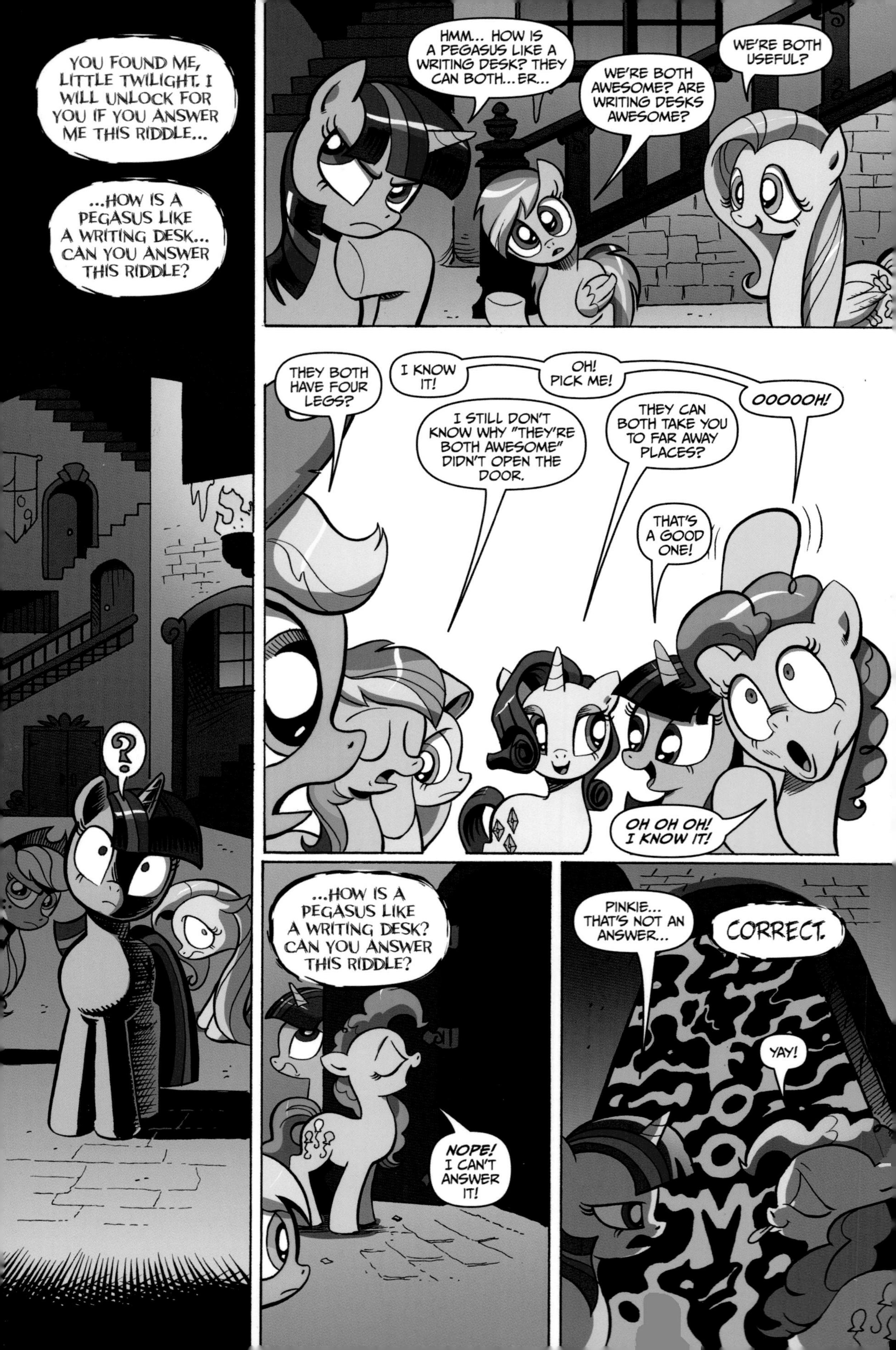
YOU FOUND ME, LITTLE TWILIGHT. I WILL UNLOCK FOR YOU IF YOU ANSWER ME THIS RIDDLE...
...HOW IS A PEGASUS LIKE A WRITING DESK... CAN YOU ANSWER THIS RIDDLE?
HMM... HOW IS A PEGASUS LIKE A WRITING DESK? THEY CAN BOTH... ER...
WE'RE BOTH AWESOME? ARE WRITING DESKS AWESOME?
WE'RE BOTH USEFUL?
THEY BOTH HAVE FOUR LEGS?
I KNOW IT!
OH! PICK ME!
OOOOOH!
I STILL DON'T KNOW WHY "THEY'RE BOTH AWESOME" DIDN'T OPEN THE DOOR.
THEY CAN BOTH TAKE YOU TO FAR AWAY PLACES?
THAT'S A GOOD ONE!
OH OH OH! I KNOW IT!
...HOW IS A PEGASUS LIKE A WRITING DESK? CAN YOU ANSWER THIS RIDDLE?
NOPE! I CAN'T ANSWER IT!
PINKIE... THAT'S NOT AN ANSWER...
CORRECT.
YAY!

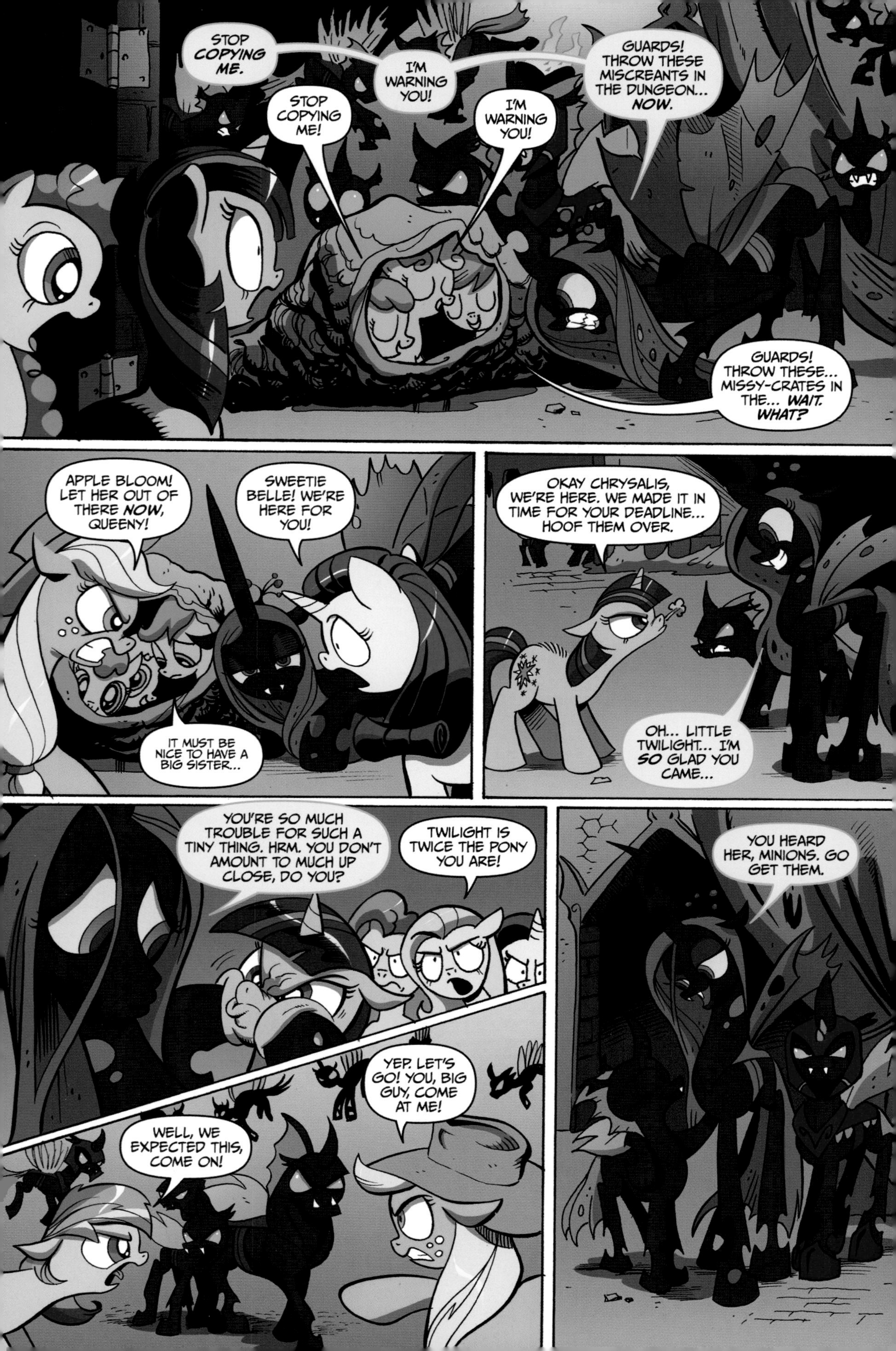
STOP *COPYING* *ME.*
STOP COPYING ME!
I'M WARNING YOU!
I'M WARNING YOU!
GUARDS! THROW THESE MISCREANTS IN THE DUNGEON... *NOW.*
GUARDS! THROW THESE... MISSY-CRATES IN THE... *WAIT. WHAT?*
APPLE BLOOM! LET HER OUT OF THERE *NOW*, QUEENY!
SWEETIE BELLE! WE'RE HERE FOR YOU!
IT MUST BE NICE TO HAVE A BIG SISTER...
OKAY CHRYSALIS, WE'RE HERE. WE MADE IT IN TIME FOR YOUR DEADLINE... HOOF THEM OVER.
OH... LITTLE TWILIGHT... I'M *SO* GLAD YOU CAME...
YOU'RE SO MUCH TROUBLE FOR SUCH A TINY THING. HRM. YOU DON'T AMOUNT TO MUCH UP CLOSE, DO YOU?
TWILIGHT IS TWICE THE PONY YOU ARE!
YOU HEARD HER, MINIONS. GO GET THEM.
YEP. LET'S GO! YOU, BIG GUY, COME AT ME!
WELL, WE EXPECTED THIS, COME ON!

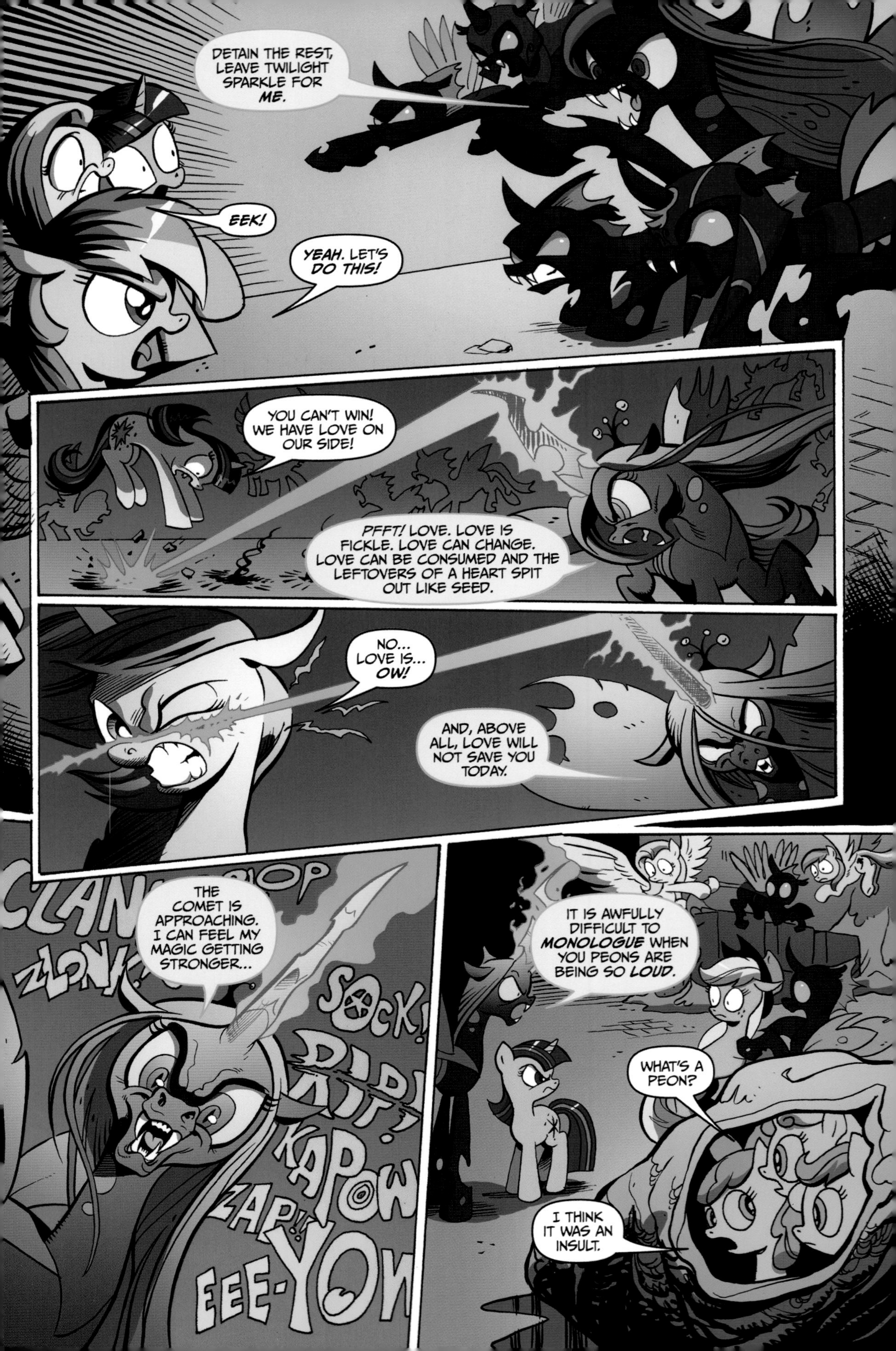
DETAIN THE REST, LEAVE TWILIGHT SPARKLE FOR *ME*.
EEK!
YEAH. LET'S *DO THIS!*
YOU CAN'T WIN! WE HAVE LOVE ON OUR SIDE!
PFFT! LOVE. LOVE IS FICKLE. LOVE CAN CHANGE. LOVE CAN BE CONSUMED AND THE LEFTOVERS OF A HEART SPIT OUT LIKE SEED.
NO... LOVE IS... *OW!*
AND, ABOVE ALL, LOVE WILL NOT SAVE YOU TODAY.
THE COMET IS APPROACHING. I CAN FEEL MY MAGIC GETTING STRONGER...
SOCK!
KAPOW
ZAP!!
EEE-YOW
IT IS AWFULLY DIFFICULT TO *MONOLOGUE* WHEN YOU PEONS ARE BEING SO *LOUD*.
WHAT'S A PEON?
I THINK IT WAS AN INSULT.

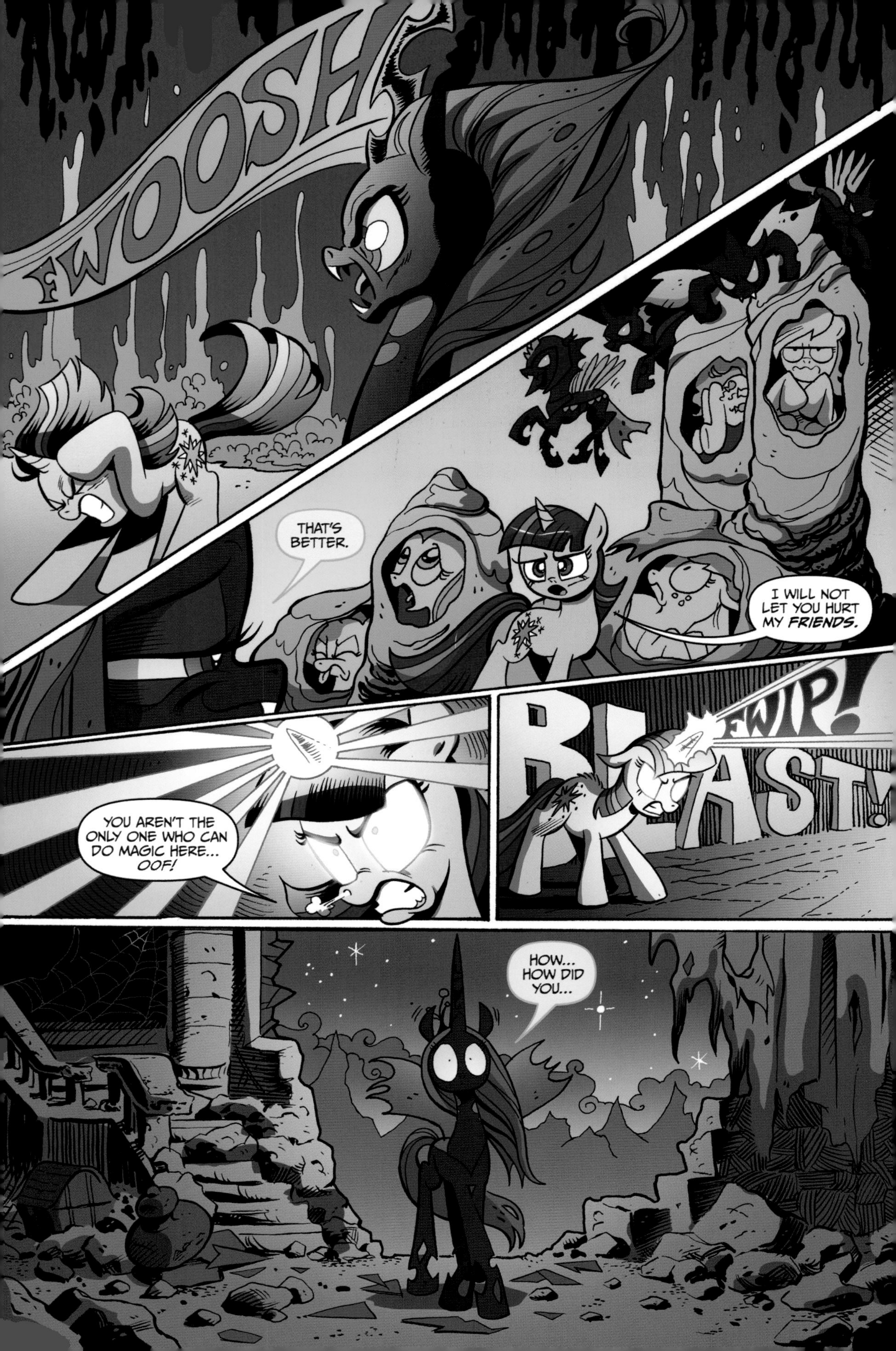
FWOOSH!
THAT'S BETTER.
I WILL NOT LET YOU HURT MY FRIENDS.
YOU AREN'T THE ONLY ONE WHO CAN DO MAGIC HERE... OOF!
FWIP!
BLAST!
HOW... HOW DID YOU...

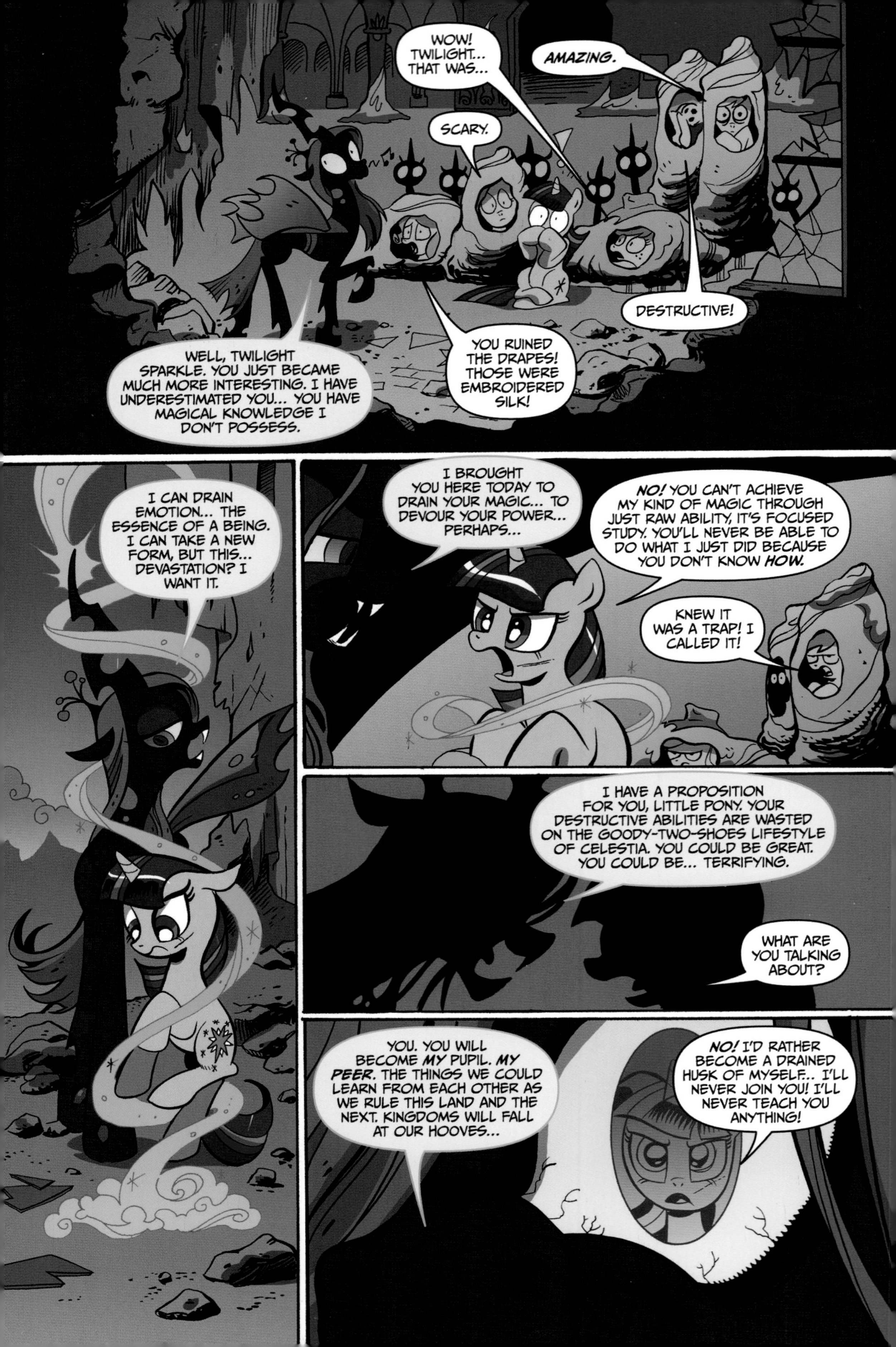

WOW! TWILIGHT... THAT WAS...
AMAZING.
SCARY.
DESTRUCTIVE!
YOU RUINED THE DRAPES! THOSE WERE EMBROIDERED SILK!
WELL, TWILIGHT SPARKLE. YOU JUST BECAME MUCH MORE INTERESTING. I HAVE UNDERESTIMATED YOU... YOU HAVE MAGICAL KNOWLEDGE I DON'T POSSESS.
I CAN DRAIN EMOTION... THE ESSENCE OF A BEING. I CAN TAKE A NEW FORM, BUT THIS... DEVASTATION? I WANT IT.
I BROUGHT YOU HERE TODAY TO DRAIN YOUR MAGIC... TO DEVOUR YOUR POWER... PERHAPS...
NO! YOU CAN'T ACHIEVE MY KIND OF MAGIC THROUGH JUST RAW ABILITY, IT'S FOCUSED STUDY. YOU'LL NEVER BE ABLE TO DO WHAT I JUST DID BECAUSE YOU DON'T KNOW HOW.
KNEW IT WAS A TRAP! I CALLED IT!
I HAVE A PROPOSITION FOR YOU, LITTLE PONY. YOUR DESTRUCTIVE ABILITIES ARE WASTED ON THE GOODY-TWO-SHOES LIFESTYLE OF CELESTIA. YOU COULD BE GREAT. YOU COULD BE... TERRIFYING.
WHAT ARE YOU TALKING ABOUT?
YOU. YOU WILL BECOME MY PUPIL. MY PEER. THE THINGS WE COULD LEARN FROM EACH OTHER AS WE RULE THIS LAND AND THE NEXT. KINGDOMS WILL FALL AT OUR HOOVES...
NO! I'D RATHER BECOME A DRAINED HUSK OF MYSELF... I'LL NEVER JOIN YOU! I'LL NEVER TEACH YOU ANYTHING!

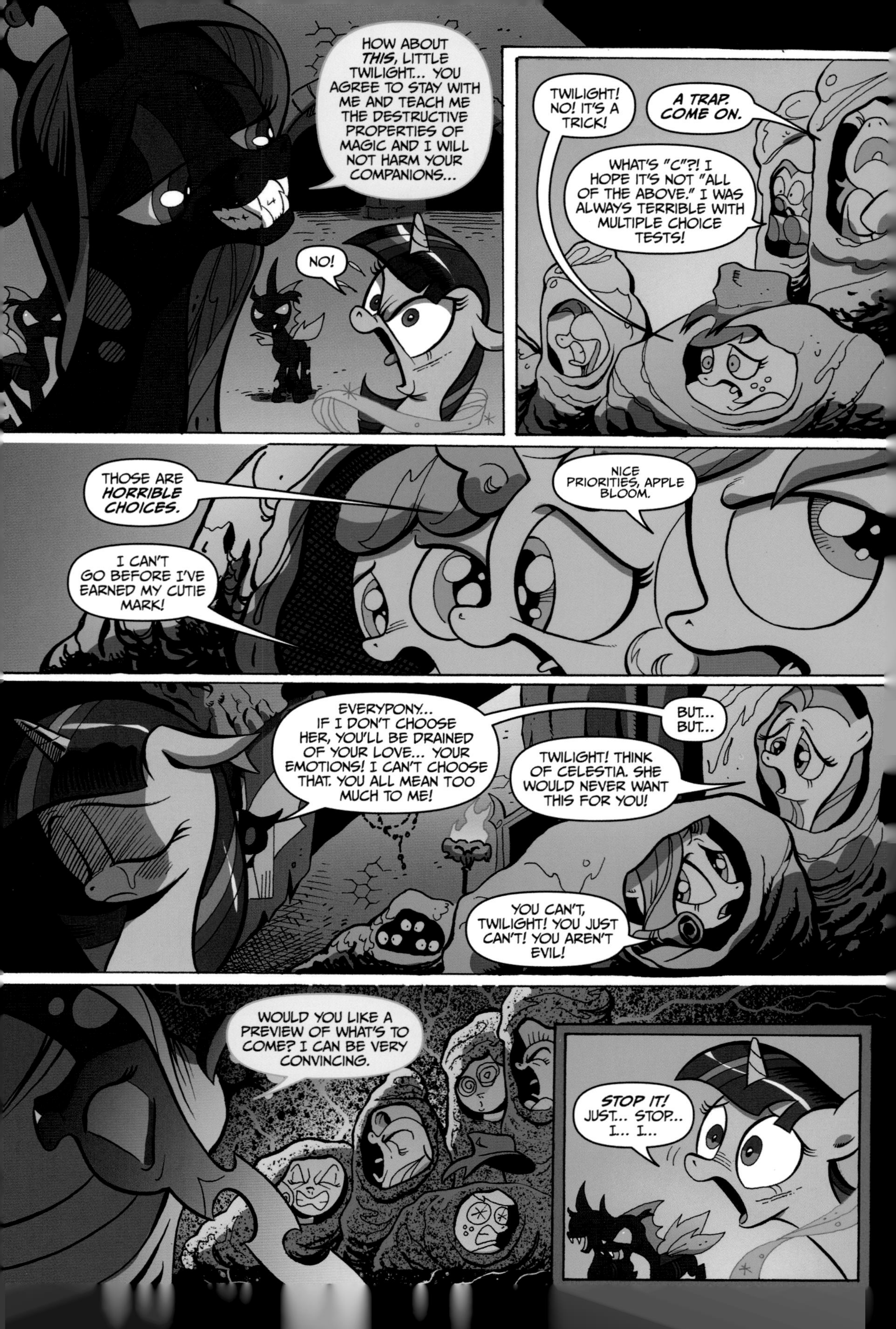
HOW ABOUT THIS, LITTLE TWILIGHT... YOU AGREE TO STAY WITH ME AND TEACH ME THE DESTRUCTIVE PROPERTIES OF MAGIC AND I WILL NOT HARM YOUR COMPANIONS...
NO!
TWILIGHT! NO! IT'S A TRICK!
A TRAP. COME ON.
WHAT'S "C"?! I HOPE IT'S NOT "ALL OF THE ABOVE." I WAS ALWAYS TERRIBLE WITH MULTIPLE CHOICE TESTS!
THOSE ARE HORRIBLE CHOICES.
NICE PRIORITIES, APPLE BLOOM.
I CAN'T GO BEFORE I'VE EARNED MY CUTIE MARK!
EVERYPONY... IF I DON'T CHOOSE HER, YOU'LL BE DRAINED OF YOUR LOVE... YOUR EMOTIONS! I CAN'T CHOOSE THAT. YOU ALL MEAN TOO MUCH TO ME!
BUT... BUT...
TWILIGHT! THINK OF CELESTIA. SHE WOULD NEVER WANT THIS FOR YOU!
YOU CAN'T, TWILIGHT! YOU JUST CAN'T! YOU AREN'T EVIL!
WOULD YOU LIKE A PREVIEW OF WHAT'S TO COME? I CAN BE VERY CONVINCING.
STOP IT! JUST... STOP... I... I...

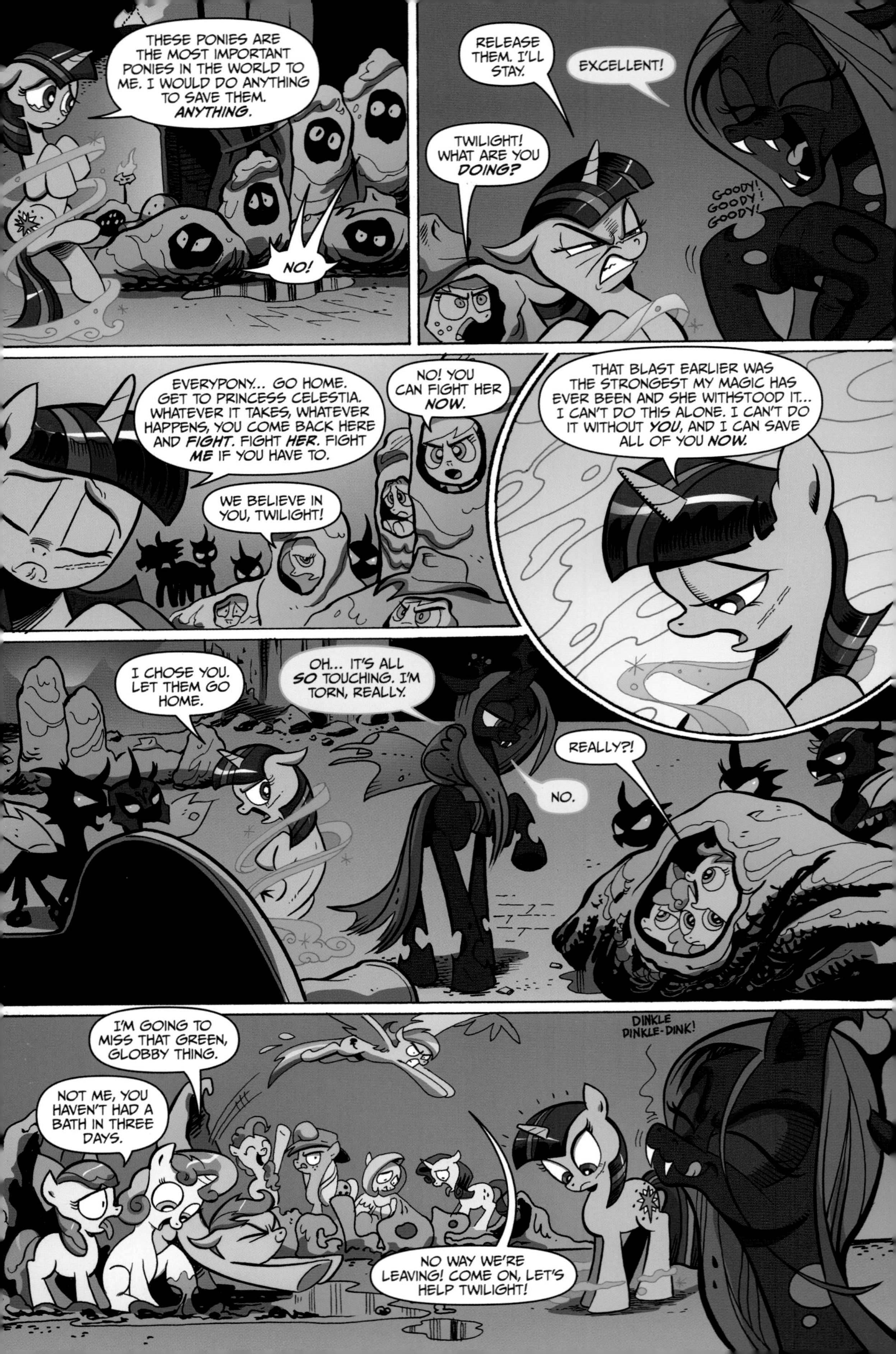
THESE PONIES ARE THE MOST IMPORTANT PONIES IN THE WORLD TO ME. I WOULD DO ANYTHING TO SAVE THEM. ANYTHING.
NO!
RELEASE THEM. I'LL STAY.
EXCELLENT!
TWILIGHT! WHAT ARE YOU DOING?
GOODY! GOODY! GOODY!
EVERYPONY... GO HOME. GET TO PRINCESS CELESTIA. WHATEVER IT TAKES, WHATEVER HAPPENS, YOU COME BACK HERE AND FIGHT. FIGHT HER. FIGHT ME IF YOU HAVE TO.
NO! YOU CAN FIGHT HER NOW.
WE BELIEVE IN YOU, TWILIGHT!
THAT BLAST EARLIER WAS THE STRONGEST MY MAGIC HAS EVER BEEN AND SHE WITHSTOOD IT... I CAN'T DO THIS ALONE. I CAN'T DO IT WITHOUT YOU, AND I CAN SAVE ALL OF YOU NOW.
I CHOSE YOU. LET THEM GO HOME.
OH... IT'S ALL SO TOUCHING. I'M TORN, REALLY.
REALLY?!
NO.
I'M GOING TO MISS THAT GREEN, GLOBBY THING.
NOT ME, YOU HAVEN'T HAD A BATH IN THREE DAYS.
DINKLE DINKLE-DINK!
NO WAY WE'RE LEAVING! COME ON, LET'S HELP TWILIGHT!

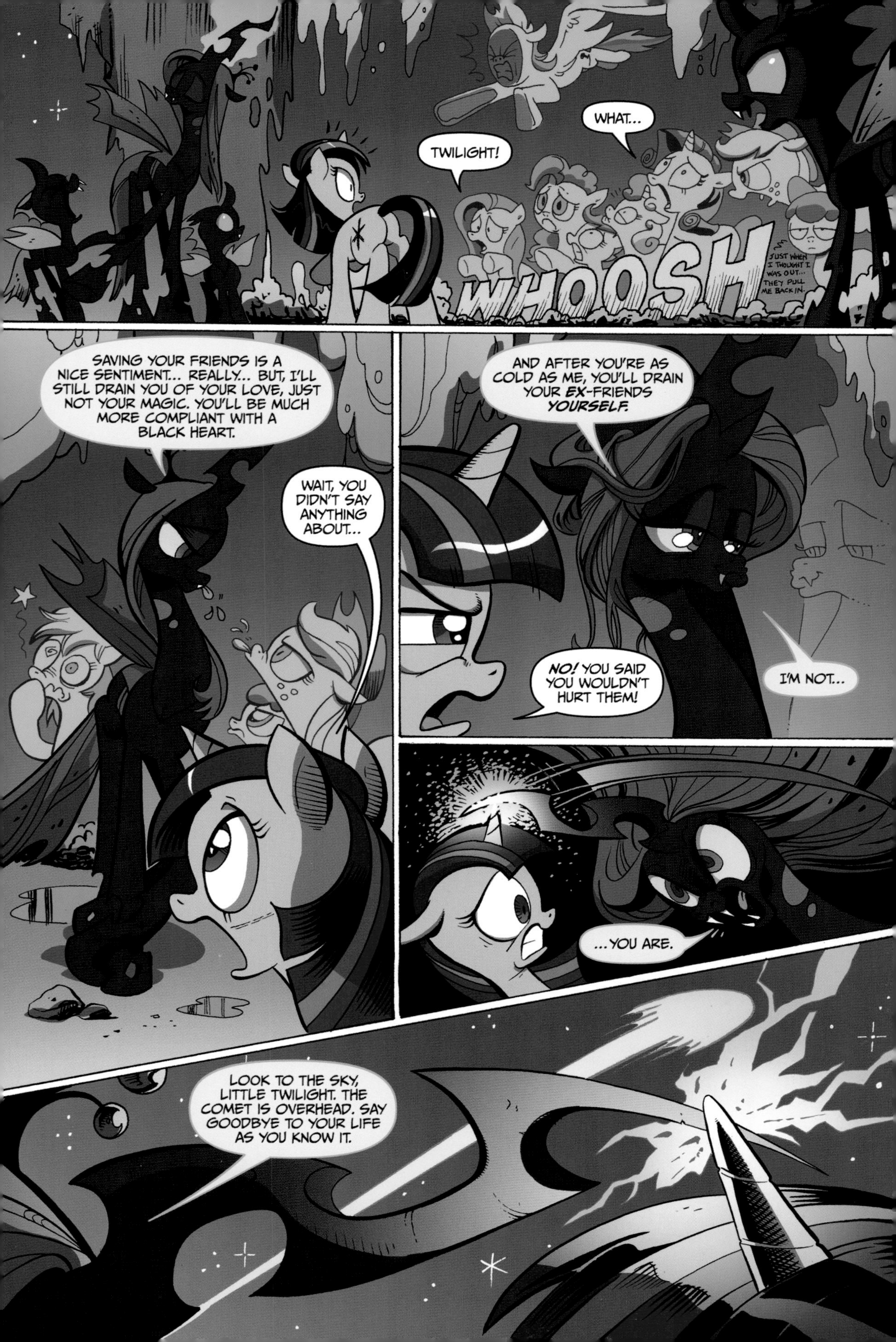
TWILIGHT!
WHAT...
WHOOSH
JUST WHEN I THOUGHT I WAS OUT... THEY PULL ME BACK IN.
SAVING YOUR FRIENDS IS A NICE SENTIMENT... REALLY... BUT, I'LL STILL DRAIN YOU OF YOUR LOVE, JUST NOT YOUR MAGIC. YOU'LL BE MUCH MORE COMPLIANT WITH A BLACK HEART.
WAIT, YOU DIDN'T SAY ANYTHING ABOUT...
AND AFTER YOU'RE AS COLD AS ME, YOU'LL DRAIN YOUR ***EX***-FRIENDS ***YOURSELF.***
NO! YOU SAID YOU WOULDN'T HURT THEM!
I'M NOT...
...YOU ARE.
LOOK TO THE SKY, LITTLE TWILIGHT. THE COMET IS OVERHEAD. SAY GOODBYE TO YOUR LIFE AS YOU KNOW IT.

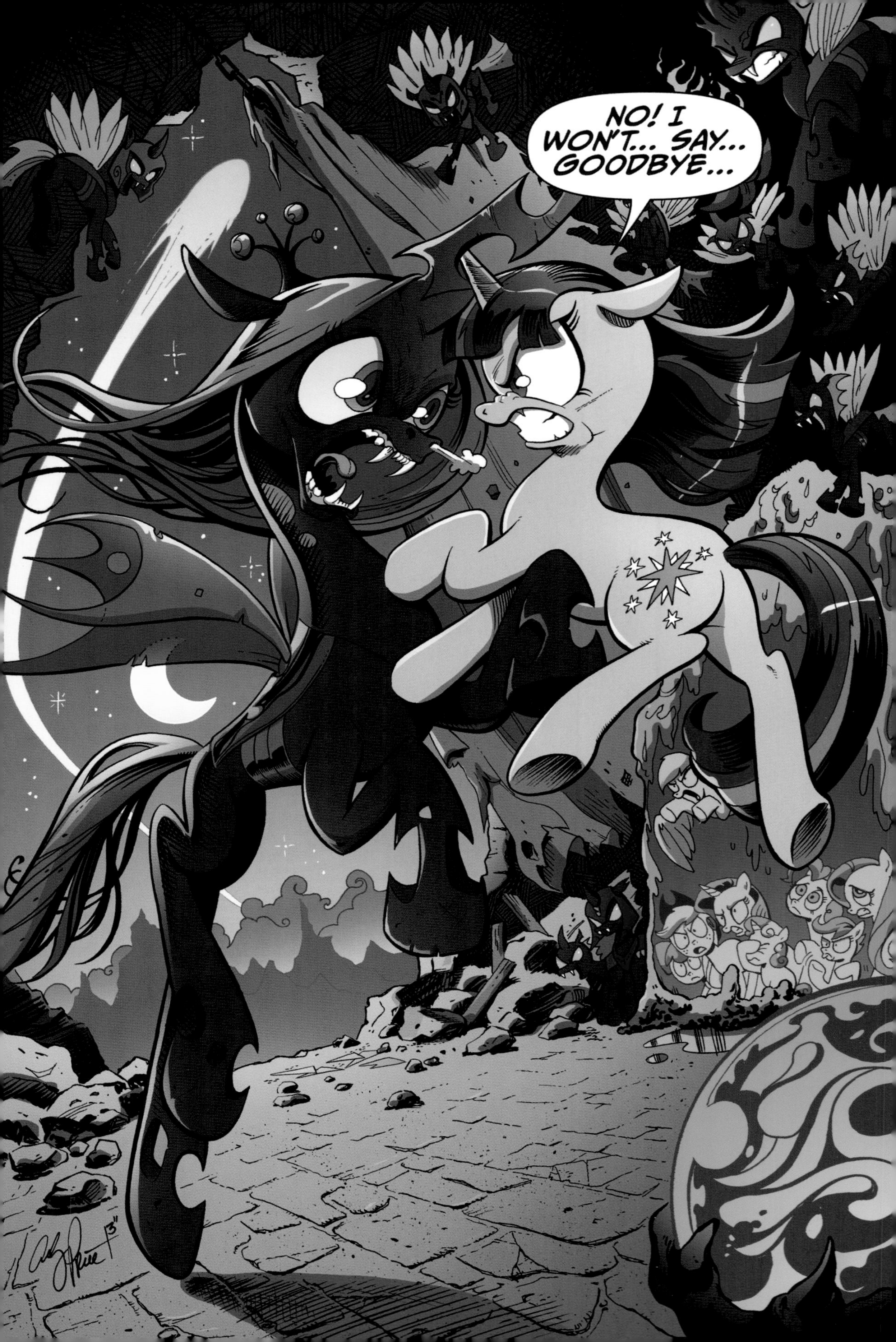
NO! I WON'T... SAY... GOODBYE...

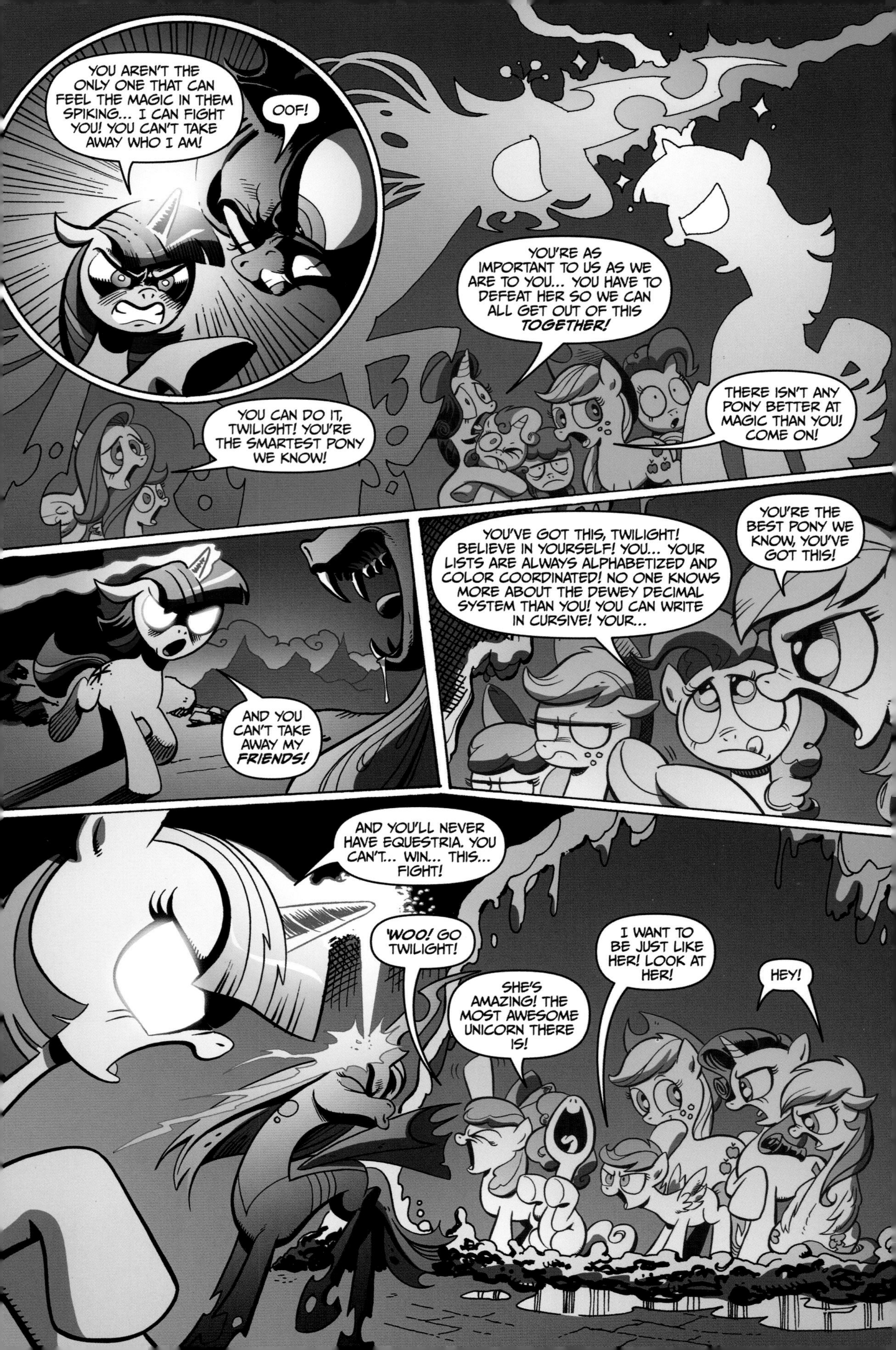
YOU AREN'T THE ONLY ONE THAT CAN FEEL THE MAGIC IN THEM SPIKING... I CAN FIGHT YOU! YOU CAN'T TAKE AWAY WHO I AM!
OOF!
YOU'RE AS IMPORTANT TO US AS WE ARE TO YOU... YOU HAVE TO DEFEAT HER SO WE CAN ALL GET OUT OF THIS TOGETHER!
YOU CAN DO IT, TWILIGHT! YOU'RE THE SMARTEST PONY WE KNOW!
THERE ISN'T ANY PONY BETTER AT MAGIC THAN YOU! COME ON!
AND YOU CAN'T TAKE AWAY MY FRIENDS!
YOU'VE GOT THIS, TWILIGHT! BELIEVE IN YOURSELF! YOU... YOUR LISTS ARE ALWAYS ALPHABETIZED AND COLOR COORDINATED! NO ONE KNOWS MORE ABOUT THE DEWEY DECIMAL SYSTEM THAN YOU! YOU CAN WRITE IN CURSIVE! YOUR...
YOU'RE THE BEST PONY WE KNOW, YOU'VE GOT THIS!
AND YOU'LL NEVER HAVE EQUESTRIA. YOU CAN'T... WIN... THIS... FIGHT!
'WOO! GO TWILIGHT!
SHE'S AMAZING! THE MOST AWESOME UNICORN THERE IS!
I WANT TO BE JUST LIKE HER! LOOK AT HER!
HEY!

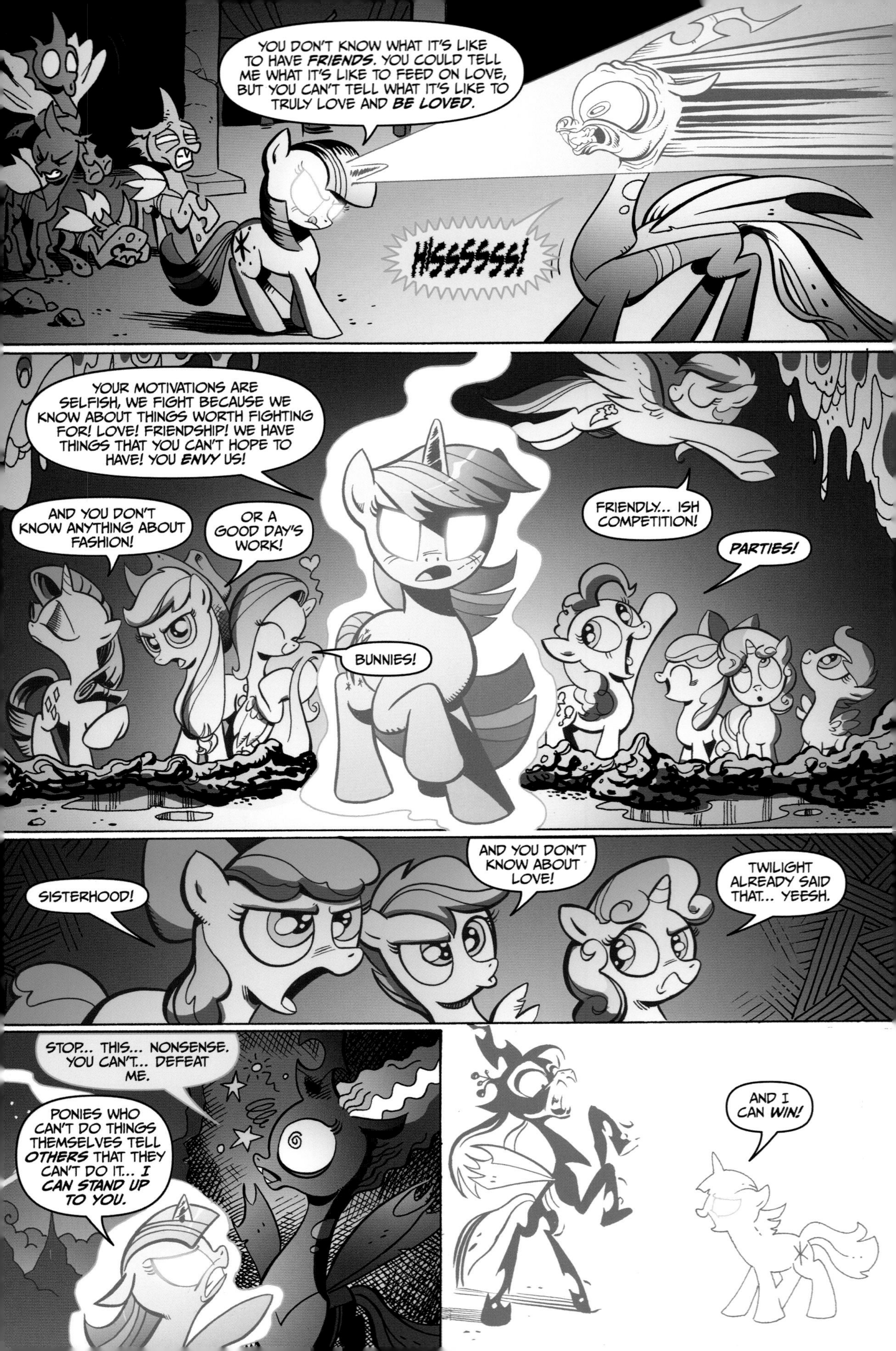
YOU DON'T KNOW WHAT IT'S LIKE TO HAVE FRIENDS. YOU COULD TELL ME WHAT IT'S LIKE TO FEED ON LOVE, BUT YOU CAN'T TELL WHAT IT'S LIKE TO TRULY LOVE AND BE LOVED.
HISSSSSS!
YOUR MOTIVATIONS ARE SELFISH, WE FIGHT BECAUSE WE KNOW ABOUT THINGS WORTH FIGHTING FOR! LOVE! FRIENDSHIP! WE HAVE THINGS THAT YOU CAN'T HOPE TO HAVE! YOU ENVY US!
AND YOU DON'T KNOW ANYTHING ABOUT FASHION!
OR A GOOD DAY'S WORK!
BUNNIES!
FRIENDLY... ISH COMPETITION!
PARTIES!
SISTERHOOD!
AND YOU DON'T KNOW ABOUT LOVE!
TWILIGHT ALREADY SAID THAT... YEESH.
STOP... THIS... NONSENSE. YOU CAN'T... DEFEAT ME.
PONIES WHO CAN'T DO THINGS THEMSELVES TELL OTHERS THAT THEY CAN'T DO IT... I CAN STAND UP TO YOU.
AND I CAN WIN!

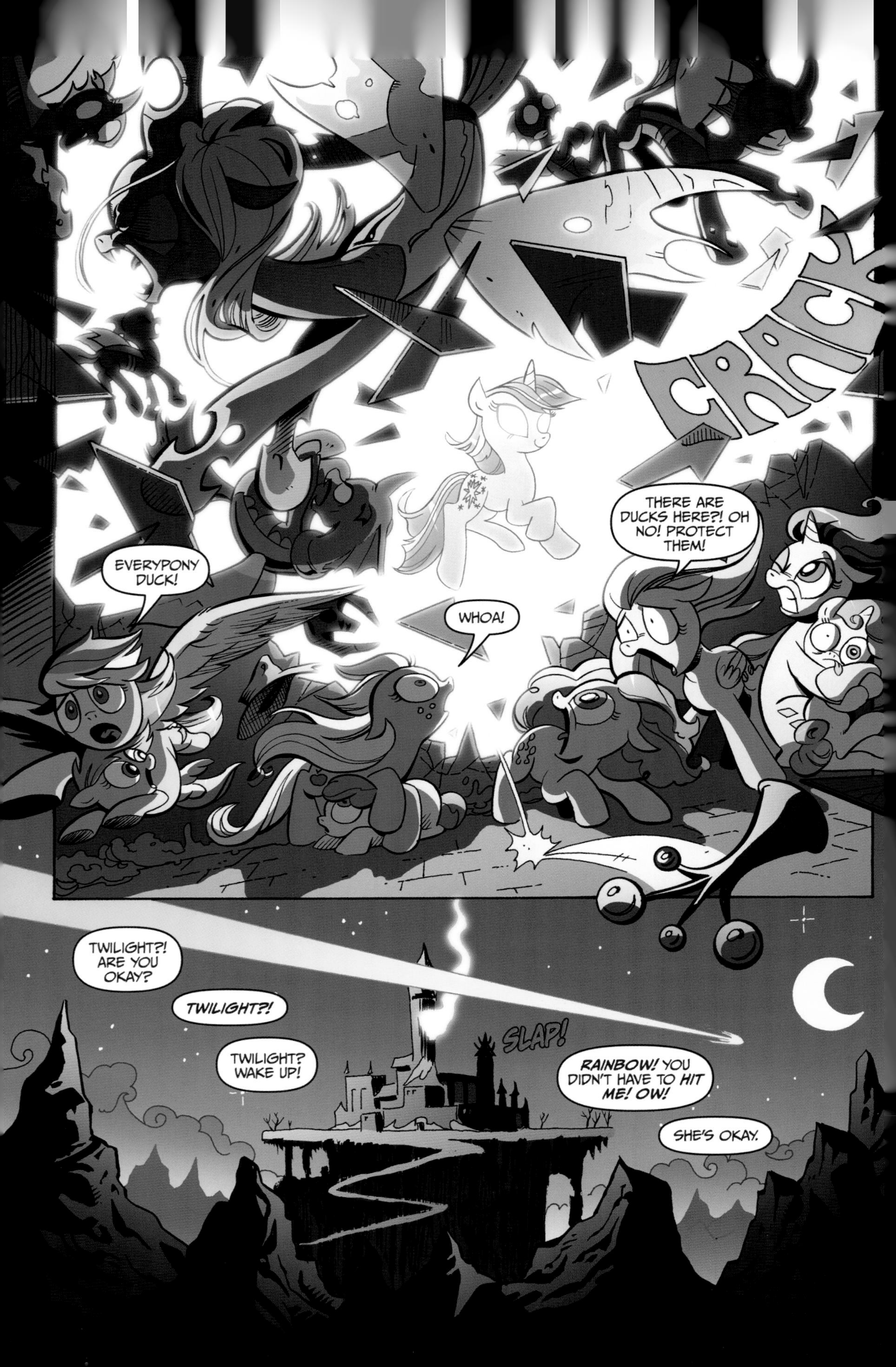
CRACK
THERE ARE DUCKS HERE?! OH NO! PROTECT THEM!
EVERYPONY DUCK!
WHOA!
TWILIGHT?! ARE YOU OKAY?
TWILIGHT?!
TWILIGHT? WAKE UP!
SLAP!
RAINBOW! YOU DIDN'T HAVE TO HIT ME! OW!
SHE'S OKAY.

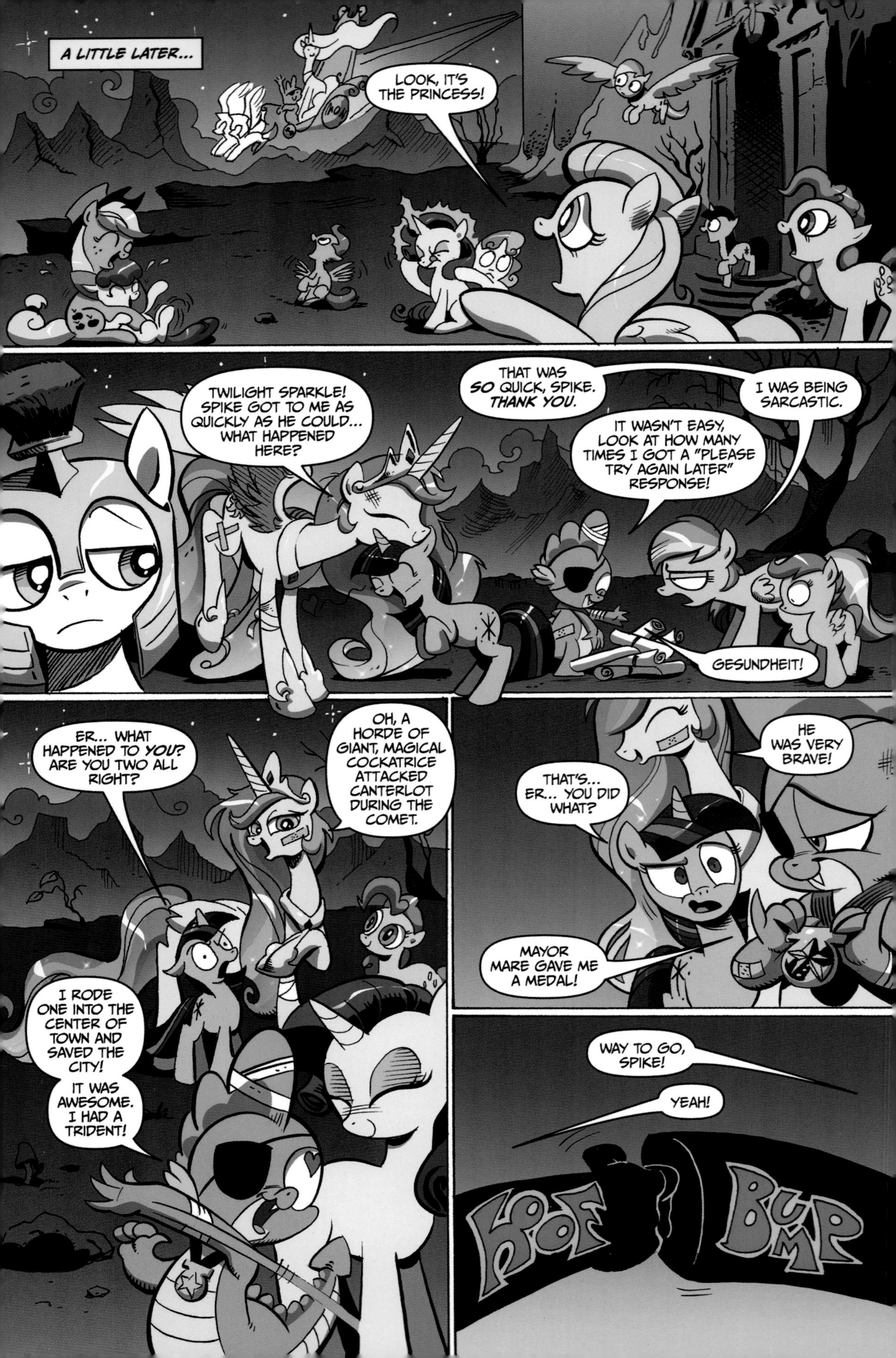
A LITTLE LATER...
LOOK, IT'S THE PRINCESS!
TWILIGHT SPARKLE! SPIKE GOT TO ME AS QUICKLY AS HE COULD... WHAT HAPPENED HERE?
THAT WAS SO QUICK, SPIKE. THANK YOU.
I WAS BEING SARCASTIC.
IT WASN'T EASY, LOOK AT HOW MANY TIMES I GOT A "PLEASE TRY AGAIN LATER" RESPONSE!
GESUNDHEIT!
ER... WHAT HAPPENED TO YOU? ARE YOU TWO ALL RIGHT?
OH, A HORDE OF GIANT, MAGICAL COCKATRICE ATTACKED CANTERLOT DURING THE COMET.
I RODE ONE INTO THE CENTER OF TOWN AND SAVED THE CITY!
IT WAS AWESOME. I HAD A TRIDENT!
HE WAS VERY BRAVE!
THAT'S... ER... YOU DID WHAT?
MAYOR MARE GAVE ME A MEDAL!
WAY TO GO, SPIKE!
YEAH!
HOOF BUMP

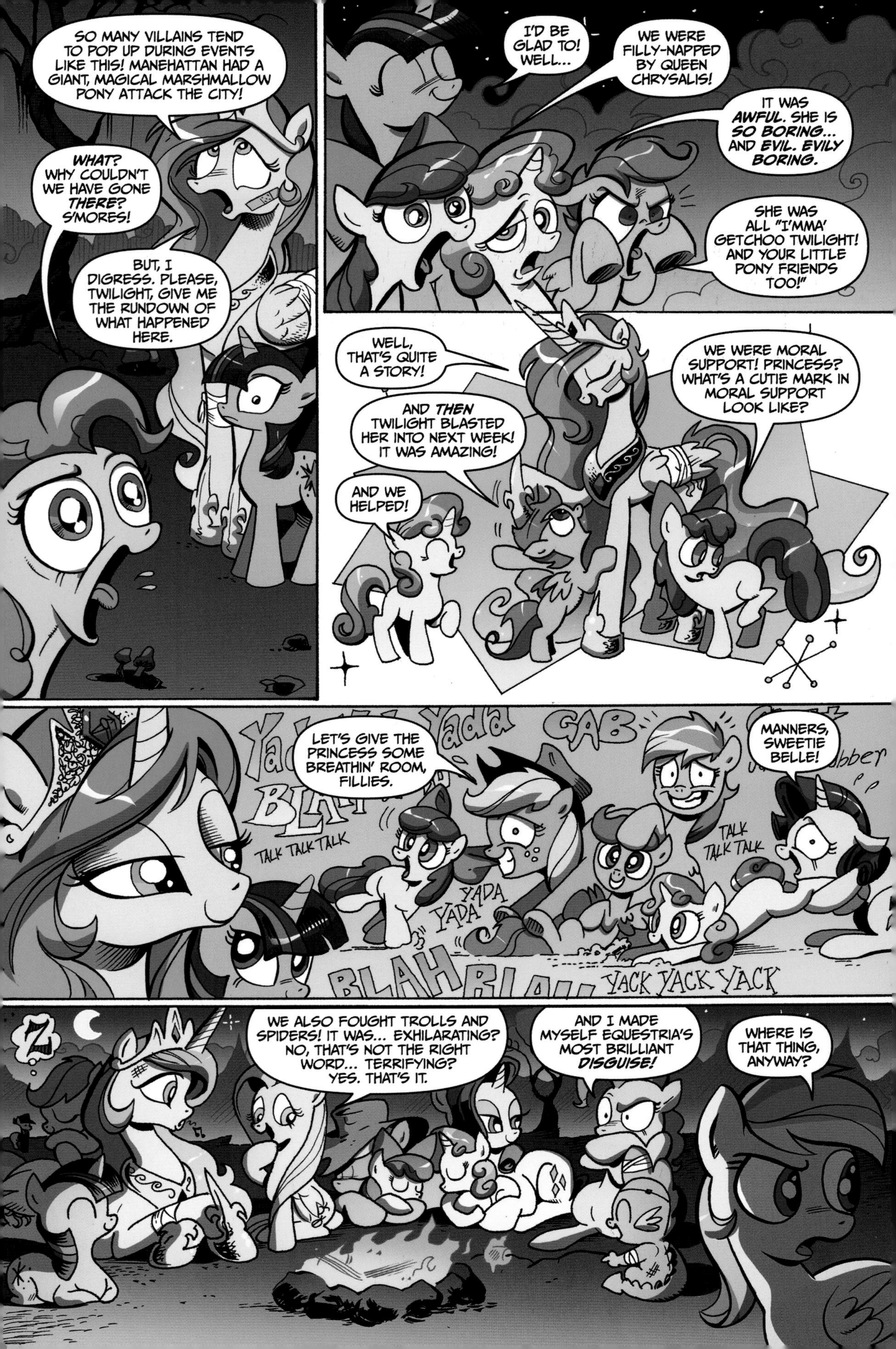
SO MANY VILLAINS TEND TO POP UP DURING EVENTS LIKE THIS! MANEHATTAN HAD A GIANT, MAGICAL MARSHMALLOW PONY ATTACK THE CITY!
WHAT? WHY COULDN'T WE HAVE GONE THERE? S'MORES!
BUT, I DIGRESS. PLEASE, TWILIGHT, GIVE ME THE RUNDOWN OF WHAT HAPPENED HERE.
I'D BE GLAD TO! WELL...
WE WERE FILLY-NAPPED BY QUEEN CHRYSALIS!
IT WAS AWFUL. SHE IS SO BORING... AND EVIL. EVILY BORING.
SHE WAS ALL "I'MMA' GETCHOO TWILIGHT! AND YOUR LITTLE PONY FRIENDS TOO!"
WELL, THAT'S QUITE A STORY!
AND THEN TWILIGHT BLASTED HER INTO NEXT WEEK! IT WAS AMAZING!
AND WE HELPED!
WE WERE MORAL SUPPORT! PRINCESS? WHAT'S A CUTIE MARK IN MORAL SUPPORT LOOK LIKE?
LET'S GIVE THE PRINCESS SOME BREATHIN' ROOM, FILLIES.
MANNERS, SWEETIE BELLE!
GAB
TALK TALK TALK
TALK TALK TALK
YADA YADA
BLAH
YACK YACK YACK
WE ALSO FOUGHT TROLLS AND SPIDERS! IT WAS... EXHILARATING? NO, THAT'S NOT THE RIGHT WORD... TERRIFYING? YES. THAT'S IT.
AND I MADE MYSELF EQUESTRIA'S MOST BRILLIANT DISGUISE!
WHERE IS THAT THING, ANYWAY?
Z

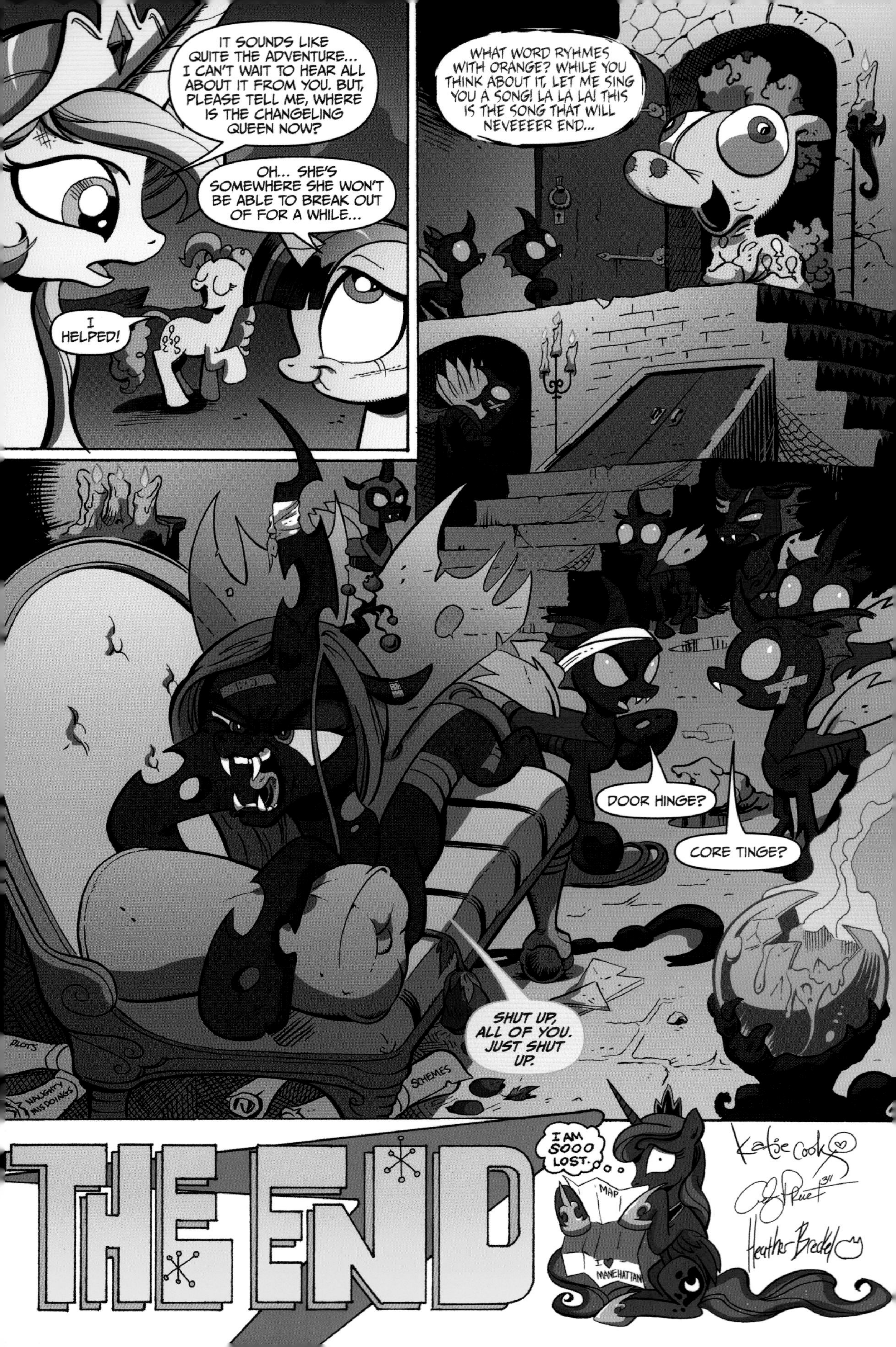
IT SOUNDS LIKE QUITE THE ADVENTURE... I CAN'T WAIT TO HEAR ALL ABOUT IT FROM YOU. BUT, PLEASE TELL ME, WHERE IS THE CHANGELING QUEEN NOW?
OH... SHE'S SOMEWHERE SHE WON'T BE ABLE TO BREAK OUT OF FOR A WHILE...
I HELPED!
WHAT WORD RYHMES WITH ORANGE? WHILE YOU THINK ABOUT IT, LET ME SING YOU A SONG! LA LA LA! THIS IS THE SONG THAT WILL NEVEEEER END...
DOOR HINGE?
CORE TINGE?
SHUT UP, ALL OF YOU. JUST SHUT UP.
PLOTS
NAUGHTY MISDOINGS
SCHEMES
THE END
I AM SOOO LOST.
MAP
I ♥ MANEHATTAN

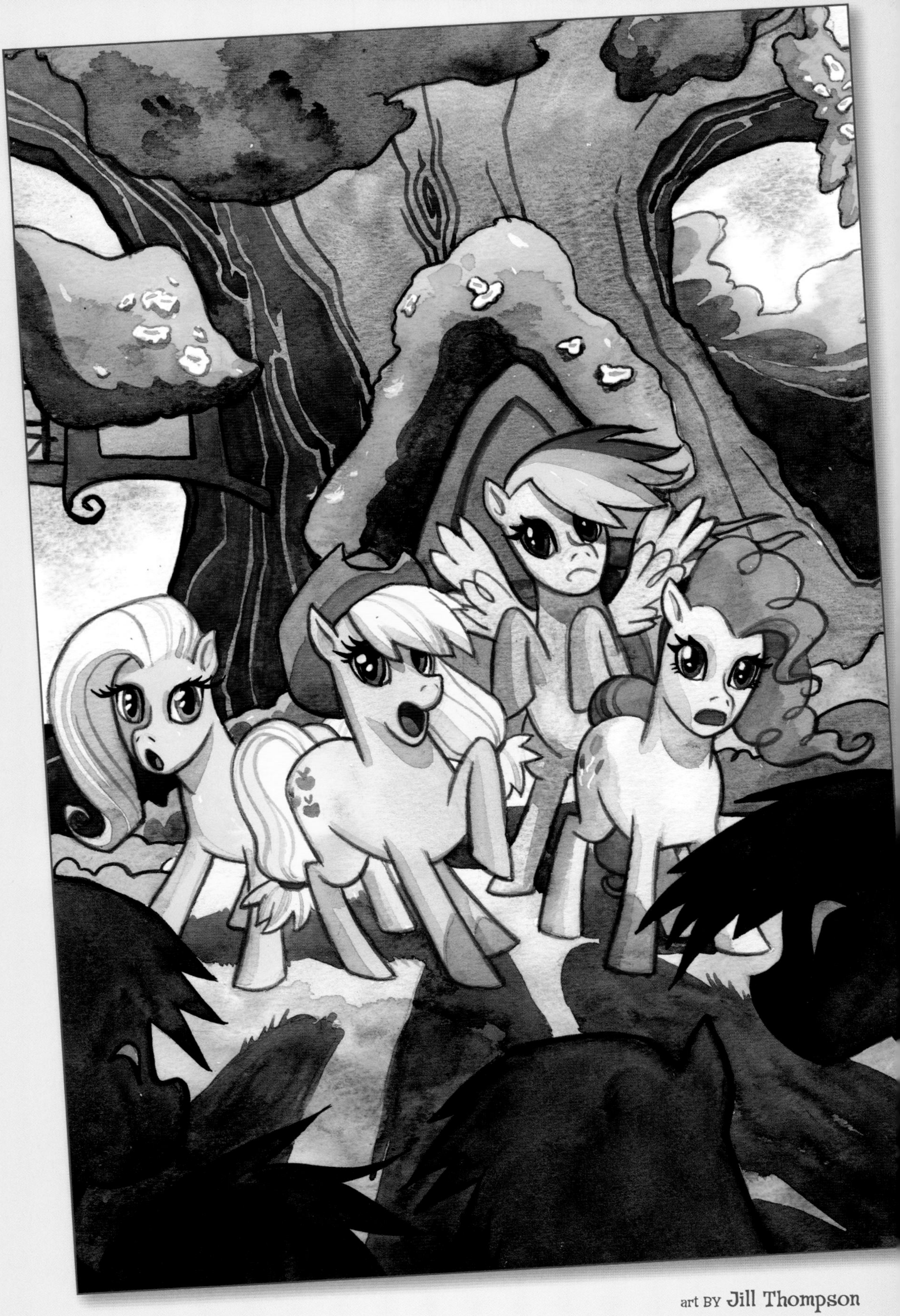

art BY Jill Thompson

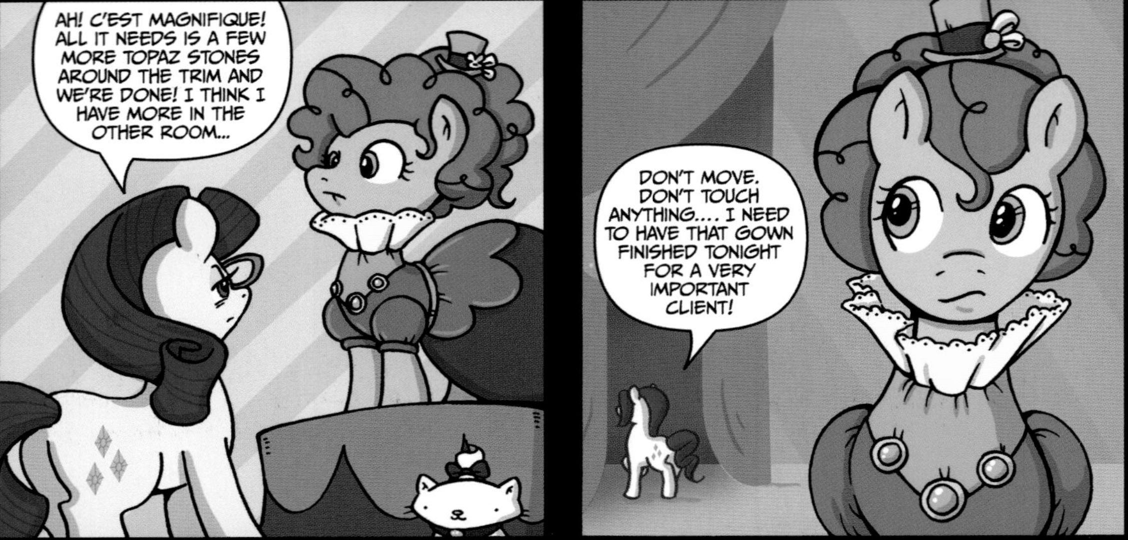
AH! C'EST MAGNIFIQUE! ALL IT NEEDS IS A FEW MORE TOPAZ STONES AROUND THE TRIM AND WE'RE DONE! I THINK I HAVE MORE IN THE OTHER ROOM...
DON'T MOVE. DON'T TOUCH ANYTHING.... I NEED TO HAVE THAT GOWN FINISHED TONIGHT FOR A VERY IMPORTANT CLIENT!

How Much IS That Pony In The Window?

Art and Story by Katie Cook

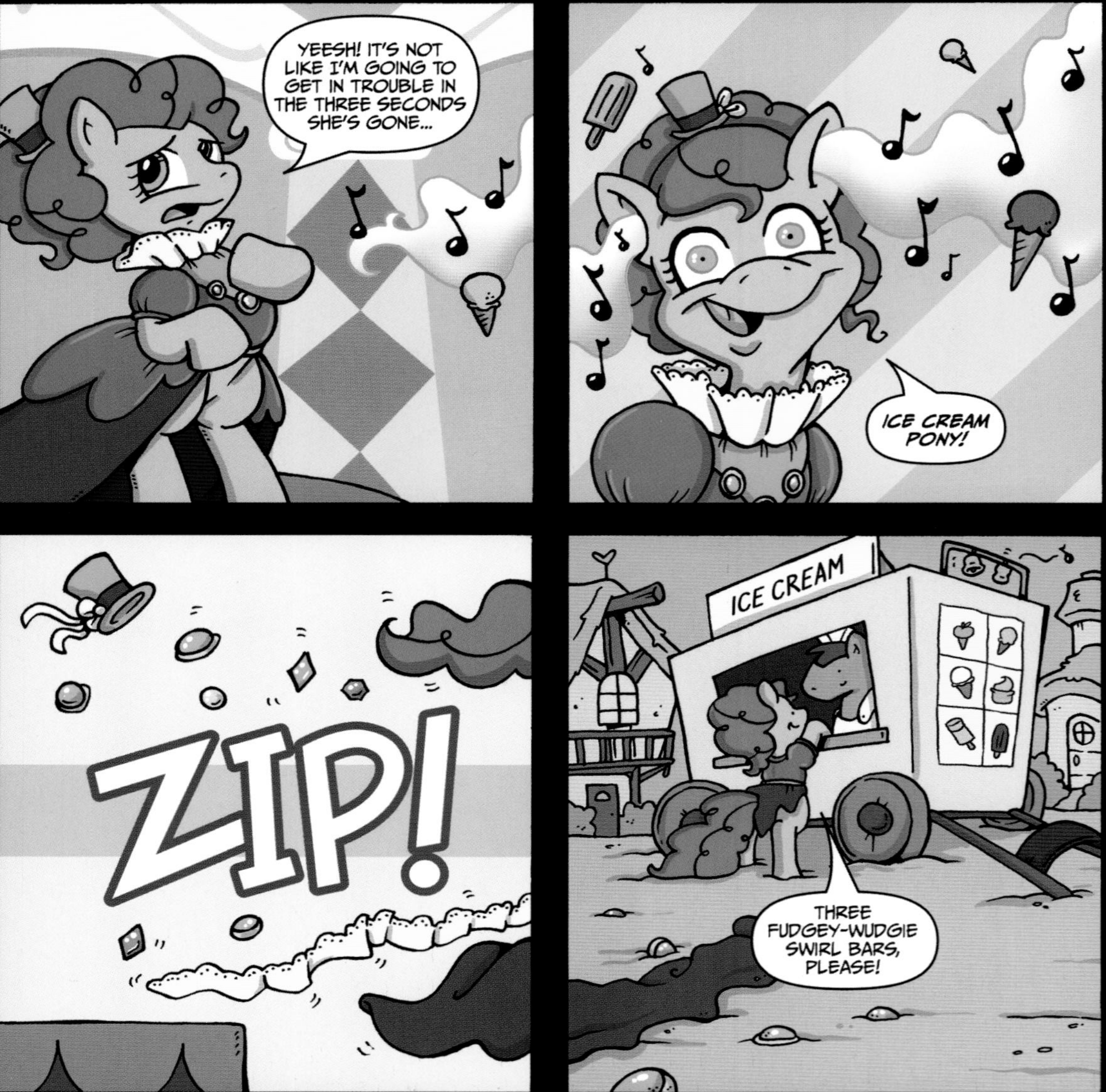
YEESH! IT'S NOT LIKE I'M GOING TO GET IN TROUBLE IN THE THREE SECONDS SHE'S GONE...
ICE CREAM PONY!
ZIP!
ICE CREAM
THREE FUDGEY-WUDGIE SWIRL BARS, PLEASE!

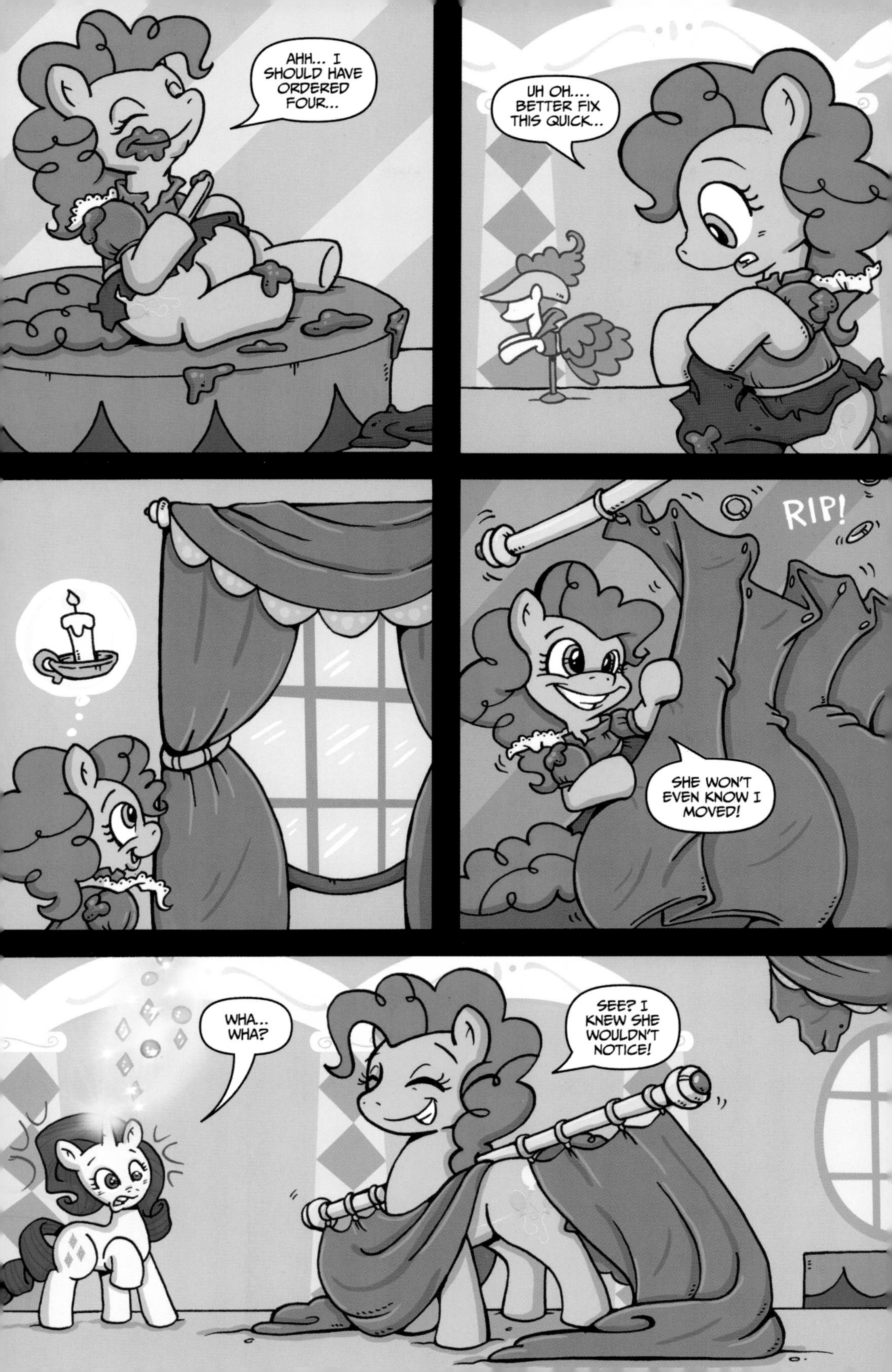
AHH... I SHOULD HAVE ORDERED FOUR...
UH OH.... BETTER FIX THIS QUICK...
RIP!
SHE WON'T EVEN KNOW I MOVED!
WHA... WHA?
SEE? I KNEW SHE WOULDN'T NOTICE!

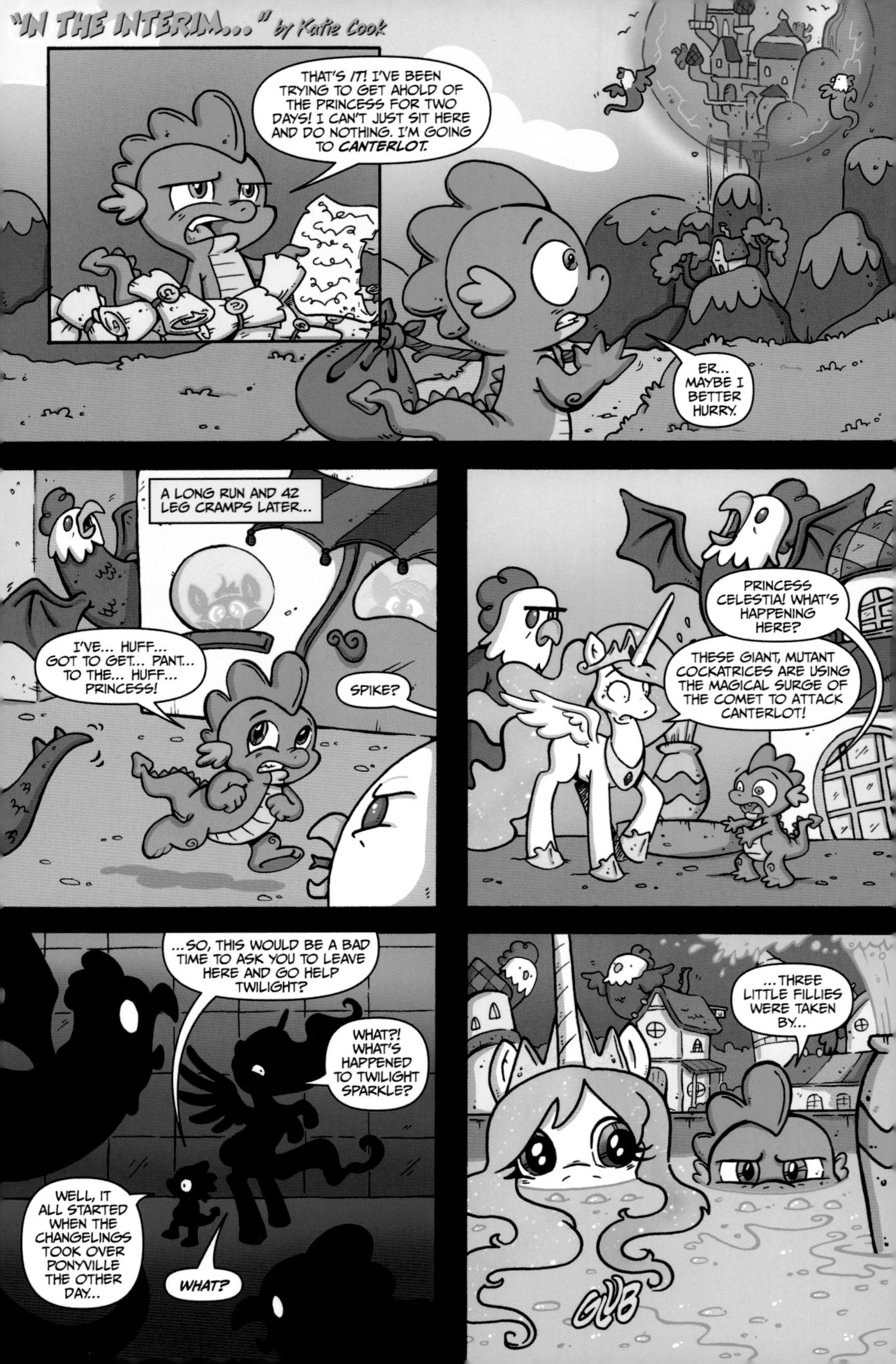
"IN THE INTERIM..." by Katie Cook
THAT'S IT! I'VE BEEN TRYING TO GET AHOLD OF THE PRINCESS FOR TWO DAYS! I CAN'T JUST SIT HERE AND DO NOTHING. I'M GOING TO CANTERLOT.
ER... MAYBE I BETTER HURRY.
A LONG RUN AND 42 LEG CRAMPS LATER...
I'VE... HUFF... GOT TO GET... PANT... TO THE... HUFF... PRINCESS!
SPIKE?
PRINCESS CELESTIA! WHAT'S HAPPENING HERE?
THESE GIANT, MUTANT COCKATRICES ARE USING THE MAGICAL SURGE OF THE COMET TO ATTACK CANTERLOT!
...SO, THIS WOULD BE A BAD TIME TO ASK YOU TO LEAVE HERE AND GO HELP TWILIGHT?
WHAT?! WHAT'S HAPPENED TO TWILIGHT SPARKLE?
WELL, IT ALL STARTED WHEN THE CHANGELINGS TOOK OVER PONYVILLE THE OTHER DAY...
WHAT?
...THREE LITTLE FILLIES WERE TAKEN BY...
GLUB

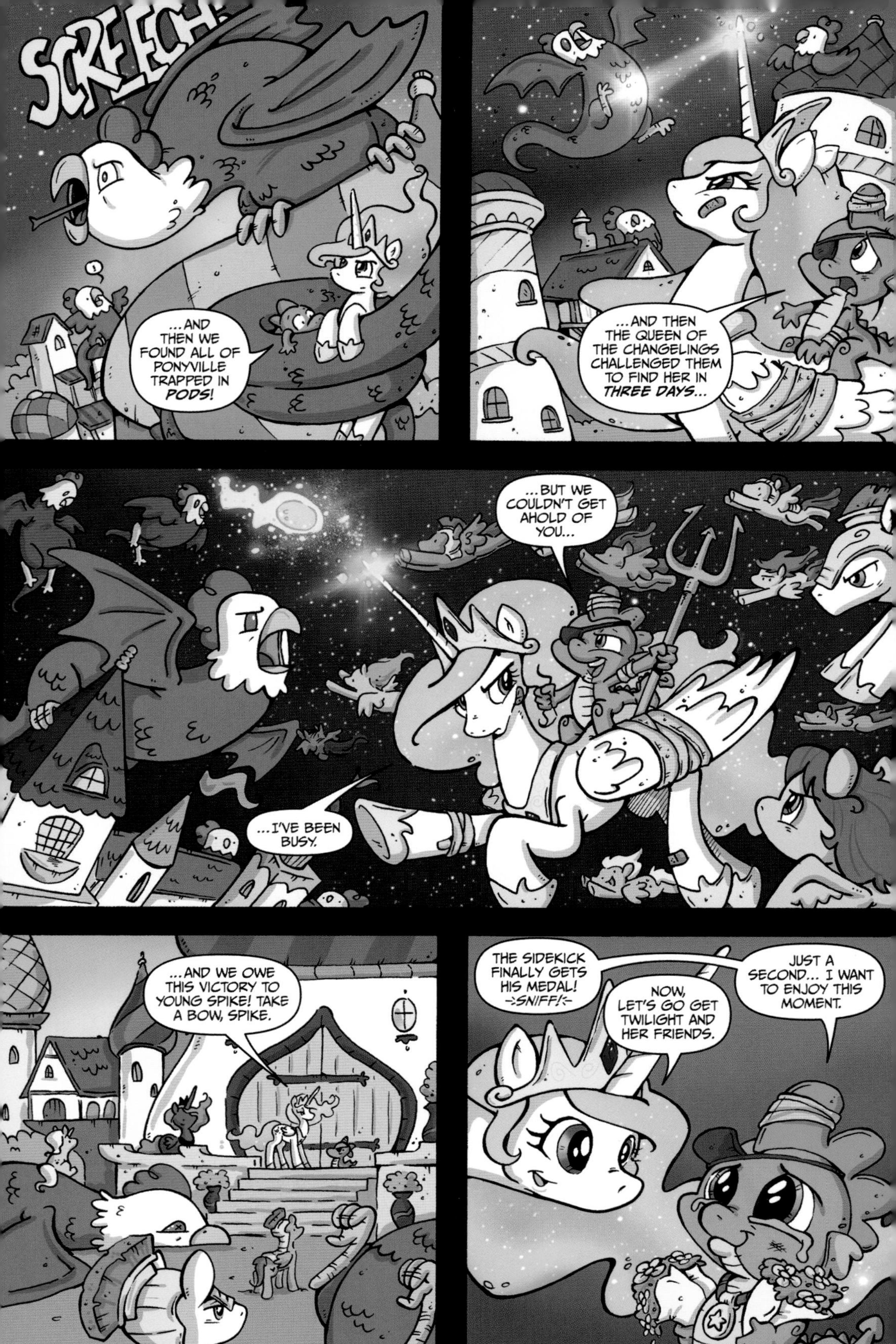
SCREECH
...AND THEN WE FOUND ALL OF PONYVILLE TRAPPED IN PODS!
...AND THEN THE QUEEN OF THE CHANGELINGS CHALLENGED THEM TO FIND HER IN THREE DAYS...
...BUT WE COULDN'T GET AHOLD OF YOU...
...I'VE BEEN BUSY.
...AND WE OWE THIS VICTORY TO YOUNG SPIKE! TAKE A BOW, SPIKE.
THE SIDEKICK FINALLY GETS HIS MEDAL! -SNIFF!-
NOW, LET'S GO GET TWILIGHT AND HER FRIENDS.
JUST A SECOND... I WANT TO ENJOY THIS MOMENT.

Art Gallery

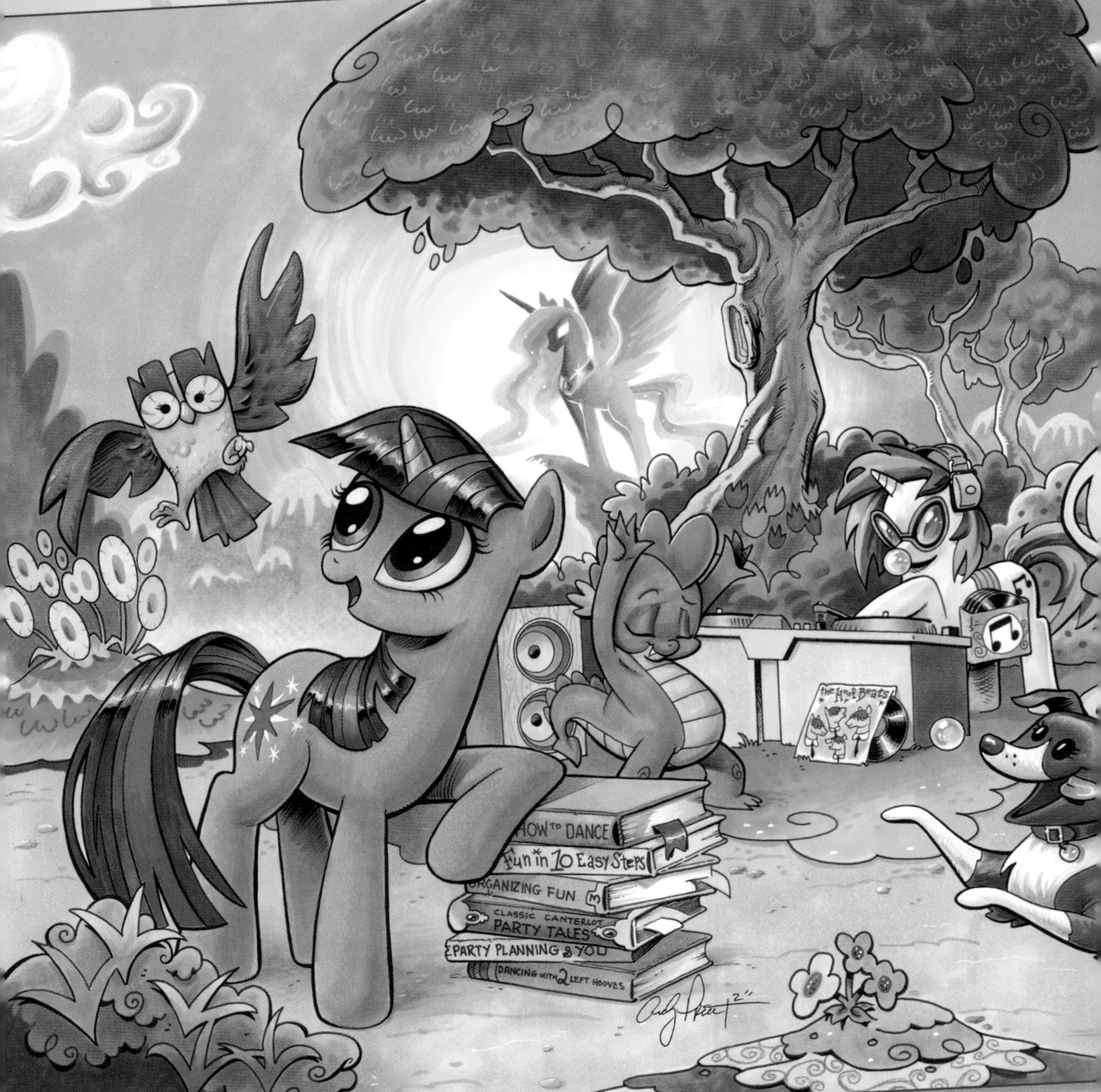

HOW TO DANCE
Fun in 10 Easy Steps
ORGANIZING FUN
CLASSIC CANTERLOT PARTY TALES
PARTY PLANNING & YOU
DANCING WITH 2 LEFT HOOVES
the Hoof Beats

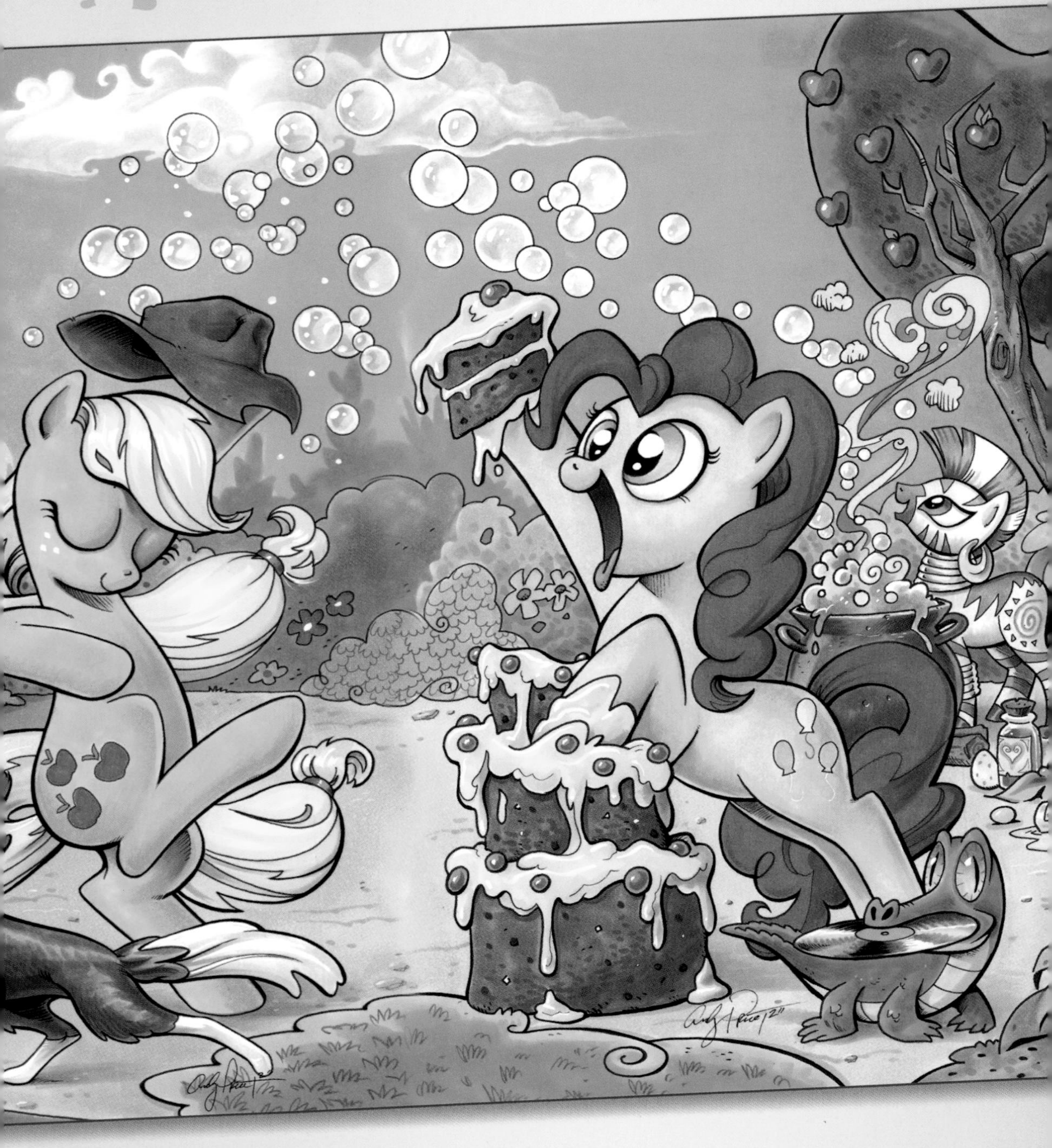

art BY Andy Price

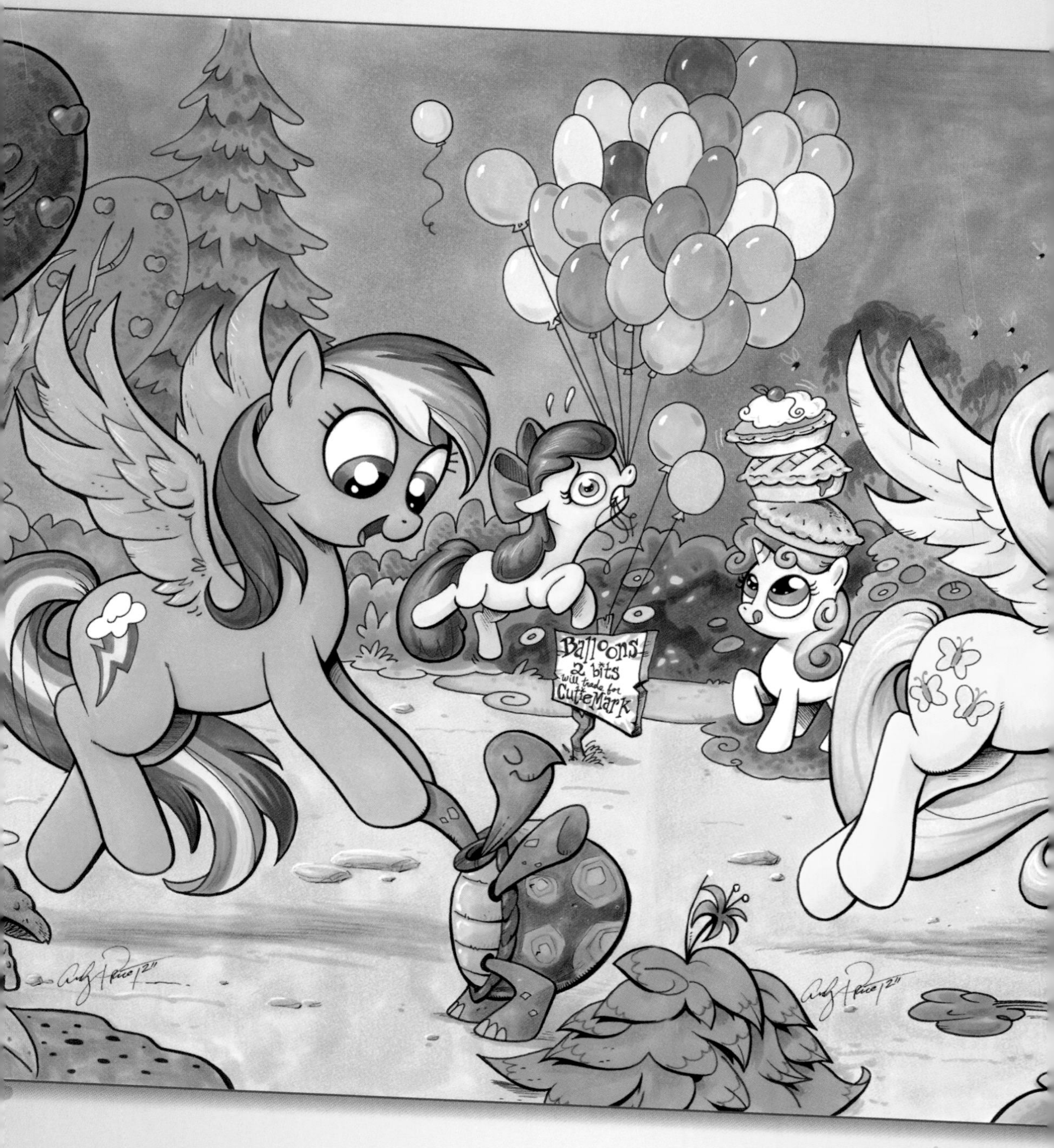
Balloons
2 bits
will trade for
CutieMark

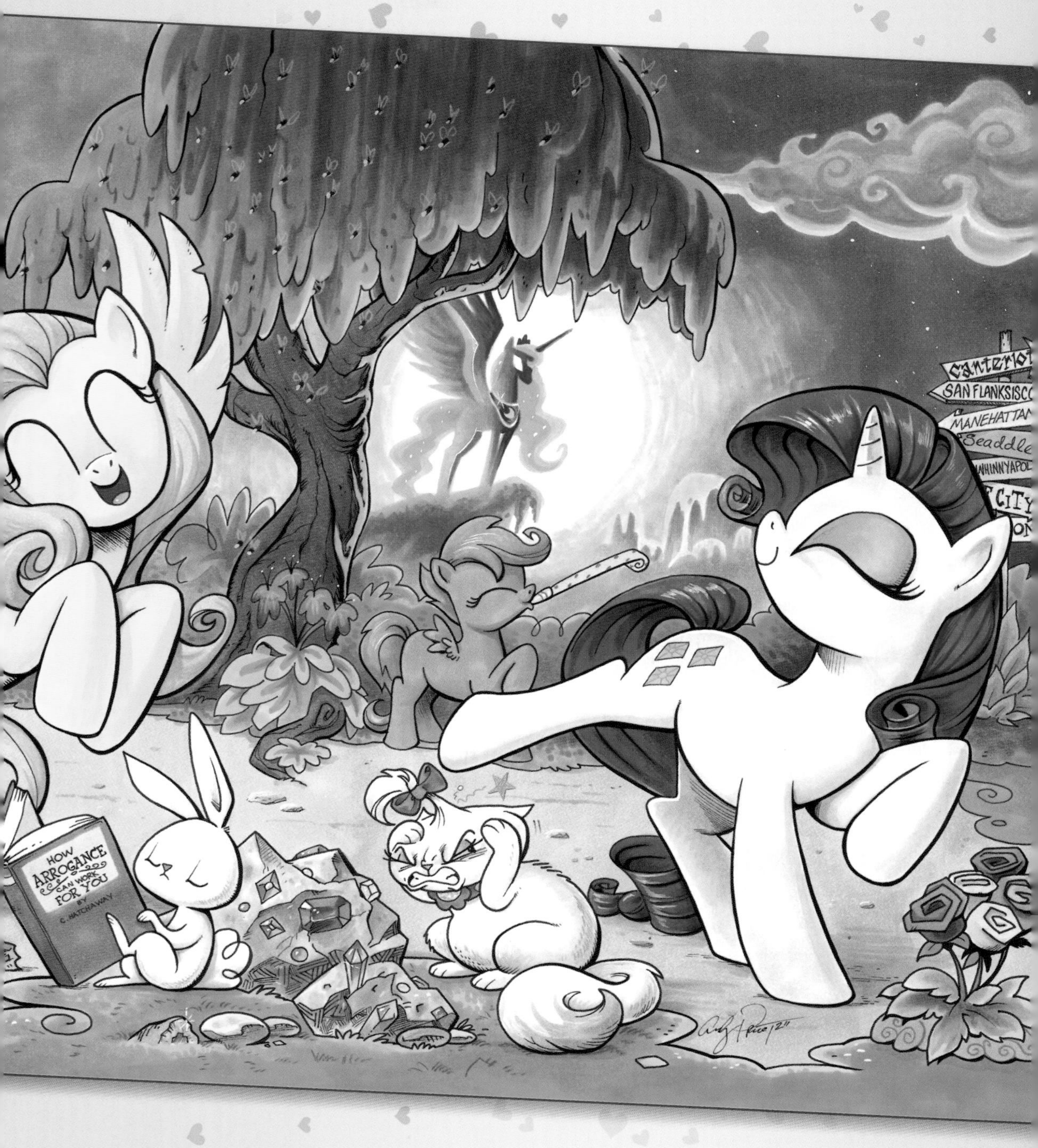
HOW ARROGANCE CAN WORK FOR YOU
BY C. HATCHAWAY

art BY Andy Price

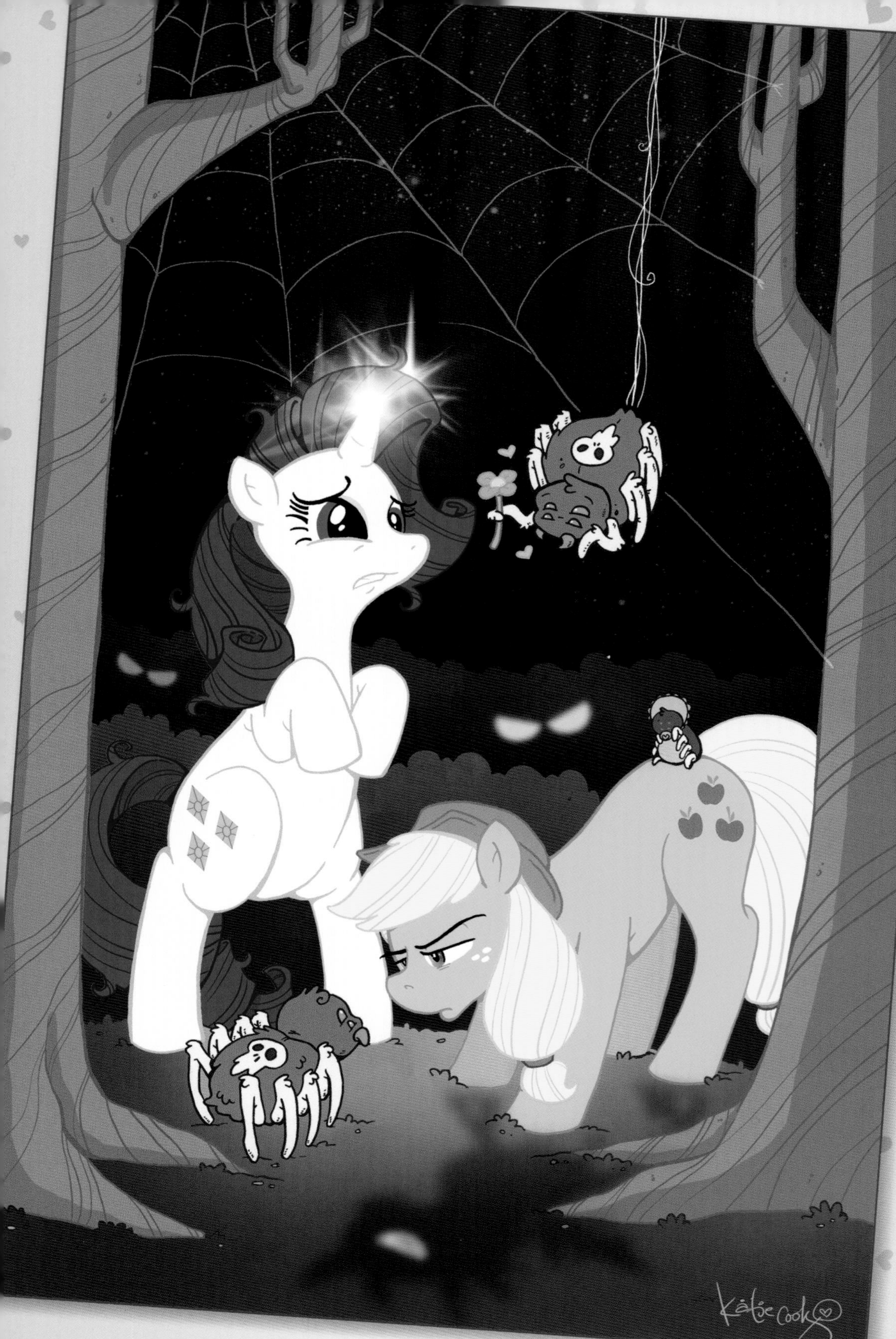
Katie Cook

art BY Katie Cook

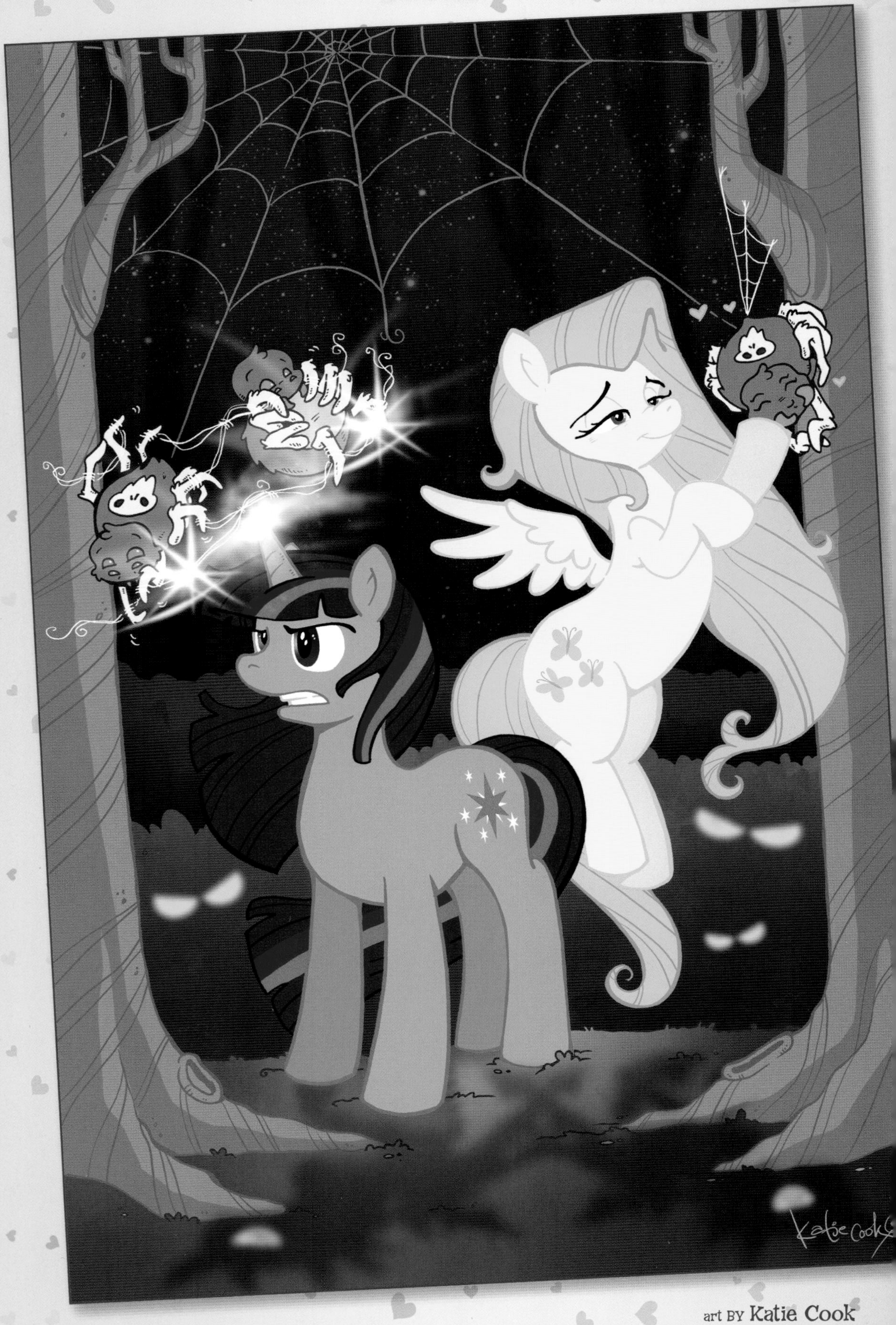

art BY Katie Cook

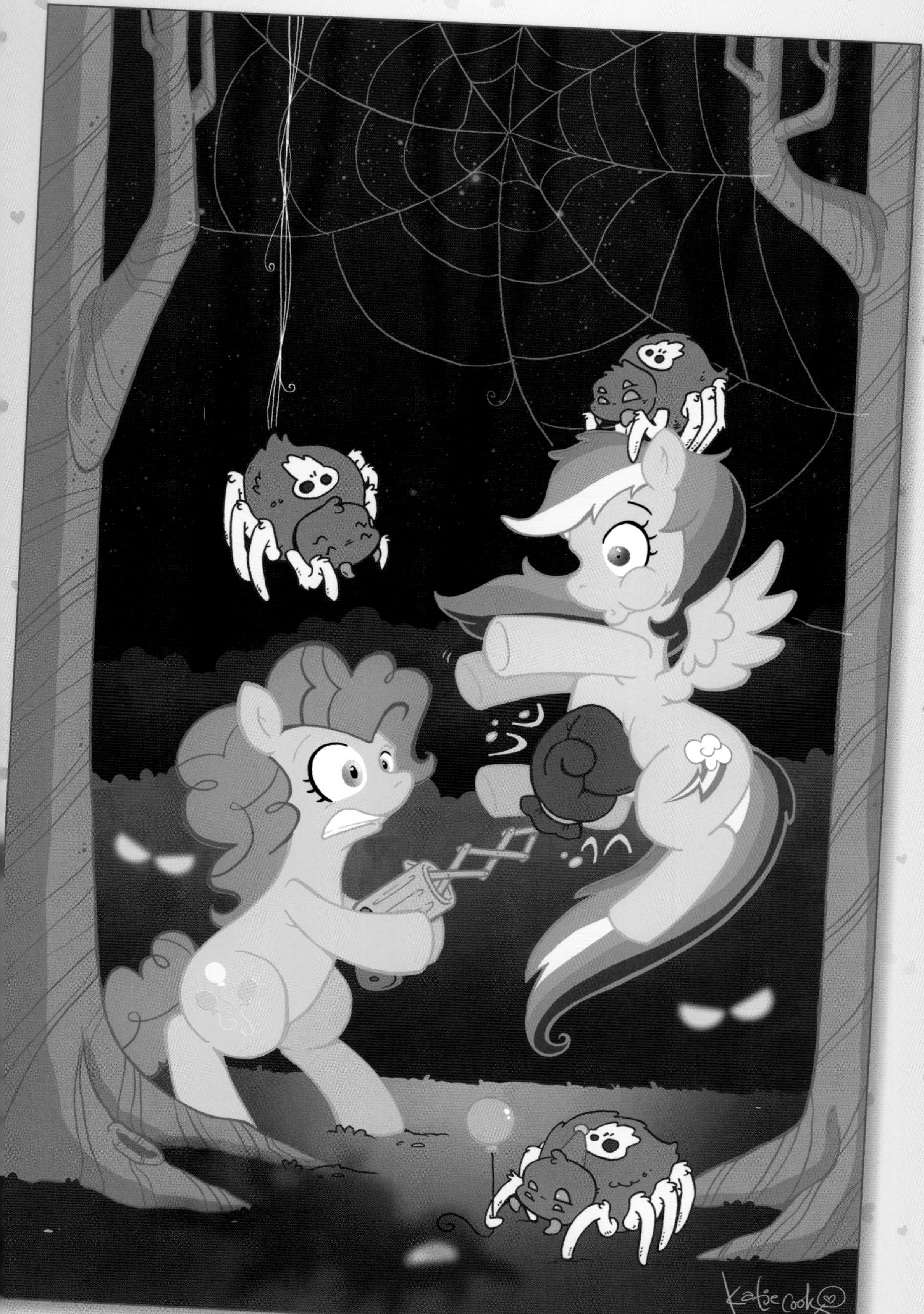
Katie Cook

art BY Katie Cook

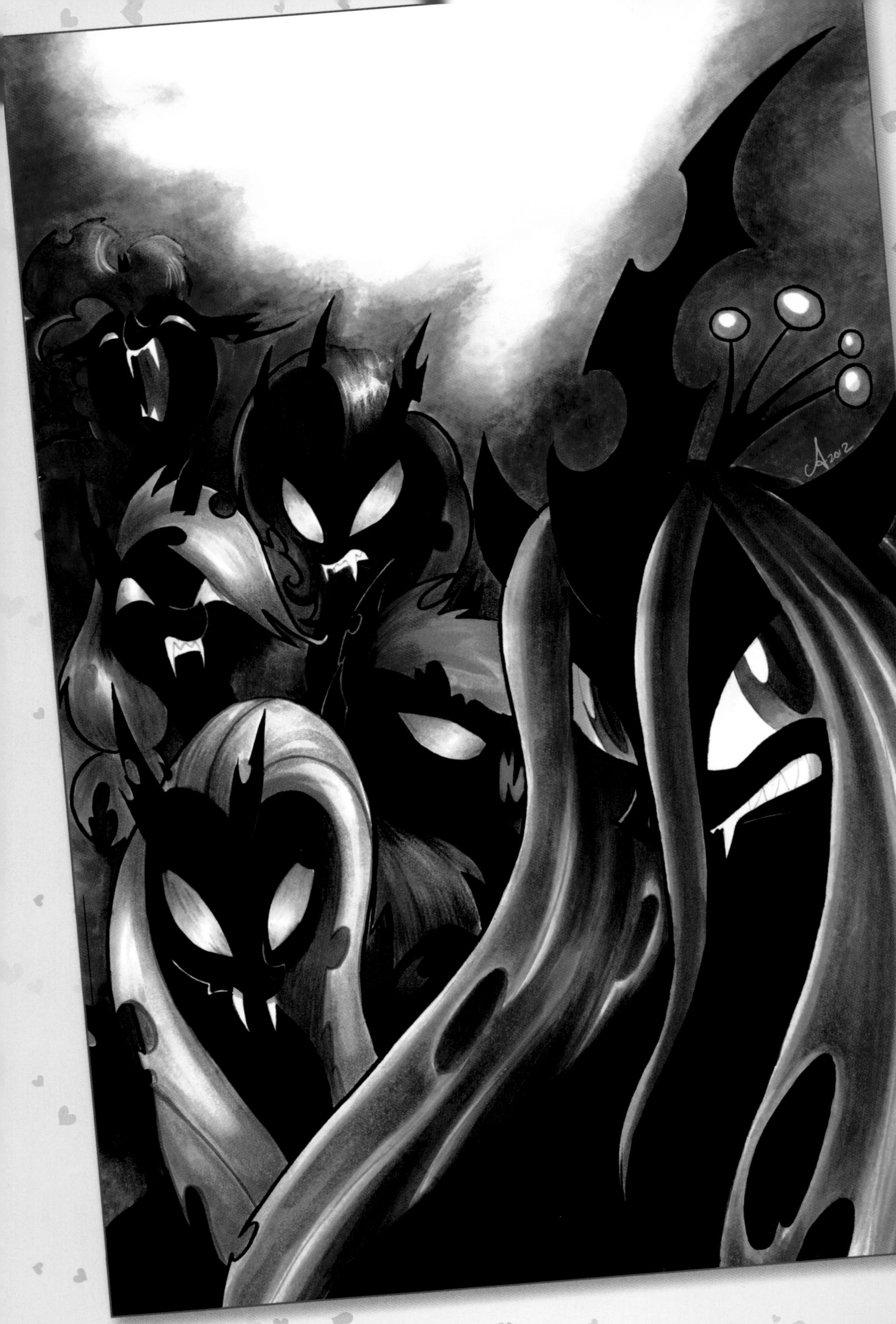

art BY Amy Mebberson

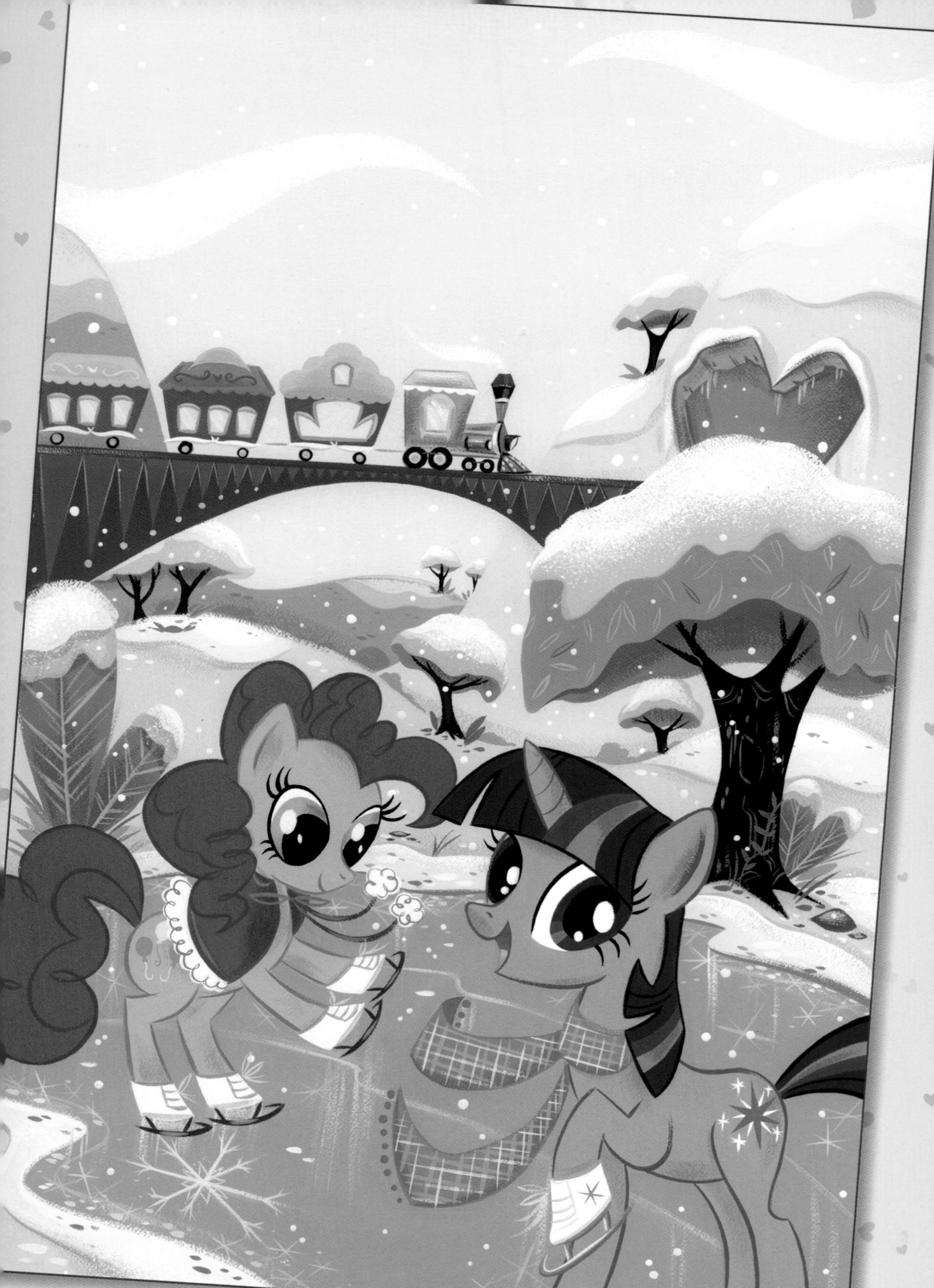

art BY Stephanie Buscema

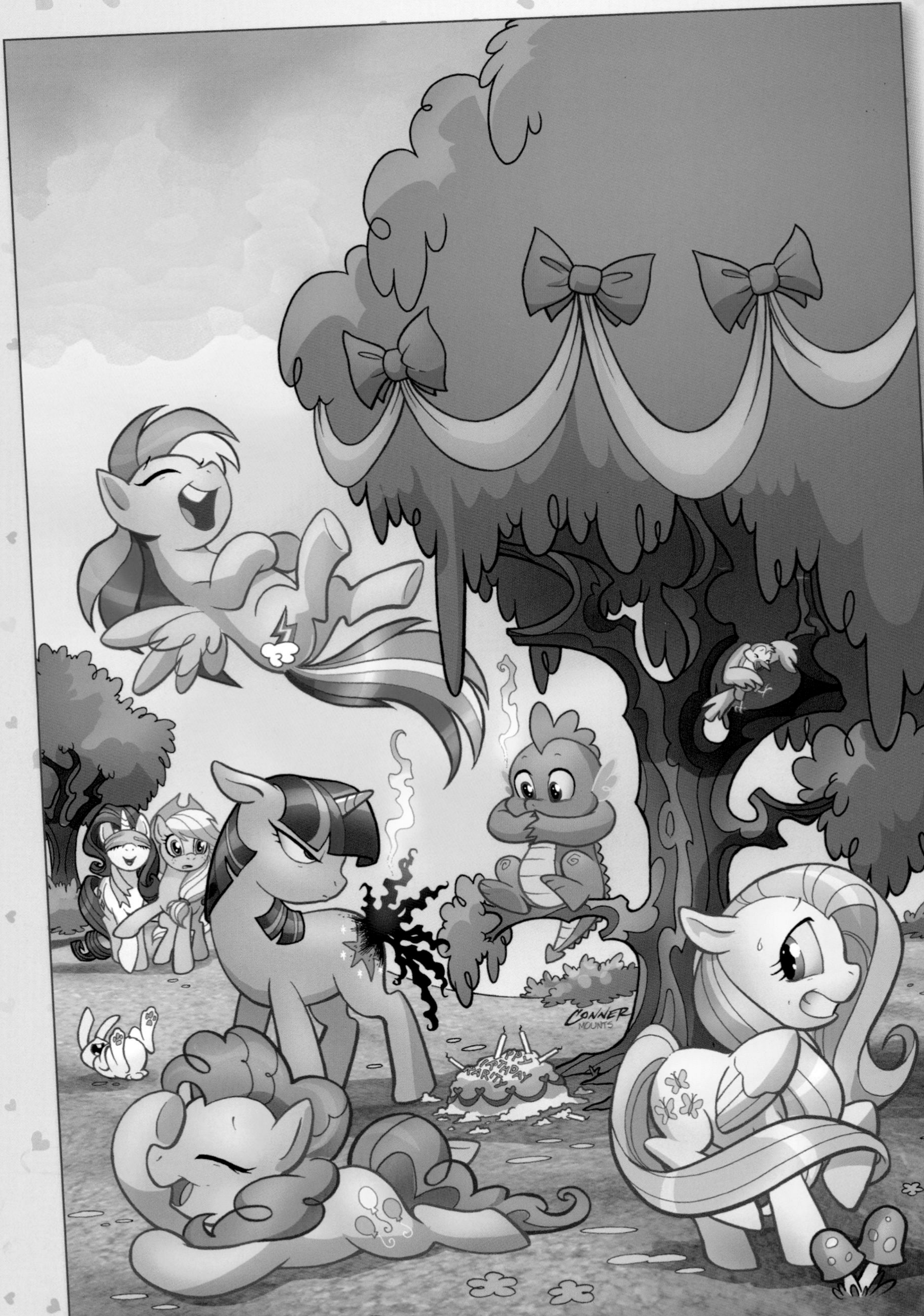
CONNER
MOUNTS

art BY Amanda Conner
colors BY Paul Mounts

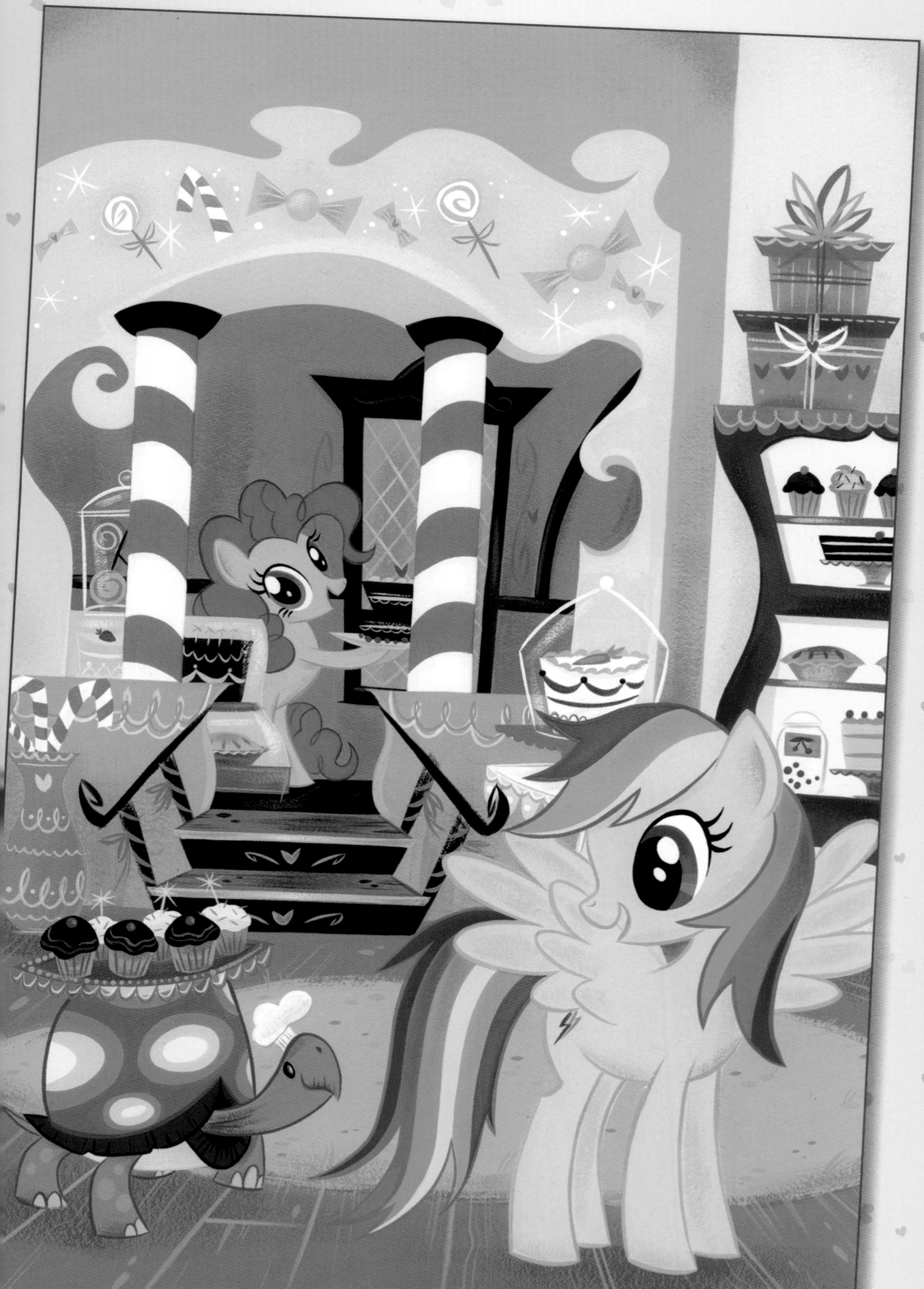

art BY Stephanie Buscema

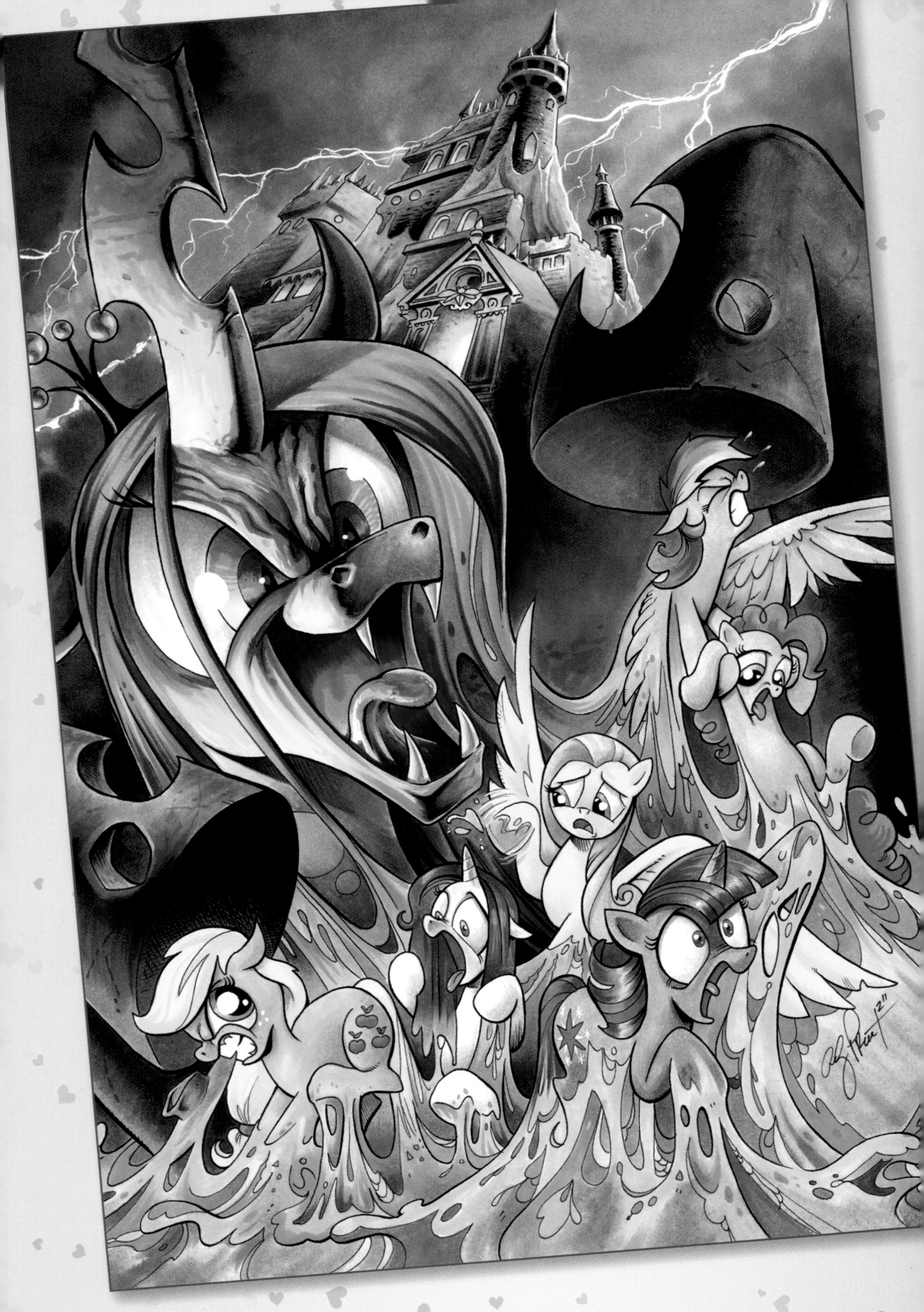

art BY Andy Price

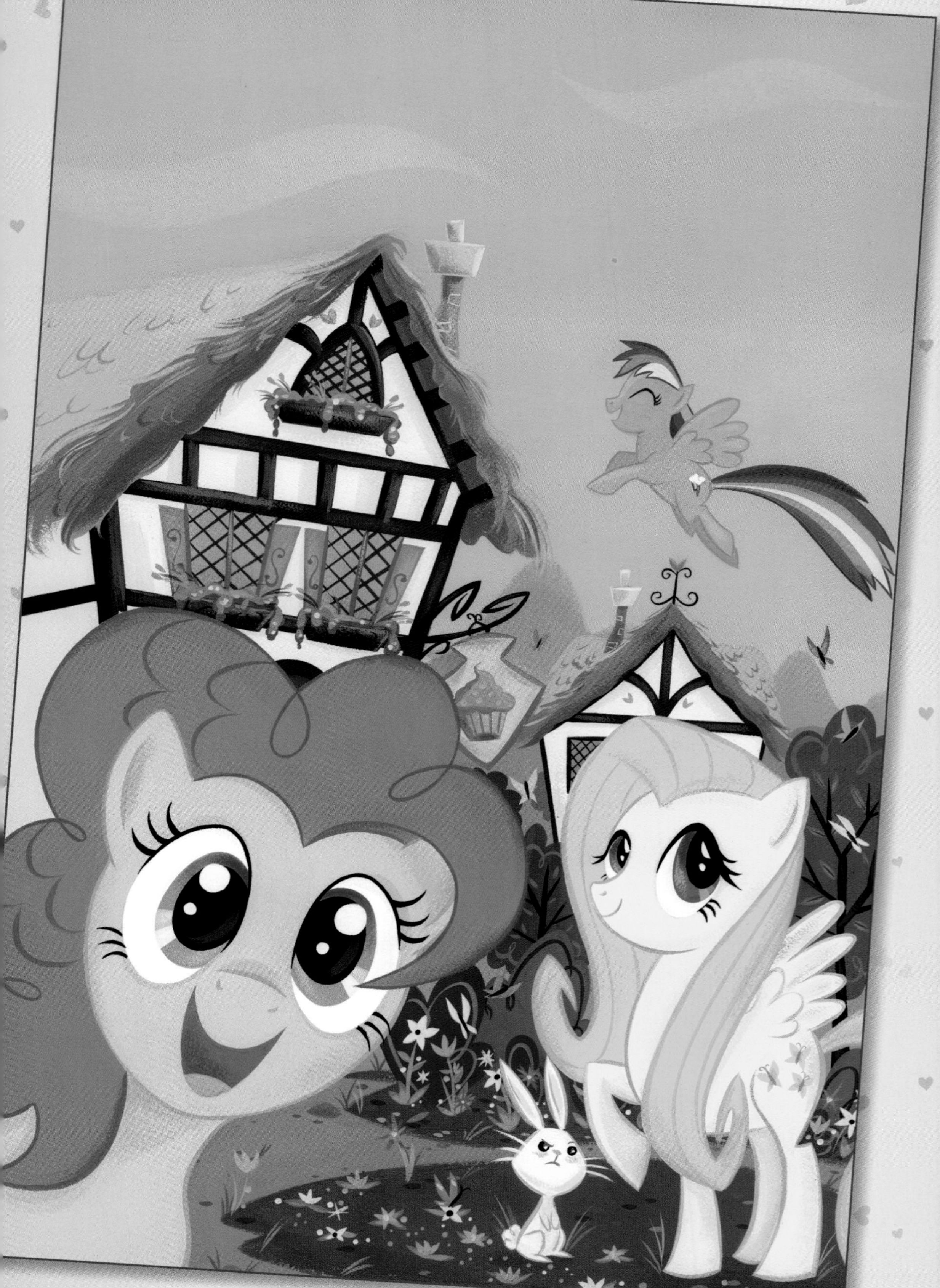

art BY Stephanie Buscema

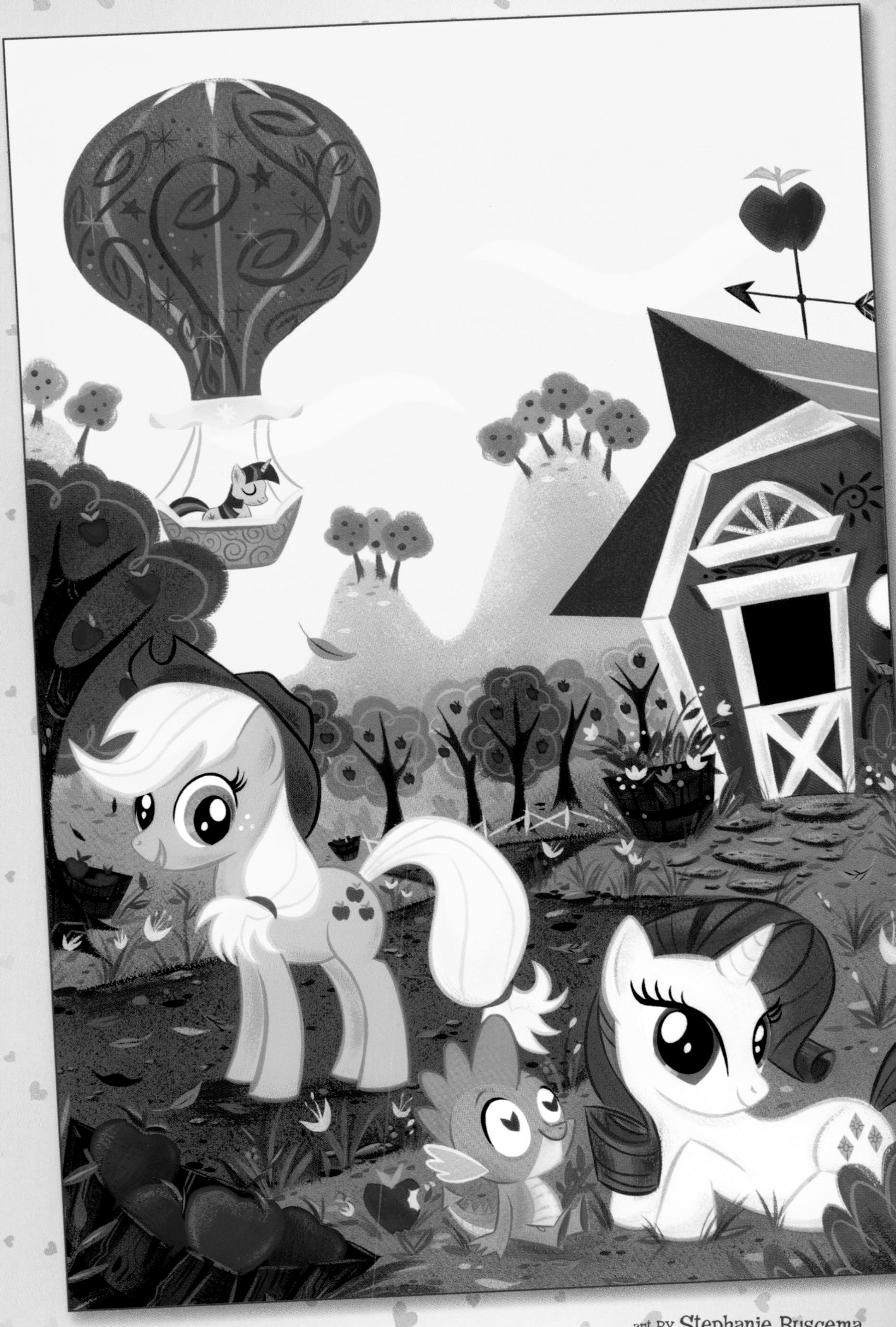

art BY Stephanie Buscema

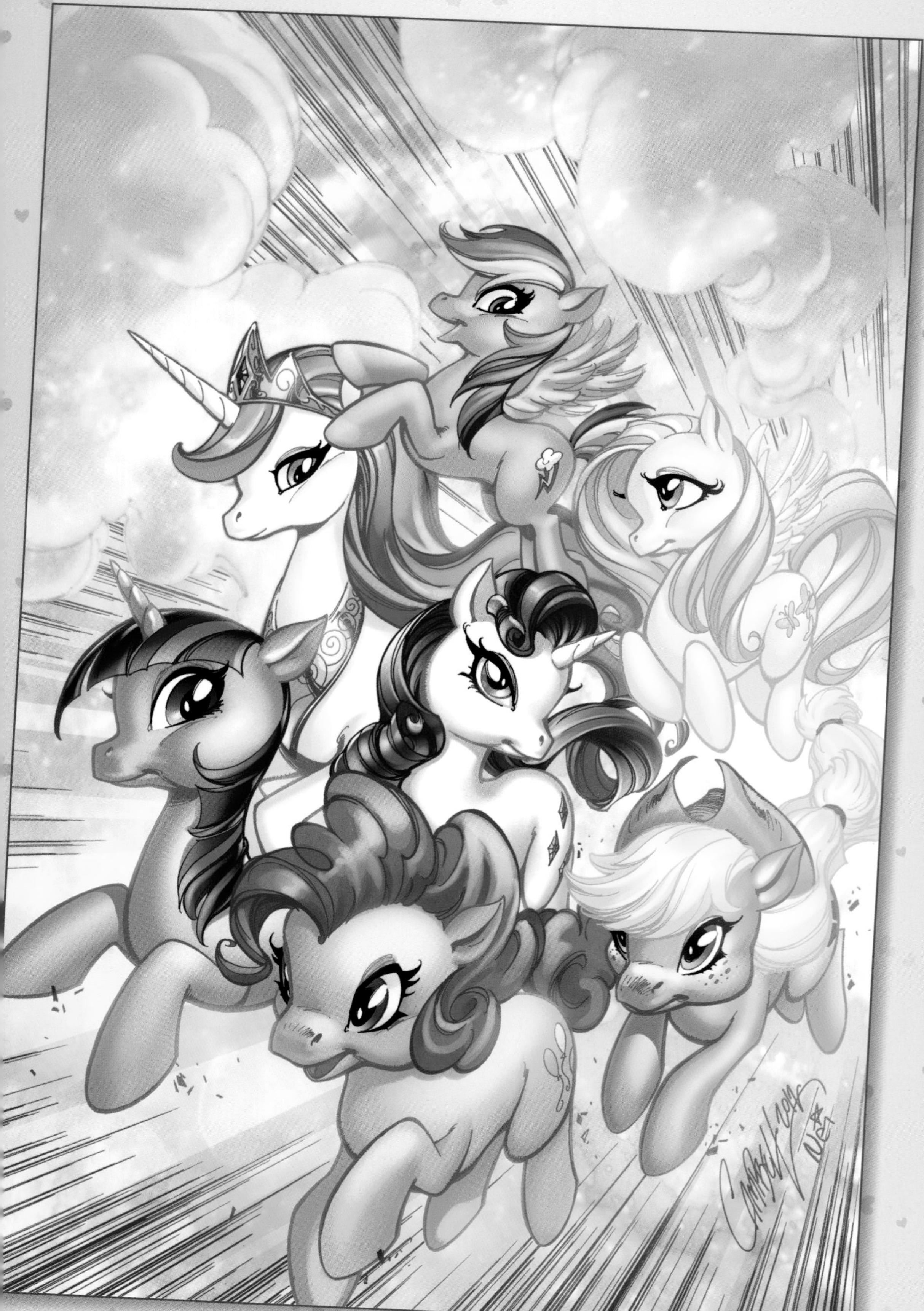

art BY J. Scott Campbell
colors BY Nei Ruffino

my LITTLE PONY™
Friendship is Magic

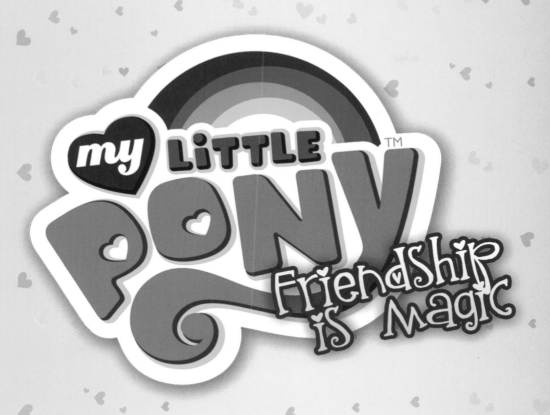

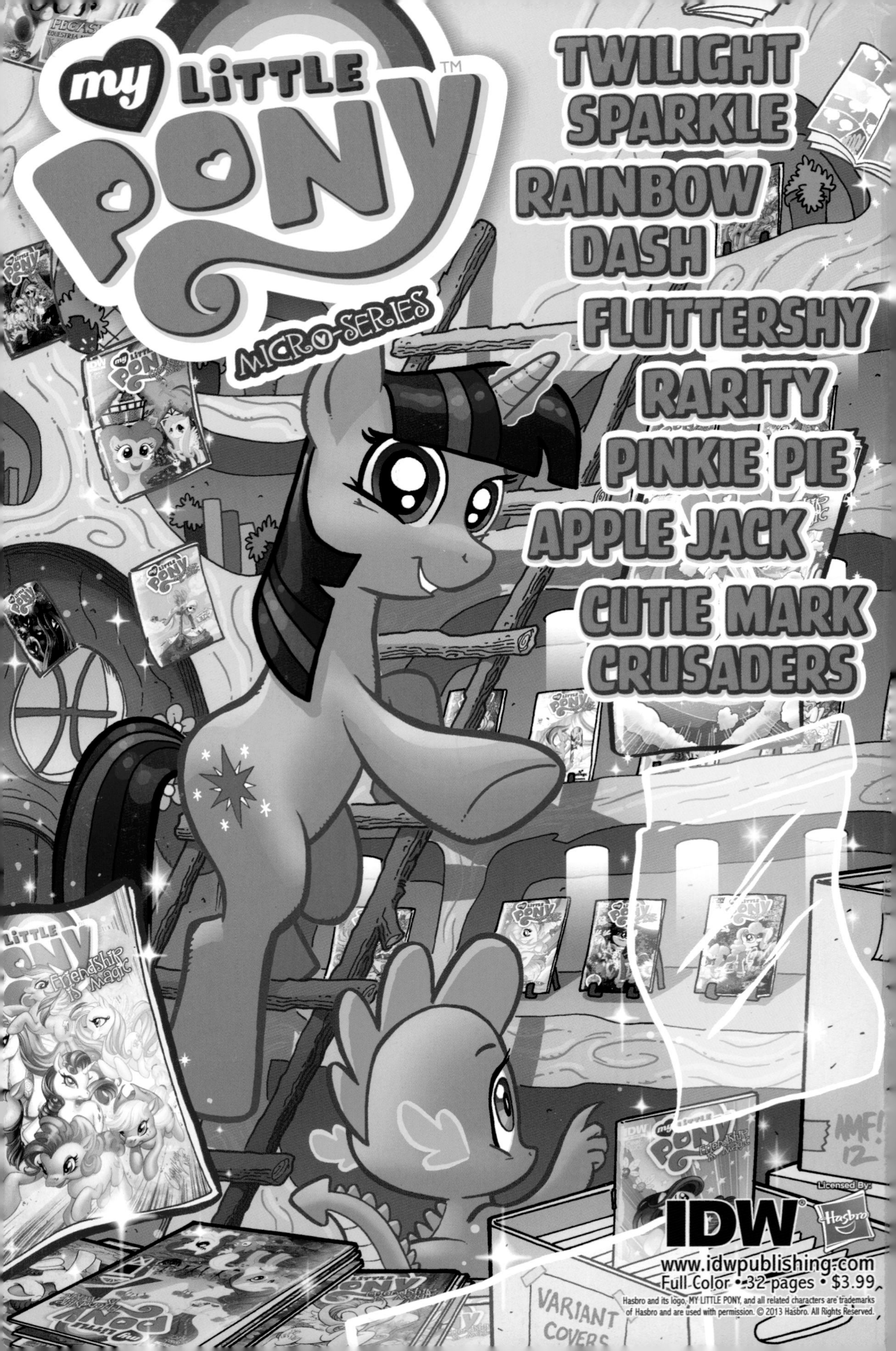

My Little Pony
MICRO-SERIES
TWILIGHT SPARKLE
RAINBOW DASH
FLUTTERSHY
RARITY
PINKIE PIE
APPLE JACK
CUTIE MARK CRUSADERS
VARIANT COVERS
Licensed By:
IDW
Hasbro
www.idwpublishing.com
Full Color • 32 pages • $3.99
Hasbro and its logo, MY LITTLE PONY, and all related characters are trademarks of Hasbro and are used with permission. © 2013 Hasbro. All Rights Reserved.

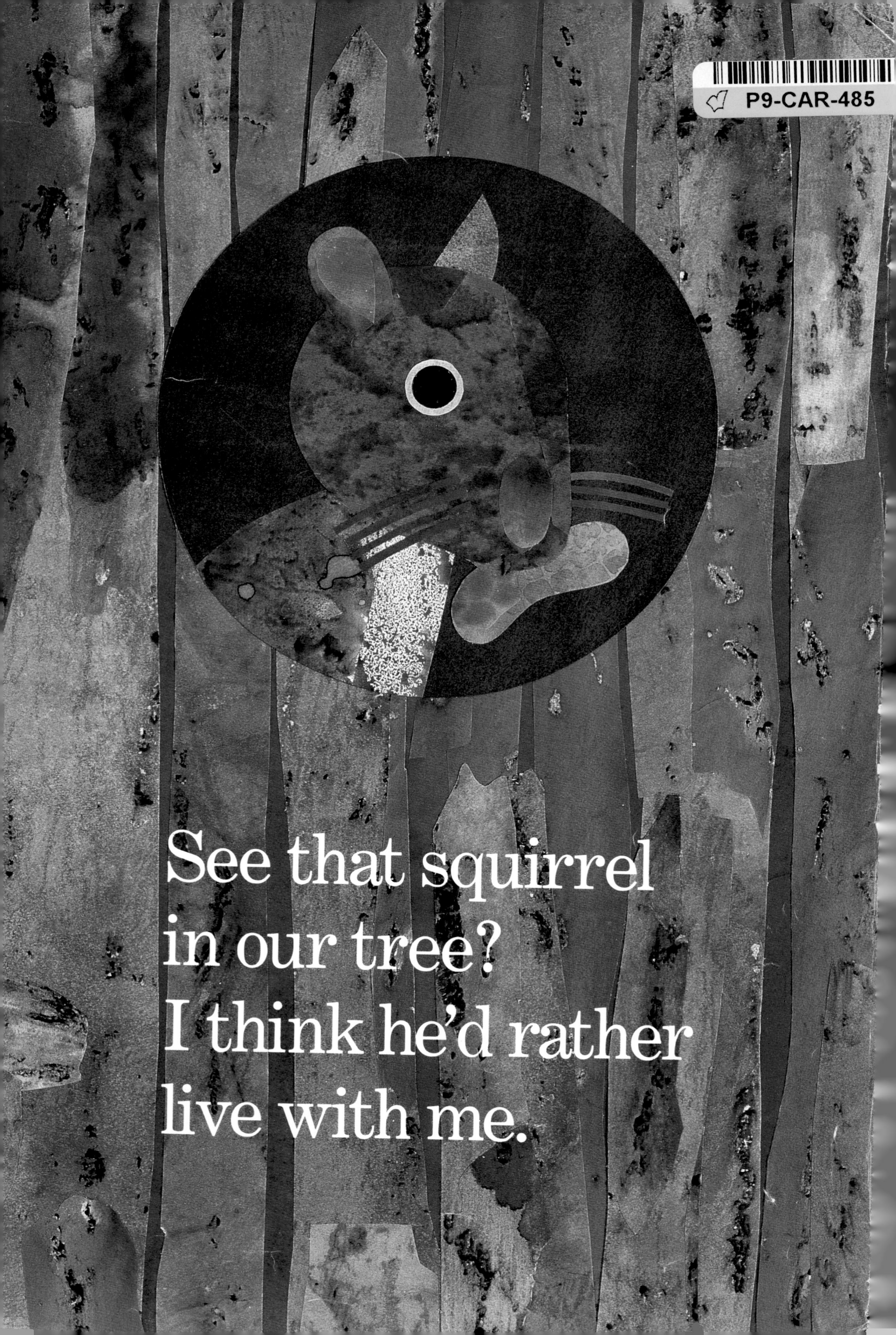

See that squirrel
in our tree?
I think he'd rather
live with me.

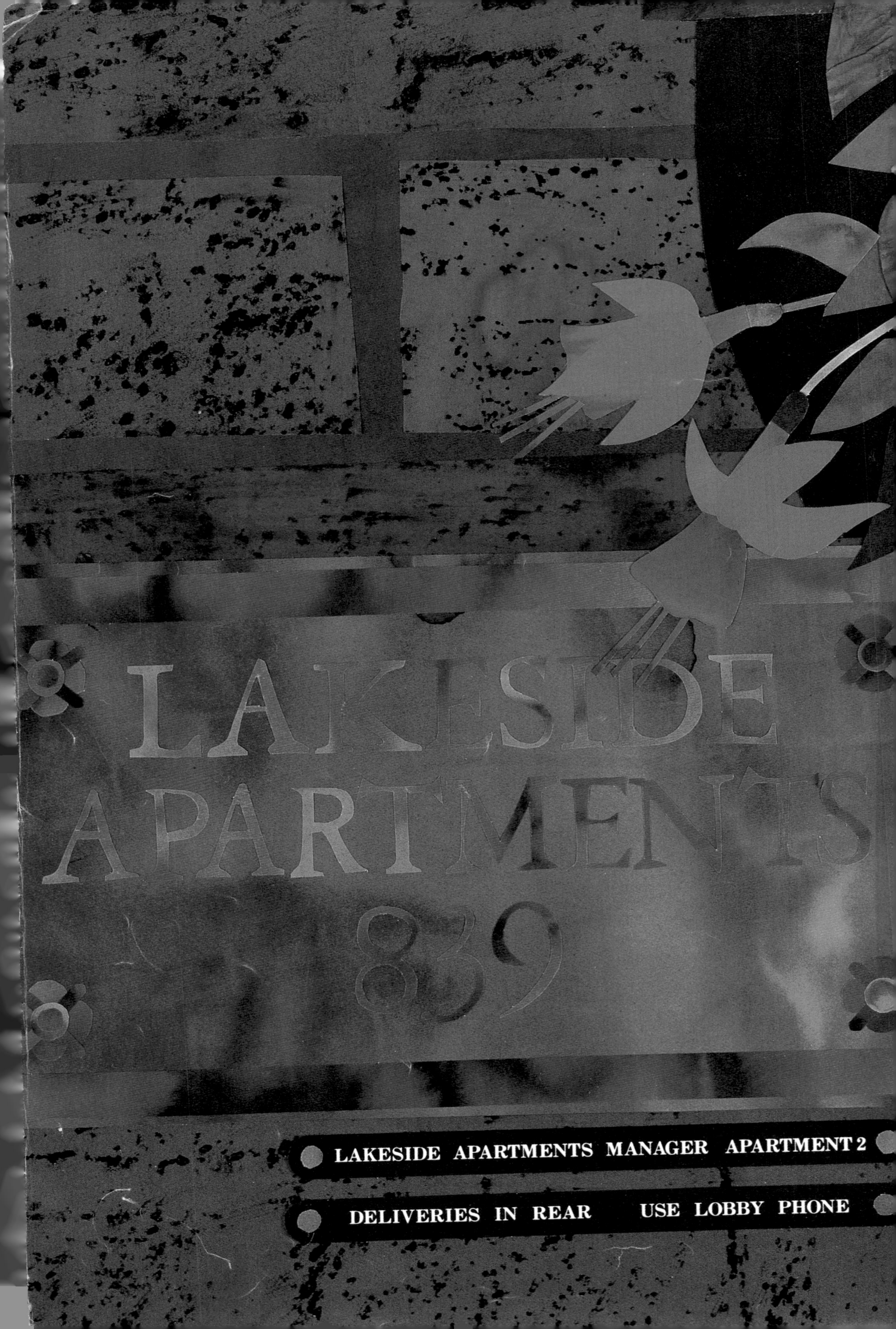
LAKESIDE
APARTMENTS
839
LAKESIDE APARTMENTS MANAGER APARTMENT 2
DELIVERIES IN REAR USE LOBBY PHONE

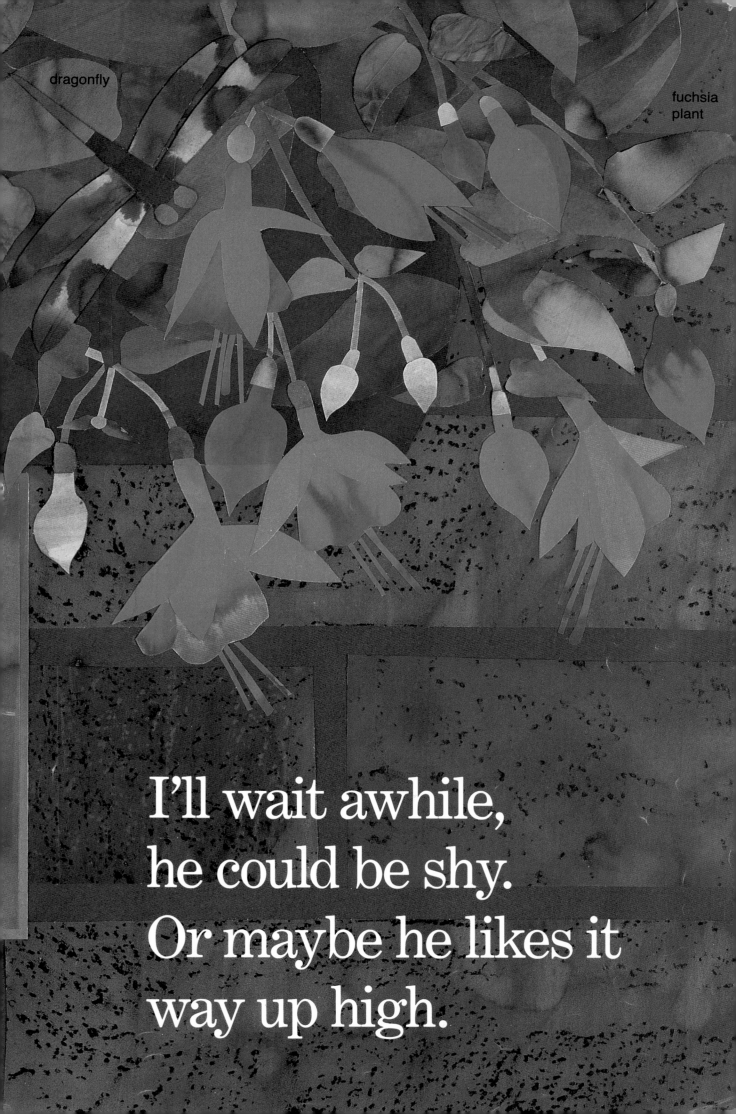

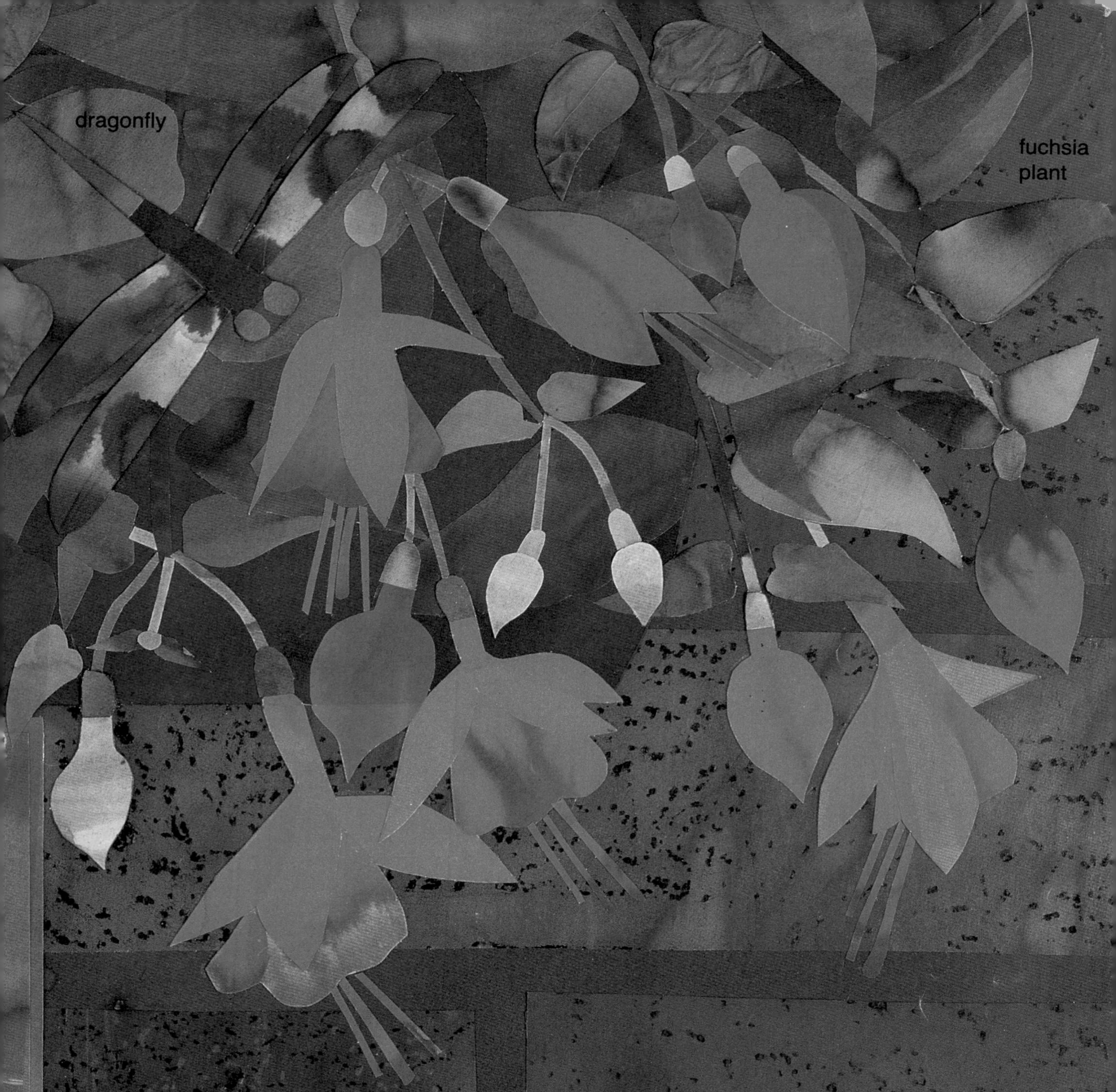
dragonfly
fuchsia
plant

I'll wait awhile,
he could be shy.
Or maybe he likes it
way up high.

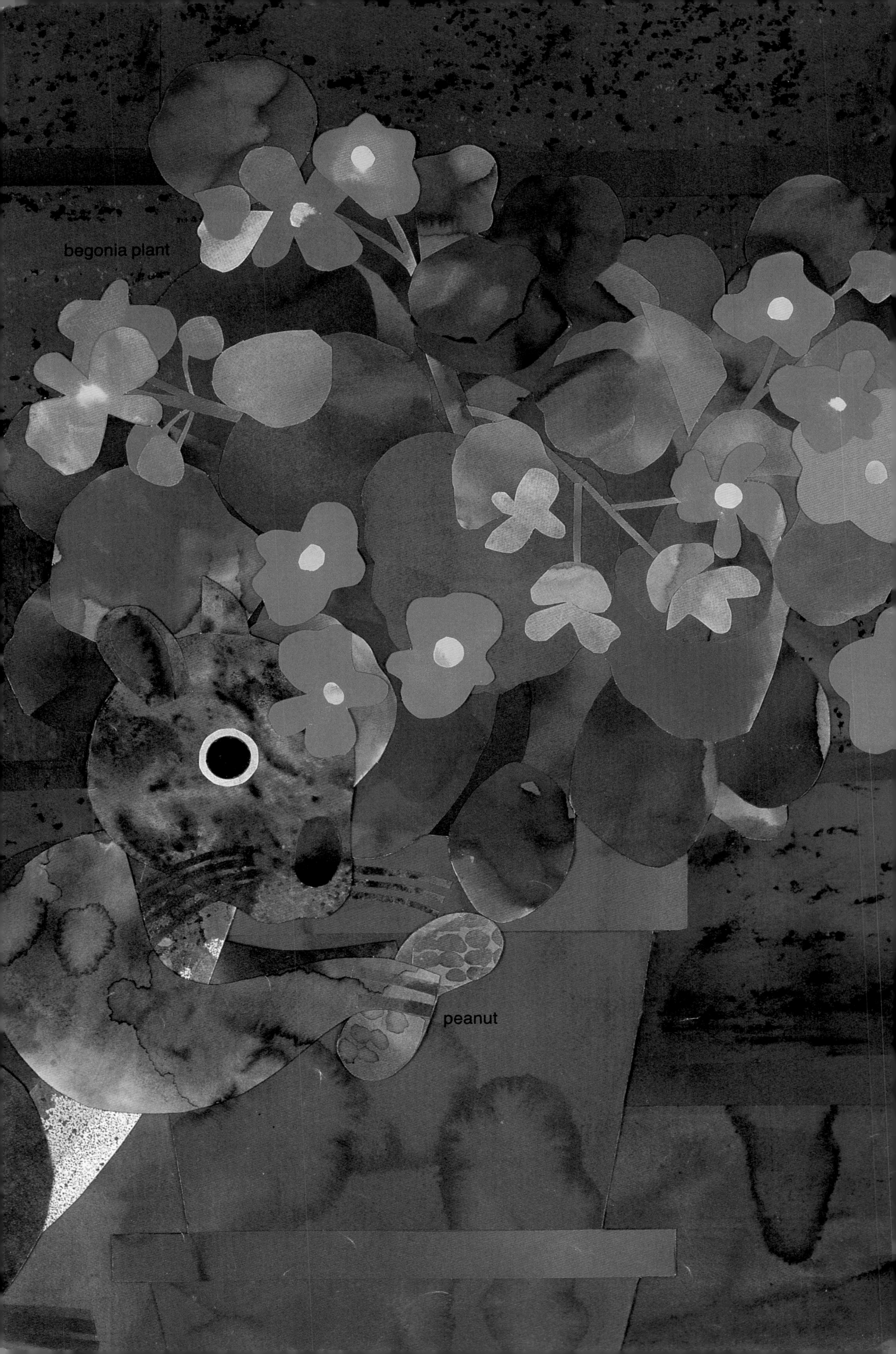
begonia plant
peanut

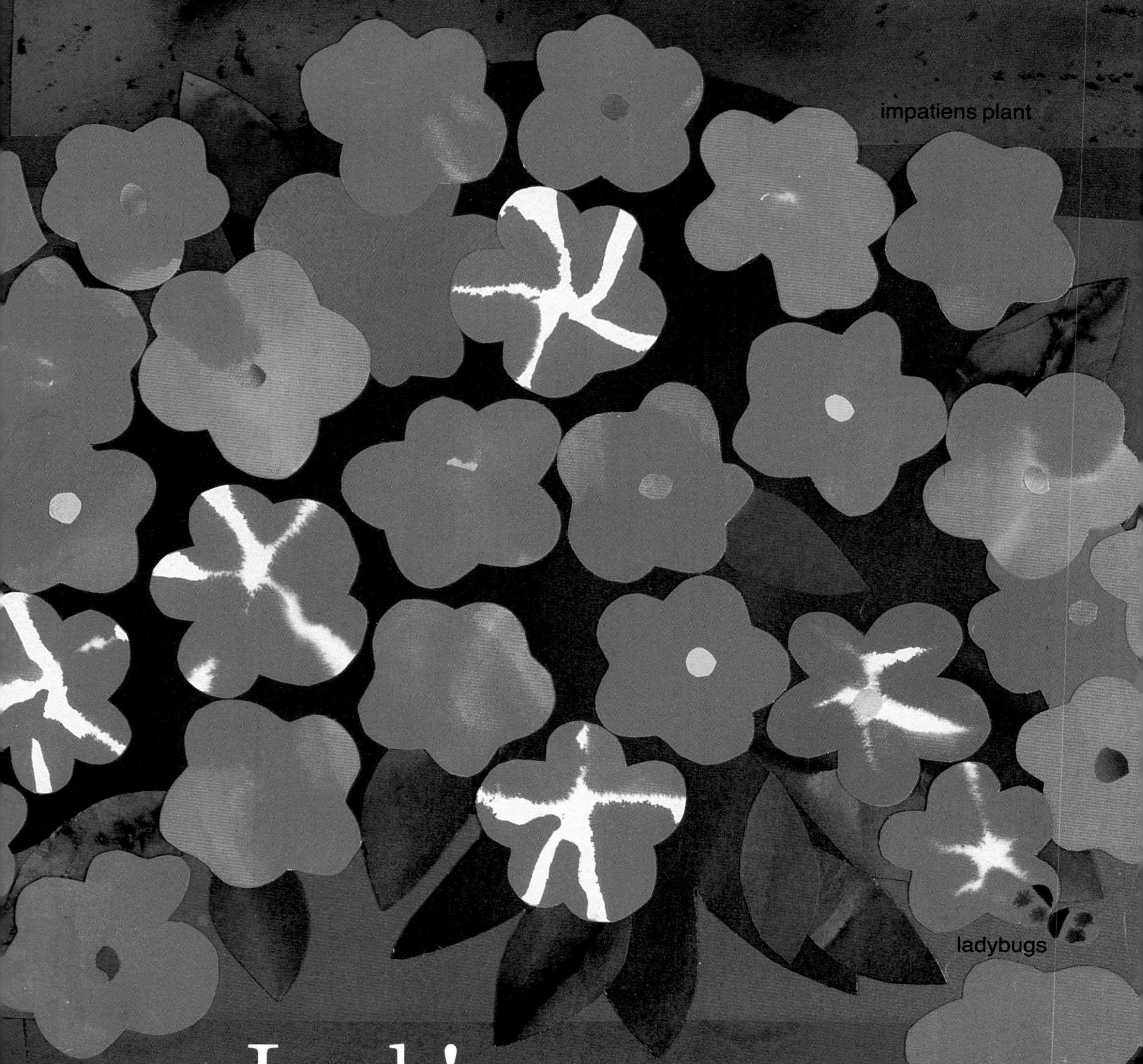
impatiens plant
ladybugs

Look!
Here he comes,
trying to hide.
He can't wait
to get inside.

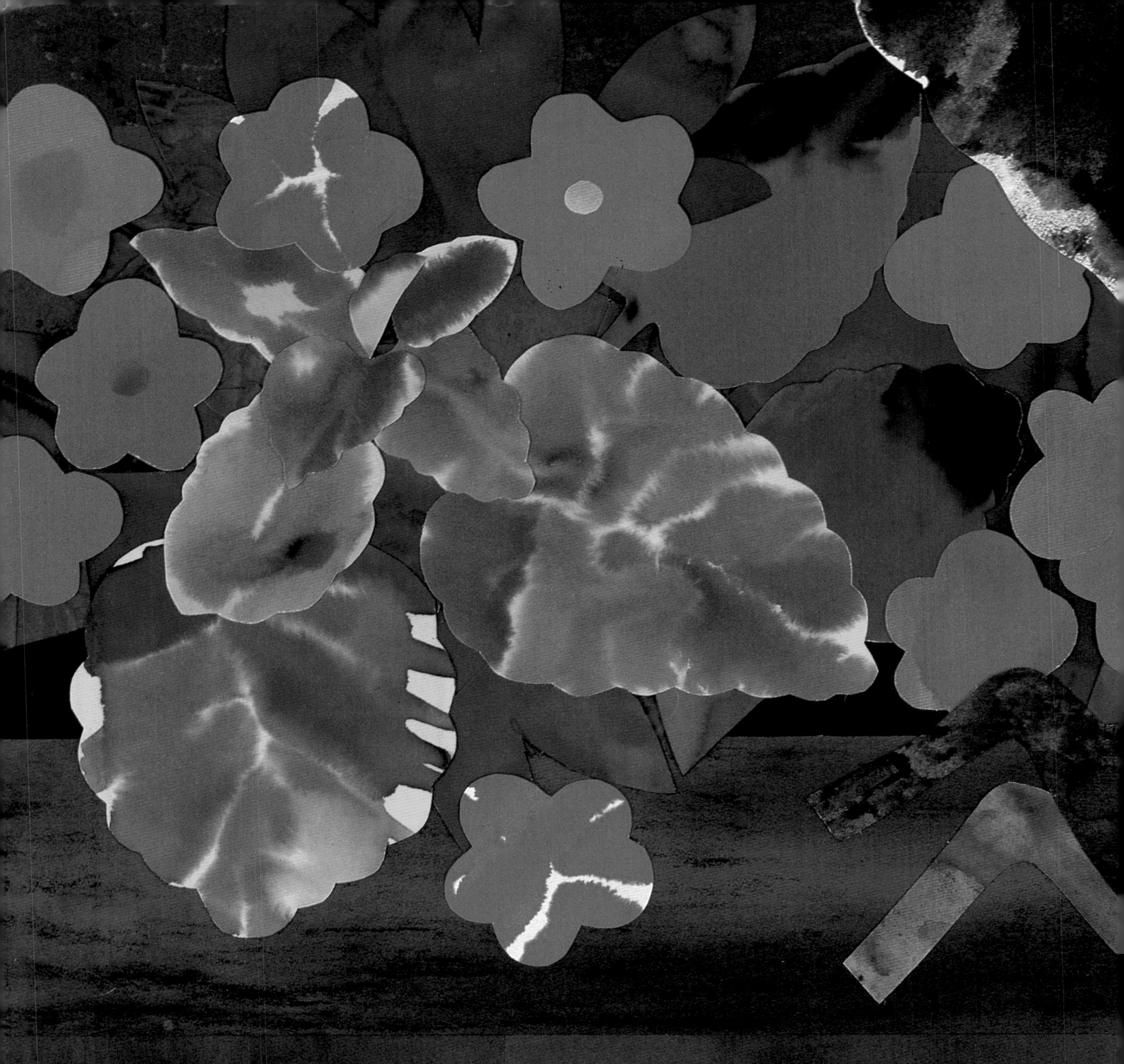

He's in the flowers,
he's really bad.
He's digging up bulbs.
My mom is mad!

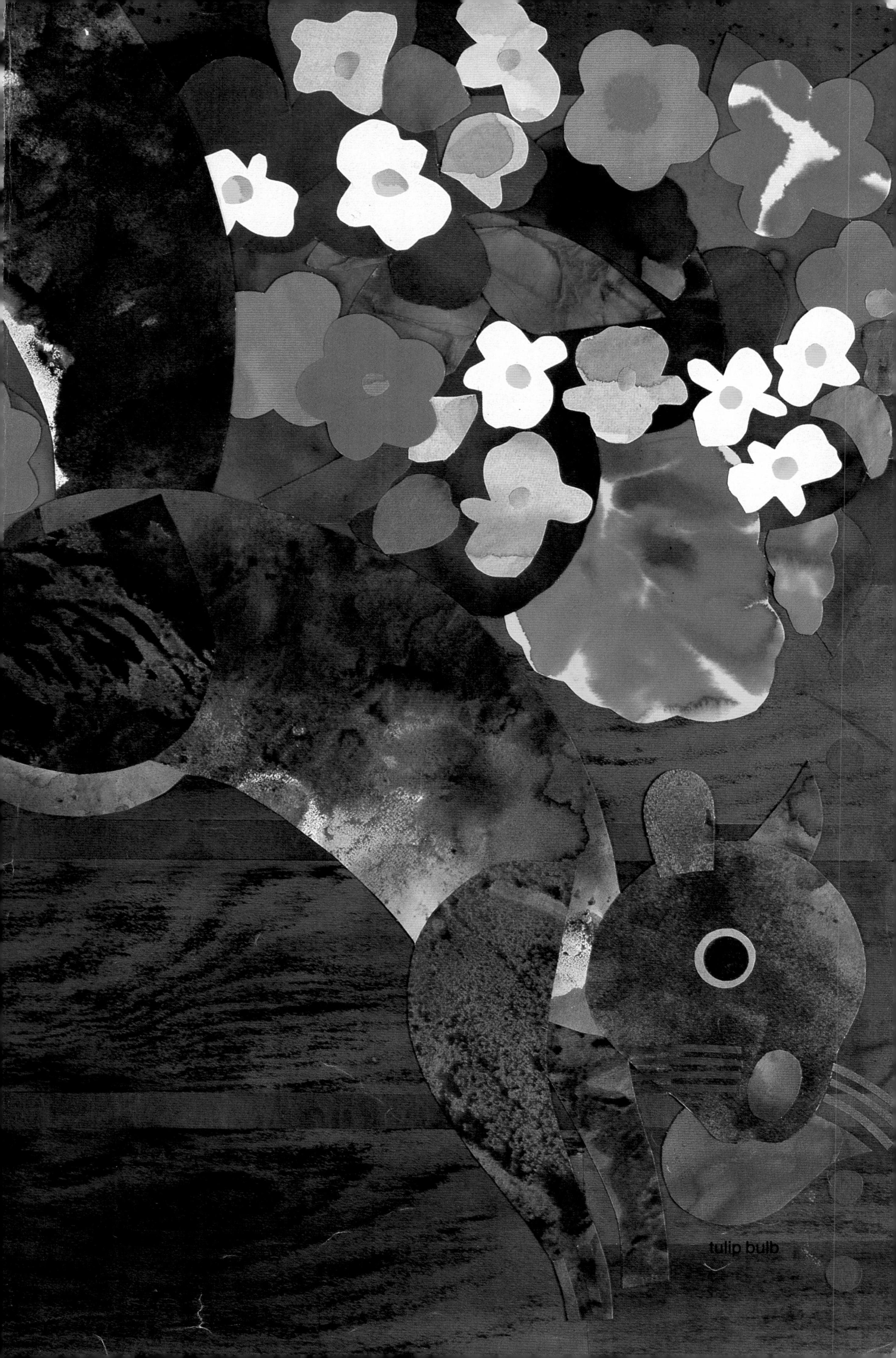
tulip bulb

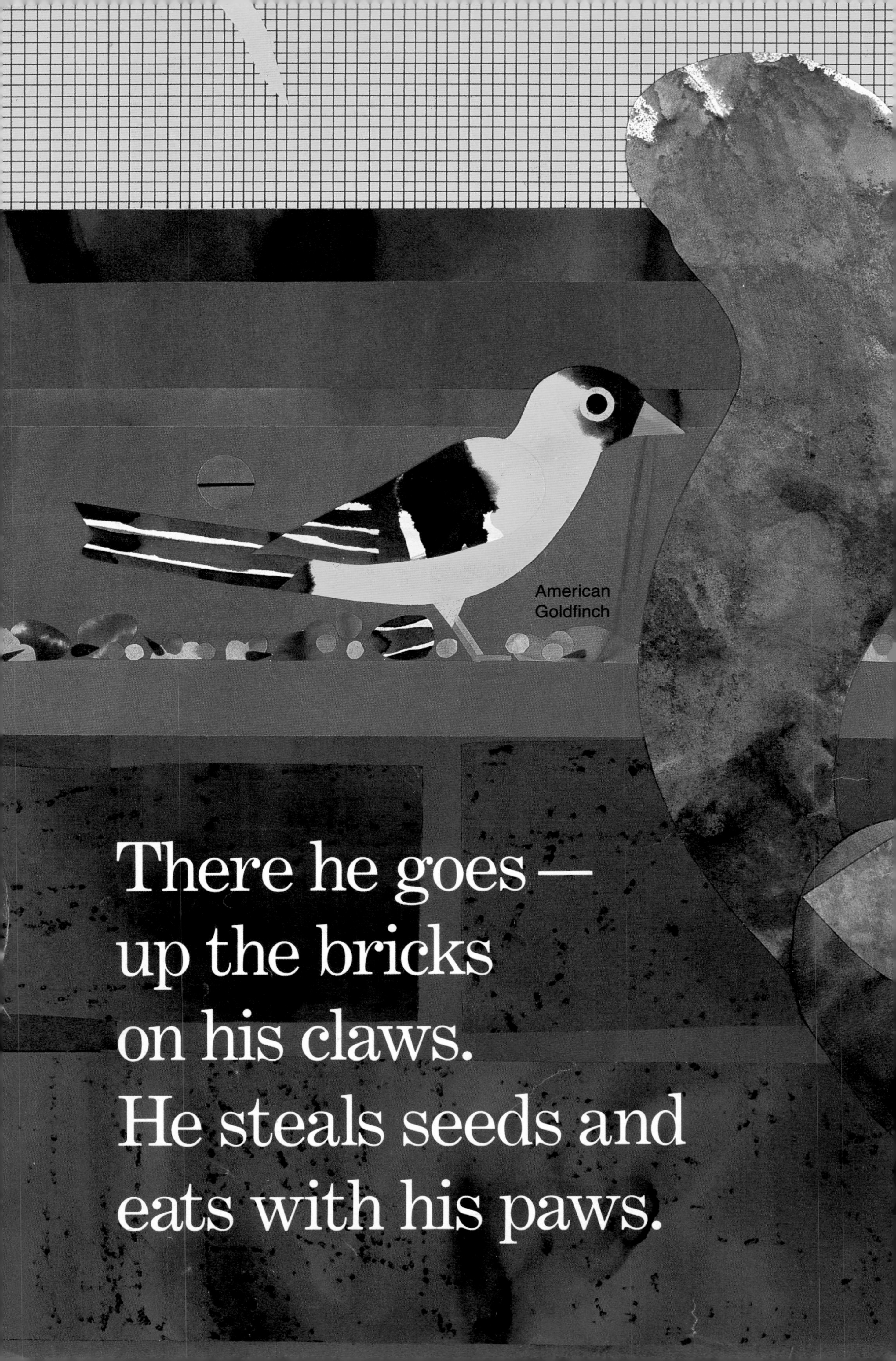
American
Goldfinch

There he goes —
up the bricks
on his claws.
He steals seeds and
eats with his paws.

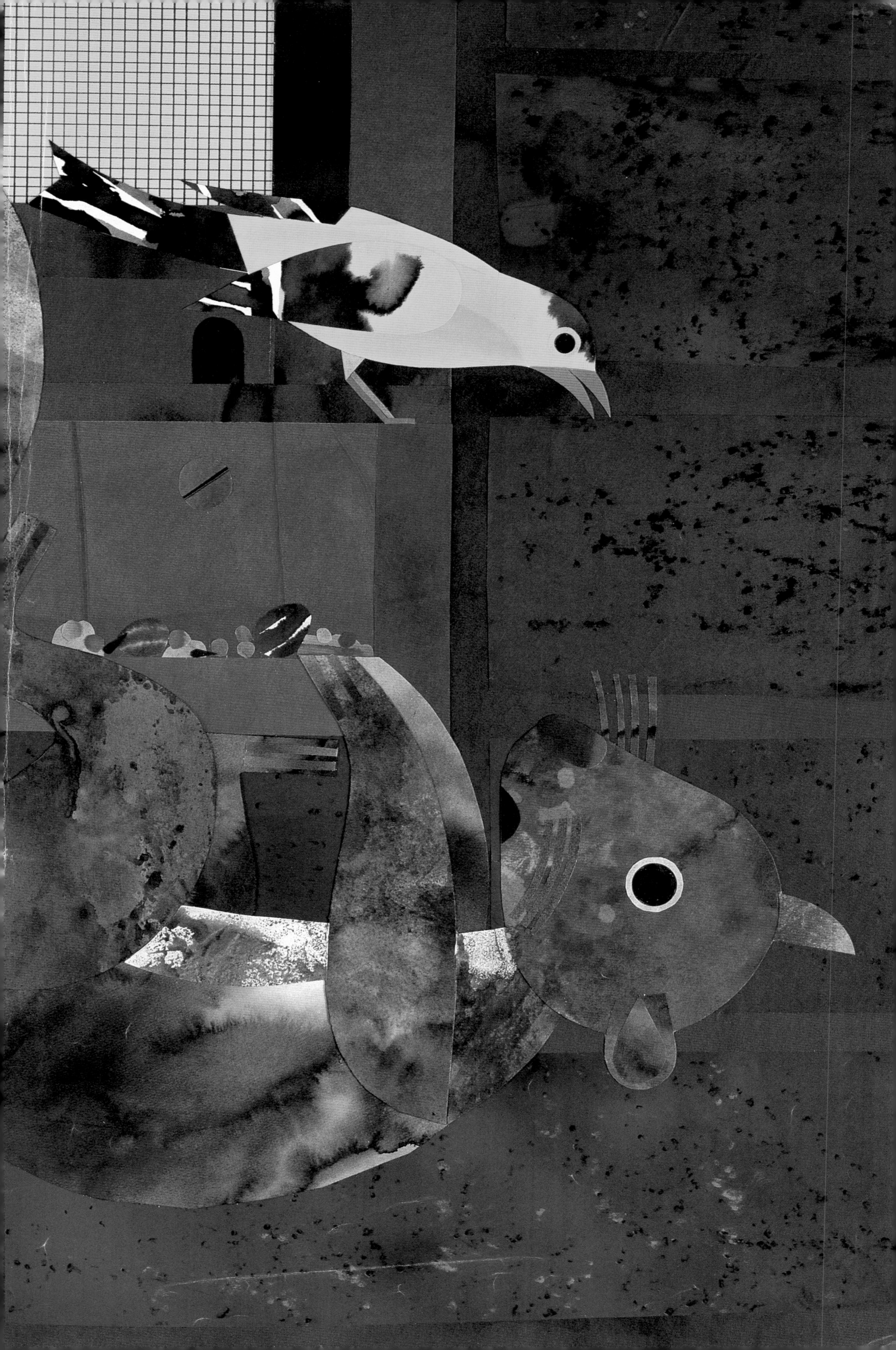

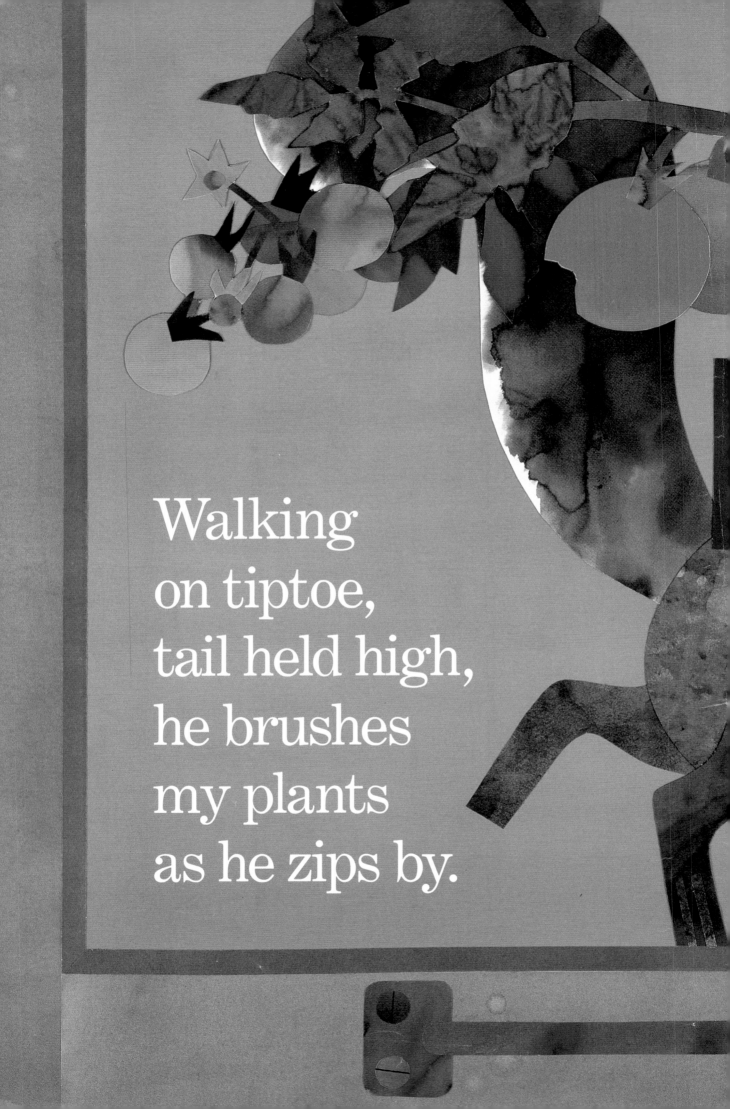

Walking
on tiptoe,
tail held high,
he brushes
my plants
as he zips by.

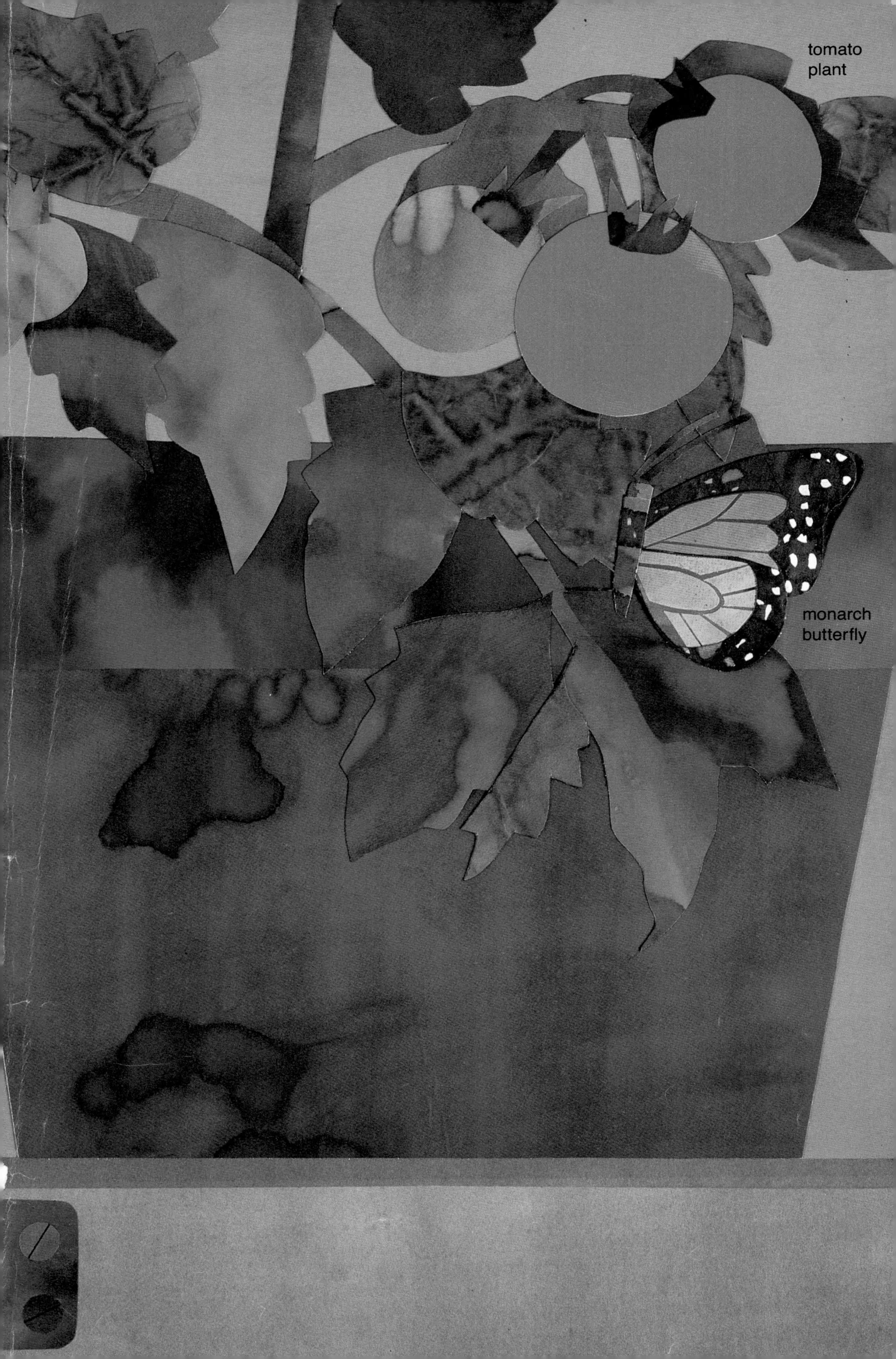
tomato
plant
monarch
butterfly

In our
window box,
watching us eat,
he sits on the flowers
and begs for a treat.

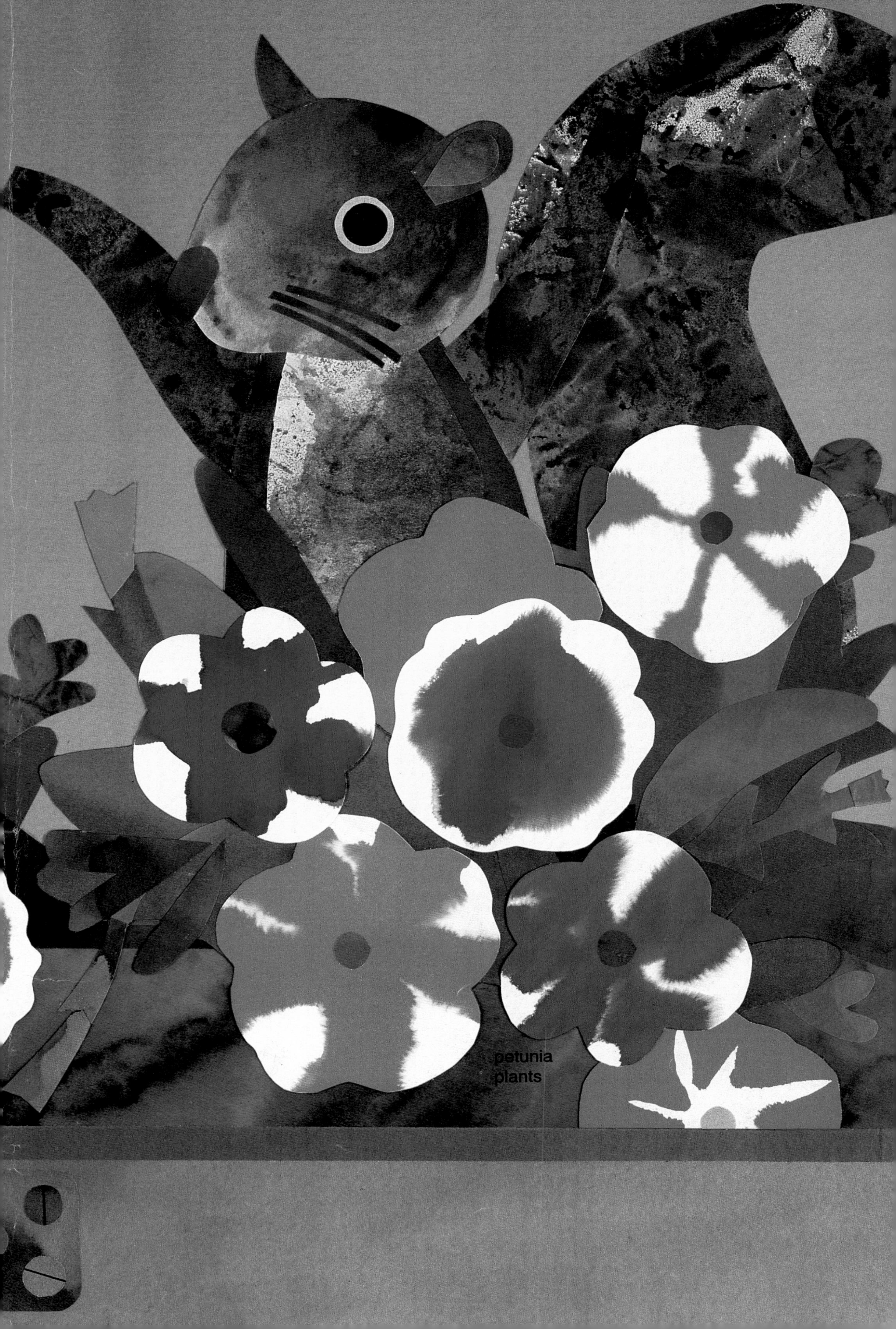
petunia
plants

I opened my window
for some fresh air,
but I forgot the screen
had a tear.

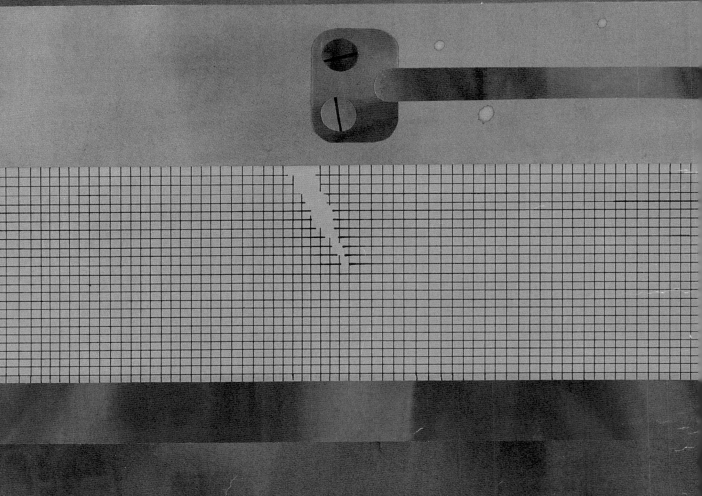

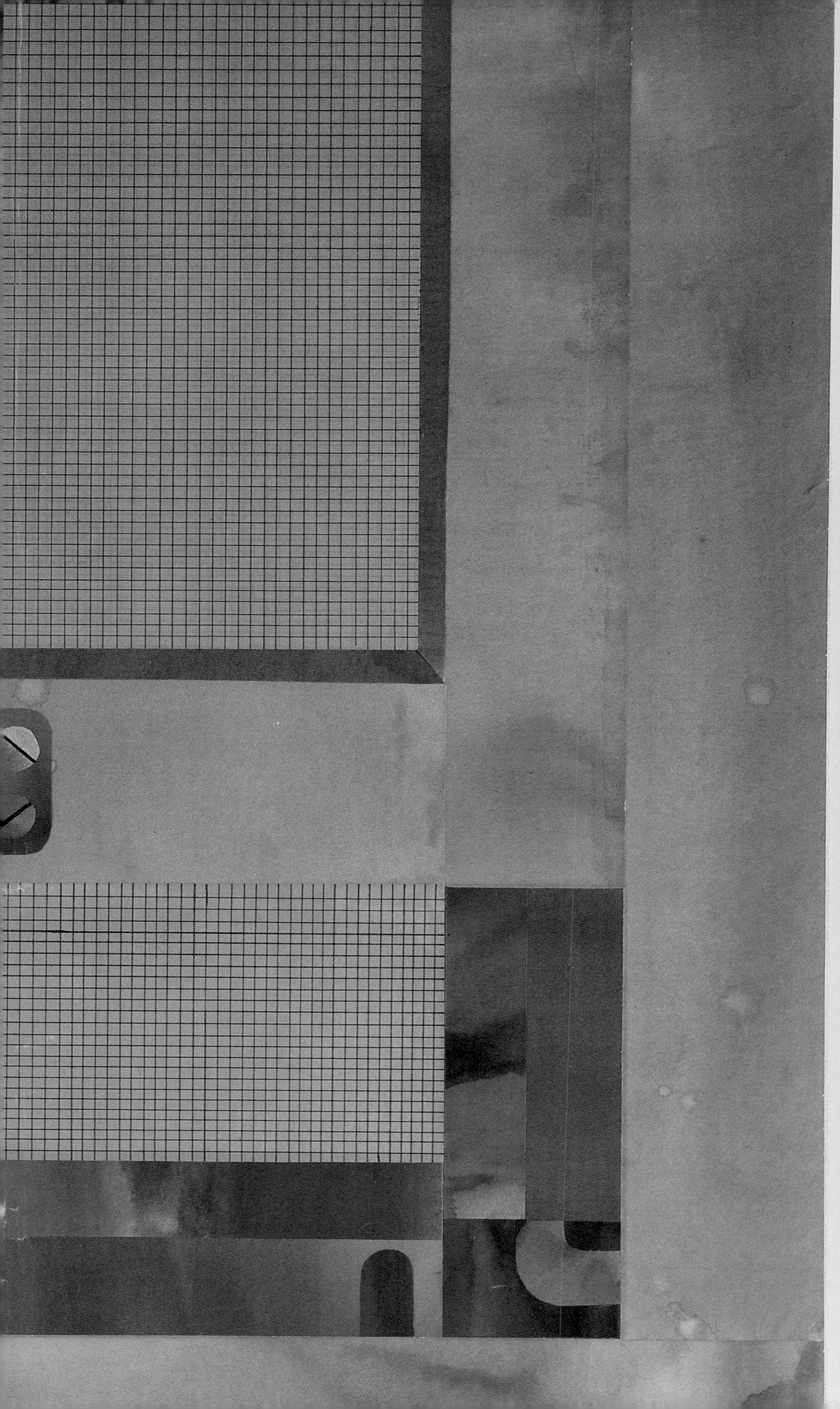

When I came back, guess what I found?

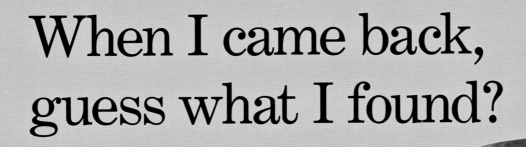

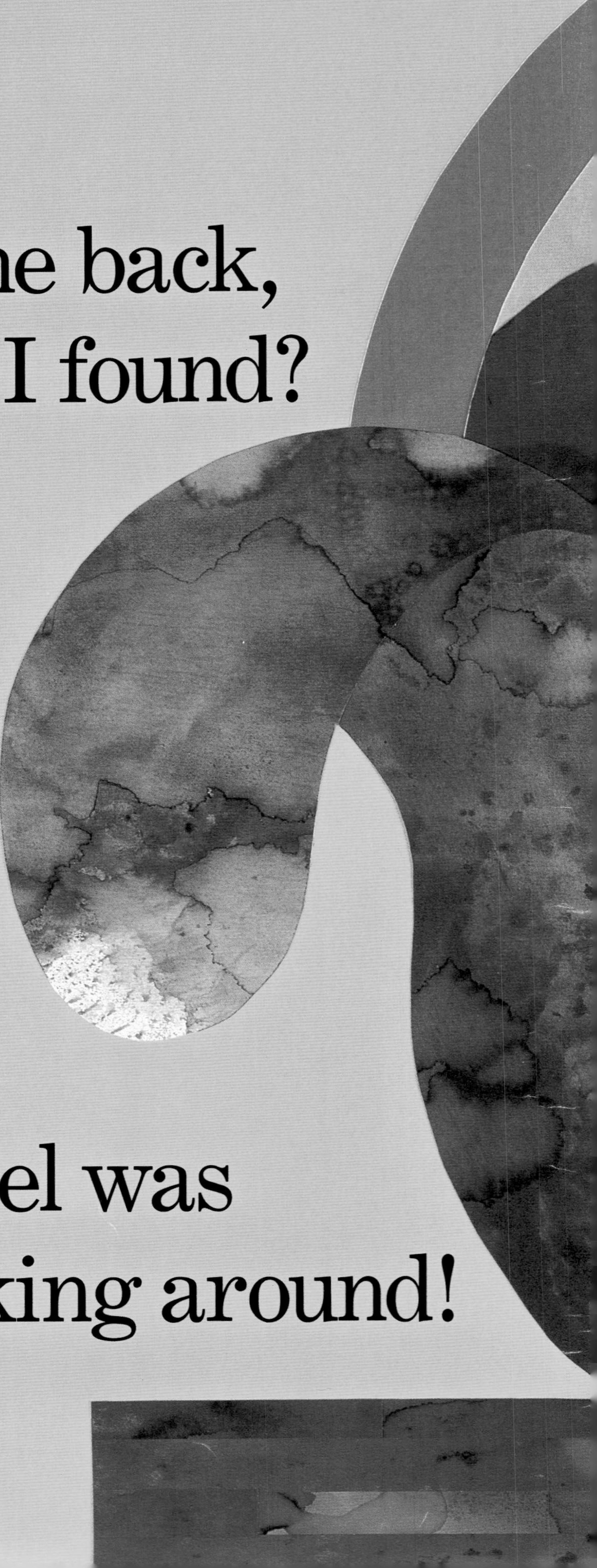

That squirrel was there — looking around!

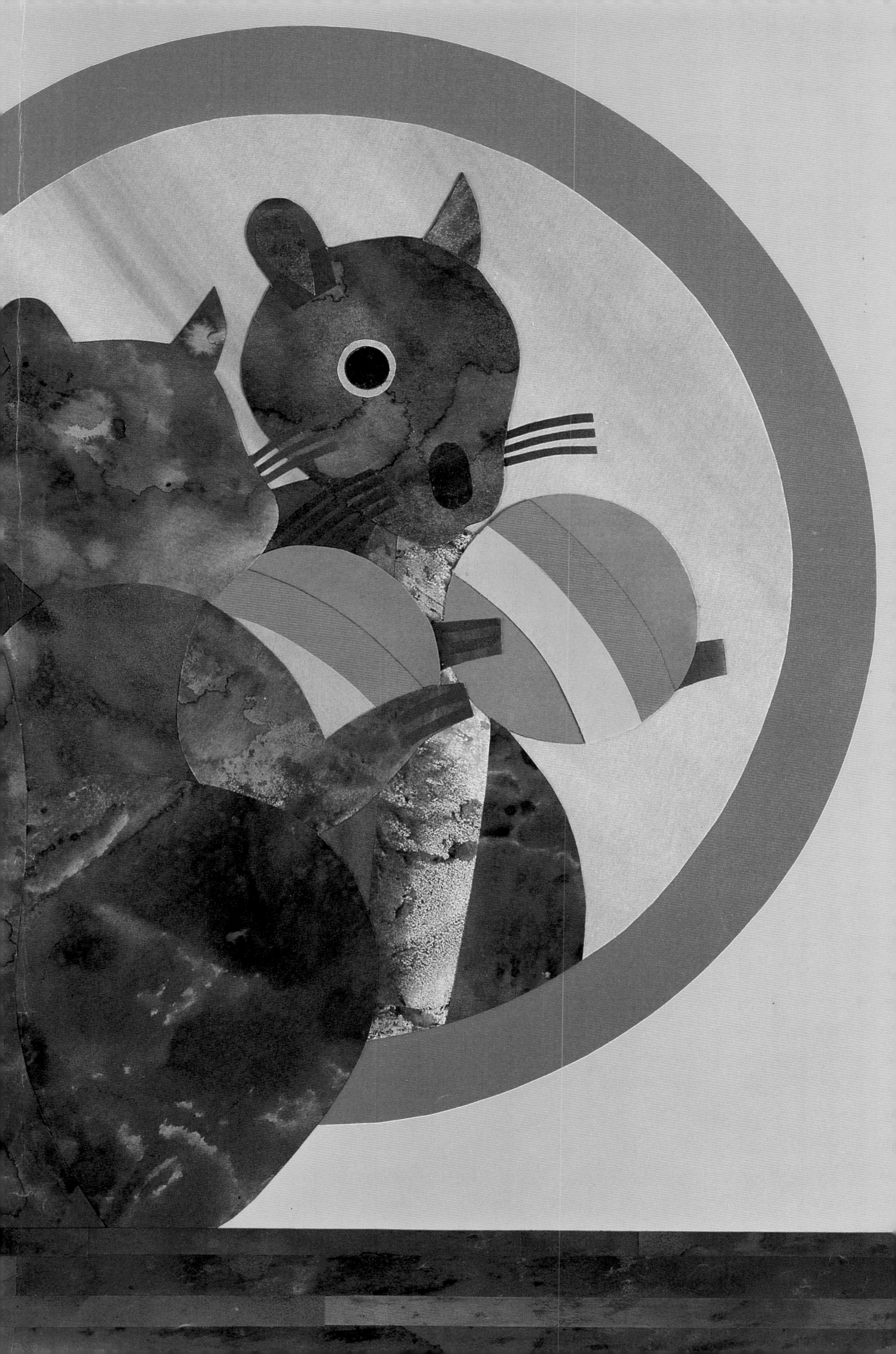

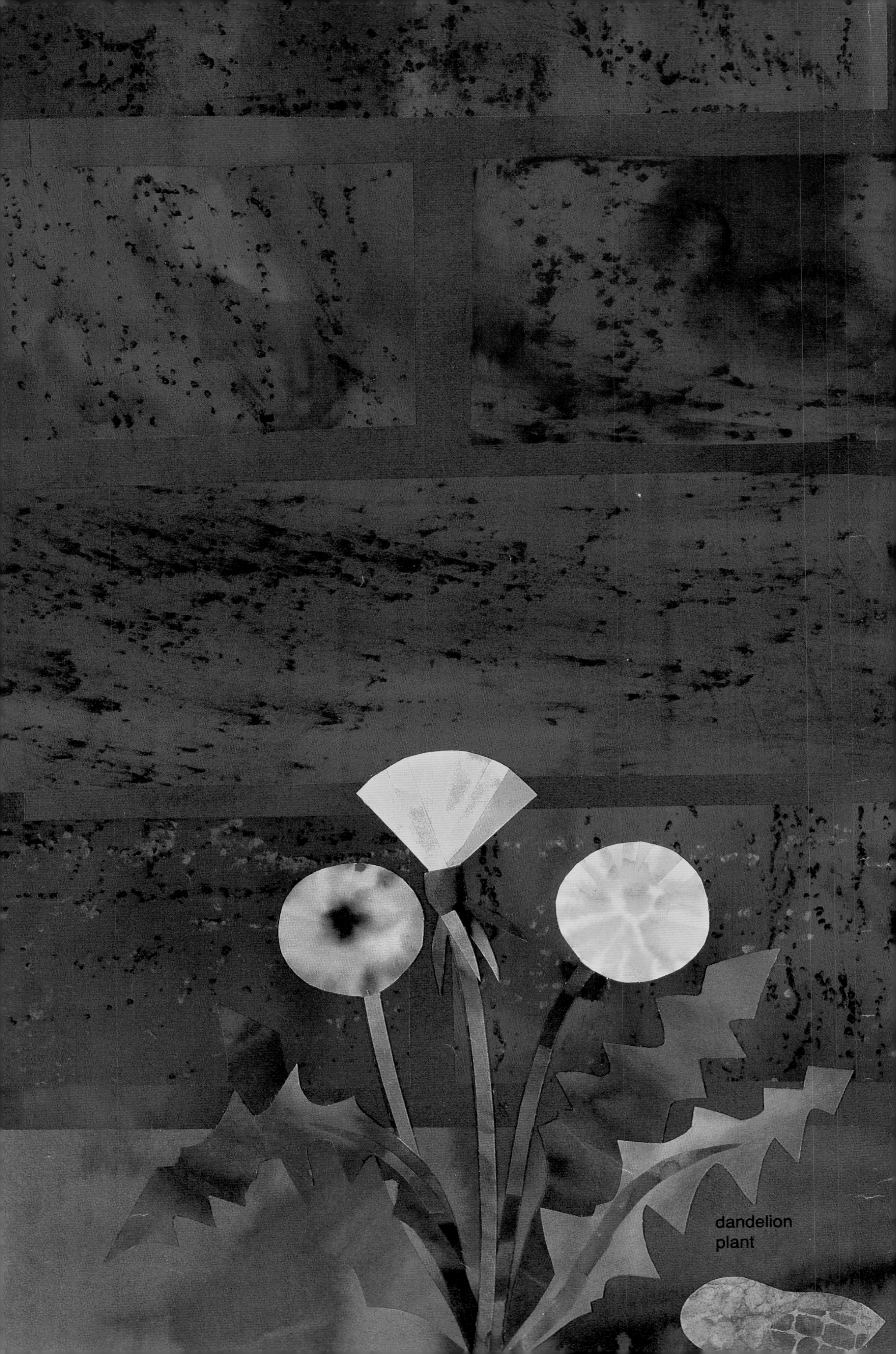
dandelion
plant

So I got some nuts,
ran out the door,
tapped one
on the sidewalk,
and left a few more.

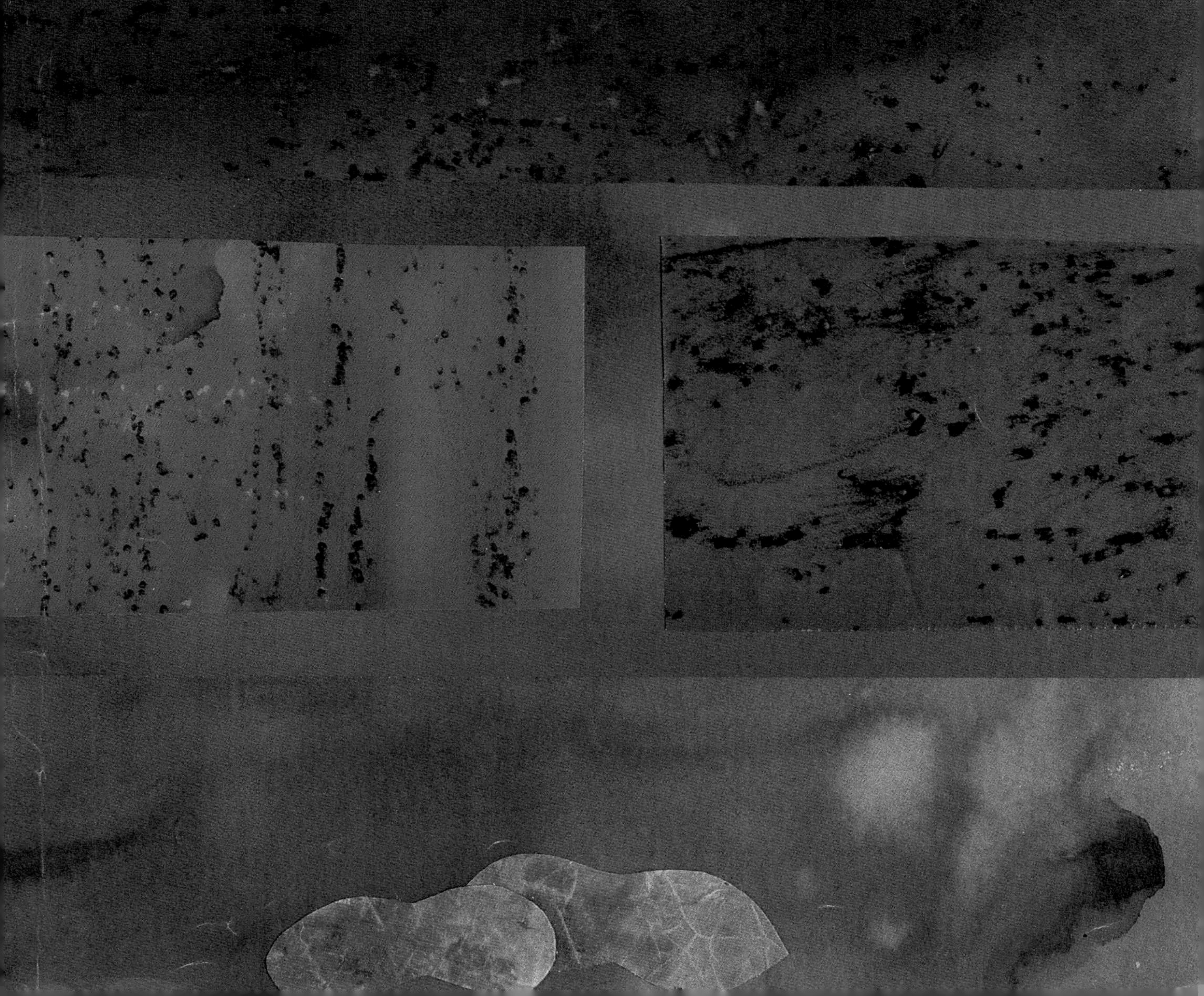

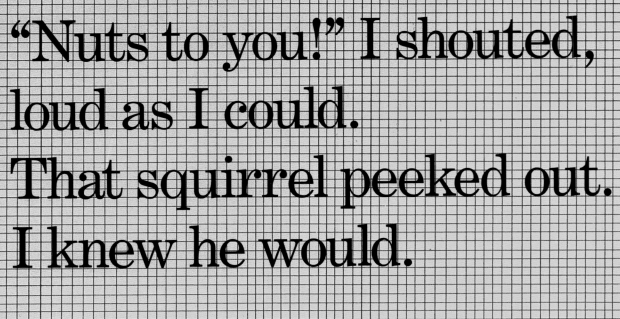

"Nuts to you!" I shouted,
loud as I could.
That squirrel peeked out.
I knew he would.

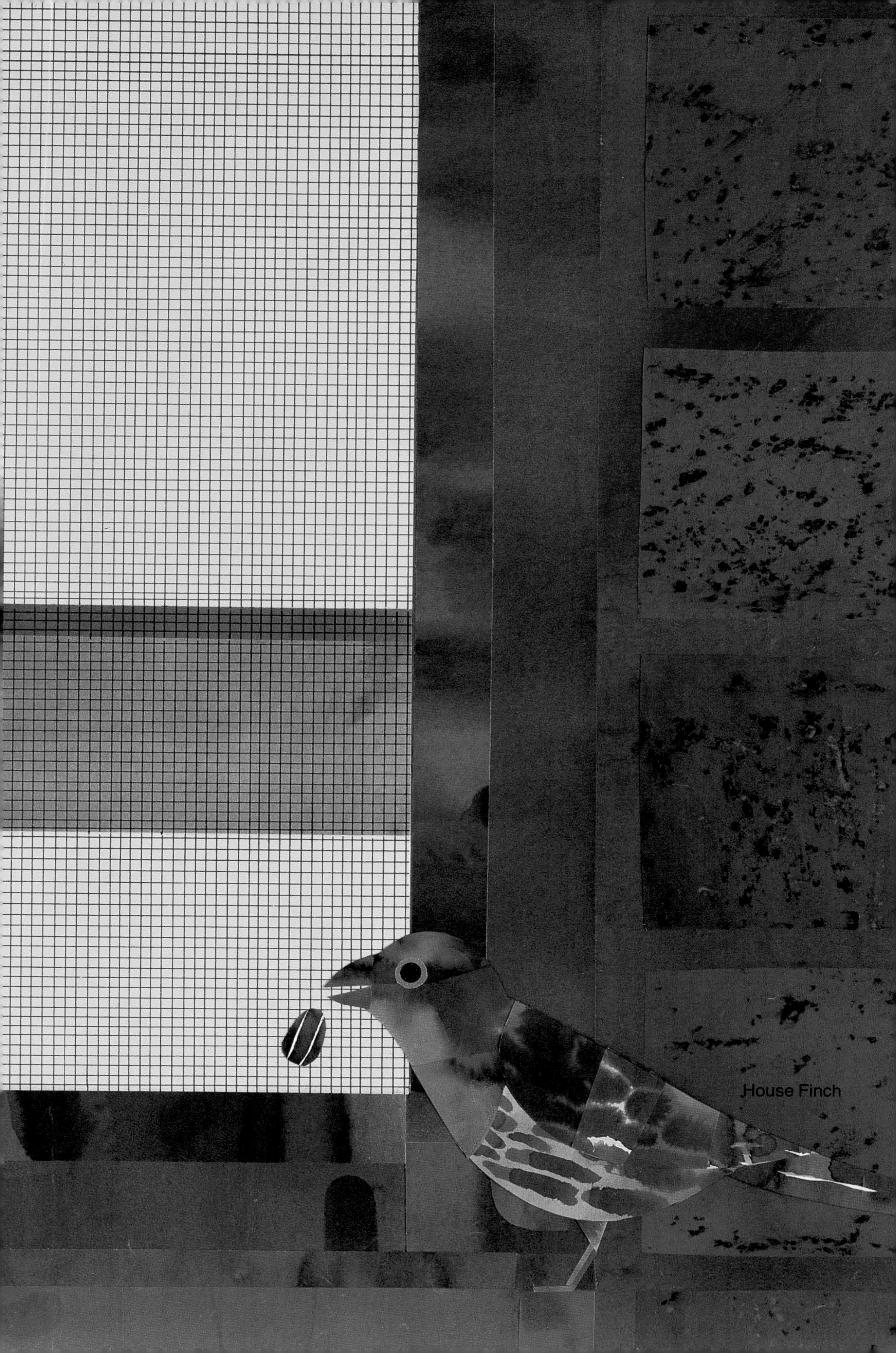
House Finch

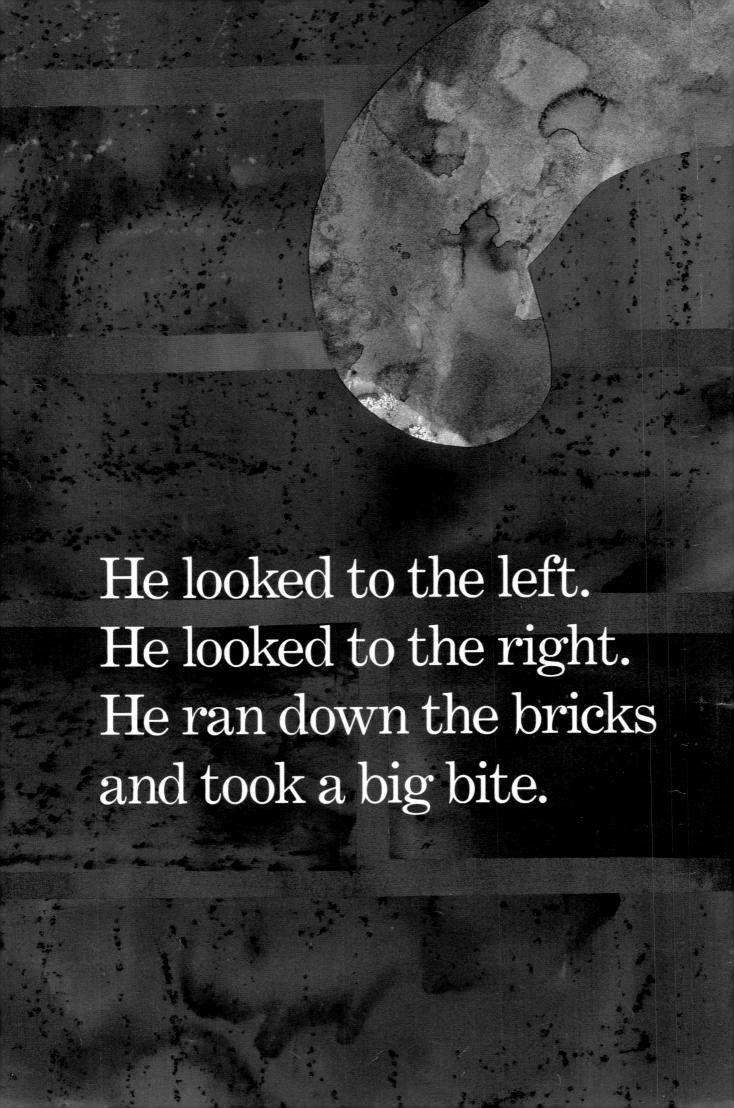

He looked to the left.
He looked to the right.
He ran down the bricks
and took a big bite.

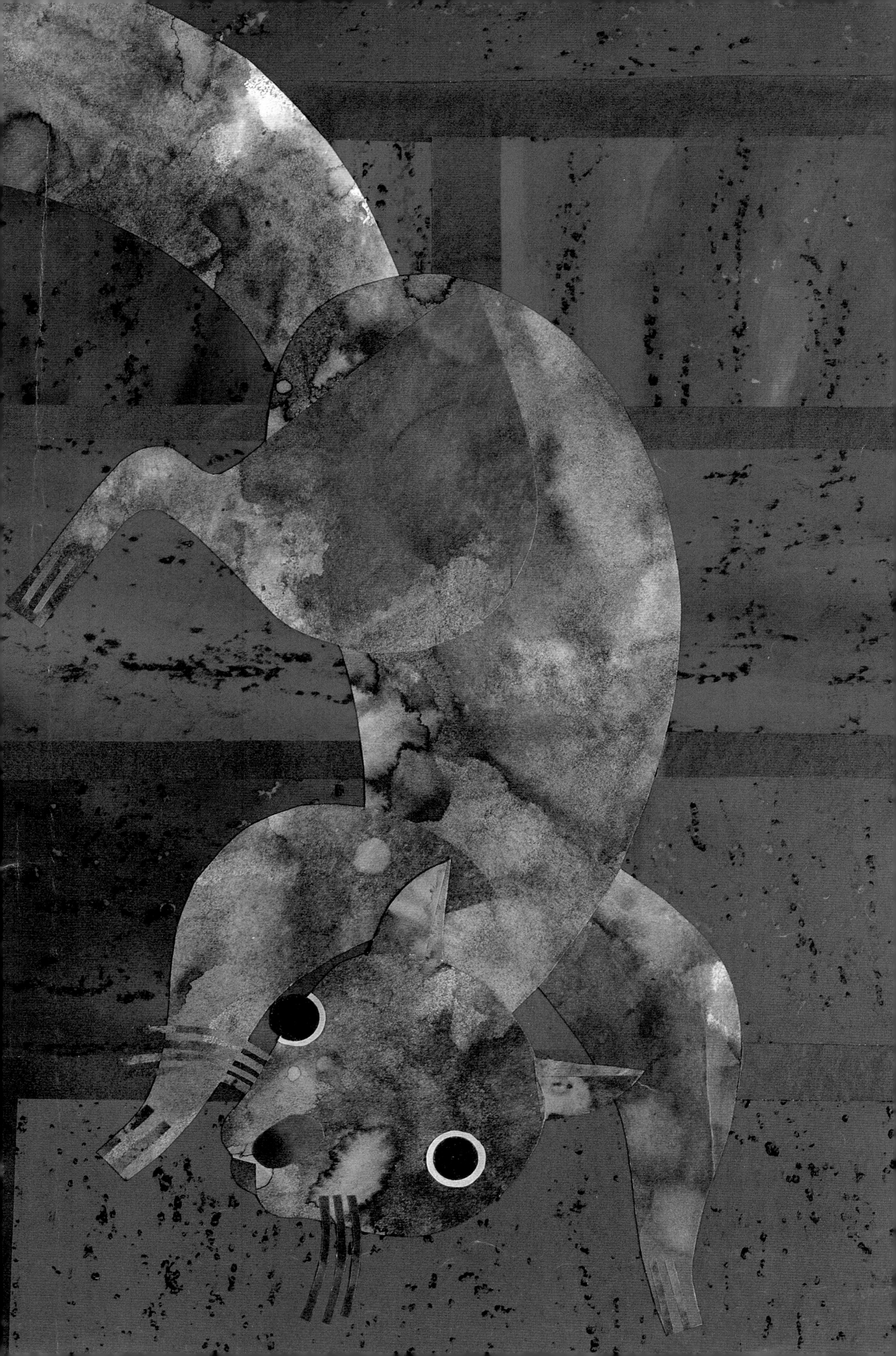

He ate all those nuts,
then scampered away,
but he'll get hungry
again someday.

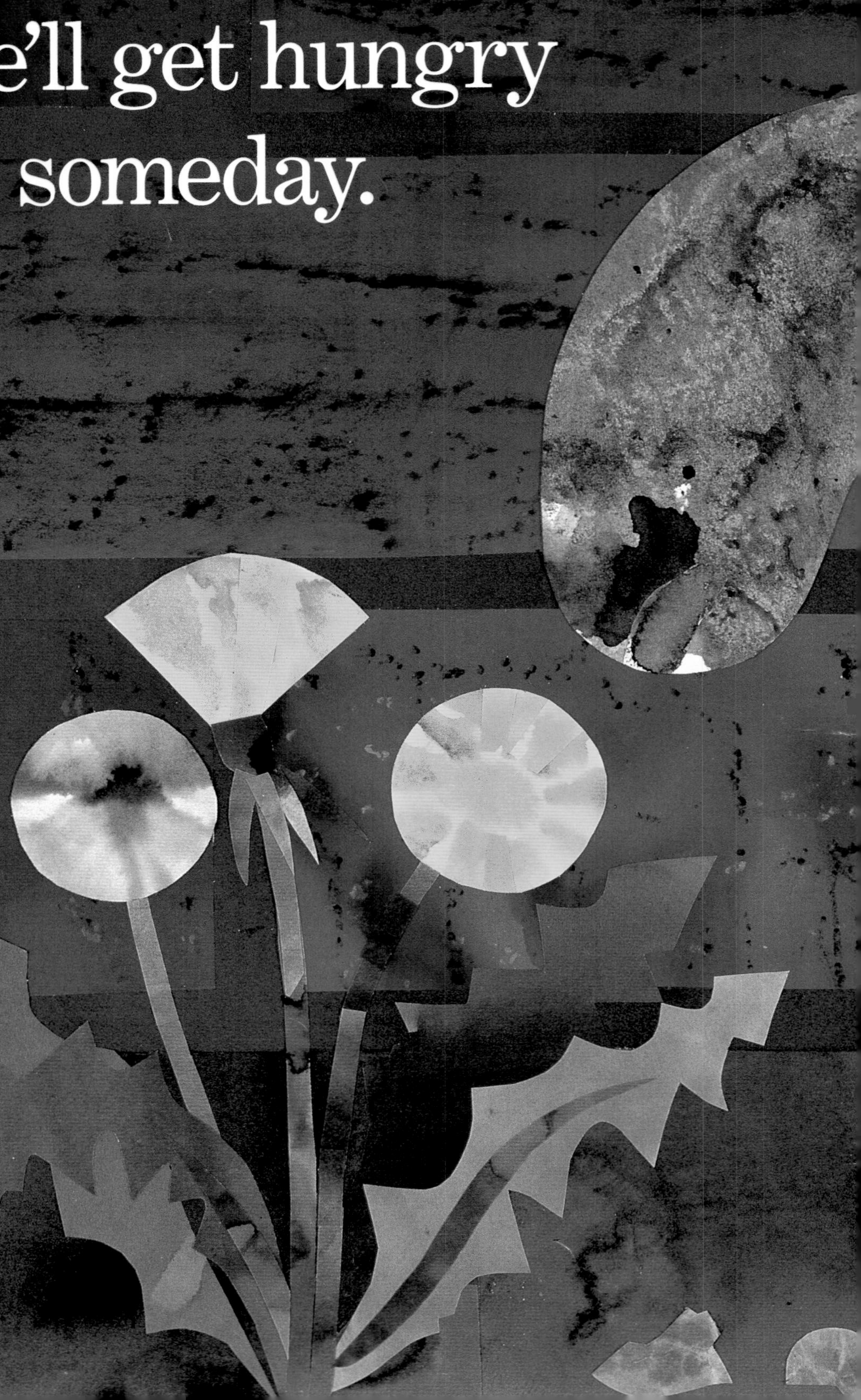

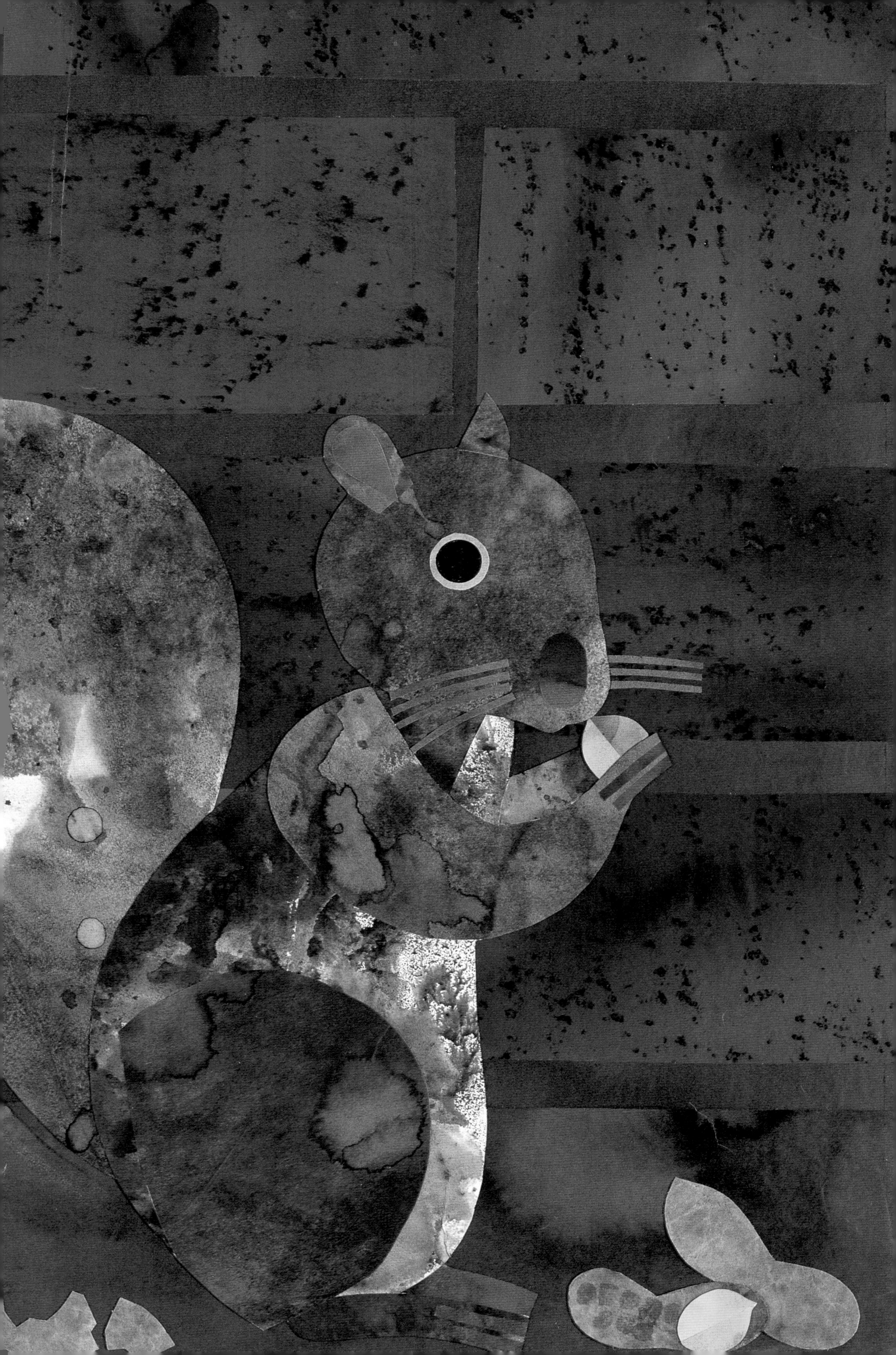

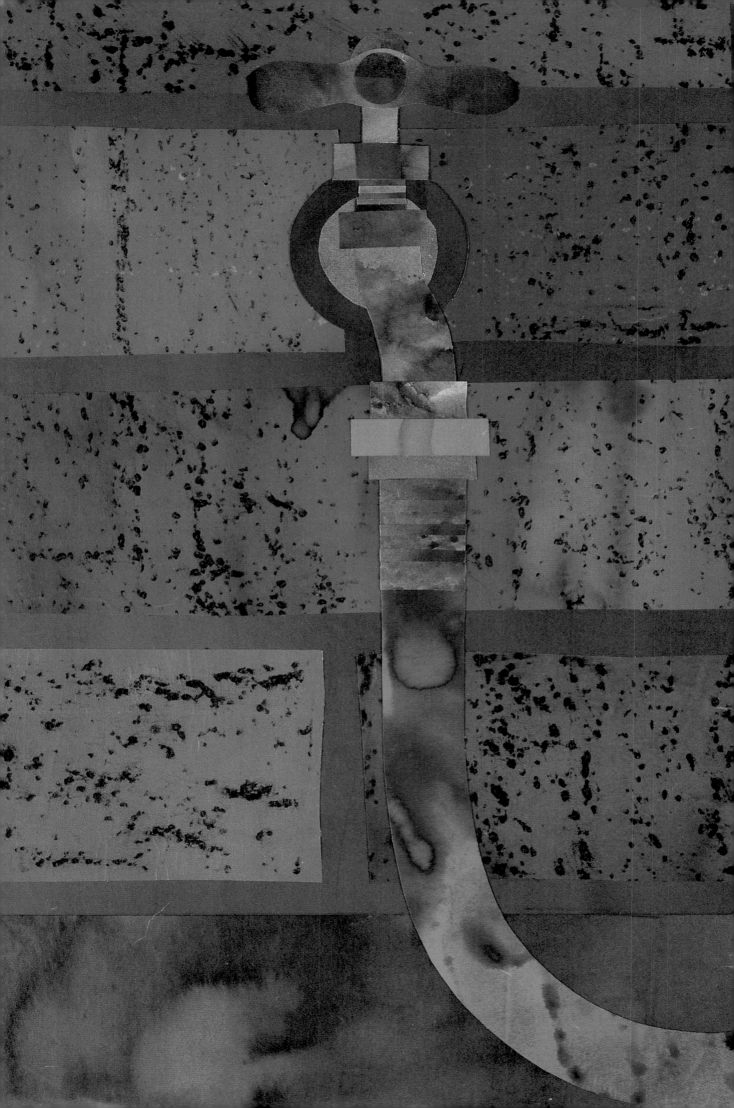

I'll keep nuts
in my pockets,
one or two,
and when I see him,
I'll say:
"Nuts to you!"

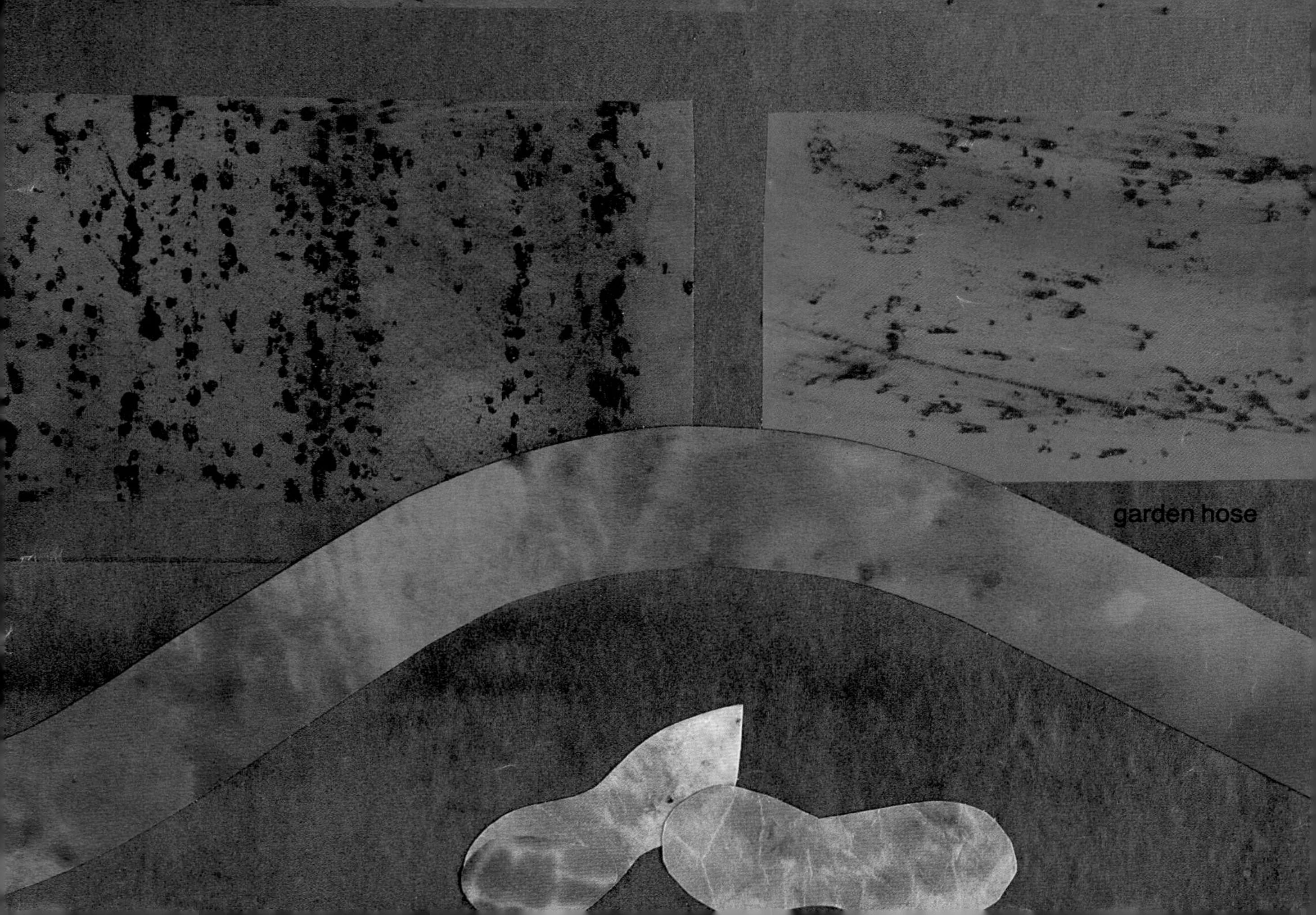
garden hose

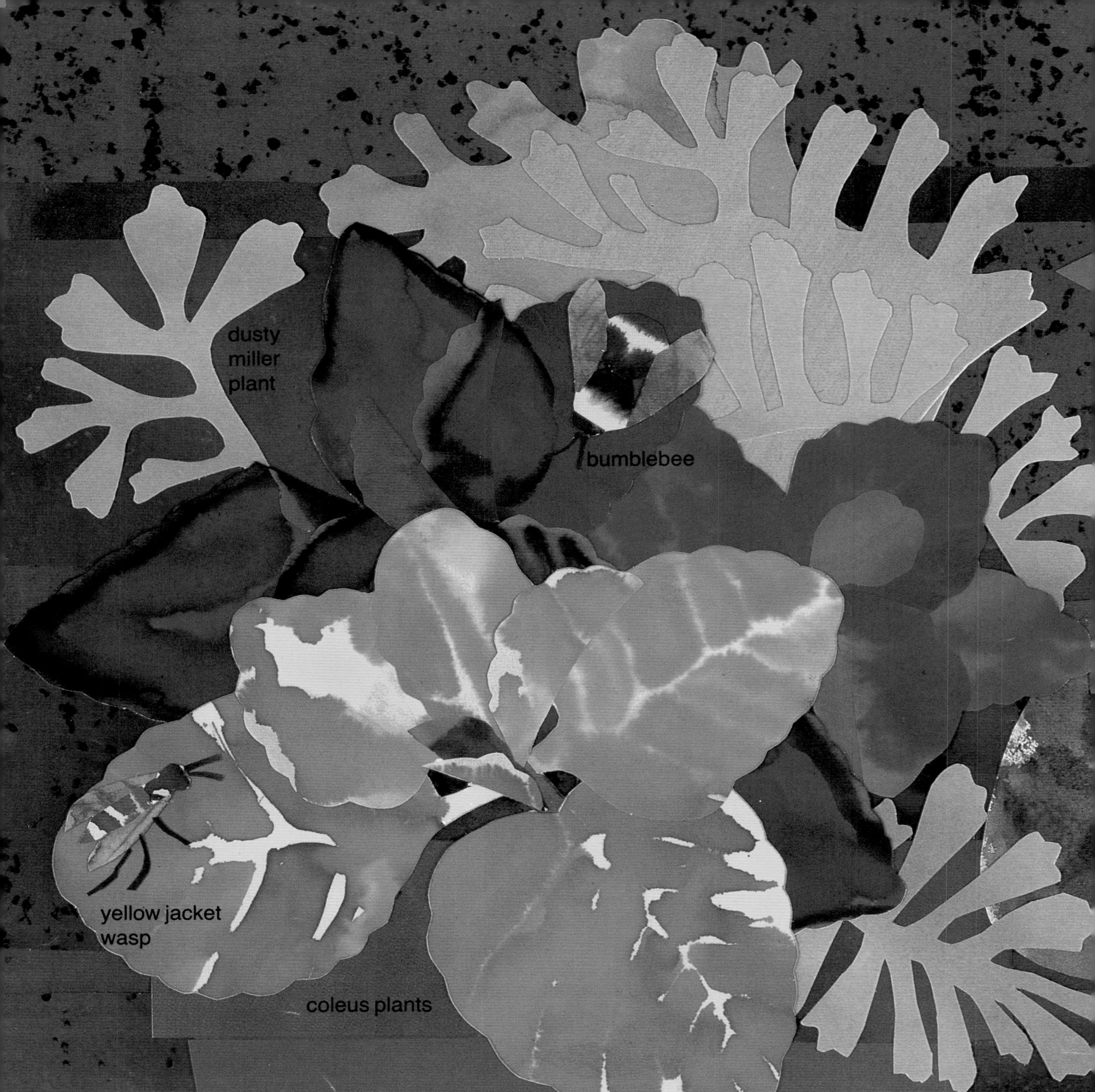
dusty miller plant
bumblebee
yellow jacket wasp
coleus plants

Identification

Squirrels are classified as mammals, the group of animals that nourish their young on milk from mammary glands, have hair on their bodies, and have warm blood.

There are many different kinds of mammals, which are divided into smaller groups. Squirrels are in a group called rodents, the gnawing mammals. Squirrels live all over the world except for Madagascar and Australia. They come in many different sizes—some are as small as mice and some as large as cats. The squirrel in this book is a gray squirrel whose head and body together measure 8 to 10 inches, and whose tail measures 7¾ to 10 inches.

Squirrel Talk

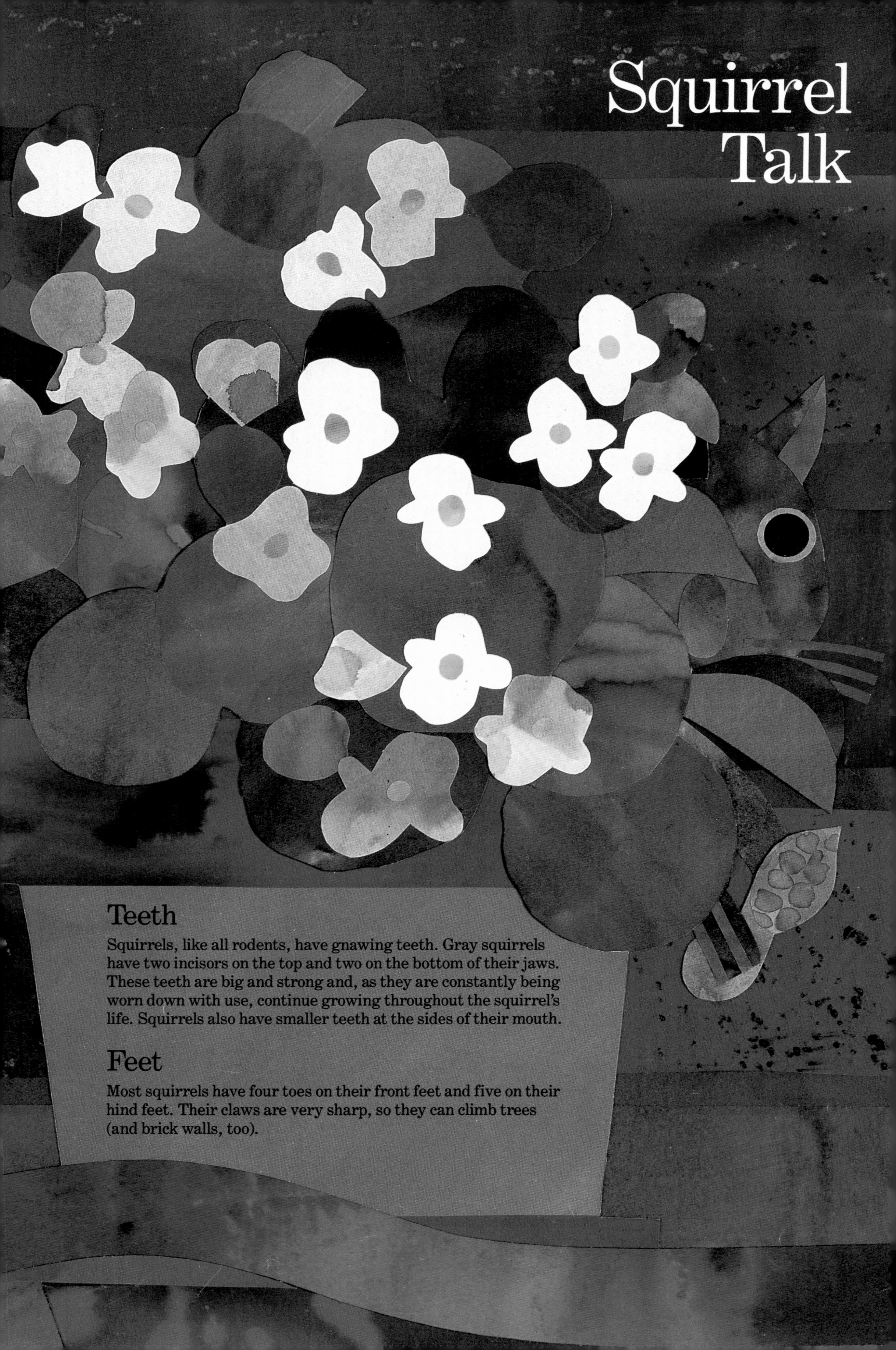

Teeth

Squirrels, like all rodents, have gnawing teeth. Gray squirrels have two incisors on the top and two on the bottom of their jaws. These teeth are big and strong and, as they are constantly being worn down with use, continue growing throughout the squirrel's life. Squirrels also have smaller teeth at the sides of their mouth.

Feet

Most squirrels have four toes on their front feet and five on their hind feet. Their claws are very sharp, so they can climb trees (and brick walls, too).

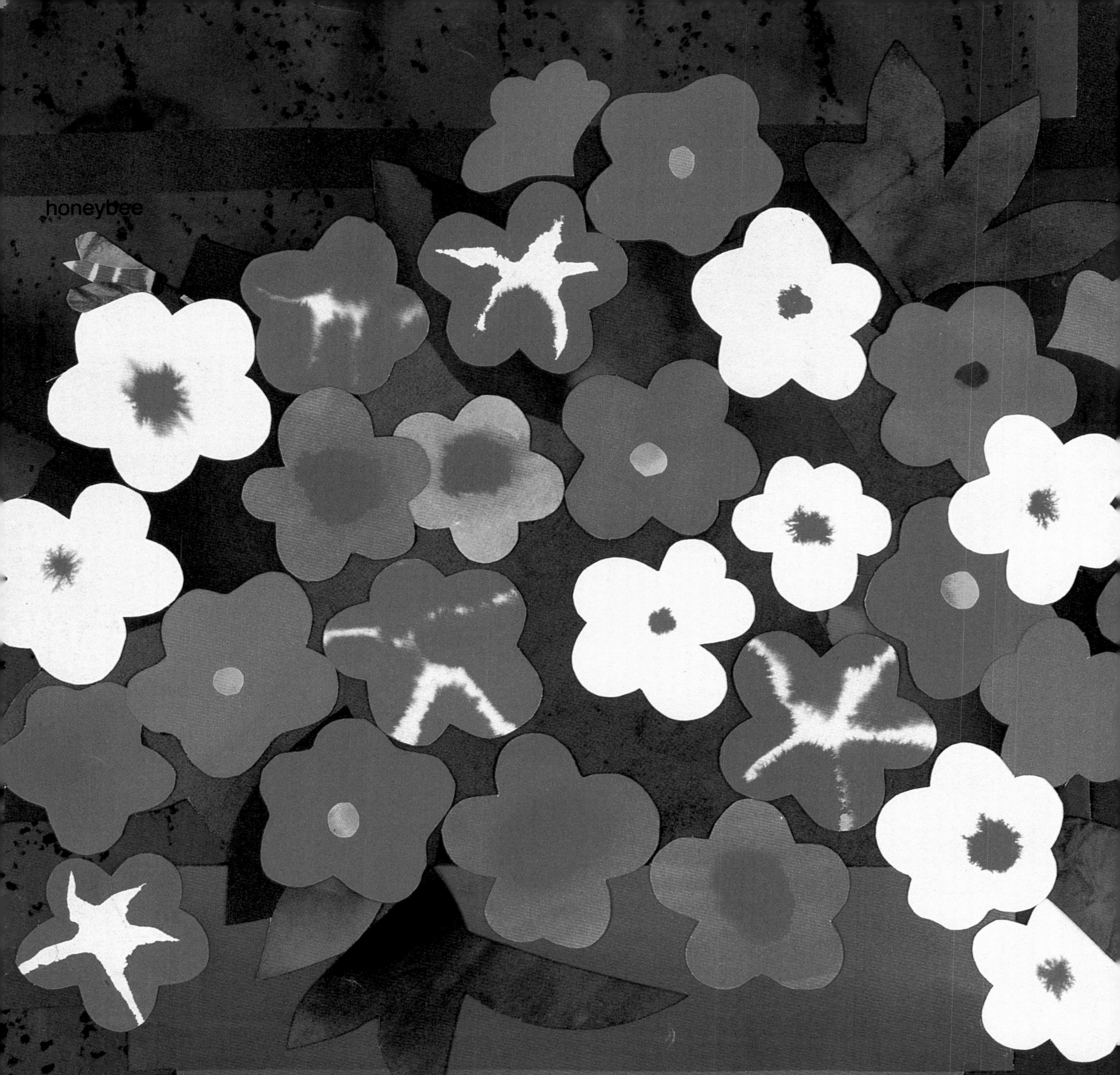
honeybee

Tail

The tail is covered with fur, can be very bushy, and is about as long as the squirrel's body. A squirrel uses its tail for many things: it's an umbrella in rain or hot sun, a blanket in winter, and a rudder when swimming. It also acts as a furry balancing rod when the squirrel is climbing or leaping from branch to branch.

Nest/Home

Gray squirrels are tree squirrels. They love trees, though you often see them on the ground. They live in holes in trees or in big leaf nests they build in high branches or in the forks of trees. You can see their nests most easily in winter, when the tree branches are bare.

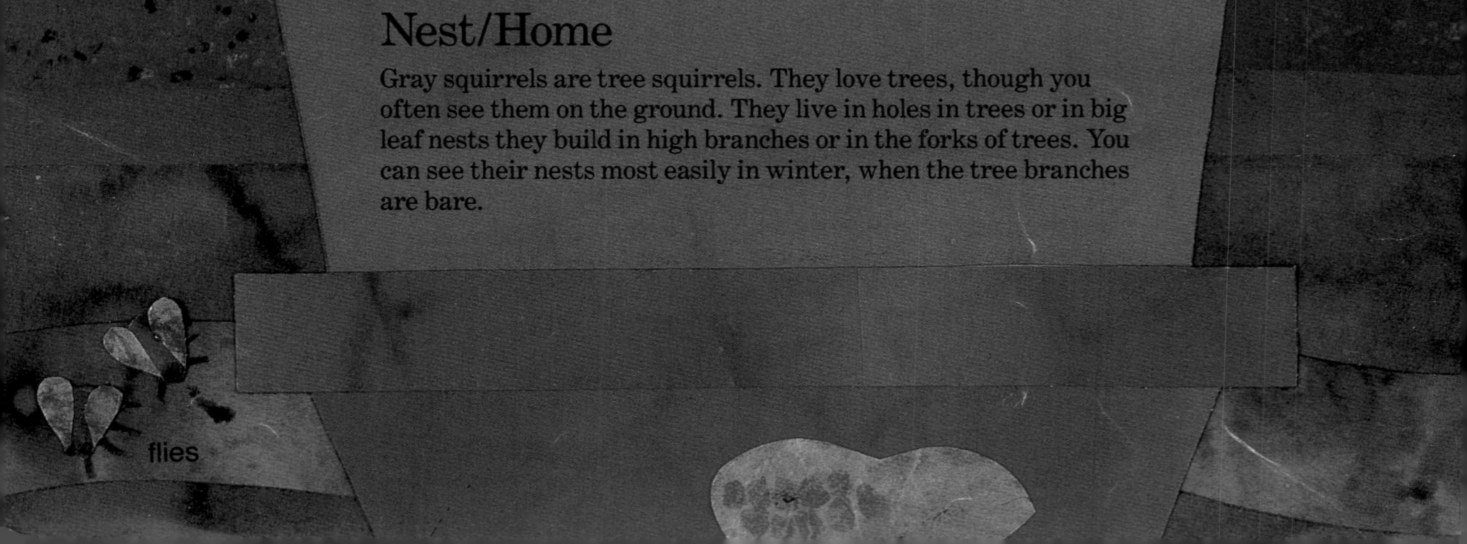
flies

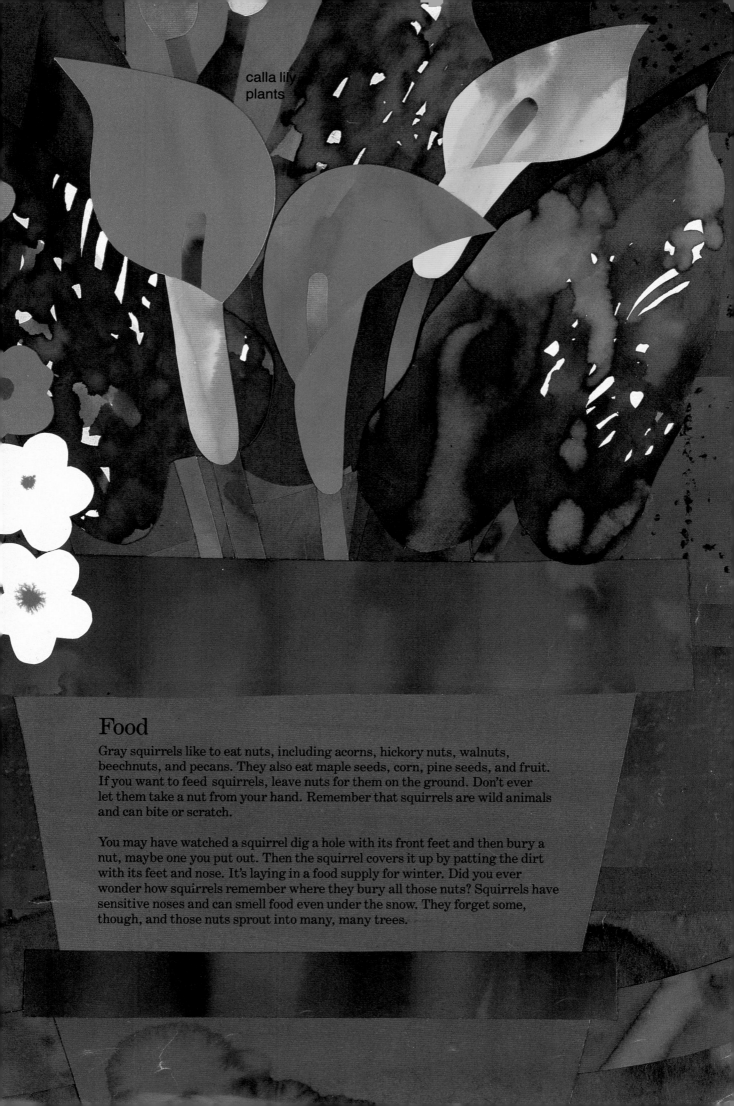

calla lily
plants

Food

Gray squirrels like to eat nuts, including acorns, hickory nuts, walnuts,
beechnuts, and pecans. They also eat maple seeds, corn, pine seeds, and fruit.
If you want to feed squirrels, leave nuts for them on the ground. Don't ever
let them take a nut from your hand. Remember that squirrels are wild animals
and can bite or scratch.

You may have watched a squirrel dig a hole with its front feet and then bury a
nut, maybe one you put out. Then the squirrel covers it up by patting the dirt
with its feet and nose. It's laying in a food supply for winter. Did you ever
wonder how squirrels remember where they bury all those nuts? Squirrels have
sensitive noses and can smell food even under the snow. They forget some,
though, and those nuts sprout into many, many trees.